Rajeev Balasubramanyam was born in Lancashire and went on to study at Oxford, Cambridge and Lancaster Universities. He has lived in London, Manchester, Suffolk, Kathmandu, Berlin and Hong Kong, where he was a Research Scholar in the Society of Scholars at Hong Kong University. He was a fellow of the Hemera Foundation, for writers with a meditation practice, and has been writer-in-residence at Crestone Zen Mountain Centre and the Zen Center of New York City. His journalism and short fiction have appeared in the *Washington Post, The Economist, New Statesman* and many other publications.

You can discover more about the author at
www.rajeevbalasubramanyam.com
Twitter @Rajeevbalasu

PROFESSOR CHANDRA FOLLOWS HIS BLISS

Professor Chandra, an internationally renowned economist, is an expert at complex problems. There's just one he can't crack: the secret of happiness. In the moments after the bicycle accident, Professor Chandra doesn't see his life flash before his eyes, but his life's work. He's just narrowly missed out on the Nobel Prize — again — and even though he knows he should get straight back to his pie charts, his doctor has other ideas. All this work. All this success. All this stress. It's killing him. He needs to take a break, start enjoying himself. In short, says his doctor — who is from California — Professor Chandra should just follow his bliss. He doesn't know it yet, but Professor Chandra is about to embark on the trip of a lifetime.

RAJEEV BALASUBRAMANYAM

PROFESSOR CHANDRA FOLLOWS HIS BLISS

Complete and Unabridged

CHARNWOOD
Leicester

First published in Great Britain in 2019 by
Chatto & Windus
an imprint of Vintage
London

First Charnwood Edition
published 2019
by arrangement with
Penguin Random House UK
London

A catalogue record for this book is available
from the British Library.

ISBN 978–1–4448–4245–6

Published by
F. A. Thorpe (Publishing)
Anstey, Leicestershire

Set by Words & Graphics Ltd.
Anstey, Leicestershire
Printed and bound in Great Britain by
T. J. International Ltd., Padstow, Cornwall

This book is printed on acid-free paper

For my parents

1

It should have been the greatest day of his life. His youngest daughter, Jasmine, had flown from Colorado to share in his triumph. There had been pieces in the *Financial Times* and the *Wall Street Journal* which were all but premature celebrations: 'Like Usain Bolt in the hundred,' the former read, 'like Mrs Clinton in November, this is one front-runner who cannot lose.' The Academy were famous for their secrecy, their cloak-and-dagger strategies to stave off leaks, but this time even the bookies agreed — the Nobel Prize in Economics 2016 belonged to Professor Chandra.

He did not sleep that night, only lay in bed imagining how he would celebrate. There would be interviews, of course, CNN, BBC, Sky, after which he would take Jasmine out for an early brunch before her flight, perhaps allowing her a glass or two of champagne. By evening the college would have organised a function somewhere in Cambridge. His competitors would be there, all the naysayers and back-stabbers and mediocrities, but Chandra would be magnanimous. He would explain how the million-dollar cheque and the banquet in December with the King of Sweden meant nothing to him. His real joy lay in being able to repay the faith shown by his departed parents, trusted colleagues and his old mentor, Milton

1

Friedman, who had once helped him change his tyre in the snow in the days when Chandra was still a lowly Associate Professor.

By mid-morning he had rehearsed his victory speech a dozen times. Still in his dressing gown, he brought a cup of coffee to his bedroom and placed it by the telephone before stretching out on the bed, his hands behind his head, in anticipation of the call. An hour later his daughter entered to find him snoring on top of the covers.

'Dad, wake up,' said Jasmine, shaking his foot. 'Dad, you didn't get it.'

Chandra did not move. He had waited so long for this, suffered through so much; his BA at Hyderabad, his PhD at Cambridge, his first job at the LSE, that punishing decade at Chicago and, after his return to Cambridge, the crash of 2008, the instant vilification of his tribe, the doubts, the pies in face, and every year afterwards the knowledge that though his name had been on the committee's longlist in April and their shortlist in the summer, that 18-carat-gold medal had still ended up in someone else's fist. This was the year his ordeal was supposed to end, the year that should have made it all worthwhile.

'And who, may I ask, was the lucky recipient this time?'

'There were two of them,' said Jasmine.

Chandra jerked his body erect, shoved two pillows behind his back, his reading glasses onto his nose.

'Names?'

'Can't remember.'

'Try.'

'Heart and Stroganoff, something like that.'

Chandra groaned. 'Not Hart and Holmström?'

'Yeah. I think so.'

'So who will it be next year? Starsky and Hutch?'

'I don't know, Dad. Maybe.'

'Well, that's that, then,' he said, pulling the covers over his body and realising that, were it not for his daughter, he would probably remain in that position until next year.

Ten minutes later Jasmine returned to tell him that a group of journalists were outside the house. Chandra met them, still in his dressing gown, and politely answered their questions. It was his daughter's idea to invite them in for coffee, which meant he ended up sitting at his kitchen table with four members of the local press: one from the *Grantchester Gazette*, one from the *Anglia Post*, and two from the *Cambs Times*.

'We're so sorry, sir,' said a young woman from the *Gazette*, who appeared close to tears.

'It was yours,' said the man from the *Times*, who smelled of gin. 'We were hoping for a fine party tonight.'

'Well, now, now,' he replied, touched by their kindness. 'C'*est la vie*.'

'It should have been you, sir,' said the woman. 'It simply *should* have been you.'

'Oh, *de rien, de rien*,' he said, wishing he could stop speaking French, a language he had no knowledge of at all. '*Laissez-faire.*'

Before the journalists left he assured them he was delighted for the winners and was glad it was all over and was looking forward to seeing them again next year. His performance fooled everyone except for Jasmine who for the rest of the morning repeated the same sentence with a seventeen-year-old's mercilessness, asking, 'Are you all right, Dad? Are you all right?' keeping at it no matter what he said until finally, on the way to the airport, he lost his temper and shouted, 'Can't you see I'm fine?'

In the past he would have assumed Jasmine's inquisition was motivated only by sweetness and concern, but now Chandra was convinced there was malice involved, that Jasmine had finally entered into the family tradition of torturing the patriarch, if this was what he still was, for she was a teenager now and lived with her mother in Boulder who blamed him not only for the divorce, three years old now, but also for the rise of Ebola and Boko Haram.

As soon as he reached home the phone began to ring with a stream of condolence calls that continued throughout the day and then, more sporadically, for the rest of the week. For the following month people he barely knew stopped him in the street to offer their sympathies, men and women who couldn't have named three economists had their lives depended on it.

By November the hysteria had died down, replaced by horror at the US election, and it was then that Chandra realised, in all probability, he would never win the prize now. The odds had

4

gone down a decade before when the Bengali had worked his unctuous charm, but even if time enough elapsed for another Indian to win, the field had changed. For years economists had wantonly obscured their profession, rendering everything absurdly technical with incomprehensible logarithms such that they were treated more like mystic seers than social scientists. Economics was little more than a poor man's mathematics now, but Chandra still struggled with calculus, considering it beneath him, a task for a penniless research assistant.

In any case, his slide to the right was hardly something the Scandinavians were likely to reward; that sub-subcontinent of mediocrity would consider it a signal of intellectual and moral deviance. It was what Chandra loathed most about liberals — their shameless self-righteousness, as if the species' failings were always someone else's fault, while anything *they* did, murder and arson included, were heroic acts in the service of liberty and justice. In point of fact, the Swedes weren't even liberals. They were neutrals, abstainers who behaved as if they had deliberately chosen not to become a superpower in the interests of preserving their objectivity.

Chandra wished he had just one Swedish student he could torment mercilessly, but the closest thing was a Dutch girl with an American accent who was, regrettably, quite bright. And so he went on giving his lectures and affecting the appearance of a man too wrapped up in his own research to notice that such a petty and trivial thing as the Nobel Prize even existed.

5

On the Wednesday morning after term had ended, Chandra walked across the meadows from his home in Grantchester to the university, something he did only when breakfasting with the Master of the college. Chandra's was at Gonville & Caius, where he was Emeritus Clifford H. Doyle Professor, a lifetime appointment that left him free to teach as much or as little as he wished. Like Professor Hawking, Chandra was as permanent a fixture at the college as the flock of stone gargoyles on the roof.

'Morning, Professor,' said the head porter, Maurice, touching his bowler hat.

'Morning, Maurice,' said Chandra, accepting his post which consisted of the new edition of the *Economic Journal* and half a dozen invitations to tea parties and functions he would almost certainly not attend.

'Master's expecting you, sir,' said Maurice who, like many porters, succeeded in being deferential and authoritarian at the same time. 'Mind your step. Heavy frost this morning.'

'Excellent,' said Chandra, and tramped into Tree Court, so named after the 'Swedish bean' trees which, now bare and spindly, lined the path.

At the entrance to the Master's Lodge, he was received by a waistcoated, poker-faced servant who took his coat and scarf while Chandra crossed to the dining room where the Master was reading *The Times* in front of the fire.

'Good to see you, Chandra,' said the Master, who always pronounced Chandra's name as if embarking upon the word 'chandelier' before losing his train of thought.

'And you, Master. Freezing outside.'

Like many English intellectuals, the Master preferred his home only very lightly heated in the manner of a *bleu* steak, claiming it 'improved the mind'.

'These are cold times,' he said, a reference to the election, in all probability.

'Quite,' said Chandra.

The Master looked younger than his years. He had a full head of hair, slicked back with brilliantine, and his eyes, though pointing in different directions, were very blue. He had been an Olympic hurdler many years ago until a rival kicked grit into his face and he lost the sight in his right eye. Rumour had it he had gone to Kenya in the early seventies to give private coaching in track to Idi Amin. From the battle lines on his face it wasn't hard to believe he was a man who had lived several lives.

The Master ushered him to the dining table, large enough for forty. As always Chandra enjoyed the surroundings, the Dutch masters on the walls, the servants standing by the doors, the solid silver cutlery and soup tureen collectively worth almost half a million pounds. Usually their conversations were about the economy, with Chandra taking on the role of therapist, gently reassuring the Master that Britain would not become a Third World country in five years' time.

'So how are things, Professor?' asked the Master. 'Recovered from your little disappointment? I must say, we were all terribly sorry you couldn't become our fifteenth.'

The college, thus far, had produced fourteen Nobel laureates. Indeed, earlier that year some of the more well-informed fellows had taken to referring to Chandra as 'Fifteen', a practice they had now discontinued.

'Oh, I'm quite well,' said Chandra, pushing his coffee cup towards the servant and nodding at the offer of fresh strawberries to accompany his croissant.

'But the last few weeks must have been difficult, eh?' said the Master. 'Rather stressful?'

'Oh, not at all,' said Chandra, who was now accustomed to spending entire weekends in bed. 'I tend to rather take these things in my stride. Medals come and go.'

'Yes,' said the Master, and put down his knife before running his fingers through his hair. 'Yes, they do, but . . . this is a little delicate, but some people seem to think you *may* have been feeling the strain somewhat of late.'

'They do?' said Chandra, sensing an ambush.

'Well, there have been complaints.'

'From whom?'

'Students,' said the Master. 'Undergraduates, mostly.'

'Oh,' said Chandra, relaxing. 'Oh, I see.'

'Yes, it seems you've made a few rather abrupt comments. Of course, they have no idea what you've been going through, but a few did take it rather hard. I mean, ordinarily this would be a matter for the Dean, but seeing as it's you, I thought I would talk to you personally.'

'I'm sorry, Master,' said Chandra. 'But I can't

recall saying anything abrupt.'

'Yes,' said the Master, taking out his notebook, which was not a good sign. 'Well, some of them are a little oversensitive. But there was one girl whom it seems you referred to repeatedly as an 'imbecile' in front of her peers, owing to what she described as a legitimate intellectual difference.'

'Yes,' said Professor Chandra, who remembered the incident well. 'You see, Master, I am often lenient with my students. I don't expect them to show up sober to tutorials; I didn't object when one plagiarised his essay from my own book; but I do expect them to acknowledge fundamental economic facts. This girl described the Keynesian multiplier as a 'trickle-down myth'. This isn't something one can have an opinion about, Master. It is a fact that if companies make higher profits they invest more and so employment increases. One can't go out in a thunderstorm and say, 'In my opinion the sun is shining.' But the student in question did exactly this, and so I pointed out another fact.'

'That she was an imbecile,' said the Master.

'Yes.'

'Well, of course, I quite understand. But in this day and age the word 'imbecile' is rather, shall we say, politically incorrect.'

'Even if the person in question is an imbecile?'

'Especially if the person is an imbecile,' said the Master, and smiled, though in a manner more suggestive of toothache than mirth. 'Look, Chandra, it's understandable that you've been feeling the strain of late. It can't be easy being such a high-profile figure, with so many expectations from so many people. That's why I did think — in fact, a few of us thought — you might benefit from a short holiday, or a sabbatical perhaps. It's up to you of course, we'd never force anything like that on you. But it might be worth considering.'

'I don't think so,' said Chandra.

'But it's worth thinking about, isn't it?'

Chandra nodded, though he had no intention of doing anything of the sort. 'Yes, it is.'

'Well, that's enough of all that,' said the Master as the servants arrived with bacon, eggs and toast. 'Let's talk about the economy, shall we?'

For the following half-hour the Master expressed his concern about Brexit, the credit crunch and China's slowing growth, and whether this would leave the world 'up manure creek'. The trouble with the last question was that it was equivalent to asking, 'Will I die in the next five years?' or, 'Will we win the Boat Race?' In microeconomic terms the correct reply was, 'It is uncertain,' but that would have left him without sufficient time to finish his second egg, which, as always, was poached to silky perfection. He decided to err on the side of positivity, which was always a good way to cope with such an encounter.

'Unlikely,' he said. 'When the US sneezes, the rest of the world catches a cold, but when China sneezes, we say *'Gesundheit'* and move on. It's a question of capital controls.'

'Well, that's a relief, isn't it?' said the Master,

brushing crumbs from his trousers. 'It's reassuring to hear it from someone who actually knows what he's talking about.'

'My pleasure,' said Chandra.

'It's the poverty I can't understand,' said the Master, going off on a potentially endless tangent. 'It's within our means to feed the entire world, but look at us. It's absurd, Chandra. I mean, will this ever change? Will we ever come to our senses?'

Professor Chandra took a deep breath.

'Certainly.'

'Excellent,' said the Master.

They shook hands and Chandra marched into the hallway, taking his coat and scarf before exiting into the sharp November breeze. His categorical assertiveness had owed little to his own feelings on the matter, which were non-existent, but to his appointment with a student for which he was now twenty-two minutes late.

He trampled across the grass, a privilege accorded only to dons, and out the college gate (the Gate of Humility, as it was called). Gonville & Caius was an oddity in that it was split in half by the road and, as was his habit, Chandra barely noticed the tourists and cyclists as he crossed Trinity Street before bounding up the wooden spiralled staircase to his rooms on the third floor.

Ram Singh, his PhD student, was sitting on the landing staring at his iPhone, which was how all his students seemed to fill up those long hours when they weren't asleep.

11

'Sorry, Ram,' said Professor Chandra. 'My bad.'

'It's all right, Professor. I was late too.'

'Good, very good . . . What the hell is that?'

The book under Ram Singh's arm was called *Statistics for Dummies.*

'Just a little light reading.'

Chandra unlocked the door and sighed. Why on earth a PhD student at the top-ranked university for economics in the country should be reading such foolishness was beyond him. But this was the root of the problem. Popular books sought to storm the intellectual barricades by 'de-jargonising' the discipline, a well-intentioned but absurd idea. You couldn't learn in three hours what it had taken others years to master. Whether the public liked it or not, knowledge still mattered. Economics was still the province of experts and not, as his thirty-four-year-old son, Sunny, was fond of saying, 'all common sense', as if any Tom, Dick or Bengali could become Clifford H. Doyle Professor at Cambridge.

'So how was Delhi?' asked Chandra as he pottered about his rooms sweeping books off the sofa, making coffee and watering his spider plant, something the bedder had neglected to do.

'Delhi was Delhi,' said Ram Singh. 'Usual stuff. Beer's getting expensive.'

'And the fieldwork?'

'Fieldwork was damn good. Got most of the data. Just a question of . . . ' Ram tapped his *Dummies* book.

'Well, not much for us to talk about then,' said

Chandra. 'Good to see things are ticking along.'

'There's still the question of Brazil.'

Ram Singh's thesis was supposed to be a comparison between Gujarat's economic performance and that of what he insisted on referring to as 'TROI'. He would just slip it into conversation: 'If you look at TROI's average growth rate,' and Chandra's mind would hurtle in the direction of Agamemnon and a thousand ships before remembering it meant 'The Rest of India'.

'Brazil, yes,' said Chandra.

This had been a point of contention between them for months. They both knew that the reason Brazil had suddenly become of such importance to the thesis was because Ram Singh's girlfriend, a Miss Betina Moreira, had returned to Sao Paulo a year ago.

Ram needed Chandra's backing for extra research funding and, thus far, Chandra had been resistant. It crossed his mind that Ram might have been one of his betrayers. After all, only last month Chandra, misquoting Churchill, had told him that if he had 'only a few more brain cells he would be a halfwit'.

'Well,' he said, 'if you can get the money, why not? It would alter your thesis dramatically, of course, not to mention the workload, but if you feel it's necessary . . . '

'You mean you'll write me a reference, sir?' said Ram.

'Well, I suppose you *could* use it as an example of what could really go wrong — Brazil's credit rating is about to go to junk, as you know.'

Ram Singh was taking notes and smiling broadly, which Professor Chandra pretended not to notice.

'And of course,' he continued, 'consider the impact of the World Cup and the Olympics and so on. All that will make a difference.'

Ram licked his lips at the mention of the World Cup, with which his last 'research trip' had coincided.

'Try to focus on the nineties for your first few chapters. Then bring in Modi. That should be enough for now.'

'Thank you, Professor,' said Ram, almost bowing. 'And my family send their regards.'

'Oh, do they?' said Chandra. 'Very good.'

'Yes, my parents insist you visit next time you're in Delhi. And I'm sure you'd love the dogs. I always miss them the most.'

'Dogs, yes,' said Chandra, who hated anything with a tail. 'Splendid.'

'And, sir . . . ' Only the subcontinentals called him 'sir', even the ones who addressed their other tutors by their first names. 'I forgot to add my commiserations, about the Nobel, I mean. I hope you aren't letting it trouble you too much.'

'Oh, I'd forgotten all about that. If awards were all I were in it for . . . '

'Yes, of course,' said Ram Singh, who was in it for the money. 'I quite agree.'

'Well, good of you to stop by.'

This was hardly any way to end a scheduled supervision, as if Ram had merely popped over to return an extension cord for a lawnmower. There were some who might even have called it

14

unprofessional, but those same bureaucratic harpies would have been unaware that Chandra had all but financed his student's conjugal visit to Brazil two years ago.

'I'll get to work asap, sir,' said Ram, pronouncing it 'ay-sap'.

Ram saw himself out while Chandra switched on his computer and stared at the ever-increasing pile of books on his desk. Remembering the coffee, he poured milk into his 'Keep Calm and Study Economics' mug, a gift from his eldest daughter, Radha, before she cut him out of her life, and reflected that he really ought to have offered Ram a cup. But it was Ram who had brought up the Nobel, a clear sign that there was nothing of any consequence left to say.

The bloody Nobel. They always made that same face, as if trying to persuade a two-year-old to put a gun down.

Chandra shifted to the sofa and put his feet on the coffee table. When things had been at their worst with Jean, he had begun shifting his entire life into these rooms: the pictures of his children, the 'standing' desk at which he never stood. He had spent several nights on the red Chesterfield sofa, conducted more than one supervision in his dressing gown and slippers. But since Jean had moved to Colorado, Chandra had begun to spend most of his evenings at home, spurning dinner invitations in favour of watching TV or reading novels he wouldn't have dared take into the SCR, as it slowly dawned on him that he was not only divorced now — that oh-so transgressive, Middle English word — but also alone, a word far less exotic. That cottage in Grantchester with its black thatched roof and seventeenth-century beams that used to be filled with children and laughter, was now the dark retreat of a tragic recluse, an Indian Miss Havisham with an Emeritus Professorship and a takeaway menu.

Sometimes he wondered if it wasn't all a giant con, the gaggle of letters after his name, the dinners with Angela Merkel and Narendra Modi, the notes of admiration from Gordon Brown and Larry Summers. They were like those fake Oscar statues bought at pound shops and given to employees, inscribed with 'World's Greatest Photocopier' or 'Best Light Bulb Changer in the Galaxy'. When he died only his writing would remain, until it was rendered obsolete when the oil and coal ran out and the species established its first settlement on Mars.

Professor Chandra was the foremost trade economist in the world, could phone any finance minister in any country at any time and have them take his call. And yet, what if he had only convinced himself that the world envied him? What if, in reality, they felt sorry for him with his swollen ego and his Savile Row suits and his sculpted tri-continental accent?

His wife was long gone now, his children too. Had he won the Nobel, life would have continued exactly as before except there would have been precisely nothing to look forward to. He seemed to have read every book worth

16

reading in his field now, so his professional life consisted only of seeking to outdo his competitors and gaining the recognition he so richly deserved and — here came the killer blow — already had.

Putting his coffee down, Chandra stomped out of his rooms, not certain where he was going, knowing only that the alternative was to sit on the sofa until lunchtime, hating his life.

On Trinity Street he turned left, heading for the Copper Kettle, hoping an early glass of wine might speed the trawl of the morning. Undergraduates were cycling to their first lectures of the day, cigarettes in their mouths, college scarfs around their necks. Outside King's, tourists from Boston, Tokyo and Hong Kong were unfurling giant Nikons in order to capture that famous five-hundred-year-old chapel.

Situated in the middle of the city, as if designed to hog all the sunlight, King's was Chandra's least favourite college. It was the intellectual equivalent of a Disney princess, fluttering its eyelashes at tourists who didn't know any better, the ones who asked questions like, 'Where's the university?' until someone pointed at King's, after which they would take several dozen pictures before going home satisfied they had 'seen Cambridge'. Of course, it boasted an illustrious roll call when it came to economics — Kaldor, Joan Robinson, J. K. Galbraith, Keynes himself — but now it was filled with half-witted undergraduates who were convinced that the Africans they sacrificed their

17

gap years to help owed their poverty entirely to men like Chandra. But this was the way it was nowadays: those who had a proper education used it for knavery, while those who lacked one did not think it important.

Professor Chandra reached Mr Simms Olde Sweet Shoppe and went inside, even though he had already made his weekly purchase. He was welcomed by a young female assistant wearing an apron and tortoiseshell glasses whom he was convinced he had never laid eyes on before until she said, 'Morning, Professor Chandra.'

'Good morning.'

'And how are we today?'

'Oh, can't complain,' said Chandra, a lie of grotesque proportions.

'So what can I get for you?'

His usual order was two hundred grams of gummy bears which he would make last all week, but today was an emergency.

'Fifty grams of chocolate-covered gummy bears, please.'

'Of course,' said the woman, and began filling a paper bag from a jar behind her.

'Cold, isn't it?' she said, putting his order on the counter.

'Terrible,' replied Chandra, handing her a five-pound note after which his phone started to ring from inside his jacket and he began his usual routine of slapping each of his pockets in turn and muttering, 'More technology, more problems,' until he finally located it and said, 'Yes?'

'Sir,' said an Indian voice on the other end,

18

'you have expressed an interest in a Samsung Galaxy J5 smartphone with sixteen gigabytes of internal storage. This is a follow-up call to confirm your interest in purchasing a smartphone.'

'I have no such interest,' he replied, accepting his change.

'Sir — '

Chandra, who as always could not seem to cancel the call, no matter how many buttons he hit, returned the phone to his inside pocket even though he could still hear that plaintive whine of 'sir' from inside, as if a pixie were trapped beneath his lapel.

'Thank you,' he called to the assistant, and walked outside into the winter sunlight.

The Copper Kettle and a fine Rioja were only metres away, but Chandra had noticed a student eyeing him from the other side of the road. He recognised her at once. The imbecile. She had looked hurt initially, but now she was smiling in that post-ironic way that always baffled Chandra. After his meeting with the Master, he supposed he owed her an explanation.

He was crossing the road when he heard the shop assistant call out, 'Professor!' and looked back to see her holding his gummy bears.

'Oh,' he said, and turned, but now the imbecile was shouting, 'Watch out!'

He turned again, but it was too late.

The bicycle had already swerved, its brakes locking, the rider able to do nothing other than throw up his hands while the handlebars wrapped themselves around Professor Chandra's

19

waist from behind like the horns of a ferocious beast, and the helmeted head collided with his back, causing them both to tumble through the air and onto the tarmac, the Professor first, the young cyclist next, the bicycle on top of both.

For what felt like minutes, all he could see was blackness, and it crossed his mind that he might be dead, though this seemed unlikely. There was blood in his mouth, and he could hear voices. Someone was pulling the bicycle off him, When he opened his eyes there was a crowd of faces peering down at him.

Professor Chandra had never thought he would die in Cambridge. He had always imagined himself in India, perhaps by a river, surrounded by weeping grandchildren instead of jubilant colleagues, idiotic students and tourists, some of whom were taking pictures.

'Professor?' exclaimed a narrowly post-pubescent voice. 'Have you been in an accident?'

'Of course I've been in a bloody accident,' he wanted to say — only an undergraduate could ask so perfectly stupid a question — but his mouth was too full of blood.

As he lay waiting for the medics to arrive it seemed that half the student body had gathered to watch this final indignity of Professor P. R. Chandrasekhar's distinguished life. Some were crying, though he suspected others were concealing smirks of triumph. Even now, he found it hard to believe these people had nothing better to do than mock him for his failure to join the ranks of those Nobel laureates whose names he had committed to memory and would recite like a mantra in moments of extreme frustration. But of course that wasn't true: all they saw was an old man bleeding in the middle of the road. How could they know how miserably he had failed at life?

'C'est *la vie*,' he told himself, fighting to shake off the oxygen mask that covered his nose and mouth. 'C'est *la* bloody *vie*.'

2

Professor Chandra awoke the next morning in a private room with a series of dull-to-sharp aches across his body. His ribs were bruised, his left wrist sprained from trying to break his fall, and his spinal cord traumatised, a word that made no sense but necessitated his immediate removal to the operating theatre to have his vertebrae realigned. He had also suffered a 'silent' heart attack, which explained much about his earlier mood. There were 'Get well soon' cards from his secretary, a few colleagues and most of his International Economics group, an email from Jasmine in Colorado and his brother in Delhi (a rare event), but nothing from Sunny, or his eldest daughter, Radha, though this was nothing new: there had been no word from her for two thorny years.

Jasmine, however, had included a short poem which made him smile:

Daddy, we're thinking of you in your hos-
    pital smock
Don't do this again, you gave us all a shock
Look left then right before crossing the
    road
You've got to be careful now, you're get-
    ting . . .
Look after yourself till you're back to your
    best

22

Keep smiling and get plenty of rest
Keep your cholesterol down but your spirits high
And if you must have bacon, please don't
   fry.

He wondered if the word 'die' had been in
there originally, but the gesture made him smile
nonetheless. Jean had written a few lines too,
implying, with that mixture of directness and
euphemism unique to the Northern English, that
this was bound to happen sooner or later and
had he been able to think about anything other
than work the accident might not only have been
avoided but everybody else's lives could also
have been far less torrid affairs. But she was
relieved he wasn't dead, and she cared about
him, albeit in a way that would baffle most
psychologists and was entirely devoid of
sympathy or affection.

When the nurse came she averted her eyes, as
if pitying his loneliness. All the other rooms were
probably filled with relatives and flowers and
out-of-tune songs strummed on hand-painted
guitars. It wasn't until a full day later that his son
called from the lobby of the Mumbai Oberoi.
Like Jean, Sunny believed Chandra to be entirely
responsible for his fate, though he took a
different line, arguing that it was the result of
something called 'synchronistic necessity'.

'It's all about the mind, Dad,' said Sunny. 'We
create our own reality.'

Sunny ran his own institute in Hong Kong
called the Institute of Mindful Business, a hugely

successful enterprise that emphasised 'positive thinking' and 'financial karma', the result of an ideology best described as 'capitalist mysticism'. Sunny always wore the same black suit with a Nehru collar, white T-shirt and sneakers. He wore glasses too, though as far as Chandra knew, his eyesight was excellent, and there were times when his voice took on a distinctly Indian inflection not unlike his father's. As much as Chandra hated to admit it, Sunny and he had become rivals. One of the reasons he'd wanted to win the Nobel so badly was to shut his son up for good.

'Sunny,' said Chandra, 'if you tell me to think positive I'm hanging up now, I swear it.'

'I'm glad to hear you sounding so upbeat, Dad.'

'Have you heard from Radha?'

'Not lately.'

'So she doesn't know?'

'She knows.'

'So you *have* heard from her?'

'I messaged her.'

'Tell her to call me, Sunny.'

This was the arrangement the others had made behind his back. They knew where Radha was but, in deference to her wishes, were sworn to secrecy. He had responded with apoplexy at first, but the whole family had proved resolute, Jasmine included. Chandra had no number for her. She would not reply to his emails. Even now, with him in hospital, the deal was unbreakable.

'I could be dead,' said Chandra. 'I could be dead and my eldest daughter wouldn't care.'

'You're not dead, Dad.'

'But Radha doesn't know that.'

'She does,' said Sunny. 'I told her you were all right, Dad.'

Chandra liked to think that had Radha walked through the door at that moment he would have turned his back to the wall after calling security, but they all knew this wasn't true. He missed her.

'I had a heart attack, Sunny,' he said. 'I could die at any time. Tell her that.'

'That's just the body's way of telling you to make some changes. Follow the doctors' orders and it'll never happen again. Trust me, Dad. You're fine.'

'I'm sixty-nine, Sunny. People younger than me die every day.'

'Not when they can afford proper hospitals.'

'I could crash my car.'

'You've got a Volvo,' said Sunny. 'It's practically a tank.'

'I could get shot.'

'In Cambridge?'

'I don't want to argue about this, Sunny. You're not actually telling me I'm safe from death, are you?'

'Theoretically, no, but the odds are that you'll live until ninety at the least. My generation will all hit a hundred unless we grow up in slums or on council estates. The way health tech is going you could make the big one-double-zero yourself, so I wouldn't worry about it. I'm not, and neither's Rad. Worry's like trying to live the future before it's happened.'

'So as long as we're alive everything's fine, is it? We need never see each other at all. I could just send an email each year saying, 'I'm fine,' and we all keep on swimming with the universe.'

'Come on, Dad, don't be like that. I'm dying for you to come visit Hong Kong.'

'I will,' said Chandra. 'I've been busy.'

'It's okay, Dad. I know you've got your work.'

It was incredible how Sunny was managing to make *him* feel guilty, an almost impossible feat of emotional dexterity. The trouble with Sunny was that he was essentially a shy, insecure, oversensitive soul who pretended to be the exact opposite, and did so with such aplomb that he fooled nearly everyone.

'All right, Sunny. Thanks. Good of you to call.'

'You're welcome, Dad. Look after yourself.'

Professor Chandra stabbed at his phone, attacking each button in turn. He could hear Sunny talking in broken Hindi, and resisted the urge to drop the phone in the vase containing tulips sent by 'the department', which meant his secretary. He looked at the cast on his wrist which no one had signed and thought about calling Jasmine, except she never answered, would only text a few minutes later saying, Missed your call. Everything okay? at which he would reply, Yes. You? and she'd write, All good. Jxx.

Jasmine had received her SAT results recently and wouldn't tell him her score, no matter how much he pleaded, yelled or emotionally black-mailed. All she would say was that she had 'fucked them up royally' and, unfortunately, he believed her. Unlike her elder siblings who had aced every exam they ever took, Jasmine had never been a natural student, always requiring extra coaching, but Chandra hadn't worried unduly because, until recently, she had always been such a happy, sweet girl. But now even that was changing.

★　★　★

Before leaving hospital, Professor Chandra underwent a thorough check-up, the results of which he discussed afterwards with his doctor, Dr Chris Chaney, a thirty-two-year-old American with Converse trainers, sparkling teeth and carefully affected stubble.

'You've got to take this very seriously,' said Dr Chaney. 'Silent heart attacks are just as deadly. You need two months off, at least.'

Professor Chandra smiled. It was obvious Dr Chaney had no idea who he was.

'The mayonnaise has to go,' continued Dr Chaney. 'And you'd be better off avoiding dairy altogether. And red meat, obviously.'

'Obviously,' said Chandra.

'Red wine, white bread, potato chips, French fries, sugar in your coffee, caffeine — '

'What's the point of telling me not to have sugar in my coffee if I can't have coffee?'

'You can have decaffeinated coffee.'

'I see.'

'Hydrogenated vegetable oil, trans fats, high-fructose corn syrup, white flour and white rice if

27

you can manage, though those are optional, bread and potatoes generally not a good idea, and obviously, cut out the cigars.'

'I did.'

'I said cut out, not cut down.'

'Cut out for how long?'

'And exercise,' said Dr Chaney. 'That's the big one. You've got to do it. You simply have to. Nothing too strenuous. You're not joining the Premier League. Even walking is enough if you do it regularly. But if I were you I'd add a little light resistance work, maybe some swimming. Can you swim?'

'Hardly.'

'Then how about yoga?' said Dr Chaney, and looked at him meaningfully.

Professor Chandra sighed. Yoga had become Jean's obsession in Chicago when it was mostly unknown to Americans. But nowadays, everyone did yoga: Republicans, porn stars, serial killers. They didn't care that he could pronounce the Sanskrit terminology they so blithely butchered but expected him, as an export from the subcontinent, to have the anatomical advantage, which was why Chandra had joined his wife for only one class before deciding his dog was better horizontal on the sofa with a Dick Francis novel than facing either upward or downward (on his gloomier days, he added this to his list of reasons why she had left him).

'I think the sutras have been misinterpreted by the secular world,' he replied.

'There's always Pilates, if you'd prefer,' said Dr Chaney. 'Have you done much Pilates?'

28

'Not a lot, no.'

'But it isn't just about exercise. It's your whole attitude to life. You need to cut back on *everything*. Work less. Relax. Take a holiday. Get some sun. Do things you like, within moderation. Stress is physical, but its origin is mostly mental. Have a little fun. Just, you know — '

'Take it easy?'

'Exactly. And I know it's easier said than done. I mean, I'm a doctor for Pete's sake. We spend our time telling patients to relax and then we work eighteen-hour shifts. It's modern life. Maybe it's just life. We can't all chillax all the time. I certainly can't. I've got two young girls and a mortgage. But you're at the top of your profession, Professor. Even I've heard of you. And you're past retirement age. You need R and R. I can give you a whole list of possibilities. There's aromatherapy, reiki, acupuncture, flotation chambers . . . it just goes on. And then there's meditation.'

'Work is my meditation,' said Chandra. 'Homo *laboris*. It's ontological.'

'I'm sure it is,' said Dr Chaney, 'but if you want to go on working for another decade, you're going to have to start enjoying yourself. You know what we say in California?'

'No,' said Professor Chandra. 'What do you say in California?'

'You gotta follow your bliss, man. That's all there is to it.'

'So you're from California, Dr Chaney?'

'Chris, please.'

'Chris.'

'Born and bred, though I lived in Seattle for years.'

Seattle was where his wife met Steve, the child psychiatrist. The memory made him scowl.

'But San Diego sure is sunnier than Seattle,' said Dr Chaney.

Professor Chandra looked out of the window. It was late November. In the forty-five years since he had left India, he had failed to develop any capacity to withstand winter. Even October left him huddled against radiators while his colleagues sauntered around as if at an embassy ball in the Bahamas. And when summer finally came he always spent the season terrified of winter's return, bracing himself for its arrival as one might a punch to the solar plexus from a prison warden.

★   ★   ★

That night, at home, Chandra pulled out his old Rand McNally atlas, purchased on New Year's Eve in Times Square in 1982, the year Sunny was born. Dr Chaney was right, he decided: he needed to go somewhere warm, and not Australia, where alligators roamed freely in the streets and lecturers gave tutorials in swimming shorts.

He thought about Florida, but Florida was too far from Colorado, where Jasmine was, and he still blamed them for failing to elect Hillary Knows-Some-Economics Clinton, which was more than could be said for the Oaf who wouldn't know a demand curve if it wrapped itself around his pizza-laden stomach. No, Dr Chaney was right. It had to be California.

Chandra hated San Francisco with its freezing, fog-ridden microclimate and those placard-carrying mummy's boys at Berkeley who paid thirty thousand dollars a year to protest income inequality. No, it had to be Los Angeles. LA was always warm, and the people were realists who actually enjoyed their lives. When Professor Chandra closed his eyes he visualised a string of parties, drives out to Malibu in a convertible with Doris Day belting out from the stereo.

Chandra didn't know anyone at UCLA, but an old colleague of his, Felix Radison, was now Professor at UC Bella Vista in Orange County. This was an hour south of Los Angeles, which might even be preferable, away from the prostitutes and drug addicts, and with starry pollution-free skies, looking out over the ocean at the end of the day with a good Napa Valley Sauvignon, And of course, Boulder would only be a short flight away.

He called a few days later.

★   ★   ★

By Christmas time it was all settled. He would start at the end of January. His official position would be Distinguished Visiting Professor at UC Bella Vista, which meant nothing more than giving the occasional lecture to a theatre packed with adoring acolytes and jealous colleagues.

Chandra would have liked to have arrived

31

earlier, but Dr Chaney had warned him not to do anything for at least two months, and so he remained alone throughout Christmas, neglecting even to attend the departmental and college Christmas dinners. Sunny said he might visit, but proved too busy in the end (Chandra called him twice on Christmas Day to make certain he wasn't actually in Boulder). Jasmine elected not to make the trip either as she was planning to resit her SATs in January although, as far as Chandra knew, it would be too late for college applications then. She insisted there were colleges who had promised they'd accept a late application but when he asked for names she told him 'Hogwarts', which he looked up online before realising it was a ruse.

He spent the first weeks of January trying to hold off work on his new book, one that would constitute a critique of the left's critique of the right (essentially a rehash of his old ideas though delivered with a more concentrated dose of bile). He had already rejected titles such as *The Importance of Free Trade* in favour of something more upbeat like *In Praise of Wealth* or *Why We Need Corporations*. The liberals would hate him for it, but Chandra didn't care what they said — he had given up trying to have a dialogue with the kindergarten of the left.

Not working proved so difficult that he ended up stuffing all his notes into the freezer along with his pencils and erasers only to discover them a week later conjoined to a packet of frozen spinach like a new and threatening life form.

He stayed in bed watching television instead,

making his way through the entire first season of *Friends*, finally understanding the jokes his children had made throughout the nineties. It was about six promiscuous yet deeply conservative youngsters who lived well beyond their means and, with the exception of the academic, lacked any ambition, drive, intelligence or common sense. In economic terms they were idiots, though this was also true of ninety per cent of undergraduates.

Days before his departure, Professor Chandra called Jean and told her of his impending sabbatical. He didn't know why he had waited so long to inform her, but it did occur to him that she might be angry with him, that she'd prefer it if he remained five thousand miles away across the water. But this turned out not to be the case.

'It'll be good for Jaz,' she said. 'She's just not herself. I know she's been sullen before, and she's a teenager and she's got hormones and, God, I know what girls are like, but this is different. She's going out of control, Charles.'

In the seventies, at the LSE, he had insisted everyone call him Charles, so impossible did they find Chandrasekhar, but as his stature had grown Chandra had rescinded his request. Jean was the only person who had never switched.

'I don't know what to say,' said Chandra. 'I had no idea.'

'Yeah,' said Jean, not unsympathetically. 'How could you?'

'You could have told me.'

'I am telling you, Charles.'

He wanted to say that she could have let him

know earlier, that he needed to know everything when it happened, not weeks later, but when antagonised Jean often cut the conversation short. It had been a long time, in fact, since they had spoken in any depth.

'Is she talking to anyone?' he asked.

'Of course she is,' said Jean. 'This is America. There's a shrink at her school.'

'And?'

'And there's Steve. He's always there for her to talk to. Oh, don't make that face, Charles. It's his job.'

He had been making a face.

'I meant,' said Chandra, 'has the shrink at school helped?'

'Well, she hates him, which Steve says is a good thing — at least she's getting her anger out.'

'And what do *you* think?'

Jean sighed. Whenever he thought of her she was sighing.

'Look, Charles, we got divorced, it shook up her whole life, and she's a teenager and angry as hell. It's hard, it's real, and we've got to deal with it as parents, which means *being parents*. We can't let her get away with blue murder.'

Chandra put his head in his hands. 'I'll spend time with her in LA,' he said. 'It's her SATs that are bothering her. It'll be all right. We'll get her into a good university.'

'She isn't you, Charles. College isn't the meaning of life to her.'

'I'll talk to her,' he repeated.

'Talk *with* her,' said Jean.

'That's what I said,' said Chandra. 'We'll spend time together in LA.'

'Teenagers don't want to spend time with their fathers, Charles. But I do agree it would be good for her to see you.'

'I know — '

'I don't think you do. You've got to be firm with her. Set the rules, Charles. Decide the boundaries. And *listen* to her, if you can get her to talk at all.'

'I've been a parent for over thirty years, Jean. I know what I'm doing.'

'Like I said, this is different. Most days she doesn't even say hello till afternoon.'

'She wants to see me,' said Chandra. 'She said so.'

'Are you all right over there, Charles?' said Jean. 'Alone for the holidays.'

'Oh, God,' said Chandra. 'I'm glad of some time alone. This year has been — '

'Well, good,' said Jean. 'It's sad thinking of you all by yourself in that house.'

Chandra thought about hinting at the presence of a significant other in his life, saying something like, 'Well, I'm relatively alone.' He wished he could have recorded a woman's voice on his answering machine saying, 'Chandra, come back to bed . . . ' but Jean would probably have seen through this at once.

'Well, see you at Jaz's graduation, right?'

'Of course.'

'Great,' said Jean. 'She'd see us together then too. The school counsellor says that'll be good for her.'

'I understand,' said Chandra, flinching at the knowledge that this would mean meeting his cuckolder again. 'Of course I'll be there. I'd never miss her graduation.'

'Good. I'm pleased,'

Feeling lonelier than ever, Chandra wished he could persuade Jean to stay on the line, to talk about something else, anything. Nothing came to mind.

'Well, *adios*, Carlos.'

He had lied and told her he was learning Spanish in preparation for LA.

'Yes, *adios*.'

'And remember your Green Cross Code.'

★ ★ ★

In 1973, when Chandra and Jean first met, he had been quite the romantic, accompanying her to ballroom dance classes even though the idea terrified him. He came close to a panic attack during the tango and might have succumbed had it not been for the smell of rose from Jean's cheek, which reminded him of India.

Seven years younger than Chandra, Jean was studying chemistry at Brunel and, like him, felt out of place in London. Jean was the only one in her family to have gone to university. She had grown up in a town called Bolton, in Lancashire, a place she described as 'like London except different in every way'.

They used to spend a lot of the time at the cinema, losing themselves in disaster films then relishing their re-entry into a world that looked far less frightening afterwards. Sometimes they would take day trips out of the city, walking along the beach at Brighton or Bournemouth, sharing ice creams and riding the Ferris wheel as the sun went down.

Neither had many friends. Jean felt cowed by the display of middle-class elocution that came so naturally to everyone around her, while Chandra, in his first lecturing job at the London School of Economics, was wrestling with his fear that the English might actually be as superior as they believed themselves to be. On the few occasions they went to parties they found themselves talking mostly to each other, and concluded they were better off at home playing board games.

Chandra remembered those early years as filled with a quiet joy. His career had felt unimportant by comparison, a necessary but trivial task like brushing his teeth or filing his taxes. But he had worked hard. He had to. Had he lost his job he would have needed to return to India, four thousand miles away from Jean.

He was nervous when he met her parents, tucking into the plate of roast beef they set in front of him as if it were his most favourite thing in the world. But they seemed uninterested in him, not unfriendly, only bored, which seemed to be how they felt about everything. They asked very few questions and replied in monosyllables to his own questions. The conversation was dominated instead by Jean's younger sister, Jennifer, who had opinions not only on India but even on economics. Britain was in recession in those days and Jennifer blamed the Arabs for hiking up the price of oil, an assessment Chandra agreed with.

'There's no point us working three fucking days a week, is there?' said Jennifer, who used such language freely in front of her parents. 'Where's that going to get us?'

'It's to save on electricity,' said Jean.

'We can't even watch TV,' said Jennifer, and again looked at Chandra as if to signify that she blamed him for both the oil crisis and the three-day week.

'She's always liked a good joust,' said Jean later.

'Yes, of course,' said Chandra, who had been telling her all year that this was the lot of the economist, that they were always society's scapegoats.

'Sorry my parents were so quiet,' said Jean. 'They'll warm up eventually.'

'Oh, I'm sure,' said Chandra.

But this never came to pass. Their wedding, also in Bolton, was just as lacklustre an affair with perhaps twenty guests, all from Jean's side except for two of Chandra's colleagues. Jean's father made a very short, perfunctory speech welcoming 'Charles' to the family before sitting down without saying another word for the rest of the evening. Jennifer made a speech too, bright and witty, but not even mentioning Chandra or the wedding.

A month later there was a second reception in Hyderabad. It was Jean's first trip abroad, Jennifer's too, though their parents elected not to make the journey, declaring it 'too far'. Chandra took the sisters to his parents' home, a three-storey villa in Banjara Hills which he described, somewhat preposterously, as his 'ancestral home' (it was only twenty years old).

He hired a driver to show them the city, trying not to leave the affluent suburbs in case the sisters saw pigs grazing in rubbish or beggars with no limbs, or barefooted sadhus, and pronounced his country a developmental failure. In the process he neglected to show Jean the places where he actually grew up, his coffee clubs and cricket grounds and book-shops, but he achieved his objective. At the reception both admitted they had expected more poverty.

'I knew it wouldn't be like on TV,' said Jennifer.

'Nothing is,' said Jean.

'Jean's a realist,' said Chandra's father, drunk since the afternoon.

'I'm a romantic,' said Chandra, desperate for a cigarette.

'You're an idiot,' said his father.

Chandra changed the subject, pretending not to have heard.

An hour later, he was huddled in a corner with two old classmates when his father walked over and extended his hand.

'I'm sorry,' he said. 'That was wrong of me.'

It was the first time in his life his father had apologised to him, or indeed to anyone, as far as Chandra knew. He was sure it was Jean's doing, but he had no idea how she had accomplished it. When he asked her she answered, 'Took his drink away.'

Chandra's father was a civil servant who had written two books on the Indian Constitution. Chandra's mother had died eleven years before and ever since his father had consumed a regular glass of rum and water at eleven in the morning. It was the reason for Chandra's strict rule about never drinking before sundown (a rule he had retired after turning sixty-five).

'I could have been so much more,' was a refrain Chandra had heard for years, but he was never sure if his father was referring to his drinking, his widowhood, his failure to become a professional cricketer, or his position within the service. All he knew was that his father was incomplete, a circle three quarters drawn, and it had made him mean.

Professor Chandra's father died four years later from a heart attack. They had spoken on the phone a week earlier when Chandra called with the news that Chicago had offered him an Associate Professorship, conveyed via a hand-written note from Milton Friedman himself who had told him he was 'enamored of' his writings. Chandra braced himself for something along the lines of, 'But Chicago's not in the Ivy League,' or, 'Why not a full Professorship?' but instead there was silence, and what might have been a sob.

'Keep going, Chandu,' his father said at last. 'You can do it, Chandu. You can do it.'

There followed a brief spat about Indira Gandhi after which his father muttered,

'Nincompoop,' and hung up the phone, but Chandra had tried to forget this. Sometimes he found himself inventing new memories, snapshots of purely imaginary kindness, as if mourning the relationship he had never had, the man his father had never been. The phrase 'I could have been so much more' was etched in his mind now, closely followed by 'You can do it, Chandu,' which he liked to think of as his father's last words.

It was at this time that he began to work with the sort of relentlessness that would become his signature in years to come. He claimed it was merely on account of being in the US. This was what they did, he said; they *all* ate dinner at their desks and ran straight from maternity wards into meetings. But Jean pointed out that he was beginning to adopt a new persona too, that he was developing a reputation for arrogance which meant that, along with admirers, he was acquiring enemies at a formidable rate.

'It's necessary,' he told her. 'They'll eat you alive here if you don't play hardball.'

Even after Sunny was born, Chandra tended to stay at the office until midnight, working on the manuscript that would eventually become his first book, *Fast Unto Bankruptcy*. He smoked more than he had in England, and drank twice as much coffee. On some mornings he would wake with his head on his desk and a cup of cold Nescafé in front of him at which he would lap before going to his first lecture of the day. Jean used to worry that he would fall asleep with a cigarette in his hand.

41

'You'll set the department on fire one day,' she said.

'That's exactly what I intend to do,' Chandra replied.

And now he was a year away from being seventy and had set not only the department but the world on fire, and yet he could not shake the feeling that he had squandered his years, drained them of all that was worthwhile. Fun! Joy! Laughter! Play! The same qualities he had so derided in his colleagues, even in his children.

Professor Chandra took off his clothes and stared at himself in the bedroom mirror. Most men his age did not like what they saw when they did this and tried to make up for it by buying sports cars or taking mistresses or making yet more money, but Chandra had no objection to his body. His paunch was gentle and inoffensive. His hair was more silver than grey and neatly parted, though with his forelock hanging wild like Denis Compton's in his Brylcreem days. He had those spindly legs common to so many South Indian men, but even they were elegant in their own way, slender and deer-like.

Most important of all, he did not look like a man who had had a heart attack, silent or otherwise. As he stared at his reflection he couldn't see the grim reaper's bony finger draped across his shoulder. Yes, he was at an age when, in days of yore, men would retire to forests for blissful austerities, but Sunny was right: this was the modern era. He could live to be over a hundred. Soon heart transplants would be as common as vasectomies, cancer no more troubling than the common cold.

'It isn't over yet,' he told his reflection and crossed to the bed, trying to whistle the tune to 'California Girls'.

3

UC Bella Vista was not what he had expected.

It resembled a glorified retirement community, row upon row of prefab homes interspersed with the occasional playground. Green deciduous plants that had no business existing in such a climate grew alongside palm trees and cacti, and every street — they all looked identical — was named after a famous writer or scientist, most of them Nobel laureates. Professor Chandra saw acres of unused land on which cranes and diggers were busy at work. He didn't want to ask what they were doing for fear they might be building a cemetery.

'Welcome to California,' said Felix who had met him at the airport.

'Where's the town?' said Chandra, peering at the horizon.

'It's all out there waiting for you. So what do you think?'

'It's quite something.'

'Isn't it?' Felix clapped him lightly on the back.

He felt better when he saw his new home, which had four bedrooms, a TV the size of a whiteboard, and a hot tub in the garden. Chandra was also provided with an SUV, his first ever, which, after a bath, he drove into town, noting that the mirror allowed him to see no more than a third of the road behind him which left him in a permanent state of anxiety.

The town revealed itself to be a giant retail outlet with shops the size of airport terminals. The same chain eateries recurred every two or three miles, and Chandra realised he could get the exercise Dr Chaney had insisted upon simply by walking from one Starbucks to the next (he counted four in the space of ten minutes). That evening, Felix and four other faculty members took him to a Mexican restaurant where, in accordance with his low-fat, low-sodium, low-sugar diet, he ate a wholewheat tortilla with grilled chicken and avocado. Felix tapped on his margarita glass and made a speech after which the waiters produced a flan with sparklers sticking out of it in Chandra's honour. It was hardly High Table.

Over the following days, the drive to LA proved neither as dramatic nor as glamorous as Chandra had hoped. He was at the mercy of the GPS which had the habit of saying, 'Turn right now,' when he was in the leftmost extremity of a five-lane highway, and on three separate occasions tattooed could-be gangsters gave him the finger (and once, the sign for a pistol). To make matters worse, he found the SUV near impossible to park and so opted for valets with their exorbitant rates until, eventually, he stopped going to LA altogether. He spent most evenings in his backyard after that, listening to the sound of hosepipes on lawns and reading Dan Brown, or else he found himself at one of his neighbours' houses, identical in layout to his own, discussing departmental politics over barbecued chicken and iced tea.

As for the university itself, it was a relief to be in less exalted surroundings, to have an office inside a twentieth-century, air-conditioned concrete block instead of a sixteenth-century castle, and to interact with staff who didn't call him sir or wear bowler hats. But the undergraduates were even worse than in Cambridge: arrogant, unhygienic and brazen, convinced that lazy platitudes and fallacious arguments would earn them nothing but praise if delivered with sufficient conviction. It remained Professor Chandra's unshakeable belief that university was wasted on ninety per cent of these unctuous recidivists but, after his reprimand in Cambridge, he tried to keep his thoughts to himself.

The best thing about being in California, however, was his proximity to Jasmine and, Jean's warnings notwithstanding, he was thrilled when, in March, he found himself waiting for her at John Wayne airport holding the bag of chocolate Easter eggs he had brought over from Mr Simms in Cambridge.

Jasmine was staring into her phone when she emerged. She was wearing some sort of pale foundation (the Gothic look; he remembered it from Radha) beneath black mascara and lipstick. Her clothes were black too, including her raincoat, ridiculous in LA. She didn't smile, but she did put her arms around his neck for at least a minute.

On the drive home he kept telling her how delighted he was to see her, prattling on for most of the journey, trying to avoid the subject of her college applications so as not to send her into a rage early on. But Jasmine didn't seem angry or depressed. She asked about his health, whether he had been smoking or eating red meat, and told him swimming was by far the best exercise.

'I can't swim,' said Chandra.

'You can, Dad. I've seen you.'

'I can float,' he said. 'It isn't the same.'

'Hey,' said Jasmine. 'Can I drive?'

She had been learning for two months. Jean couldn't drive herself, but had reported that Steve was doing 'a super job'.

'Certainly,' said Chandra, and pulled over.

Chandra watched as Jasmine settled into the driver's seat and spent several minutes adjusting the mirror, a difficult task in an SUV, before pulling away. To his relief, she proved a slow and conservative driver (which had not been the case with Sunny or Radha), and on reaching home, parked the SUV in the driveway far more neatly than he ever had, before handing him the keys.

'So,' he said. 'This is it.'

'Yeah,' said Jasmine. 'It looks all right.'

'Nothing like Boulder.'

Jasmine shrugged.

'So how are your friends?' he asked, feeling like an idiot. 'Suzie and . . . everyone else.'

'They're okay.'

'Your mother said you've been talking to someone,' said Chandra. 'Is that, you know, going well?'

Jasmine sighed. 'I don't need therapy, Dad. I'm just having it to keep everyone happy, okay?'

'That's what I thought.'

'Everything's all right. Mum's all right. Steve's all right. School's all right. Life's all right. It's not brilliant, it's not great, it's not wonderful, but it's not like I'm planning on slashing my arteries with a potato peeler. Okay?'

'Okay.'

That night as he got out of the bath, wrapping a towel around his waist, he looked out the window and saw Jasmine in the garden smoking a cigarette. She stared at him defiantly before turning her back. With that baseball cap on her head, she looked exactly as she had at thirteen; he could easily imagine a sticking plaster on her left knee, the two of them playing ping-pong on that rusty table in the garden or painting the shed while making up nonsense rhymes.

They visited the Getty the following morning, and again he let her drive, but this time the SUV got the better of her and in the parking lot she pressed too hard on the accelerator and slammed the car into a concrete wall. Sunny was right: airbags were pretty safe, if uncomfortable.

Chandra prepared himself for tears, contrition, an inconsolable child, but instead Jasmine squeezed her way past that plastic bubble, tearing her skirt, and into the car park where she began to scream, short, sharp and repeatedly, like someone thrusting a dagger. A security guard came and helped Professor Chandra out through the back seat after which the two approached Jasmine from behind, carefully, as if stalking a bear.

'I wish you'd both just disappear!' she shrieked, not even turning around.

'Now what did I ever do to you?' said the guard.

'You and Mum! You and your little lives, as if every fucking thing in the world is about *you!*'

Four women had stopped to gawk and were talking in French, which Jasmine understood perfectly.

'*Allez vous faire foutre, bande de salopes!*'

The women fled, a flurry of calf-length designer skirts and heels. Chandra looked at the security guard for help but he only shrugged and said, 'She's your kid, man.'

'I am nobody's fucking kid! Do I look like a kid?'

'No,' said the guard, who was about forty-five, with flecks of white in his beard. 'But you sure sound like one, and if you were mine I'd put you over my knee and spank you, I don't care how big you are.'

'Yeah, you'd love that, wouldn't you?' said Jasmine. 'You'd love to get your paedo hands on my ass. Be a nice change from school-girl porn!'

'Sorry, friend, you're on your own,' said the guard. 'I can call a pickup truck, but that's as far as I go.'

'I thought you wanted to spank me?' said Jasmine. 'Come on, big man, spank me!'

The guard walked away, his image receding into the darkness like the silhouette of a distant shoreline.

For the rest of her visit Jasmine was just as Jean had described. After he tried to talk to her about her college applications she went into her room and locked the door while Chandra stood outside repeating her name, trying to keep the irritation out of his voice. When he smelled marijuana he almost started shouting but checked himself and knocked again, slowly and methodically. 'All right,' came Jasmine's voice, 'I'll come down', and for the rest of the evening they watched television on the sofa in silence.

The following day he took her to the airport where she hugged him for exactly three seconds before saying, 'See you around,' and walked away, looking at her phone. Chandra stayed in the airport for two more hours, drinking lemonade and watching the planes take off. His conditioning told him to be stern with his daughter, that her behaviour was villainous, disrespectful, wanton and abhorrent — but he couldn't make that mistake again, not after Radha.

He called Jean that night and told her everything had gone splendidly, 'save for a few hiccoughs'.

'That's what I thought,' said Jean.

'Yes, she's become quite a personality.'

'That's not how I'd put it. I'd say she's shut herself down. You can't even see her personality.'

'Oh, not at all,' said Chandra. 'Come now.'

'So tell me, Charles,' said Jean, slipping into scorn. 'What did you learn about Jasmine? What did she tell you?'

'Lots of things.'

'I want details, Charles. Come on.'

'Well . . . ' said Chandra.

'Sorry, Charles,' said Jean. 'But I don't think

this is normal. I don't care what anyone says. Not you, and not Steve.'

He wondered if Steve was in the room, perhaps massaging her shoulders, whispering, 'I know you don't, honey, and that's *fine*.' Their home was nothing like Chandra's Grantchester cottage: lights and music were activated by handclaps; there were four taps, for hot, cold, filtered and sparkling water; and Jean had said there was no plastic in their house. None.

'Perhaps,' said Chandra, admitting defeat. 'Perhaps you're right.'

After Jasmine returned to Boulder, he continued to call her twice a week, but she always replied in monosyllables, or sometimes no syllables at all. He tried to focus on his lecture series instead, entitled 'The World Economy Today', but found the students too brash and outspoken for his liking, which only reminded him of Radha. They seemed to come pre-offended, forsaking any analytical content in favour of emotion and outrage. At the end of April, during his final lecture on the credit crunch, a graduate student stood up and rattled on for several minutes about how outrageous everything was, before saying:

'And surely, Professor, *someone* should have gone to jail, shouldn't they?'

'It's a good question.'

It was a horrible question, one that put him in the most awkward of positions, because the truth was that by the end of 2008 the CEO of every bank, mortgage lender and insurance company should have been in jail, along with half the faculty of Harvard Business School. But he could hardly say that in a public lecture.

'These things are complex. We could look at Goldman's and others and say they lied about their products, but in this respect they're no different from the car salesman who passes off a lemon as a plum, or the burger joint that gives you a cardboard pancake instead of a juicy two-incher. As for the credit raters, their response was that they gave their opinion, which turned out to be wrong, and how can we prove otherwise?'

'So they butt-fucked us, didn't they?' shouted someone from the balcony.

Professor Chandra took off his glasses and laughed. The entire room laughed with him; if he stopped, they would be laughing at him.

'The short answer to your question,' he said, wiping his glasses and returning them to his face, 'is yes.'

The room roared its approval.

'But there's more to it than that. The crash was a systemic problem and must be treated as such. Inadequate regulation, reckless loans to sub-prime borrowers, greed, and — a lot of the time — simple stupidity. There were economists who shouted it from the rooftops, journalists too, even traders, and they were ignored because the system made them ignorable. We have to put a system in place with proper safeguards so this can never happen again. For obvious reasons, this is a far more urgent concern than locking bankers away.'

The applause was thinner now, the audience

disgruntled. Professor Chandra blamed Radha. He blamed her for more or less everything these days, as if she were always with him, lodged inside his brain like a fragment of a bullet. Wherever he went, he could hear her taunting him, telling him he was weak, disingenuous, arrogant, ignorant, self-serving, deluded. She was with him in that voice that had shouted about being 'butt-fucked', just as she'd been there last week when a cab driver spat on the side-walk after Chandra realised he'd forgotten his wallet, yelling, 'If you can't pay for it, don't get in the goddamn car.'

And still, Chandra had no idea where Radha *was*. He doubted she was in England, but nor did America seem likely. India was always a possibility, or somewhere further afield like China or, God forbid, Russia. Presumably they would have told him if she were dead or had joined ISIS or signed up for the 2036 colony on Mars.

He had tried asking Jean, tried several times, but she always replied with, 'Sorry, Charles, I gave my word,' a grandiose way of saying, 'Sorry, Charles, but I enjoy torturing you.' When he left for Colorado, it occurred to him that Steve probably knew where Radha was. Maybe she was even a frequent visitor to their house.

* * *

In early May, Chandra returned to the airport to fly to Boulder for Jasmine's graduation. On landing, he looked at Steve's instructions,

53

forwarded to him by Jean in an email, noting the phrase:

Try to come before sunset — the ride is imperial!

Imperial! he thought. What did Americans know of imperial? And was this a sensitive thing to say to a man from a country colonised for hundreds of years by wife-stealing white men? Did the child psychiatrist even know this? But of course not. Steve was American, and in America they called all subcontinentals 'Indians' which typified their ignorance of alien lands. Oh, yes, Americans just took what they wanted without even stopping to learn who or what they were taking it from. It was their manifest destiny.

The sun was setting when he arrived. Steve and Jean lived on the ridge of a hill accessible by a dirt track. He had been there only once before not long after the divorce, to inspect where Jasmine would be living. It was a sharp-lined, modern-looking white bungalow, slightly raised on stilts, and with an open garage in which he could see a black Porsche convertible and two motorbikes. There was also a dark-skinned man dressed in dungarees staring up at him from inside the grounds, shielding his eyes against the red glare of the dipping sun. And now the man was smiling at him and opening the gates so that he could park beside the motorbikes that were polished to an alien sheen.

Chandra turned off the engine and realised his hands were shaking. He removed his tie, shoved it in the glovebox, and closed his eyes before

54

trying to recite a mantra he had learned in childhood: '*Ramaskandam Hanumantham* . . . ' Unable to remember the rest, he switched to the Leontief paradox: 'A country with a higher capital per worker has a *lower* capital/labour ratio in exports than in imports.' A tear leaked from his eye, which he rubbed into the faux leather of the steering wheel.

The man in the dungarees stepped forward to open the car door.

'*Bienvenido*, sir,' said the man. 'I am Rafael.'

'Pleased to meet you, Rafael,' said the Professor, wishing he had indeed learned some Spanish (it would be embarrassing if Jean were to mention it). 'Call me Chandra.'

'Okay, Chandra,' said Rafael, taking his hand in both of his.

They walked around the house, passing a column of rose bushes that gave the air a venomous sweetness. At the rear was a pool filled with blue-green water that appeared to tumble over the edge of a precipice beyond which Chandra could see the nascent lights of Boulder. Vivaldi was playing from hidden speakers.

There were two grey sofas on the deck and Jean was reclining on one in a white trouser suit, sandals and a green coral necklace. She had cut her hair and dyed it from dirty grey to blonde. There was a pair of Martini glasses on the table beside her and a full jug. Jean lifted her head and sat up, turning down the music with a remote control.

'Charles,' she said, rising. At the edge of the pool she clapped her hands, and circular floor lights illuminated the garden. The last time he had seen her was a year ago, on his usual lecture tour in the US. She had seemed tense around him then, but looked more relaxed now as she walked towards him and — he had to admit it — younger. He could feel the sadness in his throat, a gristled lump of poison he refused to swallow. But tonight was not the night for grief.

Jean avoided his extended hand and gave him a loose-limbed hug. He heard a cough from behind him.

'It's so good to see you again,' said Steve, who was barefoot. 'You look wonderful, Chandrasekhar.'

Like Jean, Steve was dressed all in white, wearing linen trousers and a silk shirt. It felt like a uniform, a signal that they belonged here and he did not. Steve was in his sixties but had this aura of age-defiance, as if in direct competition with the younger generation. Chandra wondered if they felt sorry for him.

'You too,' said Chandra.

'No, really, you've lost weight.'

'Well . . . ' said Chandra.

Steve shook his hand and pressed Chandra's back, which was not quite a hug.

'We were sorry to hear you were unwell,' said Steve. 'You had us worried for a while.'

'Oh, I'm all right now,' said Chandra, wanting to divert the conversation away from how, unlike Steve, he had neglected his body and paid the price. 'Your home is looking very smart.'

'We did our best, thank you, Chandrasekhar,' said Steve. 'You know, it's odd me calling you

Chandrasekhar, isn't it?'

'Is it?' said Chandra, who hated Steve's ability to pronounce his name which, when fully extended, was usually his most dangerous weapon.

'Well, it's like you calling me Benowitz, isn't it? I mean, why don't I use your first name?'

'Technically my name is only Chandrasekhar,' said Chandra. 'First and last.'

'So nobody calls you P. R.'

'Oh, no, no. Nobody has ever called me P. R.'

Steve's hair was white, but his bristly arms indicated a no-nonsense virility. It was easy to imagine him swimming forty lengths each morning. He looked like a man who had spent much of his life on a beach.

'You know,' said Steve, 'I get nervous when I meet you. I start feeling like the village idiot or something. I mean, how many future Nobel Prize-winners have I met?'

'And how many psychiatrists have I met?'

'Well, I'm mostly retired these days. I just help friends out in a crisis. The last few years have all been about the business. I guess Jean told you.'

'I don't think so,' said Chandra.

'It was a family thing. My brother died and the business was my father's, so I thought I'd better step up. Anyway, it keeps the rain off our heads.'

Jean smiled. In the past she would always smile when she was nervous, but in a tight way. This loose smile was something new.

'And what line of business is it?' asked Chandra, though he knew the answer.

'Flowers,' said Steve. 'Plain and simple. Grow

them in greenhouses, sell them in shops. We deliver, too. Restaurants, funeral homes, anyone who needs them. People always need flowers. You see flowers all day long in cities. It cheers us up like nothing else, even if we don't notice them.'

'Yes,' said Chandra. 'I also like flowers.'

'But it's serious to me. Business isn't something you can joke about these days, not since the times darkened. Anyway, I hardly need to tell you that. You're like a world authority.'

'Well, I suppose that's *my* family business.'

'Oh, so your father was an economist?'

'No,' said Chandra, flustered. 'Not exactly.'

He shot a glance at Jean who was still smiling. He wondered if she had taken a Valium, or one of the new drugs those emails in his inbox kept inviting him to try. Presumably this was a perk of living with a psychiatrist.

'Ah, but there's Sunny,' said Steve. 'I guess you could call him an economist.'

Not for the first time, Chandra was possessed by the terrible paranoiac fantasy that Sunny and Radha had both spent Christmas with his cuckolder, and that Sunny had covered his tracks by rerouting his home phone to Boulder with some new technology, a feat he was quite capable of.

'Let's sit down, shall we?' said Jean, pointing to the sofas. 'Unless you'd rather be indoors, Charles.'

'Here's fine,' said Chandra, wondering if she could actually be enjoying this encounter, like a favoured lady at a joust. 'This really is a wonderful place, Steve.'

'Well, it didn't turn out exactly as I imagined it, but nothing ever does, does it?'

'No,' said Chandra, wanting to make a joke about his marriage that would make them uncomfortable and put him at his ease, but lacking the courage.

Chandra took care not to slip on the deck; his shoes were Italian and leather, bought for the occasion. On reaching the sofas he barged in front of Jean so as not to face the cliff's edge.

'Charles has a fear of heights,' said Jean.

'I used to have agliophobia,' said Steve. 'Did I tell you? I guess not. It's hardly something you lead with. Fear of pain. Seriously. It's why I became a shrink. I was in therapy so long I thought, 'Why don't I just do this myself?' Ninety per cent of shrinks are insane when they start.'

'I was a Marxist at university,' said Chandra. 'I suppose that's comparable.'

Steve looked away in confusion. Jean did not respond. She'd had over thirty years of jokes like this.

'I was never a Marxist,' said Steve. 'I mean, there's got to be some redistribution, but all this obsession with justice . . . it's not healthy. Whenever you say, 'That isn't right,' or, 'That's not fair,' you're being violent. I didn't used to get that, but then I took a course in NVC. You know NVC?'

Chandra shook his head.

'Nonviolent communication. Fella called Marshall Rosenberg who says we got to focus on feelings and needs. If I'm always saying, 'You're making me feel . . . ' or, 'Your anger is . . . ' it'll always end up in a fight; any therapist can tell you that. NVC has a better way of going about it. Gets to the heart of the problem.'

Steve reached beneath the arm of the sofa. At once Rafael's amplified voice filled the night air.

'*Si, señor.*'

'*Rafael, la guitarra, por favor.*'

'Steve,' said Jean. 'No. Just don't.'

'Why not? Chandrasekhar wants me to, don't you?'

Chandra nodded. 'Sure. Why not?'

'He doesn't even know what you're going to do,' said Jean.

'I'm going to sing a song, of course.'

'We did the course together,' said Jean. 'The singing's got nothing to do with it. Steve just likes performing.'

'Folk was my first love. Didn't give myself a chance.'

'Steve has many talents,' said Jean, stroking Steve's cheek which made Chandra want to lower himself into the pool until the water covered his head. 'Singing isn't one of them. Trust me.'

'Oh, no,' said Chandra. 'I'm sure . . . '

Jean removed the plastic cover from the pitcher and filled two Martini glasses. Seconds later Rafael appeared with a tray of olives and two tiny wooden spoons.

'See,' said Jean. 'Rafa 'forgot' the guitar.'

'Great man, Rafa,' said Steve. 'Crossed the border when he was five. Illegal, no parents, not even twenty bucks in his pocket. Learned

60

English in nine months. *Nine.* His English is flawless now. Reads Shakespeare, Melville, you name it. We speak in Spanish for me, not him. I'm putting his kids through school. Made a commitment to see it through all the way up to college.'

'That was very generous of you,' said Chandra.

'I didn't mean to brag. I just love the guy. He's like family. That's an old chestnut, I know, but in this case it's true. He's a hero, all he's been through, all he does for other people. When I help someone I let the whole world know. Not Rafa. He'll help anyone, rich, poor, doesn't care. Doesn't think like that. He'll go as out of his way for a member of my family as he will for one of his own. A true saint.'

One of the only things Chandra and Jean used to have in common was politics. Jean had always been a conservative. He watched now as she spooned olives into the Martini glasses and handed one to Chandra. Maybe Steve had brought out her inner liberal. Maybe this was behind that loose smile and the hair.

'What about you, Steve?' said Chandra. 'Not drinking?'

'AA,' said Steve. 'Twenty-four years.'

'Right,' said Chandra. 'Well done.'

'Don't thank me,' said Steve. 'Thank my higher power.'

'Charles doesn't believe in higher powers.'

'Then you haven't been in California long enough,' said Steve.

'This is what Californians do,' said Jean. 'They

convince you to be as open as they are, and then they screw you. Crafty buggers.'

Steve puckered up his lips in Jean's direction.

'Oh, honey, you love Californians and you know it,' said Steve. 'What you described is something totally different. It's called a Canadian.'

Jean took a slug of her drink. 'Anyway,' she said, 'Steve's first love is India.'

'You've been to more states than I have, as I recall,' said Chandra. 'You were there for years, weren't you?'

'Two,' said Steve. 'Two wonderful years.'

'With his first wife,' said Jean, poker-faced.

'I wanted to talk to you about it last time, but I didn't want to sound like a fucking stereotype,' said Steve, giving Chandra a meaningful look. 'I went there in '68 to find myself.'

Chandra remembered seeing hippies in the sixties. His parents had told him never to go near them, that they were all drug addicts, the dregs of the West. It was only when he came to England and actually spoke with them that he overcame his fear and realised they were essentially anthropologists.

'The difference is,' said Jean, 'Steve actually did find himself. He almost never came back.'

'I was mostly in Bombay, Poona, Rishikesh and Varanasi,' said Steve. 'I learned Sanskrit and Hindi, though I've forgotten most of it now.'

'Steve was one of the foremost Western experts on the school of Vedanta,' said Jean.

'Oh, no,' said Steve. 'I was just in the inner circle of a wise man, a very wise man. And when

I fell out of grace with him I drifted back here. I lived at Esalen for a time, but that's another story.'

'Esalen?'

'Sorry,' said Steve. 'I forget there are people who don't know it.'

'Forgive my ignorance.'

'Oh, no,' said Steve. 'I've got a very narrow group of friends. Same old fuckers from forty years ago. There's no reason you should know Esalen. It's a spiritual retreat centre. You can go there for three days, or five days, or a week, and eat good food, relax, look at the sea, and study.'

'Study what?' said Chandra.

'Whatever you like. Yoga, dance, chakra cleansing, primeval chanting, tantra.'

'It's beautiful,' said Jean. 'I mean, I've never been there, but I've seen pictures.'

'Big Sur,' said Steve. 'One of the most beautiful places in the world.'

'Oh,' said Chandra, 'well, maybe I should visit one day.'

Jean laughed, but Steve said: 'I think that's a great idea.'

Chandra looked at his watch. 'Where's Jasmine?'

'Ha!' said Steve. 'You won't see her till morning.'

'No,' said Jean. 'She'll be back for dinner. That was the deal.'

'That was *your* deal.'

'It was our deal. She can go out with her friends tomorrow.'

'Did you shake on it?'

63

'I told her she needs to see her father,' said Jean.

'Honey, no teenage girl wants to see her father. No offence, Chandra. My kids didn't want to see me either. That's just life.'

'The deal was she'd be back for dinner,' said Jean, 'so she'd better be.'

'Rebellion's a part of it,' said Steve. 'You command, she defies.'

'You can't do without boundaries,' said Jean.

'Boundaries are there to protect us. Teenagers don't want to be protected. They'll cross any line they see, which is why we have to be careful which lines we draw. Isn't that right, Chandrasekhar?'

'I almost think it doesn't matter what we do,' said Chandra. 'We can't control our children, boundaries or no boundaries. We can't control anything really. When I think about it, when I really sit down and think about it, I realise there *are* no boundaries. No boundaries at all. We only pretend there are.'

Steve looked out across the valley. Chandra could feel Jean staring at him. He doubted she had ever heard him talk like this. The truth was he had felt this way for years but had never been able to put it into words until his accident, that sudden realisation that if there was a meaning to life, none of them would ever know what it was.

Jean walked to the cliff's edge and looked at the sky, black now with a few stars emerging.

'I used to think Jean was angry when she got like this, but she's not, is she?' said Steve.

In Chandra's opinion, Jean was always a little

angry. It was her level; a sharpness Northern Englanders had, a permanent state of depression they accepted wholeheartedly. *Life's a bitch and so's the Prime Minister*, Jean used to say, despite being a Thatcherite through and through. Professor Chandra wanted to believe Steve had just revealed something critical about how little he knew Jean, but perhaps the truth was that Jean was becoming a Californian too, or, harder to stomach, was simply happier now.

'But Jasmine's a great kid,' said Steve. 'God, isn't it funny how your definition of a kid changes as you get older? I bet you see your students as children.'

'Some of them, yes.'

'That's the thing about child psychiatry. You realise so much of it applies to yourself. Like there's always a child in you who never went away. And then after we die, we become children again. You believe that, don't you, Chandrasekhar? That we're reincarnated?'

Chandra wanted to retaliate with something vicious and witty like, 'Maybe you were a man in your former life,' but he felt compelled to tell the truth: it was that sort of evening.

'I used to believe it when I was a child,' he said, 'but then I stopped. I haven't believed in anything since then. I haven't had time.'

'Wow,' said Steve. 'I never heard that one before. 'I'm an atheist because I don't have the time.''

'In my case it's true.'

Jean was talking on the phone, her voice raised. Chandra could not see her face, but he knew it was red, a balloon about to burst. It meant Jasmine wasn't coming home for dinner. He wished he could go back to his hotel and spend the evening under the covers with a book and a brandy from the mini-bar; he had started reading *Angels and Demons* a few days ago.

'I admire that so much,' said Steve, 'your take-it-or-leave-it attitude. In the West there's a tendency to let spirituality get to the ego. We start thinking we're better than other people because we meditate. That was the counterculture back then, and it's what finally did us in. People like me went to India, grew beards, came home, then realised our grandmothers were the wisest people we knew. So we turned into conservatives. You know what I mean?'

Chandra thought of his own grandmother, a cruel manipulator who died of a chest infection after immersing herself in a supposedly holy lake at the age of eighty-three.

'Absolutely,' said Chandra.

Jean tossed her phone onto the sofa. 'Well,' she said, 'that's that then.'

'Feelings and needs, Jean.'

Steve had morphed into a professional, eyes closed, hands on his knees, breathing deeply.

'All right,' said Jean. 'I feel angry as hell and hurt and sad because my need for respect is not being met.'

'And?'

'And love, and friggin' consideration — '

'That's a judgement.'

'Then just love . . . and respect.'

'Can we isolate the two?'

'I feel hurt because my need for love is not being met, and angry because my need for respect is not being met.'

'That's nonviolent communication,' said Steve. 'It takes blame out of the equation.'

It sounded like management-speak to Chandra's ears, which had never sounded non-violent to him but more a form of silly, confusing passive aggression, like bashing someone to death with a balloon.

'So when is Jasmine coming?' asked Chandra.

'God knows,' said Jean. 'She said she'd be back by midnight, which could mean anything.'

Jean's eyes were still locked onto Steve's. Chandra hoped no one would ask how *he* was feeling.

'Well,' said Steve, leaning forward and putting his hand on Jean's waist. 'I guess I'd better see about dinner.'

Steve stood and, to Chandra's surprise, Jean pulled him towards her and they embraced like shameless exhibitionists for what felt like hours but was probably seconds. So far as he could tell it was entirely unselfconscious and not a performance. He had always thought Jean so practical, so admirably unsentimental, but perhaps that had been him all along, and not her.

'Hungry, Chandrasekhar?' said Steve.

'Always,' said Chandra, who wasn't certain he could manage even a mouthful.

'Excellent.'

'Food's very simple here,' said Jean. 'Not exactly Cambridge fare.'

He was about to reply, 'Simple is my middle name,' but hung his head instead, his anxiety finally getting the better of him. Steve and Jean proceeded into the house with Chandra following, as if connected by a slack but high-quality length of rope.

To his relief, there was a baseball game on TV that Steve wanted to watch so they ate dinner in the open-plan kitchen, talking only during commercials. Chandra tried to explain the rules of cricket but Steve didn't seem interested, so he allowed baseball to be explained to him for what might have been the fortieth time in his life.

The dinner was Indian food, dal and aloo gobi, neither authentic nor inauthentic, but obviously made from superior ingredients. 'Rafa grinds the spices himself,' said Steve, and pointed to a giant mortar and pestle by the dishwasher.

After dinner Chandra took out his iPad, sitting at the kitchen counter and pretending to look at his emails, muttering, 'Okay, okay,' and, 'I thought I'd replied to this,' though in reality he was watching Steve and Jean who, it was evident, were happy, happier than he and Jean had ever been, even at the beginning.

He left shortly after eleven, accepting Jean's assurances that Jasmine wouldn't show her face until dawn. Steve hugged him goodbye, and Jean kissed him on the cheek, which she never used to, as if she were too joyous now to feel any bitterness towards him.

'Rafa will see you out,' said Steve, but there was no one there, so Chandra opened the gate and drove through the darkness, forgetting to turn on his lights until he was halfway up the road.

4

Jean had left him for the first time in 1997, three years after they moved back to Cambridge from Chicago. She called his rooms to tell him she was in Bristol with her sister. She had made arrangements for the babysitter to pick up the ten-year-old Radha.

'Why, Jean?' he said. 'What is this?'

'We'll talk when I get back, Charles.'

He'd been Head of Department for exactly a year by then, a role he had approached like a samurai trapped behind enemy lines. Declaring it a scandal that a department as illustrious as theirs should find itself beneath the Paris School of Economics in the league table, he made it his mission to go after the department's weakest links, the ones who believed a tenured position at Cambridge gave them the right to deliver the same lecture for twenty years, or to write English so sloppy they might as well have been living in Paris.

His methods were appreciated by the brighter, more productive members of staff, but he became a figure of hate for the mediocrities, those dough-faced, black-tied port swiggers who draped their frames across the velvet thrones of the SCR as if in a Saint-Denis bordello, reading *The Times* two or even three times during those long empty hours before dinner that everyone else called 'the day'. Many had been fine minds once, but they had let themselves go in their fifties, victims of pomp, circumstance and the college wine cellar. Chandra made it his task to expose them, pinning invisible dunce caps to their shiny foreheads in the hope that this might galvanise them into becoming scholars once more. Sometimes he corrected their work himself, applying Tipp-Ex with the zeal of a house painter. And many did emerge from their torpor, but with one goal only — to destroy their new tormentor so that life could return to the way it had been before the days of tyranny.

And so his life became a war, and through it all he continued to publish, cutting back on consulting and the only other thing he could afford to reduce — time spent with family. In any case, he had become a liability in the home, a short-tempered rogue who yelled at his children when he could not find his glasses, regularly stormed out of the house on Sundays in favour of the office, and twice kicked dents in the side of the car when the engine wouldn't start.

The night after Jean left, Sunny, then fifteen, asked where his mother was to which Chandra replied, 'Stop saying the first thing that comes into your head!' Sunny shrugged and replied, 'I was only asking,' at which Chandra yelled, 'You're always only asking!' Sunny stayed in his room that night, refusing to come down for dinner.

When Jean returned three days later she behaved as if nothing out of the ordinary had happened. It was only when they were in bed with the lights off that she dropped the bomb.

'A marriage counsellor!' said Chandra. 'Whatever for?'

'Because I want to.'

'But I don't beat you. I'm not an alcoholic.'

'I'm not as content as you are, Charles. I'm not happy with our marriage.'

'My God,' said Chandra. 'You think I'm content?'

'I think you're absorbed in what you're doing. I think that's enough.'

'I didn't choose to be absorbed,' said Chandra. 'I have to be. Do you understand? I have to.'

'We'll see,' said Jean, watching him while he crushed his face inside his hands. It felt as if she were analysing him, taking notes on his symptoms for future reference.

They saw the counsellor the following week, Jean making the appointment herself without consulting him. It was a woman, a Ms Cynthia Benson, who listened quite sympathetically to Chandra's side of the story. Chandra agreed that becoming a departmental wife had not been what Jean had wanted, but she had agreed to do this, he said, agreed to move to Chicago and then Cambridge, agreed not to work after Sunny was born. To his surprise, Cynthia Benson considered this important.

'Is this true, Jean?'

Jean nodded.

'Then you have to own it.'

'Yes,' said Jean, after a silence. 'Yes, that's fair.'

'It's important to take ownership of our decisions.'

'I agree,' said Chandra.

'And do you agree with your wife that you choose to work the hours you do?'

Chandra looked from Jean, who was staring at him, to Ms Benson, who was cleaning her glasses. Of course it wasn't a choice: if he didn't work, then how would he pay for their house, or their cars, or the televisions in every room, or the sums he doled out to cousins in India, some of whom he had never even met? And did anyone have the slightest idea what it was like for him in that department, how hated he was by those mediocrats, how he had to work twice as hard as all of them, not including the Senior Common Room somnambulists who barely worked at all? If that was a choice, you might as well call breathing a choice.

'Well, Chandra?' said Cynthia Benson.

'Yes,' said Chandra. 'I agree.'

'There's more,' said Jean. 'Charles won't say this, but he doesn't think the rules apply to him. He thinks he's not an ordinary person, that his work has to come first because it's vital for humanity and if his children have to suffer, then so be it.'

It was the cruellest thing she had ever said to him. Could he help it if he was a brilliant man? Yes, why not say it? B-R-I-L-L-I-A-N-T. It was a fact acknowledged by far greater authorities than Cynthia Benson. And yes, his work mattered. As he never tired of telling Jean, he had been born into a poor country, truly poor, not the sort of kitchen-sink poverty she complained of but the sort where millions died in famines, where homelessness *meant* homelessness instead of a preference for inferior wines and an al-fresco lifestyle. Chandra's work saved lives. It didn't mean he was more important than Jean or that he didn't love his family, but it was a fact.

'My work is important,' he said.

'Important to *you*,' said Jean.

'Yes,' said Chandra, adding, 'and to the world,' in his head.

'I wonder if Jean would see it as an act of love if you were to sacrifice some work time for family time,' said Cynthia Benson.

'I would,' said Jean. 'Absolutely. I feel invisible, Charles. As though you see your work but not me. I mean, you know I'm there, but you don't *see* me. I'm just your wife. Like an armchair. Like a rug.'

Chandra shook his head. 'No,' he said. 'I do see you.'

'But you have to accept this is the way Jean *feels*,' said Cynthia Benson.

Chandra nodded.

'And what about you, Chandra?' said Cynthia Benson. 'Is there anything you'd like from her?'

He looked Jean in the eye and struck a magnanimous pose, his head tilted as if modelling a Renaissance beret. 'Nothing at all.'

'Good,' said Cynthia Benson. 'So, I think we all agree that it's healthier for Jean to accept responsibility for her own decisions and try not to blame you for the past, while you, Chandra, will agree to come home earlier and spend less time at the office. We can discuss specifics, hours, days and so on, or we can leave it at that for now. Third . . . '

For the first few weeks, Chandra and Jean upheld their sides of the bargain. Jean spoke openly about how she wished she had pursued her studies further after marriage, but how she had resigned herself to being a departmental wife because she'd been afraid to fight her own battle, not because Chandra had oppressed her into doing it. But the battle had meant very little to her anyway, she told him. Chemistry had never excited her: she had never wanted to work in a lab, or to teach, or to join some company that made a product with a name she couldn't pronounce and a function she didn't care about. She had studied chemistry because she was good at it, because women didn't usually do science, because she'd wanted to be different. Marrying Chandra had been far easier than figuring out what she actually wanted to do.

'So you married me for something to do?' said Chandra.

'That isn't what I said, Charles.'

Jean had promised not to exhibit what Cynthia Benson, and now Chandra, called 'passive aggressive' behaviour, though he was still not sure what this meant. Chandra had always found much of her behaviour simply aggressive, wasn't certain there was even a difference.

He himself was making genuine attempts to spend less time at the office. He began to work in front of the fireplace at home, or in bed, and Jean seemed satisfied with this, as did Sunny and Radha. Sometimes Sunny would sit and read drafts of articles with his father, making arcane, unintelligible comments, sharing Chandra's outrage at a colleague's idiosyncratic grammar and syntax, repeating phrases like 'This would be hogwash if it came from an undergraduate!' and 'This is actually rather good; I wonder where he stole it from.' Radha, despite her age, seemed to understand the situation better. She would put an arm around Chandra or pat him on the back as if to congratulate him for being at home. 'We really have fun with you, you know,' she'd tell him, looking at him with those planet-sized eyes.

Chandra and Jean also fulfilled the third condition of their agreement, one entirely at the behest of the therapist, which was to go on a weekly 'date'. Usually Chandra would suggest the cinema or theatre, afraid that if they went to dinner he and Jean would have little to talk about and, because these dates were self-conscious by definition, would simply stare at one another with mounting anxiety before deciding to skip dessert and go home to watch *The Poseidon Adventure* on video.

It was on one such evening that Jean dropped her second bomb of the year. They were in a Spanish restaurant and she was talking about the garden and whether they should cut down the fir tree that blocked the light to the east, when Chandra interrupted and said, 'You know what, Jean, perhaps we should just be honest and stop this.'

'Stop what, Charles?'

'These dates. We're too old for it and we know it.'

'What is it you want, Charles?'

'I just want everything to go back to normal,' he said, realising the stress he put on the last word made him sound like a child.

'You want everything to go back to normal?'

Chandra nodded, and poured himself another glass of the Rioja which Jean hadn't touched.

'If it's not too late,' he said.

He wanted to tell her he loved her, but such histrionics did not come easily to him. In Hindi movies whenever couples leaned towards one another a rose always appeared between them, a symbolic reminder that romantic love was a fictional entertainment, that real love was far less demonstrative.

'Well, I think it probably *is* too late,' said Jean.

'It is?'

Jean sighed. 'I'm up the duff, Charles.'

Looking back on it, Jean must have known such an expression would have been outside Chandra's frame of reference, but still she permitted the longest of silences until he admitted he had no idea what she was talking about. Even after she explained, all he could think about was the phrase itself, and when they came home he looked it up in *Green's Dictionary of Slang* and learned that 'duff' referred to 'dough' which referred to 'pudding' which referred to the phrase to 'pull one's pudding' which was slang for masturbation, and when one stirred all of these etymological mixers together, it meant Jean was pregnant.

'And how do you feel about it?' he asked, as a way of concealing his own confusion.

Jean shrugged. 'No point being sad, is there?'

Jean was bored, Chandra decided; that Western ailment caused by the collapse of the joint family and the invention of labour-saving devices. But now it would be all hands on deck once more, every hour usurped by a red-faced, bawling, fist-clenching little dictator which meant no one would have time to criticise the breadwinner for retiring to the office in order to fulfil his part of the bargain because all actions were now in service of the common cause. Yes, he concluded, everything could return to a state of antediluvian normality.

The following Friday, when they visited the doctor, they were warned this pregnancy might not be like the others. Jean was forty-four now. But Chandra wasn't worried. Jean had been a champion swimmer in her youth, and Radha's birth had been straightforward. 'She barely broke into a sweat,' he'd told her sister, Jennifer, on the phone.

By the end of her first trimester, however, Jean was looking gaunt and older than her years. She vomited a lot, lost her temper at least twice a day, and at night he often found her in front of the television or watering the plants. He wondered if she was sleepwalking, though she was perfectly lucid when he spoke to her.

'Leave it,' he told her once, when he found her taking out the rubbish at two in the morning. 'I'll do that.'

'What else is there to do?' said Jean, her

dressing gown flapping around her pregnant yet still underweight body.

'I'm sorry, Jean,' he said. 'Let me help. I'll do whatever you need.'

'What are you on about, Charles?' she said, tying up the rubbish bag on her knees. 'Just let me get on.'

'Do you know what time it is?'

'Why does it matter what time it is?'

'Come back to bed.'

'I'll only be awake again in the morning.'

'What?'

'I said why go to bed when I'll only wake up again?'

'Jean,' said Chandra, moving towards her to take her arm.

'Fine,' said Jean, and pushed past him, going upstairs.

When Chandra consulted their doctor he was told that no, this was not exactly normal. 'Is it possible she's depressed?' the doctor asked, but Chandra shook his head. Jean had never suffered from depression. It wasn't in her character. She had the values of a Third World migrant, though via the industrial North. Neither of them was self-indulgent enough for depression. It was one of the reasons he'd been so amazed when Jean said she wanted them to see a therapist.

It was a Sunday when Jean went into labour. Professor Chandra was in the Marshall Library looking for an issue of the Indian *Economic Journal* he didn't really need (but was nonetheless appalled they didn't have) when one of the secretaries rushed in to find him. He took a taxi

79

to the hospital where Dr Button greeted him with the words, 'Good of you to join us,' to which Chandra replied, 'Mon *plaisir*,' reverting to the pseudo-French that was his habit in times of distress.

When Jean saw him she only stared, as if trying to fathom who he was. Chandra took her hand and she held it tightly. She was in the medical profession's preferred birth position, her blue nightgown bunched around her waist. Professor Chandra had recently read that this was an entirely arbitrary posture attributable to Louis XIV's voyeuristic tendencies; crouching or squatting was far more natural and effective. He had already told this to Jean but now it was all too late — the baby was crowning.

To Chandra's amazement Jean was virtually silent throughout the birth, though afterwards she cried when she held the baby in her arms. He took a picture of the two of them but left the flash on and the baby flinched, even with its eyes closed. He often wondered about this, whether it was the reason for Jasmine's timidity later in life. He would always claim they named her after the flowers in the vase behind Jean's head, the distinctive fragrance that filled the room. 'Rubbish, Charles,' Jean would say, 'there weren't any flowers there,' but Chandra remembered a blue vase, delicate white petals stretching out to meet his gaze.

Jasmine was underweight and spent five weeks in the incubator, but by the time she came home she was still the tiniest baby Chandra had seen. Jean also lost all her pregnancy weight in a matter of weeks, turning as thin as she had been when they first met, though her skin looked looser, as if waiting for her to grow back into it. For the first time in her life she started having migraines, would lie in bed for hours with a wet towel over her face, groaning softly. Chandra hired a nanny to give her some respite, but though she looked less worn and pale, Jean's moods did not improve. She lost her temper over minor things, answered him with tight, clipped replies that felt as if he were perpetually reaching for a cigar only to have the box slammed shut on his fingers. On occasion she was silent for days, not even talking on the phone. The only times she looked relatively peaceful were when she was feeding or rocking the baby.

As a shock tactic, Chandra suggested they revisit Cynthia Benson — in truth, the last thing he wanted to do — but Jean replied, 'I'm not ill, Charles, I'm just pissed off.' When he proposed getting a dog, which she had wanted for years but forgone because of Chandra, she said, 'That's all I need, another creature to look after.'

When Chandra spoke to Mohini, his brother's wife in Delhi who was also a doctor, she assured him it would pass. 'Post-partum depression is so common,' she said. 'You mustn't take it personally. It's a chemical thing. Just be there for her. It will pass.'

In some respects, Mohini was correct. Jean did stop sleeping through the mornings and, in time, became her old, efficient, hard-working self once more. But even after eighteen months she remained angrier than he ever remembered her being, and she began to sigh regularly through-out the day, sometimes seven or eight times per hour (he counted them), always unconsciously, as if living in her own soundproof bubble.

In the meantime, Jasmine was a beautiful, charming baby, but remained fragile and small for her age, easily startled and prone to crying at the tiniest stimulus. This continued as she became a toddler. When Chandra retreated to his study in one of his cigar-and-coffee-fuelled fugs, she would walk in with her hand on her hip and point downstairs saying, 'Fun, Daddy?' Chandra would take her hand and let her guide him wherever she wanted, unless he was too absorbed in work, too tense for interruptions, in which case she would stare at him for a few forlorn seconds before making her retreat.

Jasmine usually knew whenever her mother was 'having a turn' (Jean's phrase) before Chandra did, and would say, 'Mummy sad,' and Jean would pick her up and hug her while Jasmine's face turned serious and beatific, a saint gazing out from a Renaissance painting.

In 2003, a few months before Jasmine's fourth birthday, Chandra decided to take his sabbatical at the University of Toronto, somewhere Jean had always wanted to go while they were at Chicago. Sunny was at the LSE, Radha still relatively civilised, and Jasmine young enough that it would have little effect on her schooling.

'No,' said Jean, when he put the idea to her over breakfast. 'Not on your nelly.'

Chandra, who had already accepted the position, scooped off the top of his soft-boiled egg and poured Tabasco into the dormant crater.

Jean sighed, her third of the morning. 'You get it, don't you, Charles?'

'You don't want to travel?'

'Of course I want to travel,' said Jean.

Forgetting about his egg, Chandra stared out the window into the rain. His hands were trembling slightly.

'I wanted to go to Canada twenty years ago, Charles,' said Jean.

'I know,' said Chandra. 'I'm trying to make up for it. I'm trying.'

'Maybe it's just too late,' said Jean. 'Maybe I wouldn't even enjoy it now.'

'Jean, please,' said Chandra. 'I think you will. We all will.'

'Let me think about it.'

Professor Chandra endured two weeks of uncertainty during which neither of them so much as mentioned the sabbatical. He telephoned the department in Toronto and told them there might be a complication, but did not give any further details. He did, however, attempt to sway his wife's opinion in subtle ways, buying maple-glazed bacon and leaving it in the fridge, playing 'My Heart Will Go On' first thing in the morning in the manner of a wake-up reveille at summer camp.

If Jean noticed these things she did not comment on them, but the *coup de grâce* came when he 'accidentally' told the children that they might be going on a 'long holiday' to Canada, that they'd see the tallest building in the world, that it was so cold in the winter your nose could drop off. From then on it was all the children spoke of, while Jean only became even more silent. Chandra waited in a state of just beneath terror until, finally, as he was falling asleep one night, he heard her laughing.

'All right, Charles,' she said. 'Let's go to Canada.'

He turned on the light and looked at his wife beside him who was grinning like an android suddenly gifted with sentience.

'Thank God.'

'I wanted to go from the beginning, Charles. You know that, don't you?'

'Of course not. How could I know that?'

'I just didn't like being told I was going.'

'I'm sorry. I wanted to surprise you.'

'Yes, yes, I get that. It's fine. I'm looking forward to it.'

Chandra turned off the light. He felt like the Greek Pheidippides who ran twenty-six miles from the Plains of Marathon to save his kingdom (and later died).

'But I've got one condition, Charles.'

He turned on the light once more.

'Yes?'

'We go on a road trip afterwards. I've wanted to go on a road trip for years.'

'Yes,' said Chandra, who had known this for years. 'Yes, of course.'

'With Jennifer.'

Chandra turned out the light. 'Yes,' he said. 'Yes, of course.'

Over the years, Chandra and Jean's sister, Jennifer, had maintained a cordial if frosty relationship. Jennifer had never married, and was not close to Sunny or Radha, seeming to enjoy making faces at them when they were babies but losing interest when they began to talk back. 'It's just the way Jen is,' Jean had said. 'She's not like us. She's a cool one.' Chandra had had an aunt who was just the same, but he didn't see it as coolness; he saw it as a livid misanthropy, though this was still better than believing she had an issue with him in particular.

Jennifer rarely made directly aggressive remarks to him any more, probably on account of the children, but when she and her sister got together for a few drinks they often made jokes at his expense. When Jean first left him she had gone to Jennifer's home in Bristol where Jennifer had her own company selling 3D printers. A road trip with Jennifer would not be easy.

To his relief, Jean did brighten up in Toronto. It was a pleasant enough city, but Chandra found the winter unbearable. When Jean and Radha took the train to Montreal in November, he stayed at home draped across the radiator like a cardigan left out to dry. He was relieved when spring came, although with it came Jennifer and the promised road trip in a rented Ford Galaxy, first to Vancouver, and then across the border to Seattle.

He had expected it to be difficult, but was taken aback by the sheer ferocity of the ribbing he received for the following week, with Jennifer and Jean treating him like the court whipping boy, their sharp Lancastrian tongues forever drawing blood at the expense of academics or Cambridge dons, or Chandra himself. He resented it most when they attempted to include Radha in their merry-making, a move he viewed as below the belt, a contravention of the rules of engagement (although, before arriving in Seattle, he hadn't realised they were engaged at all).

'We should go and see the Hendrix exhibit,' said Jennifer one day.

'What about Charles?' said Jean.

'J-I-M-I H-E-N-D-R-I-X,' said Jennifer, miming playing a guitar. 'You know Jimi Hendrix?'

'Yes,' said Chandra. 'Thank you. I know Jimi Hendrix.'

'FYI, Jen,' said Jean. 'Charles has no idea who you're talking about.'

'I know Jimi Hendrix and I know Kurt Cobain,' said Chandra, who had looked up the history of the city only that morning in his guidebook.

'Maybe we can see a Cobain concert while we're here?' said Jennifer, winking at Radha.

'Oh, stop,' said Jean, stifling a laugh.

'He died on 5 April 1994,' said Chandra, whose recall remained impeccable. 'A self-inflicted gunshot wound.'

'Oh, God, you're right,' said Jennifer. 'So maybe we should see Abba then?'

'Whatever you prefer,' said Chandra, knowing it was a trap and heading for the door. 'I really don't mind.'

The mockery continued the following day, becoming so unpleasant that on the Friday Chandra invented a fictitious lunch appointment with a 'Professor Gundappa Viswanath' (in reality a brilliant wristy batsman from the seventies) and wandered the University of Washington's campus with Jasmine, visiting the bookstore and reading *The Very Hungry Caterpillar* to her in a corner.

When he returned to the hotel, Jean and her sister were in high spirits. They had visited the oldest Starbucks in the USA where they had shared a table with two psychiatrists who were also brothers. They kept making jokes about Frasier and Niles, references that went over Chandra's head, and the following day they went out to a bar and came home drunk, arguing in that thick-vowelled Northern way. All he could glean was that Jennifer appeared to be unhappy with something Jean had done and, for the first time that vacation, was on Chandra's side.

By the time they returned to Cambridge, Jean had changed again. The sighing stopped, and she no longer seemed so exhausted all the time, but she did not go to bed at her usual hour any more but stayed up late staring at her computer screen, smelling of the perfume she would often apply after dinner, a possibly superfluous touch to a phenomenon Chandra had no understanding of: a twenty-first-century affair in the age of broadband. It was only years later that he realised Jean had been chatting with Steve, one of two brothers she had met in Seattle.

Steve and Jean were pen pals — if this was the correct term — for years afterwards, but they also met physically on several occasions, though Chandra only pieced this together later, realising

Jean hadn't been making solo trips to Bristol, but had been going to London, staying in a hotel. At the time, all he was aware of was that she was paying less attention to him and simultaneously seemed happier, but it had never occurred to him that another man was involved.

He still did not know about Steve until after she left him for good, when she told him everything. He began sleeping with the brandy bottle under his pillow then, calling her number at three, four and five in the morning, even though he knew she turned the ringer off at nights. When he agreed to the divorce it was only because he was convinced this was the most efficient way to win her back, that only by closing the door and locking it would she realise that true separation from the man on the other side was impossible.

The problem was that Chandra's head had been ripened by centuries of South Asian conditioning which convinced him that no matter what Jean might say, deep down she and he shared a love and devotion that was inviolable, as if they had walked hand in hand across the earth for several previous incarnations. But the hammer blow came when Jean announced she was moving to Boulder. Chandra was defiant, arguing that Jasmine was too young, that such a change would be terrible for her. But Jean had spent her whole life making compromises: this time she would not back down.

'Jaz wants to go,' she said.

'Of course she does,' said Chandra. 'She always wants what you want.'

The truth was that Jasmine always wanted what *he* wanted too. She was that sort of a child, and this was a situation that called for the judgement of Solomon. In Solomon's absence Chandra decided he had no option but to give in, for Jasmine's sake.

Jean didn't even tell him she was getting married until after the wedding. Chandra was in shock for days until he realised this wasn't about love. For legal reasons, Jean *had* to marry Steve if the three of them were to live together in the US. But Jean had always been more practical than Chandra, sharper too, when it came to what she called 'street smarts'. Looking back on it, he felt he ought to have gone to court, to have forced Steve to move to England if he wanted to be with Jean so much, and perhaps he would have done so had not part of him still believed their estrangement was temporary.

He missed his children terribly in those years. Sunny was in Hong Kong by then, and though Chandra suspected the divorce had hurt him badly, the two of them rarely spoke about it, as if neither could bear to admit their own weakness, or even simple humanity. He wished he could confide in Radha, but she had begun to hate him without mercy and he couldn't tell whether this was also about the divorce or whether it was, as she claimed, about politics. As for Jasmine, she was beginning to sound more and more American, her accent slowly bending from Received Pronunciation to generalised Midwestern, like a character from *Friends*. Every key or formative experience in her life would reach him second-hand over the phone or was narrated post-hoc during the holidays. He knew her friends' names, or at least some of them, but had never met them in person, and when he first heard about something called Facebook he joined at once simply in order to have a way of watching his daughter's life unfold.

It was around this time that his obsession with the Nobel began, his fervent belief that if only he could lift that coveted trophy then everything else would cease to matter, that he would join the ranks of the gods who never felt pain or cold or hunger or loneliness, who were drunk from morning till night on the heavenly elixir of absolute, unchallengeable intellectual superiority. It became all he could think about, all he talked about, even on grossly inappropriate occasions, and each year, when he didn't win, he felt a crushing sense not of failure but of existential terror. And now, after he had accepted that he would never win the prize, what frightened him most was the absence of that desperate, violent hope from his life. He was like a greyhound after the race has ended, forever longing for that phantom rabbit now vanished from the horizon.

5

He was woken by the telephone.

'Charles?'

Professor Chandra stabbed on the bedside light, knocking his book and brandy glass to the floor.

'Yes. Yes, what is it?'

'We can't find Jasmine.'

'Where is she?'

'I said we can't find her, Charles.'

'Oh, God. What time is it?'

'Almost four.'

'I'm coming.'

'She's in Boulder. I'll come to you.'

He went into the bathroom and began to brush his teeth. The phone rang again. Jean couldn't remember which hotel he was staying at. She had called for a taxi, she said. Steve was staying at home in case Jasmine returned.

Chandra shaved and pulled on his clothes from yesterday. In the lobby he saw a man about his age stagger through the revolving doors with his hand on the bare back of a woman who looked perhaps thirty-five and was wearing a yellow summer frock with blue heels. There was a glazed look in her eyes as she swayed towards him. The man's face was neutral to the point of emptiness.

When Jean arrived she smelled of alcohol. She had thrown a grey cardigan over her white trouser suit and her make-up was gone, more like the Jean he remembered.

'What happened?' he said.

'Her friend Suzie called. She said Jaz left the party and was acting weird. Wanted to know if she got home okay.'

'Her friend called you in the middle of the night?'

'Steve says it's fine. She'll have gone off with a boy and that's what girls do and I've got to let her grow up. He said she'll be mad as hell when she sees us.'

'Maybe he's right.'

'And if he's not?'

'I'll get the car.'

Chandra took the elevator to the parking lot and got into his rental car. When he pulled up outside the hotel, Jean was talking into her phone but hung up at once and got inside.

'Where do we go?' he said, switching on the GPS.

'I'll direct you.'

Of course: Boulder was her home now.

'I'm worried about her, Charles.'

'I know.'

'I mean, she's not happy. Steve says all teenagers are depressed at times, that it's less dangerous for them than it is for us, but I don't believe him. I mean, I believe him, but she's still unhappy. So why shouldn't I worry? Take a left.'

'I suppose he means there's no point in worrying, that it doesn't help anyone.'

'Why on earth do people say that, Charles? I mean, it's worry that made me come down here.

It's normal for mothers to worry. We worry because we love our children, and they can feel it. It's what makes them feel safe.'

'It's normal for fathers too.'

'I know it is.'

Her hand brushed his over the gear stick. They would always have Jasmine, he thought, then realised this wasn't true. Soon she would be like the other two, living a thousand miles away, contactable only by email, perhaps with a family of her own. And that meant Jean and he would have nothing to connect them any more. In the final stage of his life he would be on his own and would look back on it all like a builder surveying a house he'd spent decades on before handing over the keys.

Jean led him to a two-storey suburban house with a large driveway into which at least six cars were crammed, two more on the narrow strip of grass that served as a front yard. It was half past four in the morning, but there were lights on in the windows, shapes moving behind the curtains upstairs.

'Right,' said Jean.

The door was stained glass and above the letterbox it said, DON'T EVEN THINK OF PUTTING ANYTHING RELIGIOUS IN HERE. They could hear music, something jazzy with a beat. Chandra knocked, heard a voice shouting about the cops, and pulled open the letterbox, saying, 'This is Jasmine's father.'

'Great,' muttered Jean.

The door opened. It was a blonde girl with dreadlocks, her large blue eyes magnified by glasses. She wore denim dungarees, bright red lipstick and an ecstatic grin.

'So how can I help you folks?' she said, clutching on to the door frame.

'Is Suzie here?' said Jean.

'Yeah,' said the girl, sucking on her finger. 'Suzie!'

Chandra watched as a brunette of about the same age came down the stairs. She was wearing only a long black T-shirt with RAMONES printed across the front.

'Hey, Mrs Benowitz,' she said. It took Chandra a moment to realise who she was talking to.

'Hi, Suzie,' said Jean.

'Jeez, it's like so good to see you,' said the girl. 'I mean, wow, you're here, that's like so . . . wow.'

'You called me, Suzie.'

'I didn't call you, Mrs Benowitz. I mean, it doesn't mean I don't like you. I just didn't call you.'

Someone behind her shouted, 'You never call anyone, bitch,' and Suzie put her hand over her mouth and giggled again.

'You called me, Suzie. I know it was you because I know your voice. You said Jasmine went out and you wanted to know if she'd come home.'

'Oh, yeah, Jaz,' said Suzie. 'You're Jaz's mom, Mrs Benowitz. Of course you are. Oh, my God,' she said, looking at Chandra. 'Are you her dad?'

'Wherever she is, just tell us,' said Chandra. 'We're worried.'

'You looking for Jaz?' said a tall shirtless boy with a spike of black beard sticking out of his chin.

'Yes,' said Chandra. 'Where is she?'

'She left about two hours ago. But she wasn't, you know, all there. I mean, she looked really out of it. Really whacked. We got worried when she didn't come back.'

'What does that mean?' said Jean, angry now. 'What do you mean 'whacked'?'

'Tell her about the 'shrooms!' shouted someone from inside.

'Shut up, Josh,' said Suzie.

'She'd taken mushrooms, sir,' said the boy. 'Thing is, I don't think she was used to it. And she was all, like . . . '

'Fucked up,' said Suzie, and put her hands over her mouth again.

'She was pretty messed up,' said the boy, nodding, 'and she just went out and nobody was too sure where she went, and we thought she must have gone home, but then someone saw her car was still here up the road, so we thought she'd taken a cab.'

'I can't believe you'd let her just walk off like that,' said Jean. 'And as for taking drugs! Do you want us to call the police? Do you?'

'Jesus, no!' said Suzie. 'We called because we were worried, Mrs Benowitz. We should have stopped her, I know. There was just too much going on.'

'And none of you thought to look for her?' said Jean.

'We called. But her phone was in the house,'

95

said the boy. 'I should have gone after her. It's my fault.'

'And we were kind of in the middle of a party here,' said Suzie, returning. 'I mean, people are free to leave. It's a free country.'

'We don't mean any disrespect,' said the boy, holding up his hands as if it were a robbery.

'Give us her phone, for God's sake,' said Jean.

Suzie swayed in the doorway, then turned and went upstairs. When she returned she had it in her hand and handed it to Jean.

'Good luck, Mrs Benowitz. Like I said, we're really sorry.'

'We hope you find her, sir,' said the boy to Chandra.

Jean closed the door. She was breathing very heavily. Chandra couldn't tell if it was from anger or anxiety.

'It's all right,' said Chandra, putting his arm around her. 'It's a warm night. She'll be okay. Let's go and look for her.'

'Yes,' said Jean. 'Yes. You take the car. I'll look around here. Have you got your mobile?'

Chandra nodded. 'I could call the police, if you want.'

'Let's look for her first,' said Jean. 'If we don't find her in half an hour we go to the police. Okay?'

'Okay.'

Jean walked around the house into the pocket of blackness that must have been the back garden. Chandra saw the silhouette of pine trees, ramrod straight like high-court judges, a watery moon behind them. He got into the car and wound down the windows. He could hear Jean calling Jasmine's name.

Chandra began circling the neighbourhood. When he saw a woman walking her dog he slowed down.

'Excuse me,' he asked her. 'Have you seen a girl about seventeen years old?'

The woman glared at him and said something that sounded like 'sleaze'. A few minutes later he passed two women in their twenties who were holding hands. 'I'm looking for my daughter,' he told them.

These women were more helpful, asking what she looked like and for his number, saying they would call if they saw her.

Chandra had been trying to keep the worry from his mind, but now it returned in force. What if Jasmine had been raped, or hit by a car, or was lying with her throat cut in a ditch? He turned on the radio, hoping it might calm him down. A Sam Cooke song was playing. It was called 'Cupid'. He and Jean had danced to it at the LSE, the first time he had kissed her — or anyone — in public. He could smell her perfume, even now.

Professor Chandra's phone was lit up with a missed call, a number he did not recognise. When he called back, a woman answered.

'Hi, it's Shelley.'

'Who?'

'The one you met on the street, looking for your girl.'

'Oh, yes, right.'

'Look, we don't know if it's her, but there's

97

someone sitting by a dumpster by Cornell and 4th. She won't talk to us.'

'Her name's Jasmine,' he said, trying to work the GPS and cursing.

'Jasmine,' he could hear the woman saying. 'Is your name Jasmine? Honey, are you Jasmine?'

It was two and a half minutes away. He put the car into gear.

'She won't say anything. Just keeps staring.'

'It's okay. I'm on my way.'

Chandra tossed the phone onto the passenger seat. He could smell blood, which happened when he was terrified. But why? They had found her, hadn't they?

He parked on 4th Street and saw the two women standing on the corner. He couldn't see Jasmine anywhere and was beginning to panic once more until one of them pointed to an alley on their left.

'She's down there,' she said. 'She won't talk to me.'

Chandra nodded, forgetting to thank her in his anxiety. He still couldn't see Jasmine, but when he reached the dumpster in the middle of the alley, he found her sitting on the ground beside it, her knees hunched to her chin, looking at the wooden fence in front of her. Chandra wanted to tell her to get up, that the ground was dirty, that she had caused enough trouble for one night, but when she didn't so much as look at him his anger disappeared. He took out his mobile to call Jean instead.

'Dad,' said Jasmine. 'Stop it. Put it down.'

Her words came out slowly, as if costing her

great effort. But she did not sound unwell. In fact, she sounded calmer than he had heard her in a long time.

'I'm calling your mother.'

'Not yet.'

'She's worried. I'm worried. What are you doing?'

'Let her worry a few more minutes. It won't kill her.'

'No. I'm calling her, Jasmine, then you are going home.'

'Home? Where's home, Dad?'

'What? What is this? Let's go. Get up.'

'Do you have a home?'

'Get up, for God's sake. It's freezing. What are you doing sitting on the ground like a hobo?'

'Have a seat, Dad.'

'Get up!'

'You can have a seat or go away. But I'd prefer it if you had a seat.'

Moonlight was falling onto the near side of Jasmine's face, making her look like a statue. He sat down in his pressed trousers and jacket, his shoulder almost touching his daughter's. The ground was cold, but it was dry at least, and there was enough light from the watery moon to verify there weren't any rats.

She was wearing black again, but there were streaks in her hair now, he couldn't tell what colour. Orange, perhaps? Jasmine was darker-skinned than her siblings, who were sometimes mistaken for Greeks or Italians, but she was still wearing that ghostly foundation. Her make-up notwithstanding, she looked like him, her nose, her forehead. He didn't understand her any more. He wanted to love her, but didn't know how.

'So what is this?' he said. 'Are you trying to get back at us?'

'Get back at you for what?'

'I don't know. Whatever you think it is we did to you.'

'And what would that be?'

'I don't know,' he said, slapping his palm against the ground and wondering whether anyone could hear them.

'Maybe I just wanted us to sit here and look at the sky. Why don't you try it, Dad? Look at the sky. Go on.'

Chandra looked up.

'Yes, I've looked,' he said. 'It's a sky. So what?'

'It's all in there,' she said. 'Everything you need to know. It's all in the sky.'

There was an emptiness at its edges, colour draining away. Dawn was coming. To the right he saw spirals of grey on the horizon, rain somewhere out west.

'Why does everything have to be something?' said Jasmine.

'I don't understand.'

'I mean, why do I have to be doing anything? I'm just sitting here, and it's got you so angry.'

'We were worried.'

'But you're not worried now.'

'I'm still worried.'

'Why?'

'I don't understand what you're talking about.'

'I'm hardly saying anything, Dad. Can't you

100

see that? I'm just being here. All I did was walk over here and be here. And you're freaking out like something catastrophic has happened. Just be here with me, Dad, for a few minutes.'

'Your mother's so worried.'

'For a few minutes.'

He sat in silence, his eyes open, staring at the fence. He kept fidgeting, trying not to look at Jasmine, wanting to take out his phone but fearing what she might say if he did. He tried closing his eyes but this made it worse. From somewhere, a baby was crying.

'I'm the only one who isn't anything,' said Jasmine. 'Sunny's trying to be you. Radha's trying to be your opposite. Me, I'm not anything. I'm not like you. I'm not like Mum. I'm just nothing.'

'You're not nothing.'

'I am nothing, Dad. You always thought I was nothing. It's okay. I don't mind.'

Was this really what she thought? Was it true? Chandra didn't know any more; all he knew was that he needed his daughter — he hadn't realised this till now — and he was losing her.

'I don't think you are nothing. You are everything to me. Everything. I haven't got anything. No wife. Nothing. *I'm* nothing. You are everything to me.'

She leaned her head against his shoulder.

'It's all right, Dad.'

'I don't understand,' he said.

'Neither do I. Neither do any of us.'

He picked up a stone and threw it at the fence. It slipped between the slats and he did not hear it hit the ground. He found another one. This time it slapped against the wood.

'It's not your fault, Dad.'

'What isn't?'

'Anything. Nothing is. It doesn't work like that.'

He took out his phone once more. Jean hadn't called.

'I guess you'd better call Mum,' said Jasmine.

'Jasmine, are you sick? Do you need a doctor? They said you ate mushrooms.'

'Magic mushrooms. They're a drug, Dad.'

'Drugs?'

'Like LSD,' said Jasmine, 'but natural. They're not dangerous. I flipped out a little but I'm okay now. Really.'

'Where did you get them?'

'They were meant to share but I thought, fuck them, they're going to college. So I took them all.'

'What?' said Chandra. 'What does that mean?'

'I took them all.'

'You're also going to college.'

'I fucked it all up, Dad. My SATs. I can go to a community college but nothing else. I'm stuck in this place.'

'No. Jasmine, no. You can go to England. Anywhere. We can pay.'

'Not without the grades. You don't know how badly I fucked up. I'm going nowhere.'

'It'll be all right, Jasmine. I'll make it all right. I'm a Professor. I can sort it out.'

He wanted to put his arm around her but he couldn't; physical affection was hard for him, especially when it was most needed — he would always freeze, afraid of rejection.

'Everything *is* all right, Dad. Everything just is. Can't you see that?'

The moon had gone. He dialled Jean's number.

'Right,' she said, when he told her he'd found Jasmine. She did not sound surprised.

They walked to the car, he and his daughter. Professor Chandra remembered what he had said by the pool about boundaries, how they didn't exist, how if there was any meaning, none of them would ever know what it was. Wasn't that exactly what Jasmine was trying to tell him? Was it possible she had come to the same realisation fifty years earlier than he had?

Once inside the car he said, 'I think I understand, Jasmine.'

She looked at him, half-smiling. 'You do?'

'Sometimes I feel like this too. As though I made a mess of it all. As though maybe none of it mattered in the first place. I know.'

'Yeah?'

'But drugs will not help, Jasmine. Not at all.'

'How would you know, Dad?'

'Drugs are dangerous, Jasmine. Everyone knows that. There are other ways to solve problems.'

'When you think about it, Dad, who really cares?'

'I care.'

'But do you? Do you really?'

'Yes, I do. Sometimes I forget. Sometimes I say silly things. But I do. It's the only thing I'm sure about.'

103

They were driving away, the windows down, Jasmine staring into the street. The sky was a dirty white now, dawn perhaps half an hour away. When they reached Suzie's house, Jean got in the back and, to his surprise, said nothing to him or to Jasmine.

At Steve and Jean's house the gate was already open. Jasmine took Jean inside without a word. Chandra, not knowing what else to do, wandered around the building to the back. Steve was standing above the pool on the low diving board, completely naked in the early-morning chill, breathing deeply: 'Hoo-hoo-hoo.'

'Good morning,' said Chandra as Steve pulled himself back from the brink, wheeling his arms like a propeller.

Chandra tried to keep his eyes off Steve's penis, but could not help noticing that his pubic area was shaved clean.

'Morning, Chandrasekhar,' said Steve, leaving the diving board and crossing the pool's perimeter. 'Guess you didn't get the sleep you were hoping for.'

'We had to look for Jasmine.'

'Yeah, and you found her? I said she'd be fine.'

'She wasn't fine,' said Chandra, drawing closer, which made it easier not to look at Steve's penis. 'She was on drugs.'

'Drugs?' said Steve. 'Really?'

'Magical mushrooms.'

'Ah, yes. We spoke about this.'

'You spoke about mushrooms?'

'About drugs in general,' said Steve. 'She's experimenting, you see.'

104

'And what did you tell her?'

'I told her to stay away from the hard stuff. That's what killed the sixties.'

'And what did you say about magical mushrooms, Steve?'

'Hallucinogens are different, my friend. They open the doors of the mind. It's what brought Eastern spirituality to the West, you know.'

'No, Steve, I don't know.'

'I was just being open with her. Being honest. I told her hallucinogens, in small quantities, won't hurt her. Nor will smoking pot.'

'You told her that?'

'Yes, Chandrasekhar. I told her the truth.'

'You know where I found her, Steve?' he said. 'In a dumpster.'

He could see her now, face up on a heap of garbage, blood dribbling from her mouth. The image was so clear it even convinced him.

'Look, Chandrasekhar, young people get up to all sorts of things. Wait till we sit down and I tell you some of *my* stories.'

Steve was afraid; Chandra could tell. He had even taken a step backwards, towards the edge of the pool.

'She could have died, Steve.'

'No, no, no, no, no, my friend, not from psilocybin. Jaz will be fine, I assure you. Just another story to tell.'

'I don't ever want you to tell my daughter to take drugs again, Steve.'

'Oh, my friend, you've got me all wrong.'

'Never again, Steve.'

'All right, buddy. Never again, I promise.'

Chandra stepped towards him until they were facing one another.

'And I want you to apologise, Steve. To me and to Jean.'

'Come on, Chandrasekhar. It's just a misunderstanding. Let's go inside and drink some coffee and laugh about it.'

'Say you're sorry, Steve.'

'I'm sorry. Truly. Come now.'

Steve put out his hand. Chandra stared at it. What did it mean, this hand? If he touched it, would that mean he agreed that teenagers should take drugs?

'Sorry, Steve,' he said. 'I reject your hand.'

'Oh, well, that's all right,' said Steve, putting his arms by his sides. 'But I had expected more from you, Chandrasekhar.'

'More from me?' said Chandra, watching as morning feelers of light crept over the edge of the pool.

'I'd expected a more enlightened approach. Rather less 1950s. Still, each to their own.'

'Jasmine *is* my own.'

'Yes, well, I've always been of the belief that children don't belong to anyone. That's the mistake we all make, you see.'

'Well, you're wrong,' said Chandra. 'She belongs to me and I belong to her. You're the one who doesn't belong.'

'This is my home,' said Steve. 'But I see what you mean. You feel angry because your need for power hasn't been met.'

'My need for what?'

'Power. That's what this is all about, isn't it?

You feel powerless and you're taking it out on me. That's quite okay. I understand. I would hate to be in your position.'

'And what position is that?' said Chandra, thinking that if Steve took one more step backwards he would fall into the pool.

'With Jean and all that,' said Steve. 'I don't want to upset you.'

'This is not about Jean,' said Chandra, leaning forward. 'This is about my daughter whom you encouraged to take drugs. I have been out all night looking for her. She could have died, and you, Steve, do not care.'

'I care, of course I do. I just think you're projecting your pain, Chandrasekhar. We both know Jasmine was in no danger. We both know this is all because your wife left you, because she's with me now. It's hard to adjust. I get it. I feel for you.'

'I don't think you get anything,' said Chandra. 'I feel for *you*.'

'So let's call it quits,' said Steve, extending his hand once more.

'Let's call it nothing,' said Chandra, and punched Steve on the nose.

Steve covered his face with his palms. A tablespoon of blood slipped between his fingers and fell shining on to the sparkling tiles. Chandra wrung his hand: punching a face, it turned out, wasn't so different from punching a fridge. And now Steve was falling, the back of his head hitting the water first, and then his back, before he disappeared altogether.

Seconds later, Steve rose to the surface,

107

spread-eagled in the sunlight with a pink halo around his head, which swelled into a cloud. He turned himself over and swam sideways to the deck where he put out his elbows and dabbed at his nose with his fingers.

'Steve,' said Chandra. 'Are you all right?'

'Fine. It's nothing. I'm all right. Just hand me that towel, please.'

Chandra walked around the pool, fetching the towel from the sofa. The sun had risen. An aeroplane was cutting its way through the solid blue sky above them.

'Here, Steve,' he said, tossing the towel.

'Thanks.'

Steve's voice sounded funny, as if he had swallowed helium, The blood was still visible in the pool, fainter now, dissolving. Chandra turned his back and entered the house through the screen doors.

Jean was sitting at the breakfast bar with her back to the pool. She half-turned her head as he entered. 'Well,' she said, 'that was quite a night.'

'How is she?' said Chandra, avoiding eye contact.

'She's asleep.'

'Do we call a doctor?'

'No. She's okay. But she doesn't want to go to her graduation. I had to say yes in the end. I mean, it's up to her.'

'Oh,' said Chandra, as Jean took a seat beside him.

'I'm sorry, Charles. You came all this way.'

'Oh, no,' said Chandra. 'We can't force her. I understand.'

'Christ,' said Jean. 'Did we ever do anything like this?'

'We couldn't afford to.'

'I think she really wanted to see us together,' said Jean. 'Maybe it all got too much for her.'

'It's about college,' said Chandra. 'She told me.'

'No, Charles. She only said that because it's what you wanted to hear.'

'It's her future,' said Chandra. 'She's thinking about the future.'

'She's thinking about right now,' said Jean. 'She just needs to see that you and me and Steve can get along. We can spend the day together at least, when she wakes up. Let her see we're all okay with each other. It won't be the end of the world if she goes to a community college for a year.'

Chandra closed his eyes. To him it would be. But the question was a test. Jean wanted him to be more accepting, like Steve.

'I suppose not,' he said.

'I'm sorry, Charles,' said Jean. 'I know you want them all to go to the best universities, but it's more important that she's happy. And right now she isn't. Another year at home might even be good for her.'

'A good education *is* happiness in the long term,' said Chandra.

'I don't disagree,' said Jean. 'But it isn't everything. You can't just tell her what's good for her, Charles. You have to see her. You have to listen to her.'

Chandra was sure Jean wanted to say, 'Like

Steve does,' or, 'Like Steve listens to me,' or talk about something that happened twenty years ago and use it as proof of his inability to understand her, or anyone. He, in turn, wanted to tell her he'd just punched Steve into the pool like something from a Hindi movie.

'You said boundaries,' said Chandra. 'One boundary is she goes to university, she studies hard, she doesn't throw her future away.'

'I agree,' said Jean.

'Would Steve agree?'

'No,' said Jean. 'But Jasmine isn't his child.'

Steve was pulling the screen doors open, stepping inside. He was wearing flip-flops and a dressing gown and had cotton wool stuffed inside his nose, which looked red and swollen but not broken.

'Lo lo lo la la la,' sang Steve.

'Oh, my God,' said Jean. 'What happened?'

Chandra's body went rigid. For a fleeting moment he considered making a run for it, getting into his car and driving through the gates while shaking his fist and yelling, 'Hi ho, Silver!' or something equally triumphant. Instead he turned to look at Steve, who was smiling at him.

'I hit my face,' said Steve, 'doing one of those stupid tumble turns.'

'Oh, love,' said Jean, taking his hand and leading him to the stool she'd been sitting on.

'It looks easy on the TV,' said Steve.

'Does it hurt, Steve?' said Chandra, in as kindly a voice as he could manage.

'I'll get you some ice,' said Jean.

'It's nothing,' said Steve. 'I didn't hit it hard.'

Jean crossed to the fridge and put some ice cubes inside a tea towel which she pressed to Steve's face.

'It's all right, love,' said Jean. 'It's just bruised.'

'How's Jaz?' said Steve.

'She doesn't want to go to her graduation,' said Jean. 'But she's fine.'

'Well,' said Steve, 'I can hardly blame her. Commencement's a drag. Three hours of pure misery.'

'She'll never have another one,' said Jean.

'And thank God for that. First you listen to the valedictorian telling you their life is gonna be way better than yours, and then some sap tells you to follow your dreams even though his generation killed any possibility of that happening. Isn't that right, Chandrasekhar?'

'Yes,' said Chandra, deciding it was best to agree with anything Steve said. 'I suppose that is right.'

'Jaz is better off at home. She had her fun with her friends last night. That's enough.'

'Steve,' said Jean. 'I don't think she had fun.'

'I know, honey,' said Steve. 'I just mean high school isn't where life's real lessons are learned. And neither is college. Jaz is a smart girl. She knows that.'

'So where are life's real lessons learned?' said Chandra, in spite of his resolution.

'And please don't say the university of life,' said Jean.

'Well, like I said last night, I learned half of what I know studying Vedanta, and the rest at Esalen.'

111

Steve put his hand over Jean's, lowering the ice pack.

'Yes,' said Chandra. 'You said.'

'It was founded by two Stanford graduates actually,' said Steve. 'Interesting story. One of them was diagnosed psychotic and put in a mental hospital. The other travelled to Pondicherry, Aurobindo's ashram.'

'What's the difference?' Chandra wanted to say, whose disdain for hippies was surpassed only by his hatred of sadhus; those ash-smeared, ganja-imbibing beggars who contributed nothing to society while expecting reverence from ordinary working people.

'Anyway,' said Steve, 'when they got back to San Fran, in '62, I think, they got together with a few other guys, Huxley, Watts, and opened the Esalen institute, named after the tribe who used to live there. It's just a hop, skip and a jump for you. You could be there in a couple of hours.'

'Oh, my God,' said Jean, putting her hand over her mouth. 'You're not actually suggesting *Charles* . . . '

'Oh, I'm sure Chandrasekhar's game for anything,' said Steve. 'Pass me the iPad, would you, honey?'

Steve shuffled over till his elbow was touching Chandra's.

'Look,' he said. 'Here are some pictures of the site. Beautiful, isn't it?'

Chandra looked. He saw gardens, and a swimming pool that faced over the sea. Steve clicked on the list of former teachers. They were mostly PhD's from Ivy League schools; Richard

Feynman's name was there, the first Nobel Prize-winner Chandra had ever met, back in the seventies.

'And here are the upcoming workshops,' said Steve. ' "The Natural Singer: Solo of the Heart', 'Advanced Yoga', 'Tantric Massage for Couples', 'Being Yourself in the Summer Solstice', 'The Path of Tibetan Mahamudra', 'The Way of Zen', 'Ecstatic Dance for Women', 'Overcoming Addiction: Six Steps Not Twelve'. Anything catch your eye?'

Chandra shook his head, then caught *Steve's* eye. There was only one word for his expression: devilish. This was payback, blackmail for his silence.

'Addictions, no,' said Chandra.

'Unless you count work,' said Jean.

'Which I don't,' said Chandra, who found the word 'workaholism' as oxymoronic as 'liberal intelligentsia'. 'Yoga, no.' Since coming to California he had begun to view yoga as the greatest evil of modern life. 'Couples, no. Singing, no.'

'How about this?' said Steve, and clicked on 'Being Yourself in the Summer Solstice', a course which lasted three days and cost two thousand dollars. ' "Often we take the biggest leaps in personal development when we learn to ignore the critical voices inside our heads, when we stop believing that wisdom is outside and look for it in ourselves instead. This workshop will help us finally listen to our own voices." '

'I don't think so,' said Chandra.

'It would be my treat,' said Steve.

113

'Oh, God no,' said Chandra. 'No, no, no.'

'I insist,' said Steve.

'Don't be silly, love,' said Jean. 'Charles would never *dream* of doing something like that. Not in a trillion years.'

This would have been true half an hour ago, Chandra reflected, but now he had no choice. He had punched Steve in the face and this was his comeuppance and both of them knew it.

'I'll do it,' said Chandra. 'But I can't let you pay, Steve.'

'Good Lord,' said Jean.

'Wonderful!' said Steve. 'And you'd be with Rudi Katz. Rudi's majestic.'

Chandra was looking at the celebrity endorsements: Arianna Huffington, Bob Shapiro, Alanis Morissette and, to his astonishment, John Galbraith, an economist Chandra had known well in the eighties. '*I'm biased,*' Galbraith had written, '*but what I'm about to say comes straight from the heart — I'm probably the best student he ever had.*'

'I hope you know what you're letting yourself in for,' said Jean. 'It's not Cambridge, Charles.'

'Yes,' said Chandra, bridling. 'Yes, I know that.'

'Good for you,' said Steve, on whose head Chandra could now visualise horns. 'Excellent.'

'Well,' said Chandra, 'we can talk about this later. I should be getting back to my hotel now.'

'Yes,' said Jean. 'We all need some sleep. Charles and I have been up all night.'

'Yes, of course,' said Steve. 'But we'll see you this afternoon, won't we?'

'Give me a call when Jasmine's awake,' said Chandra.

'Rest well, Charles,' said Jean, holding Steve's hand.

'You too.'

He circuited the house until he reached the garage and his SUV, spending several seconds looking for his keys until he spotted them in the ignition. As he drove to the gates he saw Rafael watering the plants nearby and waved goodbye.

'*Adios*,' said Chandra.

'*Adios*,' said Rafael.

As he drove down the hill, Professor Chandra remembered how it had felt when his fist made contact with Steve's face, the way the sun seemed to brighten into an explosion as Steve's body struck the pool, how the water had turned pink afterwards while Chandra wrung his hand, his knuckles smarting. He felt giddy now, *alive*, as if his enormous car might float off the road and into the sky at any moment.

It's happening, he told himself. I'm doing it. I'm following my bliss.

6

Professor Chandra returned to his hotel room
and tried to sleep, but his body was too full of
adrenaline. He stood in front of the mirror,
trying to re-enact the punch, Professor Chandra
the Master Blaster versus Whimpering Steve
Benowitz; that beautiful moment when he'd felt
freer than he ever had in his life as he watched
Steve fall backwards, propelled by the force of
his sixty-nine-year-old fist.

Finally, by about eleven o'clock Professor
Chandra dozed off, awakening at three and
ordering room service. Jean called after he had
finished eating and was drinking a second cup of
coffee.

'Charles,' she said, 'have you eaten?'

'Not really,' he said, looking at the remnants of
his crab cakes.

'Good. Jaz is up.'

'So she's not going to graduation?'

'No. We can have an early dinner instead.'

Chandra arrived an hour later. Steve was
wearing a black polo neck this time, which
made him look more like an international
narcotics smuggler than a practitioner of
Vedanta, and his nose was still bruised, though
not grotesquely. He seemed in high spirits.
Jasmine, on the other hand, looked depressed
and close to tears.

After dinner, Chandra sat beside her on the

116

sofa and they watched *Forrest Gump* with their shoulders touching. He wanted to ask her if she was still high, if they should take her to a doctor (though Jean had insisted this wasn't necessary) but Jasmine fell asleep before the end of the movie. Chandra covered her with a blanket and, after Jean left to take a shower, Steve sat opposite him on the ottoman and handed him a glass of Prosecco.

'Well, well, well,' said Steve, in the manner of a circus drum roll.

'How are you feeling today?' said Chandra.

'Very good,' said Steve.

'I'm glad.'

Chandra reached out towards Steve's face, his middle finger almost grazing his nose and said, *sotto voce*, 'Is it okay?'

'You know, Chandrasekhar,' said Steve, loud as a ringmaster, 'I made a call to Esalen on your behalf. It seems Rudi's workshop was full but they agreed to allow one more, for me, meaning for you.'

'Oh, that was very generous of you.'

'All we have to do is call and confirm.'

'Well, I'd have to check my schedule.'

'The semester's over, isn't it?' said Steve.

'Yes,' said Chandra. 'Yes, it is.'

'So you have no commitments.'

Chandra shook his head.

'Excellent.'

Steve appeared to have the institute's number pre-programmed into his phone.

'Hello, hello!' he said. 'Benowitz here. How're you keeping, Leia? Breathing the joy? I'd expect

117

nothing less! Listen, I called yesterday. Want to talk to the man himself? Excellent . . . '

Chandra accepted the phone as if he'd been handed a small but quite genuine lump of plutonium. The woman on the other end explained that all Chandra needed to do was show up on Friday before dinner time. His workshop was fully paid for, though if he wanted to upgrade to a better room he could do this. When asked if he had any questions he gave a curt, 'No', before returning the phone to Steve. Jean, he saw, was standing in the hallway and had been watching all the while.

'I can't accept this, Steve,' he said. 'It's too much.'

'Not at all, my friend. It's my gift to you.'

Chandra wanted to reply, 'As are my wife and child to you,' but instead he said, 'Thank you, Steve.'

When Jasmine awoke Chandra sat with her for a few more minutes. He told her that everything would be all right, that he wasn't angry at all, that a community college would be fine for a while, and that under no circumstances should she resort to consuming any other edible fungi in the future but call him if she had a problem. Jasmine, who looked pale and weak and very, very young, did not answer, but she heard him out which, he supposed, was the best he could have hoped for.

He flew back to Orange County the following morning and called the Esalen Institute from the airport, upgrading to a premium room and telling them to put the difference on his credit card. On reaching home he emailed Sunny, realising it was a masochistic move, but not knowing whom else to contact:

I've gone and booked myself up for this thing, and all I want to know is, will everyone there be stark raving mad, and if so, what on earth will they think of me? I'm guessing you've been there, right?

Sunny's reply came through within the hour, as Chandra suspected it would (sensing weakness, the red-tailed hawk swoops to kill).

To:prchandra101@cam.ac.uk
From:sunnysideofthestreet@imb.co.hk
Subject: Esalen?

Whoa Dad,

Esalen! That's wild. Who'd have thought it? I'm proud of you, Prof. All those years of being so identified with the mind. This is a real step forward, or inward, I should say. You're deepening, changing. It's the great shift. We're all a part of it, but only some of us respond to the call. Even if you're scared or apprehensive, that's a good thing. You're responding. You have to feel the fear but step anyway, and step and step and step. Just keep moving in, no matter what.

To your questions: no, everyone will not be crazy there, but I think you know this already. That

119

isn't what you're afraid of, am I right? They're serious professionals and scientists, but they've transgressed boundaries traditional academia cannot comprehend.

No, I've never been there, but I know people who have and of course I'm in the loop. They've been wanting me to run a course there for a while actually but I've been time poor of late, which happens during periods of transformation.

Anyway, my advice is don't think too much, just give yourself to the experience with a whole heart and remember to say your affirmations. But good on you, Dad. Enjoy it.

Yours,

Sunil

P.S. If you're still struggling with yourself, ask yourself this: 'What have I got to be afraid of?'

P.P.S. Make sure you visit the hot tubs.

Chandra was pleased with Sunny's response. For years now he had been asking Sunny the same question, 'What does spiritual mean?' and had never once received a satisfactory answer. But he was glad his son hadn't laughed at him and, to his surprise, it felt good to hear Sunny say that he was proud of him.

As for the question, 'What have you got to be afraid of?' his immediate answer was he was scared of meeting someone he knew. And yet the only person from his world who had any connection to Esalen was he of the glass jaw. There might be people there who knew Steve, but it wouldn't be hard to diffuse any potential embarrassment: 'Oh, him, yes, nice fellow but a little crude for my taste, had to teach him a lesson, if you know what I mean.' And they would laugh and say, 'You gotta follow your bliss, man.'

No, his biggest fear was that there would be people there who hadn't the slightest interest in economics, or even in universities, who would ask him questions he couldn't answer, didn't *want* to answer, like the last time he cried, or touched a woman, or fell to his knees and prayed. In fact, he wasn't afraid they would be crazy; he was afraid they would be normal, and *he* would be revealed as the eccentric, a term he hated. A rebel chose not to conform, while an eccentric had no option; an eccentric did not know how the rest of society lived. But Chandra's exposure to the outside world was limited, he had to admit: when, after all, was the last time he'd interacted socially with someone who wasn't an academic?

He replied:

Thanks, Sunny,

Glad you approve, and I shall certainly give it my all. Not sure about all this 'great shift' stuff, but shall give a full report back when it's over. Of course will mention you to them. They'd be

121

lucky to have you and I shall impress this upon them.

Love, Dad

After he pressed send it dawned on him that there might be another reason he was going, apart from his obligation to Sir Bleedsalot. Punching Steve had been the first truly honest thing Professor Chandra had done in years, and he had liked the way it felt. Honesty was exciting, but fraught, at his age. He had become used to wearing so many overcoats, one on top of the other, that he had no idea how it might feel to go outside without one any more. He wondered if this was a sentiment he could share with the others in his workshop.

★   ★   ★

Esalen was a six-hour drive from Bella Vista. When the day came he took a handful of Nana Mouskouri and Harry Belafonte CDs and rolled down the windows so that he could smell the sea while heading up the coastline on Highway 1. Big Sur was beautiful, but Chandra had been told it was beautiful by so many people already that it felt as if he were staring at a Photoshopped postcard instead of at actual clifftops and lagoons. In any case, he was too anxious to really enjoy it and stopped only once, when he thought he saw a group of whales (which turned out to be clumps of seaweed, bobbing like body bags atop the breakers).

When he reached the turnoff for Esalen he had to manoeuvre his SUV down a narrow, private road until he ended up inside a small car park with the sea in front of him. There was a manicured lawn to his left, people reading or meditating on preter-naturally green grass. He couldn't see anybody else wearing a blazer, or even trousers. Taking his bags, Chandra crossed the park and headed into the lodge to his left where a ponytailed man grinned at him from behind a desk.

'Hello,' said Chandra.

'Welcome! I'm Ronnie.'

Ronnie had tea-coloured skin, grey hair, and an expression redolent of a man staring at his newborn daughter moments after she'd been placed in his arms. He handed Chandra a clipboard and asked him to sign in and write the name of his workshop on the form.

'Wow!' said Ronnie. 'You're with Rudi. You're so lucky, man. He's in demand, that guy. Has been for forty years. Used to do a lot of encounter work with acid until he got in trouble.'

Chandra was imagining a group of naked hippies flinging concentrated hydrofluoric solution at each other's flesh-stripped faces, but his expression must have betrayed him because Ronnie added, 'But not any more. They learned a lot of things the hard way, those boomers.'

Ronnie took his bags and they strolled through the vegetable gardens. There were pine trees and flowers to their right, the ocean only metres away on the left. All the colours were very intense, as if drabness had been outlawed.

123

They came to a ravine, the path turning into a footbridge. Chandra could see a white sword of water at the bottom, its point pressing into the sea. Ronnie indicated a house cut into the cliff on the other side, the sort the Swiss Family Robinson might have lived in.

'Rudi used to live right there,' said Ronnie. 'They were all a lot more intense back then. I guess that's how pioneers are. It's what's earned them so much respect.'

Professor Chandra wished this were true of economics. The *Guardian* had referred to Milton Friedman as a devil only last week, and once called Chandra himself 'an unreconstructed market fundamentalist'. It was small wonder he'd ended up here, at the Technicolor Funny Farm.

'That's the meditation zendō.' Ronnie pointed to a hut under the bridge. 'You do much meditation?'

Chandra shook his head.

'And here's your room,' said Ronnie, as they crossed the river. 'Premium single, walk-in shower. Towels are inside, champagne if you feel like it. And don't forget the hot tubs. You'll love 'em. Get yourself relaxed for tonight's workshop.'

'Sure,' said Chandra. 'Thank you.'

'Just be in your flow, okay. Don't worry about a thing, and have a wonderful, healing stay at Esalen. All righty? Ciao ciao.'

'Ciao.'

Chandra shaved for the second time that day, and changed into beige slacks and a Hawaiian

124

shirt, hoping he looked like a man in casual attire as opposed to a professor in fancy dress. Stuffing his swimming trunks and the *Economist* into a shoulder bag, he retraced his steps over the river and past the lodge.

He had to walk an extended gangplank to reach the hot tubs which were perched on the cliff's edge, looking out over the misty Pacific. There was only one changing room, for men *and* women, but it was empty and so he changed into his swimming trunks and slung his towel over his shoulder.

There were perhaps fifteen people on the deck, bathing or lounging on sunbeds, but it took him a few moments to realise that, with the exception of himself, everyone was naked, an inversion of his worst schoolboy nightmare.

He had two choices, he realised: he could be brash and American, not caring a damn what anyone thought, jumping into that tub filled with pride at his non-conformist, avant-garde attire; or he could take off those offending trunks, fling them over the cliff and say, 'If God wanted us to have trunks he'd have made us elephants,' while the entire deck roared with naked, gut-wobbling laughter.

The third option was to go back to the changing room, put on his slacks, and return to his cabin to lie on the bed reading the *Economist* until his workshop began, which was exactly what he did.

★ ★ ★

125

Professor Chandra's workshop was in a yurt a hundred metres away from his room. When he entered, the teacher was sitting on a chair with his eyes closed. Twenty others sat facing him, mostly women in their thirties and forties. As Chandra had feared, they didn't look like academics, not even sociologists. They looked like ordinary people. Some were sitting on cushions on the floor and the rest on white patio chairs. Chandra sat on one of these, towards the back.

Rudi Katz himself was on a chair, fists on his knees. He was older than Chandra, but looked very fit, barely an ounce of fat on his pale body, wearing a short-sleeved cream shirt with matching pants and white canvas shoes, an outfit that would not have looked out of place on Steve.

'For those arriving,' said Katz, his eyes still closed, 'find yourself a seat and, when you're ready, close your eyes. Take a deep breath. Feel all the tension in your body flow into your feet and out into the earth. Completely relax.'

Professor Chandra was well-known for his impatience with students, and would open seminars by writing on the whiteboard, IF YOU DON'T DO THE READING, DON'T COME TO CLASS. He would sometimes end lectures by intoning, 'Tomorrow's lecture is at nine o'clock, nine o'clock, nine o'clock.' But now he found himself unable to comply with the simplest of instructions. All he could do was wonder whether everyone else had their eyes closed, or if they were staring at him. Chandra had often

126

heard it said that people who sat their A levels in middle age were terribly inspiring and brave, but he'd always feared they were deluding themselves, that it was too late — one simply couldn't start from zero at such an advanced age. He wondered, not for the first time, if he'd been a fool to come here.

'Wonderful!' said Katz. 'We'll start every session with silent meditation. Please don't open your eyes until you hear my voice. And so, friends, welcome to Esalen and to 'Being Yourself in the Summer Solstice'. This class is about embracing the new and letting go of the pain and suffering we've caused ourselves by asking, 'Who am I?' 'What do I really want?' 'Why have I allowed so much pain and sorrow into my life?' 'How can I make my life better?'

'The way we'll do this, initially, is to talk about something I call strings. It's very simple. Our strings are the beliefs we have about ourselves that hold us back. So for our first string, our primary string, we try to find a core negative belief we have, a message we give to ourselves that hurts us, that we'd like to let go of but can't.

'It could be 'I'm stupid,' 'I'm ugly,' 'I'm lazy,' 'I'm selfish.' And then we add a second string and we say, 'And that's why my boyfriend left me,' or, 'And that's why I still live with my parents,' or, 'And that's why nobody's ever going to love me.' If we're going to be happy, we've got to learn that those thoughts aren't true. They have no outside legitimacy, no existence other than the existence we give to them. We can literally be anything we want to be, but only once those critical voices are gone.'

Chandra gave a mental snort. Of course those thoughts were true. He knew undergraduates who spoke like this; telling themselves they failed because their parents didn't love them or they were struggling with their identity, when in reality they were bone idle or half-witted or both. In his opinion, all this talk of self-esteem that Sunny was so fond of only caused mediocrities to convince themselves they were geniuses, the ones who asked for their exam papers to be remarked and ended up with even lower grades before filing formal complaints citing bullying or discrimination or eurocentrism.

'So, let's go around the room,' continued Katz, 'and introduce ourselves and tell each other our first string, and then add a second string, like, 'I'm selfish and *therefore* nobody will ever love me.' Everybody got that? We can start with me.

'My name is Rudi Katz and I'm a spiritual teacher and a therapist and for many years I have held the belief about myself that I'm not a responsible parent. It's a belief I had for years and years, and in some ways it's true, but my second string is, 'That's why my daughter's not happy and why I don't deserve to be happy.' And that's the rub. That's the one that's got to go.'

Rudi Katz looked around the yurt, making eye contact with each of them in turn before grinning at a large woman in her forties. The woman, clearly taken with Katz, grinned back.

'My name is Sally. Hi, everyone. I'm from Miami, Florida, and I'm a massage therapist and a mother, though not necessarily in that order. I'm here because I've been big since I was a teenager and recently I've gotten a whole lot bigger, and I just can't shake this voice in my head that tells me, 'I'm repulsive,' 'I'm a whale,' 'I'm a monster.' And I *am* fat. I know it, but that doesn't mean I have to think of myself as repulsive, does it?'

The room murmured its disapproval; even Chandra muttered, 'Of course not,' though the truth was that he wasn't entirely sympathetic. With the money she had spent on coming here this woman from Florida could simply have joined a decent gym. In Chandra's opinion, problems *did* have solutions.

'And as for my second string,' continued Sally, 'well, I guess it's like you said; I'm repulsive and *therefore* I don't have a boyfriend, and I'll never have one 'cause who'd want to be with this?' She indicated her body with a flourish of both hands. 'And that's all. Thank you, and it's good to be here with you all.'

'Thank you, Sally,' said Rudi.

Sally was dabbing at her eyes with a tissue. Chandra had always been astonished at the ability of women, particularly Americans, to cry so easily and with so little shame. The words 'emotional striptease' came to mind. Rudi Katz said nothing, only looked at the thin woman in her sixties sitting beside Sally on a bean bag, her legs folded to her chin, her grey mohair cardigan pulled down to her knees.

'Hi,' said the woman. 'I'm Madeleine, and I'm from Sacramento, California. I'm a retired teacher and I'm here because I have cancer and I can't shake the voice in my head that tells me every day, 'You're sick, you're dying, you're sick.' I mean, I am sick and I am dying. We all are, I guess, though I'm doing it faster than any of you, but does that really mean I have to tell myself that every day? I mean, aren't I other things besides sick? Aren't I still a person? Aren't I a mother and an artist and a friend and a wife and all sorts of other things? I suppose I know I am, but I keep telling myself I'm sick every day so it seems like the only thing that matters is that I have cancer. And I hate it because I'm ruining however long I have by feeling like shit all the time. That's it. That's all I have to say.'

Chandra nodded. Cancer was different, he supposed, though he still didn't understand why this woman needed to come here to say this. Perhaps she was one of those people who needed . . . what was it called? Validation. Chandra remembered how lonely he had felt in hospital. But he'd wanted his children then, not a roomful of strangers. Americans were different, perhaps.

'Thank you, Madeleine,' said Rudi, as Sally leaned her head against Madeleine's shoulder. 'And who's next? Yes, sir.'

'Well,' said a bald, middle-aged man, sitting cross-legged and leaning on his fist. 'Well, I feel a little funny following that, but maybe that's synchronicity at work, 'cause the truth is I feel like an asshole. Sorry, my name's Dan. I'm not working right now, though I used to be in movies in different capacities, and yeah, I tell myself every day, 'You're an asshole.' And why am I an

130

asshole? 'Cause I'm *not* dying. I mean, I'm not sick. I'm perfectly healthy and I've lost *eight* friends to Aids in the last twenty years, though I'm the one who *should* have got it, and that includes my lovely sweet straight friend Alice who slept with maybe four people in her whole life and was a good Catholic till the day she died — God knows how she got it — and then there's me, who had sex with most of New York before moving on to California, and not a scratch! Not a damn thing wrong with me and I just can't forgive myself, no matter how many times I say, 'Nam-myōhō-renge-kyō,' or tell myself I'm not to blame or it's up to the universe. I just can't stop hating myself, and I guess that's my second string. And what really stinks is I've got a great life otherwise. I've got money; I've got a beautiful apartment; I've got a great partner; my family's loving; I live in the hills. I've got everything in my life except joy, but hey — you can't have it all.'

'Well, we can talk about that,' said Katz, nodding. 'But thank you, Dan, and I think we all know you're not an asshole, but, as we're learning, that isn't the point. Yes, ma'am.'

With a start, Chandra realised the girl Katz had pointed to was Indian and, judging from her skin tone, possibly South Indian like him. 'Hi, my name's Pam,' she began, 'and I'm a little embarrassed that I don't have anything half as important to say as any of you guys, but I guess my critical voice tells me I should have more money. I mean, it's not like I haven't got money. I'm the daughter of a pretty well-to-do dad, and

131

I'm in law school, and I'm a part-time hair model, but all the time I just think, 'You could be living in Bel Air, and you could be driving a Cayenne or something — I don't know much about cars — or you could be dating Brad Pitt, but instead you're just little old you,' and you probably all think I'm a spoiled bitch.' She laughed. 'And I guess that's my second string.'

'You don't have enough money and *therefore* you're a spoiled bitch?' said Katz.

'Well, like, *yeah*,' said Pam.

'Now that's one I haven't heard before,' said Katz, and the whole room laughed.

'At least I got something right,' said Pam, waving her hands in the air. 'That's me. Miss Originality, California.'

Everyone laughed again.

'Well, thank you for sharing that with us, Pam,' said Katz. 'And let's see if we can't think up some ways to get you a few more bucks before the weekend is out.'

And on it went around the room, each person telling their tale. In spite of himself, Professor Chandra found himself becoming more and more involved. Apart from the Indian girl, he had to admit that these people did have real problems, more serious than his own in most cases, and they told their stories with such candour that, on occasion, he found himself deeply moved. There were people in the room who were crying, however, which he found absurd, and it did seem to him that nearly every one of them thrived on the attention, the drama of it all.

The woman beside him was an exception. She was sitting with her back very straight, her hands by her sides, and had barely moved for the last hour save for when Chandra swivelled to look at her and she jerked her head in the other direction. When it came to her turn Chandra wasn't surprised to learn that she was the only other non-American in the room.

'Hello, everyone,' the woman began. 'My name is Elke and I'm from Holland, but I've been living in Arizona for twenty years. Actually, I've been living in the care of the state of Arizona for the last nine because, unlike most of you, I actually did do something wrong. A decade ago I killed my own baby daughter. She ingested a fatal dose of morphine through my breast milk. I was convicted of child abuse, involuntary manslaughter, and unlawful conduct towards a child.

'I lost my nursing licence for obtaining morphine illegally and ultimately, I believe, I got what I deserved. It's a long story, but needless to say it's hard for me to get work now. I'm sleeping on the floor of the conference room tonight and I can barely afford that, but I just felt it was either this or I kill myself. I don't even want to tell you what my critical voices say, because it'd be like hearing the devil speak or something. I just . . . I'm sorry for what I did, though maybe not sorry enough, and I wish I could see a future, but I don't. That's all.'

'Thank you, Elke,' said Katz, 'and I think this is a good time to state that whatever is said in this room stays in this room, and that's a code of

133

honour we've all got to keep to, for obvious reasons. But thank you, Elke, for sharing, and I hope we can work on this over the weekend so we can put at least a little hope into the despair you've articulated so eloquently. And now to you, sir, please.'

Professor Chandra was staring at the back of the chair in front of him. He could hardly believe he was sitting beside a convicted murderer, and of a baby. Surely she hadn't meant to kill her child, but she had; she had spoken with such coldness about herself, such absence. Yes, he thought, he could imagine her killing herself. After speaking she had shuffled her body an inch or two away from him, as if convinced he were judging her. Chandra looked at Katz, who returned his glance. Of course, thought Chandra; it was up to him not to make this worse by lengthening the silence that had permeated every corner of the room. He was nervous, he realised, so out of his depth that if he didn't speak soon he'd drown, but still, nothing was coming out of his mouth. Chandra looked at Katz once more who was smiling, nodding at him. He cleared his throat.

'My name is Chandra,' he said, his voice barely audible. 'I'm from England, though right now I'm on a visiting professorship in Los Angeles. I'm an academic, an economist, and I'm, well, I suppose a lot of people would say I'm at the top of my profession. I'm an Emeritus Professor at Cambridge. I earn more money than I need. I'm staying in a premium room.' Everyone laughed, and Chandra smiled in response, feeling more at ease now. 'But the truth is that I consider myself a failure. That's my first string. That's what my critical voice says. It says, 'Chandra, you're a bloody failure,' and no matter what I do, no matter if I do win the damn Nobel Prize next year, I think I'll still feel like that.

'And now to the second string,' he continued, raising his head to make eye contact with Madeleine and Dan and Rudi. 'It's simple. I'm sixty-nine years old and the voice in my head says there's nothing to live for. I've screwed it up, my life — as an economist, as a father, and as a husband. I might as well just give up the ghost. My life is worthless. I've never said this out loud. I've never told anyone this. Because the truth is, I am not a sincere person. I look around and see so many wonderful people, so much honesty, and it seems to come so naturally to you all, but all I can think is that I have the biggest ego in this room, and I'm the least honest of anyone here.'

'But you're being honest now,' said Rudi.

'Yes,' replied Chandra. 'Yes, I am.'

Chandra heard nothing of what the next speaker said. He felt exhilarated, weightless, as if he could float into the air if he exhaled hard enough. So this was why Americans loved confessing so much . . .

After a few minutes he was able to regain some composure, listening while the remainder of the group introduced themselves. He even found himself beginning to enjoy himself, feeling like a child of four or five, sitting on the floor and listening to stories.

135

When the exercise was over Rudi Katz thanked them all for being so brave and said, 'And before we go, one last exercise, and then we can meet again in the morning, prepared and in the right frame of mind. I want you to turn to the person next to you, though not somebody you came with, and shut your eyes, think about what they said about themselves, and try to find its reverse, its opposite. If you need them to remind you of their strings then do so, but don't spend too much time talking.

'So: I said I was an irresponsible father who didn't deserve to be happy. One way to reverse this would be to say, 'You are a loving, responsible parent who deserves a happy life.' That's one way. But you can say it another way if you prefer. The important thing is not to rush it. Take as long as you need. We've got time. Just close your eyes and picture the person. Try to feel them, their essence, and then let the words come out.

'Any questions? All right. When you're finished I want you to look towards the front so I can see. We won't stop until everyone is finished.'

Professor Chandra looked to his right but his neighbour, Chester, from Texas, was already talking to the short mousy woman beside him. Chandra had no choice. He took two deep breaths and turned to his left, saying, 'Elke, isn't it? I'm Chandra.'

'I know,' said Elke.

'Do you need me to remind you of my strings?'

'No. I think I have it. How about you?'

136

'No,' said Chandra. 'It's all right.'

'Good,' said Elke. 'That's good.'

'Well,' said Chandra. 'Shall we begin?'

But the question was redundant as Elke had already closed her eyes, her hands folded in her lap. Chandra closed his too. Had it been anyone else, he realised, his cynicism might have returned.

He thought of what this woman had done, that she had taken morphine while breast-feeding, injected it. Probably she'd been addicted; it would have been hard for her to stop, but why hadn't she tried to get help? Why hadn't she gone for rehabilitation or to her family? Had she been a drug addict while she was pregnant? She must have known she could harm the baby. But she had gone on taking the drug and her daughter had died, a baby girl, like Jasmine, like Radha.

How the world must have hated her! It would have been in the papers, surely, and her family, her friends, people in the street, at work, everyone would have known. She used to be a nurse — didn't she say that? How would she have felt at that moment when she realised her baby was dead? Had she been high at the time? Had she even cared?

Chandra's fists were balled. He unfurled them, placing his palms on his knees. He wondered if Rudi Katz was watching him, but he did not open his eyes.

'You are a successful, attractive man,' said Elke beside him. 'Your life is a wonderful gift to be celebrated and enjoyed.'

137

Her voice was so cold. Did she even mean what she'd said? And 'attractive', where had that come from? He had said nothing about his looks. Was she mocking him?

'Once more please,' he said.

He counted to seven before Elke spoke.

'You are a very successful and good man,' she said. 'You have your life ahead of you at this moment. Celebrate and cherish it.'

Yes. To her this was probably true, she who had destroyed her own life. To her he would seem successful. He had not gone to jail. He had not killed anyone, least of all a tiny, blameless baby. But who was she to tell him he was a good man? She didn't even know him, and what did this woman know about goodness? And why the hell had he been given this one? Was it some sort of a trap? Had everyone else known who she was and avoided her, or had she sat next to him because she wanted to land a rich man, and hence that ludicrous comment about his being attractive even though he was practically twice her age? He should never have been so candid. He did not know these people. Who else had murdered someone in here? He wanted to shout it: 'Who else?'

But this was not the exercise. Chandra inhaled and exhaled, tried to concentrate on his breathing but found his attention shifting to the 'teacher' at the front who had played with their emotions like a child with a bag of marbles, sitting there in his stupid cotton playsuit thinking he knew something about people because he had taken drugs and spent a couple of years in India, probably in Rishikesh which was where most of them went, like Steve.

But back to Elke, whose breathing he could hear from beside him.

She would have hated herself, that was for certain, would have wished herself dead, longed for someone to come up behind her in prison with a rope or a knife. The other prisoners would have known. They would have bullied her for it, would have called her 'baby killer' or taunted her by making the sound of babies crying or calling out 'Mommy' in the middle of the night. They would have gone for her in the showers or the canteen, banged her head against the walls. And she would have been cold the entire time, cold like she was tonight, because she did not feel she deserved to suffer or cry, did not deserve feelings, did not deserve life, not after what she'd done.

She would have mourned for her baby, her daughter, her little girl. She would have asked God — because everyone believed in God at times like these — to take her life, to give her baby's back. She would have gone over everything a million times in her head, all the different things she should or could have done but didn't, the treatments she could have received, the help she could have asked for. She would have come to see herself as the embodiment of evil, the walking dead, someone too impure for this world, someone who did not even deserve the peace that would come from taking her own life, just slime, waiting to be washed down the drain of existence one day.

139

And yet she was here, sitting beside him, breathing.

'You are a mother and you can love,' he said. 'There is still hope.'

He opened his eyes. Elke's were closed.

'Thank you,' she said, and looked towards the front.

7

When he entered the yurt the following morning, Chandra saw Elke kneeling on a cushion by the wall. He sat on a chair at the back as before and closed his eyes, though he made no attempt to meditate. He had slept poorly, kept awake by the braggadocio of the sea which he had hoped would prove soporific. When he had left his room, however, he'd been shocked to see the water only metres away, so vast, so unchanged, so indifferent, and was struck by the realisation that he was somewhere quite new, an environment whose purpose had been alien to him until now.

'And now gently open your eyes,' said Rudi Katz, which caused Chandra to wonder how one violently opened one's eyes. 'And take a breath,' which also seemed extraneous, for they would hardly have asphyxiated in their chairs without this instruction.

'Last night was a warm-up,' said Katz, who was wearing the same cream shirt and pants as yesterday. 'Today we begin the real work. I've been running the following exercise for years and, believe me, it goes deep, so if at any moment you feel it's getting too much for you then go outside, take a walk by the sea or a drink of water, and come back when you're ready.

'I'm going to divide you into groups of four. You'll need to sit in circles, preferably on the floor, and talk. That's all, just talk. But you've got to be absolutely, strictly honest. No cop-outs. We're looking to break through today, to get to what we really think, how we really feel.

'We're going to repeat what we did yesterday, tell each other what our critical voices say, and you're going to respond to each other. Speak from the gut. There are no restrictions on language here. The only thing we don't tolerate is physical abuse of any kind. That is out of the question.'

Katz raised his eyebrows so high they looked like hairpins.

'If anyone isn't prepared to do this then say so now. Don't worry. Some people aren't ready for it, and we respect autonomy here.' Katz seemed to be looking at Chandra, who fingered his car keys in his trouser pocket. 'But if you're not sure, give it a try. The worst that can happen is someone will say something you don't like, but then you have the opportunity to observe your reaction, which is where it gets interesting. You might be surprised by how liberating you find it.

'I'll be walking around, intervening from time to time, just guiding, nothing more, but if you need me snap your fingers or call me over and I'll be there. I'm not going to leave this room.'

Pam, the Indian girl sitting in front of Chandra, raised her hand, keeping it raised while she asked her question.

'So we're allowed to insult each other?'

'You're allowed to say what you feel, Pam. How the other person reacts is their business.'

'Can you write that on the board?'

'I think it's pretty clear.'

Pam looked hurt, and lowered her hand.

'Do we have to inform you if we leave the room?' asked Sally.

'No,' said Katz. 'Just go. It's up to you. Okay. Let's start. I'll come help divide you into your groups.'

Professor Chandra knew this trick. Katz had said, 'Okay,' almost instantly in order to prevent further questions. They were all uneasy, that much was clear: questions cushioned, or rather delayed, the blow.

Elke was too far away to be in Chandra's group, but he did find himself with Pam, the Indian girl. Also in Chandra's circle was a man in his thirties called Bryan with blond curls that hung over his eyebrows, and a woman called Daisy, perhaps ten or fifteen years younger than Chandra, with a thin but perfectly symmetrical face and long grey hair down to her tailbone. She was wearing a flowing white dress that reminded him of a merciful, yet powerful, witch.

They sat on cushions in a tight circle at the back, Chandra leaning against the wall beside Daisy. He would have preferred a chair, but he didn't want anyone to think he considered himself superior.

Bryan, sitting cross-legged, was smiling, making eye contact with each of them in turn, while Daisy did the opposite, looking pointedly past Pam who was biting the nail polish off her fingers. Chandra resisted the urge to tell her to stop.

'I don't want to begin,' said Daisy, 'but none

of you are speaking so I kind of feel I have to. I don't know why. I've done workshops with Rudi before; I guess that's why.'

'I think we've got to say our strings first, haven't we?' said Bryan.

'Oh, that's right. You go ahead,' said Daisy, looking down and smoothing her metre-long cylinder of grey hair.

'My first string,' said Bryan, 'is that — like a lot of people — I'm kind of selfish. I don't spend enough time with my son, though there are reasons for that, and now I work myself so hard because I feel guilty, which means I still don't have much time for other people, and this makes me not as happy as I could be.'

He hadn't stopped smiling all the while, and now he rubbed his hands together.

'Anyone want to respond?' said Bryan. 'Or do we keep going?'

'I'll go,' said Daisy. 'My first string is that I don't think I'm a people person. It's just not my thing, but most people feel there's something wrong with me, like I'm this antisocial old hag who's not alive or something. I don't care. I'm fine with it. I mean, I know people feel sorry for me and say stuff like, 'She must be so miserable,' and whatever, but I don't feel like that. I used to be married — I didn't say that yesterday — and I have a son who's sick. I love him, but I don't think about him all the time and I don't tear out my hair. I just accept it. I don't miss my husband. I don't even miss my son much. I *like* being alone. That's all. Thank you.'

'Well, I guess you remember me,' said Pam, undoing and redoing the second button of her blouse in a way that suggested highly performative but perfectly genuine neurosis. 'I'm a lawyer. I mean, I will be. I live in Fremont with my parents, but I'm going to move to SF soon, and it's going to be expensive but I need my own place. And my thing is I just don't think I have as much money as I need, or as I want, and I spend all day wishing I had more and thinking my life's dull and boring and I won't be happy till I've got more, a *lot* more, and soon I'll be earning pretty well but I know it won't be enough, not for another twenty years at least, and I hate that I have to wait that long and I guess that makes me shallow, but . . . '

Pam grinned, giggled, and was quiet. It was Chandra's turn. He had waded in up to his neck, it felt, was about to take the final, definitive step.

'My name is Chandra,' said Chandra. 'And I've had a good career. I have three children, but I'm divorced now and I hardly see them. I think of myself as having accomplished nothing in life, and the truth is I may not be around all that much longer. Who can say? I used to be so confident that I was right and everyone else was wrong, but now I think maybe it was me who was wrong, especially now that I see how happy my wife is without me. If this is a mid-life crisis, it's happening too late. I'm sixty-nine years old. But I'm here, and I never thought I would be in a place like this.'

Chandra was pleased with his speech. Forthrightness was coming more easily to him now. He was almost disappointed when Pam turned to Daisy instead of him.

'So you really don't feel anything, Daisy?' she said. 'No emotions? Nothing?'

'I feel things,' said Daisy. 'I just don't need people the way others do. I like my own company and my solitude.'

'But you said your son is sick,' said Chandra.

'Yeah,' said Pam. 'Don't you feel anything about your son?'

'I didn't say that,' said Daisy.

'Say how *you* feel,' said Rudi, hovering behind Bryan.

'I feel you might not be as cold as you say you are,' said Bryan, with his Californian grin.

'No,' said Rudi. 'How do *you* feel? Don't say what you think she feels.'

'Well, I guess I feel a little sorry for you,' said Bryan.

Daisy raised her eyebrows, a passable imitation of Rudi Katz.

'Why do you feel sorry for her?' said Chandra.

'Maybe she wants to reach out to people but she's scared. It's tough being alone. It becomes a habit. I know. I've been there.'

'I like being alone,' said Daisy, her eyes harder now.

'Do you feel sorry for Daisy, Pam?' said Rudi.

'Kind of. But I'm pretty creeped out too. It's like . . . it's weird; like she doesn't care about the rest of us, like we could all die and she wouldn't care.'

'Since when did liking being alone become wanting you all to die?' said Daisy.

146

'I didn't say you *wanted* us all to die,' said Pam.

'And I didn't say I don't have any feelings.'

'You said you didn't really like people,' said Pam. 'I guess I find that hurtful.'

'Good,' said Rudi.

'I mean, we're all people here, and you're saying you don't like us.'

'I never said that,' said Daisy.

'And if you don't like us then why should we like you? I mean, you get what you put out in the end, isn't that true?' said Pam.

Chandra nodded; he also found Daisy cold, but it didn't bother him as much. He wondered if this was an age thing, if older people were simply more tolerant.

'You're pretty hostile, Pam,' said Daisy.

'I don't mean to be hostile,' said Pam, her eyes becoming marginally wetter.

'But you are. You've got a lot of rage inside you.'

'And?' said Rudi.

'And I don't like it. It makes me uncomfortable. You started judging me after thirty seconds and it's because of your rage. You didn't even listen to what I said. I just said I'm not a people person and I like being alone. You've made it all about you.'

'What's wrong with your son?' asked Chandra.

'He had a psychotic break eleven years ago. He's schizophrenic. He was at home for a long time but now he needs permanent care.'

'And how does this make you feel, Chandra?' asked Rudi. 'How do you feel about Daisy?'

'It's a sad story,' said Chandra. 'It makes me feel sad. We can't control what happens to our children. I'm very sad about my own children.'

'I feel sad listening to both of you,' said Pam. 'Sad and depressed. I don't want to get old.'

'Okay, that's good,' said Rudi. 'You're getting it. Holler if you need me.'

Katz walked away. Chandra turned to face Pam. She was on the heavy side, dressed in a light pink blouse and a white skirt, and she wore a lot of make-up, but underneath that, Chandra could see a girl, a child.

'Are you South Indian, Pam?' asked Chandra.

'I'm me. I'm Pam.'

'But Pam isn't an Indian name?'

'Pam is my name,' said Pam.

'I know, I was just wondering where you're from.'

'I told you. I live in Fremont. I'm from the Bay.'

'But your parents are South Indian?' said Chandra, knowing he should stop.

'Why don't you ask about Bryan's parents?' said Pam. 'Or Daisy's?'

'I feel uncomfortable now,' said Bryan. 'Like something's going on.'

'I'm just asking about her name,' said Chandra.

'You're trying to place her,' said Daisy. 'And why not? It won't kill her, will it?'

'I want all of you to back off,' said Pam. 'I feel attacked.'

'Nobody is attacking you,' said Daisy.

'Then why do you need to know what I am?

I'm me. I'm Pam. I've told you.'

'Why are you being defensive?' said Daisy.

'I'm not being defensive.'

'You are. It's obvious.'

'It's okay,' said Bryan. 'You're just protecting your own space.'

'I don't like being interrogated,' said Pam. 'I'm not on trial.'

'I was just asking a question,' said Chandra. 'I didn't mean anything by it.'

'That's bullshit,' said Pam. 'Sorry, but it is.'

'How do you feel, Chandra?' asked Bryan.

'Like I'm talking to my daughter,' said Chandra.

'Well, I'm not your daughter,' said Pam. 'I'm me. I'm Pam.'

'Christ, we get it,' said Daisy.

'Excuse me?' said Pam.

'I've just never heard anyone say their own name so many times.'

'My name's Pammi,' said Pam. 'Yes, it's Indian. I'm half Bengali. My name means lovable.'

'And half what?' said Chandra.

'Punjabi!' said Pam. 'God!'

'Do you feel you know her better now, Chandra?' asked Bryan.

'I don't know,' said Chandra. 'I was just curious. I didn't want to make her angry.'

'But you could see it was annoying her,' said Daisy.

'Yes, but I didn't know why. It was an innocent question. My daughter is the same. Whatever I say to her she gets angry.'

149

'And you feel angry back?' said Daisy.

'I feel confused. I don't understand why they have to get so angry all the time.'

'Why did you have to know those things?' said Pam. 'Why can't you just talk to me like I'm a person?'

'I was talking to you like you're a person. I just wanted to know if you were Indian. I'm Indian. You look like you are Indian. I was curious. Why is that wrong? I don't understand it. I said one thing and you flew off the handle.'

'Do you feel he's projecting his daughter on to you, Pam?' said Bryan.

'Actually, I feel like I'm talking to my dad. I've had enough of talking to my dad.'

'Do you feel ashamed of being Indian?' said Daisy.

'Do you feel guilty for having a psychotic son?'

'Yes,' said Daisy.

'Wow,' said Bryan.

'Wow what, Bryan?' said Pam. 'Do you really think anyone buys that you're this chilled-out happy-go-lucky surfer dude who loves everyone and himself twenty-four-seven?'

'I never said I was any of those things,' said Bryan. 'I said I work too hard, and I'm carrying a lot of guilt about my son, and I don't spend any time with my boyfriend even though we live together, and I don't know how long he'll take that for but I'm unable to stop because if I did I'd have to face myself. So yeah, I have problems, and I'm not happy all the time.'

'Yeah, you're human, we get it,' said Pam. 'The rest of us are unhinged dysfunctional lunatics but you've just got regular normal-guy stuff which means you can sit there smiling while we all bawl and yell and tear each other's faces off.'

'No,' said Bryan, his smile vanishing. 'That isn't how I feel.'

'That's how it looks,' said Pam.

'You see?' said Daisy. 'Hostile.'

'And what else?' said Pam. 'What is it you really want to say?'

'You're a spoiled, hostile little bitch,' said Daisy, whose body looked so brittle that if Pam did slap her, as she was shaping up to, Chandra thought she might shatter like a stage vase.

'I'm feeling uncomfortable now,' said Bryan. 'I don't know where all this came from.'

'It came from me,' said Chandra. 'I started this.'

'So you feel guilty?' said Bryan.

'Yes,' said Chandra, wanting to sit on a chair but not daring. 'I feel guilty.'

'How's it going?' said Rudi, manifesting to their right.

'It's getting hot in here,' said Bryan.

Rudi sat beside Daisy with his back to the wall so he could see everyone except Chandra, who was on Daisy's other side.

'How are you feeling, Bryan?' said Rudi.

'Like I always feel when I'm watching other people fight.'

'Which is?'

'Like I want to be somewhere else.'

'Did you watch your parents fight?' said Rudi.

'Yep.'

151

'And how did that make you feel?'

'Like I wanted to disappear. Like it was my fault. Like they could turn on me at any time.'

'How about you, Chandra?' said Rudi, leaning forward to make eye contact. 'How's it going?'

'I upset Pam,' said Chandra.

'He feels guilty,' said Daisy.

'I don't care,' said Pam. 'It's nothing. It's not important.'

'So that's how you feel, Pam?' said Rudi. 'That your feelings aren't important.'

'I'm emotional!' said Pam. 'I got emotional. Sometimes I blow things out of proportion.'

'We don't have to apologise for our emotions in here,' said Rudi. 'We are our emotions. If we say our emotions aren't important, we're saying we aren't important. If we say our emotions are nothing, we're saying we're nothing.'

'Was that how you felt as a kid, Pam?' said Bryan. 'Like you were nothing?'

'I guess.'

'Was that how you felt when Chandra was talking to you?' said Rudi. 'I mean, I don't know what he said, and it probably doesn't matter that I don't know. I just want to know how you felt.'

'I felt like he wasn't seeing me,' said Pam. 'Like he thought he was more important than me. Like he could just tell me who I was and tell me what to do and I should shut up and listen because I'm stupid and pointless and I'll never be as good as he is.'

'I didn't say any of that,' said Chandra. 'I just asked if she was Indian, for God's sake.'

152

'Why is it important to you?' said Rudi. 'What does her ethnicity matter to you?'

'Because she's the only other Indian in the room and . . . '

'Yes?' said Rudi, leaning closer.

'And I supposed that might mean we had a connection.'

'And when she responded in the way that she did, how did that make you feel?'

'As if she was rejecting that connection, as if she . . . didn't like me, maybe because of it.'

'So you were reaching out to her and she was pushing you away and you felt hurt.'

'Yes.'

'And how do you feel about all this, Daisy?' said Rudi.

'I feel we're being sidelined, Bryan and I. Like these two have started up all this father-daughter Indian-not Indian stuff, and we just have to shut up and watch them play out their dramas, like it's all about them.'

'Oh, I'm so sorry,' said Pam. 'I'm so sorry all this minority shit is getting in the way of you taking centre stage. We'll just shut up and let you get on with it, shall we?'

'I didn't say that,' said Daisy.

'You didn't have to,' said Pam.

'Feelings, please,' said Rudi.

'I feel angry,' said Daisy. 'Mindy Kaling here thinks the whole world revolves around her.'

'And I feel you're a racist bitch,' said Pam. 'Do you know how many times I've been called Mindy Kaling? Do you? Because I'm brown and I'm not a size zero and I like to shop! And Mindy Kaling

153

isn't even dumb, she just plays dumb.'

'Whereas you actually *are* dumb?' said Daisy.

'I don't think so,' said Bryan. 'I think you play dumb too. I think it's a defence mechanism.'

Pam was rubbing at her eyes now and sniffing. Chandra couldn't see any tears. He wondered if she was pretending.

'I feel this was all my fault,' said Chandra.

'Because everything's about you,' said Pam.

'What?'

'Why am I here with my fucking *father*?' said Pam. 'The minute I saw you . . . '

'That's the law of karma,' said Rudi. 'You get what you need, not what you want.'

'I'm sorry,' said Daisy. 'I shouldn't have said the Mindy Kaling thing. I actually said it because I thought it was funny and it might ease the tension, but obviously I was wrong.'

'Who is Mindy Kaling?' asked Chandra.

'Never mind,' said Pam.

'She's a comedian,' said Daisy.

'She's Indian,' said Pam.

'Ah,' said Chandra.

'You know,' said Bryan, 'we seem to have forgotten everyone's strings. We all just went off about thirty seconds into the thing. Maybe that's okay, but I want to point it out.'

'I'm a cold bitch. She's shallow. He hates himself, and you're a cop-out,' said Daisy. 'You didn't tell us one thing about yourself, Bryan. We all saw it.'

'How do you feel, Bryan?' said Rudi, lifting himself to his feet before stretching to touch his toes.

'I feel scared,' said Bryan, putting his fingertips together, a Californian yogi posing for a cover shoot. 'I feel scared of being judged.'

'Good,' said Rudi. 'Good.'

Rudi Katz wandered off. Chandra, whose knees had been hurting since they began, fetched a chair and sat on it, waiting for someone, probably Pam, to tell him how superior he looked on his throne, but nobody did.

'Why are you scared, Bryan?' he said.

'I know the point of this exercise,' said Bryan. 'I've done things like this before. The whole point is to let us go after each other. And — I don't know — I guess words can't kill you, but I'm afraid that they can. I'm afraid one day someone will say something that destroys me.'

'What I can't understand,' said Chandra, 'is how he can be so sure that everything is happening for a reason. How does he know?'

'He doesn't know,' said Daisy. 'It's faith.'

Chandra shook his head. 'I don't think I have faith.'

'Course you do,' said Bryan. 'You couldn't get through any minute of any day without faith. If we didn't have faith we'd kill ourselves.'

'I don't know,' said Chandra. 'I only believe what I know.'

'That isn't possible,' said Bryan. 'It's like how our eyes pick up only about forty per cent of what we think we see. Our brain fills in the rest. That's faith.'

'Yes,' said Chandra. 'Maybe you're right.'

Pam rolled her eyes and said, 'God.'

'Why are you so angry with me?' said Chandra.

'I'm not angry with you.'

'You are. You were angry with me before I spoke.'

'I told you. It's not about you. It's about my father.' She looked at Daisy. 'I may be dumb, but I know that.'

'Then why are you so angry with your father?' asked Chandra.

'What's it to you?'

'He brought you up. He clothed you. You wouldn't even exist if it weren't for him. How can you hate the person who gave you life? What sense does it make to hate him? Why does everyone of your generation have to hate their parents? Does it make you more intelligent?'

Pam stared at him.

'I never hated my parents,' Chandra continued. 'I wouldn't have dreamed of hating my parents. They gave me everything. They weren't perfect, but why does that matter? They gave me everything I had, everything I have now. Nothing can repay that debt.'

'Did you ask to be born?' said Pam.

'I think you are ungrateful,' said Chandra. 'I think your whole generation is ungrateful, as if you think you invented the world and everyone else should thank you for it, as if it was you who created your parents instead of the other way around. All you know is the last twenty years, and you think that's all you need to know, as if nothing of any consequence happened in this world until you were born, that you are the sun

156

and the rest of us are orbiting around you. You are not a bad person. You are not dumb. And you are not this Mindy woman. But you are selfish and ungrateful and that is why you are unhappy. And if I sound like your father then I'm sorry, but perhaps you should listen to your father.'

Pam stood up and left the room. It was like watching his daughter's receding back and yet it felt liberating, if only for an instant.

'Wow,' said Daisy. 'I couldn't have done that.'

'It's all right,' said Bryan. 'She's okay.'

'No,' said Chandra. 'I shouldn't have spoken. That was wrong.'

'It's okay,' said Daisy.

'No,' said Chandra. 'I'll go after her.'

'Look.' Daisy put her hand on his wrist. 'All this time Pam has been prodding all of us, trying to make us angry. It was obvious to me because I used to be just the same. You said exactly what she needed to hear and she knows it. She's just gone to process what you said. It'll do her good. Of all the people here, you were the one in a position to help her, and you did help her. So don't beat yourself up.'

'Hear, hear,' said Bryan.

'Rudi saw everything,' said Daisy. 'He was laughing, and if Obi-Wan Kenobi says it's okay, it's okay.'

'Who is Obi-Wan Kenobi?' said Chandra.

Bryan patted his leg.

'You're quite a character, Chandra. I've never met anyone like you at a place like this.'

'Yeah,' said Daisy. 'Kudos for coming here. That takes guts.'

Chandra felt irritated, as if they were telling him he didn't belong, that he was making a fool of himself, that he should have stayed at home. He did not want to be the joker, or the fool.

'So why did *you* come here, Bryan?' he asked. 'If you don't want to talk about yourself?'

★   ★   ★

At lunch, Chandra kept hoping to catch a glimpse of Pam. He was concerned she might have left, a diminutive firearm tucked inside her Prada handbag.

'My daughters are just the same,' he told Bryan. 'I don't understand them. Even my wife, my former wife, I mean. I used to know her, but now I only think I knew her. She left me for someone else. His name's Steve. I think he understands her. I don't think I ever did.'

'It's a bit cliched, isn't it?' said Bryan, whose grin seemed to have prevailed for three hours now. 'The ageing male whose wife left him all alone and now women are this giant cosmic mystery . . . '

'So now I am lonely and a cliche?'

'I don't think it's about understanding women. You're just up against a universal conundrum. Look, I have a partner, right? I like him. I love him. But I don't *understand* him. Sometimes I think I don't even know him. And that's not because he's an atheist or Hispanic or an only child. It's because he's another human being. Humans don't understand one other. *Punto*. That's the way it is. But start saying you

158

don't understand women and you're making yourself the problem. Let it go. You're just a human like anyone else. This is what happens. We fall in love and then one day we realise we have no fucking clue who that other person is, and sometimes it falls apart and sometimes it makes us stronger. Yours fell apart. She left you for Sean.'

'Steve,' said Chandra, looking at the sea.

'Well, I can tell you this. Steve doesn't understand her either. He might pretend to, and he can come up with all the psychobabble he wants, but he doesn't. And he's not better than you. He just came after you. It's not your fault, man. Let it go. Nothing is anyone's fault.'

'My God,' said Chandra. 'You people are as ideological as economists, aren't you? Everything happens for a reason. Follow your bliss. Nothing is anyone's fault.'

'Yeah,' said Bryan, laughing. 'That's California. I wasn't into any of it till I got to the Bay area and then . . . it just kind of happens to you. You go to one thing, then you go to another, then you go to some sort of couples rejuvenation therapy, then both of you are into it, and then you get a whole set of friends, and before you know it . . . you're a Californian. But, hey, it's happening to you, Chandra. You can't deny it. You're here, aren't you? You *gave* yourself to that workshop, man. You didn't hold back. It was awesome what you did.'

Chandra pushed his plate away. Lunch had been excellent: organic chard and kale from the garden, parsnip and coriander soup, a large fruit salad with yoghurt, the sea air. He was feeling healthier already.

'The thing is,' said Chandra, 'when I saw Pam I knew something would happen. I knew we'd end up in some sort of . . . situation. I just knew it.'

'She said she knew it too,' said Bryan.

'But I don't think she and I made it happen. It was like we couldn't help it.'

'The Universe made it happen,' said Bryan, leaning forward and grinning. 'That's the word people traumatised by religion use for God.'

'I'm not traumatised by religion, but I can't believe God has nothing better to do than see that Pam and I yell at each other.'

'Well, let's not call it religion then,' said Bryan. 'But it's something spiritual, the whole workshop is.'

'It didn't feel spiritual to me,' said Chandra. 'It was just . . . arguing.'

'It was group therapy,' said Bryan. 'But they're kind of connected. It's like Jack Kornfield says about Westerners: if you've got so much unresolved shit floating around, deep meditation's wasted on you.'

'I don't know if I'm Western,' said Chandra, 'but I think troubled childhoods and problems with relationships are universal. Anyway, India's not as religious as it used to be. We economists used to say that India suffered from the Hindu rate of growth, you know that?'

Bryan shook his head.

'But not any more. It was 7.1 per cent last year.'

'You're quite a character, Chandra.'

Professor Chandra smiled. He had no idea why Bryan kept saying that.

★ ★ ★

When they returned for the afternoon session Pam was already present and meditating. She was wearing a bright blue cobalt necklace, which Chandra thought might be a good-luck charm, or perhaps to ward off evil (meaning him). She opened her eyes and, for one breathless second, seemed to smother him in her gaze, before returning to her meditation.

'Well,' said Rudi, once they were all seated. 'We had quite a morning, didn't we?'

There were calls of 'Amen' amidst much laughter.

'You see what happens when we're honest about our feelings?' said Katz, pausing to do some facial exercises. 'Not a pretty sight, is it?'

There was further laughter, of a more nervous variety.

'This afternoon,' continued Katz, 'I want you to use your notebooks and write down all the judgemental things you can remember yourself saying about other people this morning — forget what anyone else said. Find a quiet spot outside, or stay here if you like. After you've done it, sit quietly and think, 'Whose voice was that? Where did I get that voice from?' Try to remember. And when you've done that, write down anything you can remember them saying about you in that same judgemental tone. We'll meet back here at a quarter of four. Any questions?'

Professor Chandra knew where he wanted to go: the bench a few yards away from his room. He took a cushion and, afraid someone might take his spot, practically ran down the steps towards the sea. But when he got there he was the only person in sight. It appeared that most of them had remained in the yurt.

He opened his notebook and looked at the ocean. So: what judgemental things had he said? Pam, of course. He had told her she was ungrateful and selfish, that her whole generation was like that, that her father was right.

Had he judged anyone else? How about Bryan? Yes, they were thick as thieves now, but at the beginning?

No, he hadn't judged Bryan; everyone else had judged Bryan. And he couldn't recall having said anything to Daisy. He'd been too afraid of her. It was only Pam. He had asked if she was Indian — that was what started it all — and she had taken this as a judgement. But he couldn't write, *Judged Pam for thinking she might be Indian.* Was it still a judgement if it was true? But surely judging someone meant saying they were stupid or selfish or ungrateful, not *Indian.* How could that be a judgement? Unless you considered being Indian a terrible thing? Was that it? Was that why Pam reacted? Because she secretly believed all Indians were devious, plotting, smelly, oily, lascivious, repugnant beasts, good only for cheating and begging and making nasty comments down here in the Black Hole of Esalen?

162

Radha used to call him a racist, said he had swallowed the colonial world view, that he was the brown poster child for global corporatism. When he thought about this now, the first thing that popped into Chandra's mind was Sunny, who actually was the brown face of global corporatism. The difference was that Sunny plotted and planned these things; Professor Chandra simply did what he believed was right. And if Radha judged him for it then to hell with her. Everyone couldn't agree with everyone. In any case, there were plenty of Indians who weren't rabid Marxists. But Radha hated being called a Marxist now. She was a P.O.C anarchist ('Pests on Campus', Chandra called them), a Third World cyberpunk, an Eco-Womanist. He couldn't keep track of all her twists and turns through the Walmart of ideological juvenilia.

The problem with Radha was that she had too many choices. She said she didn't believe in duty or obligation; but obligation, by definition, wasn't something you believed in. It was something you did because you had to. Belief was irrelevant. However, when life became some kind of giant hotel buffet — which happened when your father had a chair at Cambridge and you went to private school and had holidays in Oman because the south of France was 'too cliched' — then the minute anyone hinted that you should 'Sit your spoiled backside down, and eat what your mother gave you' you started wailing about child abuse. You talked to therapists who made you write letters telling your parents you forgave them even though they'd wasted the most potentially wondrous years of their lives running after you like a pair of underpaid waiters at that same hotel buffet you didn't even know you were sitting at.

But Radha hadn't done that. That was Jasmine. Radha had turned around and said she didn't want all the advantages he'd practically killed himself to give her. Radha had decided she wouldn't be happy until the whole world took holidays in Oman, and until then she would blame him for caring about her and not 'them'. He wanted to ask her whom she had helped, whose life she had made a difference to, how many students she had sat with while they cried about missing their parents or lack of money or their inability to understand first-year calculus. How many? Yep. The Indian contribution to mathematics. Zero. Om. *Nada*, Radha.

Chandra wrote in his notebook:

You've done nothing to help others. And you've contributed nothing to society except antipathy and rage. You're a professional complainer who still benefits from the economy you claim to want nothing to do with and so frankly, dear Radha, go to hell

Chandra looked up, hoping to see whales blowing froth in front of him, but instead it was still the same old sea with its giant know-it-all grin. He tried to recall what he had said to Pam but the only word that came to mind now was 'ungrateful', which she was, and 'Indian', which she was too.

164

He decided to read his paragraph aloud. When he reached the final three words he whispered them into the breeze, just to see how it felt. To his surprise, it felt good, so good that he set down his pen and pad, took a deep breath, stared into the sea, and yelled, 'Go to hell, Radha, you spoiled little brat. I wish you'd never been born!'

He looked over his shoulder. There was nobody there. He looked over his other shoulder, towards the yurt. Elke was sitting on the steps, watching him. He wondered if his words had carried. Probably. But she of all people would not care.

8

In the old days, Radha used to be the only one he would soften for, the only one who could drag him away from his desk. In Chicago he would take her for what he called 'road trips', which in reality were ten-minute drives around the block until she fell asleep. After they moved to Cambridge, when she was six or seven, she would come into his study and gaze up at him with her enormous eyes and say, 'Road trip, Daddy?' and on a good day he would put down his pencil and say, 'Why not?' and off they would go, on longer jaunts around the East Anglian countryside, Radha talking incessantly from the back seat.

A couple of years later, he decided to tell her the facts of life:

'The West has twenty per cent of the world's population,' he said, 'but consumes *eighty* per cent of the world's resources.'

He doubted his words had much effect until, a full three weeks later, he was standing outside her bedroom door while she was playing with two friends who had come for a sleepover.

'Do you know,' he heard her saying, 'America eats eighty per cent of the world's food, and has only twenty per cent of the world's people?'

Close enough, he thought.

Radha had always taken after Chandra. She was the most adventurous of his children, the most rebellious. Even at sixteen when she cut her hair into sharp, upstanding tufts and wore a dog collar around her neck, he still felt he understood her. By the time she turned eighteen, however, she began to spend less time with him. Everyone assured him this was normal. She was getting ready for university, for life; she would come back when she was ready.

The problem was that Radha didn't go directly to university. Shortly after receiving her acceptance from SOAS she announced her intention to go to India by herself for the summer. Chandra had put up a token resistance, but he was actually quite excited by the idea. He had regularly criticised his children for being too Western; Sunny for his refusal to eat anything even moderately spicy, Radha for mispronouncing her own surname, Jasmine for her inability to lisp even a sentence in any of the four Indian languages Chandra spoke fluently. It was not their fault, but there was a nationalist in him who refused to pipe down, unable to get over his guilt at having joined the great transatlantic brain drain in the first place. He wished they could have visited India more often as a family, but it wouldn't have been fair to Jean, or to any of the children whose friends went on holidays to Europe or Hawaii.

'I just don't think you're getting it, Charles,' said Jean. 'She's not an Indian girl searching for her roots. She's a Western girl looking for action, which means drugs. They've been doing it since the sixties.'

Chandra listened, but he wasn't so sure. To

him, Radha did have an Indian side. It was there in the way she dispensed with social niceties in favour of verbal tactility, as if she did not see the boundaries between herself and others. It was there in her physicality too, how she would massage his forehead without having to be asked, the way she related to children via touch instead of that stilted British baby talk. The truth was that he couldn't wait to see how the experience changed his daughter. Yes, he decided, Radha *should* go to India. It was a cultural, even moral, imperative.

Radha left with a list of his friends and relatives in various parts of the country, from Trivandrum to Darjeeling, photocopied from his old address book. She would travel alone for six weeks and in August she would meet Chandra in Delhi where he had a conference. He would show her his old haunts. Actually, he'd worked so hard at Delhi School of Economics that he hadn't really had any, but he'd make something up. Maybe she would have discovered haunts of her own by then. Maybe she would be speaking Hindi, would finally understand where her father was coming from, would throw her arms around him and say, 'Okay, Daddy, I get it now,' to which he would ruffle her hair and they'd jump into an air-conditioned Ambassador and head off for Agra or Jaipur while he explained why a human capital-intensive export promotion strategy was the only possible way forward within the context of a globalised economy.

And all of this might have happened had it not been for Prakash.

Professor Chandra and his brother had never been close. Prakash was five years older, serious, bookish and moody. He had left for university when Chandra was twelve and the two had seen little of each other since. By the time Chandra was in his thirties, however, it became clear that Prakash resented him, which, to Chandra, made no sense: Prakash had never wanted to leave India, or to stay in academia; he had quit his PhD in his third year to pursue full-time political activism and then, after a brief jail term during the Emergency, writing.

Prakash's first book was published a year after Chandra's own *Why the Third World Matters* and with a not dissimilar title: *No Bronze Medal for Third World*. But it did poorly, gained no international distribution, suffered low sales in India and, unlike Chandra's book which earned a thick sheaf of both scathing and glowing reviews, was simply ignored by most reviewers, or else dismissed as 'standard Marxist fare'.

Both had written several books since, but Prakash had never gained the renown Chandra did. He had a following among young people who liked his uncompromising attitude, his bare-knuckled debating style, but among his peers he was viewed as a colourful yet unhinged character whose chief occupation was the hoisting of his own flag in the name of the poor and downtrodden, a reputation only exacerbated when it came to the attention of his fellow party members that he had earned quite substantial sums of money consulting for the World Bank in the nineties (a gig he had never thanked

Chandra for securing).

Prakash had never visited America or England: 'I have no interest in capitalist countries,' he always said, but Chandra suspected he was afraid of being found lacking, unable to cope with the codes of another culture, that his anti-colonial ire would be revealed as a colossal inferiority complex proving that he wasn't at war with the West at all — but with himself.

It was impossible for Chandra to visit his brother without an argument ensuing, usually within the first ten minutes. No utterance was innocent. To request a cup of tea was to invite a debate on Monsanto and 'big sugar'; to talk about the weather was to risk a diatribe on the hypocrisy of the Kyoto Protocol. And staying silent was not an option either: Prakash would view this as an invitation to explain why Chandra's world view was symptomatic of advanced colonial brainwashing and would proceed to rectify this with several hours of merciless fraternal re-education.

After Chandra's parents died, Prakash became his closest relative, but their 'bickering' as Jean termed it (a choice of words Chandra found unfair) made all visits painful, drawn-out affairs. Mohini, Prakash's wife (a doctor who, in truth, was the sole breadwinner) made it easier, but she tended to say very little during his visits, would just watch with an expression more pitying than disapproving. On this occasion, Chandra hoped that Radha's presence would bring out a more human side in Prakash, who had never had children. With Radha around he might let his

170

hair down (what little he had left of it), eat ice cream, tell jokes, visit the zoo.

★ ★ ★

Radha had been in Delhi for three weeks by the time Chandra arrived. He was supposed to get there in the afternoon but his flight was delayed and it was after midnight when he reached Saket.

Prakash answered the door, clad in the eveningwear of the politically immature: khadi khurta, ill-fitting jeans, a glass of rum pani in his hand. He had grown a full beard, which was new (the last time Chandra saw him — eighteen months ago — he'd been sporting a Stalinesque moustache), but he was still skinny as a teenager; Prakash never put on weight, even though he ate and drank recklessly, a side-effect, perhaps, of perpetual outrage.

'I brought you some whisky,' said Chandra.

'Good,' said Prakash, his way of saying thank you.

'Where's Mohini?'

'In bed. She needs to be up early.' Prakash clapped Chandra on the shoulder. 'Come on, your daughter's in here.'

Radha was sitting on the sofa dressed exactly like Prakash. She too had a glass of rum pani in her hand and, arrestingly, a cigarette. Her eyes remained focused on the book in her lap even as Chandra stood in front of her, staring. But the moment she looked up, he knew.

The girl he used to chauffeur around

171

Chicago's suburbs, the one who later wore dog collars and listened to punk rock music, the only one he could talk to about economics or his colleagues or even, on occasion, his wife, had gone. There was a look in those big chestnut-coloured eyes that was all too familiar to him, that seething sense of superiority, as if her mind were perpetually absorbed with matters beyond his puny comprehension. Yes, Radha hadn't become a drug addict, and nor had she discovered her roots. She had become a Marxist. No, worse. She had become a Prakash-ist.

The arguing began in earnest the following evening, when Chandra returned from his seminar. Mohini was home and he was glad to see her, helping her in the kitchen while she cooked dinner for everyone despite having just completed a twelve-hour shift. They were both complaining of exhaustion while they carried the food into the living room, and this was how it began.

'This is bourgeois exhaustion,' said Prakash. 'There are workers who've been sitting in front of machines since yesterday without toilet breaks.'

'Bourgeois or not,' said Mohini. 'I'm tired.'

Professor Chandra smiled, an expression of sympathy from the only other person in the house who actually worked.

'Even communists get tired,' said Chandra.

'That depends on your definition of communism,' said Prakash, tearing his roti in half.

Chandra knew he shouldn't rise to the bait, but he also knew his brother was about to tell him that workers in socialist states never felt tired (Prakash had made far more outrageous claims in the past).

'So let's go to a factory in North Korea,' said Chandra. 'Let's see.'

'Why is it always North Korea?' said Radha. 'Why should North Korea always be the cardboard villain in the room?'

'Not card,' said Prakash. 'Straw.'

'Exactly,' said Radha. 'The strawman.'

'Yes,' said Chandra, closing his eyes with the air of a man diagnosed with a disease too polysyllabic to remember. 'I have drawn the short strawman.'

As the evening progressed the arguing continued, which was normal when Prakash and Chandra were together, only now he was up against Prakash 1.0 and Prakash 2.0, a laboratory-created clone who bore a horrifying resemblance to Professor Chandra's daughter.

'It simply isn't true that colonialism is 'over',' she was saying, that Prakash-ist smirk never leaving her lips. 'That's nonsense. The WTO is nothing but primitive accumulation under the guise of — ' she made the dreaded air quotes — ' 'free trade'.'

'It's more complex than that,' said Chandra.

'Free trade benefits the most powerful economy,' continued Radha, 'which means — ' she lifted her fingers once more — ' 'the West'.'

'We Marxists know better,' said Prakash, and put his arm around Radha who nodded with grotesque gravity while Mohini spooned ice cream into Chandra's bowl.

'Prakash,' said Chandra, 'what have you been filling her head with?'

Prakash clapped his hands. 'We've only been talking! She's a very bright girl.'

'*She* can think for herself, Dad,' said Radha while Prakash nodded.

Chandra looked at Mohini. 'What do you think?'

'I think we need more ice cream,' said Mohini, which was her way of telling him to give up. He had lost. He had lost everything.

★ ★ ★

It was only when Radha returned to England that the true extent of her Kafkaesque metamorphosis became apparent. Chandra tried to look on the bright side. Dinner times were livelier affairs now, full of debate and repartee, their duels enhanced by the fact of their occupying near opposite ends of the spectrum. But it was not long before he realised that there was a far graver problem at hand. Prakash had taught Radha more than Marxism. He had taught her how to hate.

'Imperialist' . . . 'the West' . . . 'bourgeois' . . . 'capitalist' . . . these words would fly from her lips like tiny little swastikas, her knuckles turning white, her jaw clenched, her eyes hard as Siberian pickaxes as she sentenced most of the world to the gulag for their crimes against ideology. Any counter-argument was met with contempt, the automatic response of the recent convert. 'Trickle down! It's trickling *up*, for

God's sake!' or, 'Do you think the workers are so stupid they can't manage their own factories?' or, 'Have you talked to any peasants about that?'

Prakash seemed to have convinced Radha that her father was not only her enemy, but also the enemy of all that was good and true in the world, of babies dying of malnutrition, of the blacks in South Africa, of the children incinerated at Hiroshima, of decent, humble, self-sacrificing leftists everywhere who simply wanted to right the wrongs that men like he and Pinochet had caused in their infinite malevolence.

Jean didn't help with comments like 'God, you're so brain-washed, Radha,' or Sunny, who simply waved fifty-pound notes in her face. It was Sunny who gave her the nickname Radical Rad, late in his year of triumph in which he'd proved his net salary exceeded that of his father.

'So you're a proletarian, are you, Rad?' he asked once.

'No, knob-head,' said Radha, which was how she usually addressed her brother in those days (that or 'prick-face'). 'Middle-class intellectuals who've become aware of the nature of the system become automatically conjoined with the revolutionary proletariat.'

'So why don't you conjoin yourself with a two-up two-down, outside-toilet council house?' said Sunny. 'Or I could find you a lovely little spot in the Bronx? You could live over a crack den and get a face tattoo. It's all the rage with New York proles.'

'Because, dick-for-brains, I'm not fighting to lower my own circumstances but to raise

175

everyone else's. How would living in a crack house benefit anyone?'

'All Sunny's trying to say — ' began Chandra, but with both of them in full flow he rarely finished a sentence.

'I didn't ask to be born into a bourgeois family. That's out of my control. But now that I have seen the correct — '

'I have been to the promised *laaand*,' said Sunny. 'I have seen the light on the mountaintop and someday *aaall* my people will be free.'

Radha had her hands raised in front of her now, palms outward like a bear in attack mode.

'Well, what would you know about it, you selfish, money-grabbing fuck-wit? Anyone can make money, Sunny. Any jerk-off can play the system. It takes *brains* to understand it.'

'Yes, it does,' said Chandra from his armchair, a stupidly self-satisfied statement that, fortunately, went over his daughter's head.

'So you understand the stock market, do you, Radha?' said Sunny. 'Or gold or crude oil or options or insurance?'

'Or unemployment or inflation or the money supply,' said Chandra, knowing it was wrong of him to take his son's side.

'I don't want to understand it,' said Radha. 'I want to — '

And then she stopped, as if only just realising her father was in the room. When she spoke her voice was much deeper, as if she were in the process of transmuting, a Marxist lycanthrope under a full moon.

'So basically, Dad, if you don't have a PhD in

176

theoretical economics then you shouldn't be able to vote, or have an opinion, or have children? Is that it?'

'What I am saying,' said Chandra in his softest bear-whispering voice, 'is that it's hard to understand the economy without knowing much economics.'

'And I don't know much economics?'

Sunny coughed the word 'understatement'.

'I think you're doing very well, Radha,' he said. 'You are learning; you are passionate. It's good. But you still have things to learn. That's all.'

'Like . . . what?'

'Like a few more facts,' said Chandra.

'Oh . . . facts?'

'It's something that comes with experience.'

'Is . . . it . . . now?' said Radha. 'The older one gets, the more one becomes . . . like . . . you.'

It was always this way. Radha's fights with Sunny were mere sideshows, deflections from the true source of all evil: Professor P. R. Chandrasekhar, Clifford H. Doyle Professor Emeritus of Economics who, until then, had believed his daughter was proud of his accomplishments.

He was relieved when she left for university, confident SOAS would straighten her out, that a good education would guide her towards a more thoughtful position so that in later years they'd be able to laugh together at her 'Prakash phase'. But he had forgotten that nothing is more dangerous to a fanatic than a little knowledge . . . except for a *lot* of knowledge. And over the following years, this was what Radha acquired.

After she graduated from SOAS their relations seemed to be improving. She visited India once more but was disillusioned with Prakash on her return, talking about 'petty tyrants' and 'authoritarian patriarchs'. But the politics continued, especially after she moved into a tumbledown wreck of a house in Hackney with six other lost souls who did minimum-wage work in the day and harassed the better off at night.

But all this was during the heyday of neoliberalism when the opposition consisted of mostly middle-class contrarian ingrates who could still make money if they chose to (and usually did) entirely because of the efforts of people like Professor Chandra. Economists and policy-makers were respected technicians back then, the ones who made things work, the ones without whom the system would fall apart. Yes, it wasn't perfect — they all knew this — but no amount of rage or egg-throwing would change that.

And then came the crash.

Nowadays every economist and their dog claimed to have seen it coming, but this was not the way Chandra remembered it. Part of his problem was that he had never considered finance a legitimate discipline, so it wasn't until 2008 that he even knew what a Credit Default Swap was. Unfortunately, the ones who *did* know were in the pay of banks or foreign treasuries, a practice Chandra considered vulgar, though it was only recently that he'd learned what these people were paid, untenured lecturers earning six figures for single papers.

In 2009 Chandra began to consult for the British Treasury Department in the manner of a concerned citizen volunteering for military service. Millions had lost their homes in the US, and ten million factory workers in China had been made redundant. Chandra could only speculate on what lay in store for India, and for this, as always, he blamed himself, a thought he did not share with Jean, who would have called him an egomaniac.

One Sunday, after Hank Paulson's bailout act, Radha came for lunch. She, Chandra, Jean and the ten-year-old Jasmine sat around the kitchen table eating shepherd's pie.

'I hope you're being careful, Rad,' Jean was saying. 'Everyone I know in Hackney has been mugged at least once.'

'Hackney's not what it used to be, Mum,' said Radha. 'Anyway, mugging isn't the worst thing that could happen.'

'Oh?'

'They just snatch your bag and run. And I don't keep much in my bag.'

'Or they stab you and run,' said Jean.

Jasmine looked frightened. Chandra wanted to change the subject but couldn't think of a safe area.

'Have you ever been mugged, Dad?' said Radha.

'Not yet,' said Chandra. 'Touch wood.'

'Yes, you have, We were all mugged. A bunch of bankers in shiny suits pulled a knife on us and took a trillion dollars from our back pockets.'

'Oh, God,' said Jean, while Jasmine squeezed a glob of ketchup onto her plate. 'No, they didn't, Radha.'

'Yes, they did.'

'What else could they do?' said Chandra. 'Let the banks go under? There'd have been anarchy.'

'So let there be anarchy,' said Radha. 'Enough is enough.'

'Grow up, Radha,' said Chandra. 'Just grow up.'

'Meaning what, exactly?'

'Meaning,' said Chandra, 'that without capital injection we'd have a global run on the banks which means key industries would fail, which would mean no food, nationwide blackouts, rioting in the streets, homelessness, suicide and starvation. I think the bailout is an acceptable price to pay.'

'Bullshit, Dad,' said Radha, dropping her fork onto her plate. 'Thieves are in control and they're royally fucking us over, and none of you care!'

'I will not have this language!' said Jean. 'This is unacceptable. Do you hear, Radha?'

'I don't care about the language,' said Chandra, throwing his napkin down. 'But I don't have time for this. Some of us don't have the luxury of railing at Daddy. Some of us are actually trying to fix the problem.'

'Yeah, you shaft people for a living, take every penny they've got, then ask them to pay your gambling debts. Problem fixed.'

'What the hell are you talking about?' said Chandra.

'You,' said Radha. 'You and your kind are perfectly happy to have a world run by blood-sucking bankers so long as they call you Professor and fly you first class and pay your big fat salary.'

Professor Chandra stood, lifted his plate above his head, and dropped it onto the floor, an absurdly theatrical gesture that resulted in Jasmine bursting into tears while Jean said, 'For Christ's sake, Charles,' and Radha smirked in triumph, the same smirk she had learned in Delhi.

Chandra went upstairs, locked the door, and did not come down until Radha had left. For weeks afterwards he refused to answer her calls, screening with his answering machine or, if she called the department, walking over to his secretary's office so that he could bellow, 'Tell her I'm not in!'

When he finally relented it was because he realised he missed their fights. None of his students dared speak to him the way she had, and debates with colleagues were never about anything other than departmental politics, which meant professional jealousy. It was good to talk to someone who spoke their mind, someone who actually cared about something.

★   ★   ★

In 2010 Radha got her first real job as a campaigner for a group called Domestic which provided safe spaces for women and children at risk from abuse. Radha's role was to petition the

181

government to bring about policy changes.

'Splendid!' said Chandra, when she told him the news. 'That all sounds very laudable.'

He knew this was patronising, but he was genuinely pleased. This was real work in the real world.

But instead of becoming sensible and practical, Radha discovered a new form of political idiocy, one far more pernicious than Third World Marxism. It was called 'identity politics', and it defied all rational explanation.

Under the auspices of identity politics, all statements were narcissistically transformed from 'I am against' to 'I am'. Radha's rants became prefaced with, '*Speaking as a Woman* . . . I find that completely offensive,' or, '*As a Person of Colour* . . . I can assure you that isn't true.'

Whereas previously she had been possessed of a righteous wrath, she now was in possession of a *self*-righteous wrath, a neat shuffle forward from Old Testament to New, from rabble-rouser to firing squad that exterminated even the possibility of debate in favour of the supremacy of 'being'.

He had preferred it by far when his daughter had merely been a leftist — their problems, after all, were largely emotional. They were angry and wanted to stay angry, and refused to compromise even when it was in their interests, which was something Chandra even admired on occasion. A few years ago at a GATT summit one of them had thrown a cream pie in his face and, while he licked his lips, had bared her teeth in a gesture of simultaneous hate and respect, a muscular leopard snarling at a great elephant. The two had remained like that, locked in queasy equilibrium, for several seconds before the police arrived to whom Chandra reported, with a wink, that his assailant had already fled.

This was how he had viewed his sparring matches with Radha until now. They merely had different opinions. He could even accept her need to take out her anger on him, but what he could not bear was this anti-intellectualism, this insistence on dismissing his point of view not only as wrong but as irrelevant. He tried to tell her that his goal had always been the same as those leftists who so despised him: to alleviate poverty, to put food in the mouths of those who had none, even to reduce the gap between the haves and have-nots. But Radha didn't seem to care about goals any more. All she cared about was blame. There were the guilty, and there were the victims, and his daughter, it seemed, was judge, jury and, if she had her way, executioner. It hardly needed to be said into which camp he belonged.

Unlike when they used to fight about economic policy (or 'capitalism' as Radha reductively called it), Chandra was out of his depth in these new debates. More often than not Radha would rage about films or books Chandra had never heard of, but would defend anyway. The breaking point, however, was an incident that he would always refer to afterwards as 'Poohgate'.

Radha was visiting and had come to his rooms to use his printer. She was sitting on the sofa sorting some flyers (for a demonstration; he didn't ask for details) into piles, when her gaze fell on the small Winnie-the-Pooh that Chandra usually kept on his bookshelf. It had been hers as a child and she had loved it (which was why Chandra kept it), but now she glared into its black, beady eyes and declared, 'I hate *Winnie-the-Pooh*.'

'What?' said Chandra.

'Every character is male, Dad,' said Radha. 'Have you even noticed that? Except for Kanga who's defined exclusively by her motherhood.'

'Well, she happens to be a mother,' said Chandra.

'But why is she the only one who's a mother?'

'Because men can't be mothers!' said Chandra, hoping nobody could hear them.

'She does nothing else,' said Radha. 'Nothing! Just sits around and tells off the boys for being silly and reckless because boys will be boys and girls will be mothers, right, Dad?'

Chandra hated it when she said, 'Right, Dad?' He had a tendency to nod without even realising he was nodding which, to Radha, was the equivalent of severing a finger in a seventeenth-century duel.

'But she is one,' said Chandra. 'What do you want her to do? Be a father?'

'So why isn't Owl a woman?' said Radha. 'Or Rabbit?'

'Because he's *not*!' said Chandra, his voice turning hoarse as their conversation crashed through the boundaries of sanity. 'And in any case, he's a rabbit! And not even a *real* rabbit!'

184

'Text is real in effect,' said Radha, unfurling one of those statements that so baffled Chandra. 'Little girls read *Winnie-the-Pooh* and grow up believing that all they're good for is making babies. It's called gender annihilation.'

'No,' said Chandra. 'Little girls read about talking animals and they have a good time and then, *hopefully*, they grow up!'

He looked at the red-jerseyed, yellow-faced figure on his sofa which looked back at him mournfully.

'What makes you so sure, Dad?' said Radha.

'Because Winnie-the-Pooh isn't important!' said Chandra. 'For God's sake, there are people starving in the world, and you're talking about stuffed toys!'

'It isn't important to you,' said Radha, 'as a cisgendered, heterosexual, middle-class male.'

'Fine,' said Chandra. 'I am a male-gendered cissy. And what about you? You're a bloody Eeyore!'

'Eeyore was male!' said Radha.

'You're crazy!' said Chandra.

But Radha was already on her way out, slamming the door after delivering her customary death blow:

'That's what men have been saying about women since they burned them at the stake!'

⋆ ⋆ ⋆

In 2014 Radha quit her job to go travelling around Europe with three friends. When Chandra asked why she felt the need to do this, she

185

told him she was 'burned out' and needed time to 'reassess'. He wanted to put a few hundred pounds in her account, but knew she would yell at him if he did, so he took her to dinner at a new Indian restaurant in Mayfair instead.

They spent much of the meal in silence, so aware were they that nearly any topic of conversation would end up in mutually assured destruction. He wished they could talk about sports but, like Sunny, Radha had no interest. This only left health and the weather, which could lead, respectively, to the privatisation of the NHS and the inevitability of global warming under the free market. At last, unable to hold his tongue any longer, Professor Chandra asked her:

'So, are you seeing anybody these days?'

Radha, who had ordered a slab of paneer with nothing on it for her main course, stared up at him, her paneer untouched.

'Why?' she said. 'Are you?'

He shook his head. 'No. I am not.'

'So your question,' said Radha, 'is am I *seeing* anyone?'

'I mean,' said Chandra, sipping at his Merlot as casually as he could, 'do you have a boyfriend?'

'Why should it be a boyfriend?'

'What?'

'Why do you assume it's . . . a . . . boy?'

'Oh, God,' said Chandra, putting his head in his hands.

'So the thought that I could be with a woman is so unbearable to you, is it, Dad?'

'No,' said Chandra, straightening his back and

186

rearranging his blazer. 'No, the fact that you have to do this to me is. All I am trying to do is have a civilised dinner with my daughter and you have to make it so . . . horrible.'

'Horrible?'

'It never stops!' said Chandra. 'All the time, Radha, with this nonsense.'

'So my life is nonsense, is it?'

'Yes,' he said, slamming his fist against his thigh. 'All this obsession with he, she, P.O.C. There are serious problems in the world. You've had a good education, a good upbringing, and all you do is complain.'

'What's nonsense,' said Radha, 'is your refusal to even contemplate that I may have ideas and principles of my own. Have you ever considered that, Dad?'

'Why do you hate me so much?' he said, putting his glass down. 'What did I do to you?'

Radha fixed him with her eye. She had started to wear a lot of eye make-up again, as she had in her teens. Her eyeliner extended outwards into her face; a 'cat's eye', he believed it was called.

'Can you see me, Dad?'

'Yes,' he said, angrier than it was safe to be in public.

'When did you ever see me, Dad? When did you ever see any of us?'

'Nonsense,' he said. 'This is nonsense.'

'When did you ever see Mum?'

'What?'

'Why do you think she left you, Dad?'

'How dare you!'

'Right. You never even thought it could have

anything to do with you, did you?'

'What do you think you are?' said Chandra. 'You little hussy!'

'Yeah, that's all you've got. Cheap slut-shaming slurs. And then you'll take out your credit card and slam your blood money down and everything's taken care of. Man make bill. That's all you need to do, right, Dad? God forbid you actually notice anyone else's existence, or listen to anyone, or give a shit about anyone except yourself and your oh-so-important career. Go on, Dad, do your thing. Pay the bill.'

'You pay it,' he said and threw his napkin in her direction before walking out of the restaurant.

He had no idea whether Radha paid the bill or not. It must have come to well over a hundred pounds (he had ordered a very good bottle of wine). He always wished he had looked back. No, he wished he had *gone* back, paid the bill, said goodbye. But he didn't. He went home to Cambridge and when Radha left for Europe *she* did not say goodbye. He assumed that when she returned they would make up in their usual way, pretending neither could remember having argued, starting again from square one (even though square one had long since been torn up from its foundations).

But Radha did not return, nor did she email, and eventually Jean told him that his daughter did not want him to know where she was.

'This is absurd,' he said.

'She made me promise, Charles.'

'She can't do that.'

'She said you'd say that.'

'What?'

'She said you'd say she belonged to you and I guess this is her way of proving she doesn't.'

'So what the hell am I supposed to do?'

'Let her prove it. It's the only thing you can do, Charles. Wait it out.'

'Tell me where she is, Jean. I won't contact her. Just tell me where she is.'

'I'm sorry, Charles. I can't. I promised.'

In a fury he called Sunny who told him the same thing, and from that moment on Chandra refused to believe a word that any of them said. He also refused to believe that Jasmine could be in on the conspiracy, so he never asked her, though he was dimly aware that he was almost certainly deluding himself on this front. He gave himself to frenetic Google searches for 'Radha Chandrasekhar' instead, but came up only with information prior to her disappearance, as if she had paid the NSA to erase all trace of her. It was impossible to find any information on Facebook either. She didn't even have a proper photograph, only a quote by Audre Lorde: *There is no such thing as a single-issue struggle, because we do not live single-issue lives.* He couldn't see her page or her friends, only the words, From *North Pole, Alaska.*

He emailed every other day, and then every day, sending increasingly desperate messages consisting of statements like:

Where are you? Worried. Please write.
Love, Dad

No word for seven months. What is this? Not
good.
Dad

And:

Reply!
Best, Chandra

When a year had elapsed, he began writing
bundles of three or four messages at a time. He
told her how sorry he was, how he loved her and
couldn't they just talk about it and maybe he was
wrong and Marxism was correct and he was just
a silly old fool with too much pride and if she
would only reply with one line telling him she
was all right he would finally be able to sleep at
night because the only thing that mattered to
him was her health and happiness.

Except he didn't send these messages, not one
of them. They just lay there in his drafts folder
like withered pieces of his heart while Radha
remained in Europe, or was it India now?

In his darkest moments, he remembered all
those vicious words in the restaurant, his
daughter staring at him with those Anubis-like
eyes, sleek and lean with hatred. Somewhere,
along the way, he had done something terribly
wrong; this was the only conclusion he could
come to. He just wished he had a way of
knowing what it was.

9

Putting his notebook in his pocket, Professor Chandra marched away past the vegetable gardens and the lodge and onto the ramp that led to the hot tubs. At the entrance he grabbed a towel, stripped off his clothes, and walked into the sunlight, trying to fight away a vision of everyone else dressed in cocktail attire turning towards him like Marie Antoinette and her chambermaids, parasols pointed at his append-age before ordering its precipitate removal.

In reality, there were two overweight white men and an older, darker-skinned woman who was looking at the sea while Chandra eased his body over the edge of the tub. The men were talking finance, using language Chandra under-stood and did not want to be reminded of, although, short of sticking his fingers in his ears, it was impossible not to hear them. They kept saying that Obama was 'racking up the national deficit', which irritated Chandra no end. He tried to hypnotise himself by staring at the sea as the woman was doing, but eventually he couldn't help turning around and saying:

'Deficit is when the government spends more than it receives in revenue. National debt is how much the government owes. You can't confuse the two.'

The younger of the men smiled before turning away so that Chandra could see the tattoo on his back — a depiction of *The Last Supper*, in its entirety — before returning to his conversation.

'You sound kinda British, honey,' said the woman, who was about his age with frizzy white hair and freckled, near cylindrical breasts that rose from the water as she spoke.

'I usually live in England,' he said, averting his eyes.

'But you're from South India originally?'

'Yes,' said Chandra. 'How did you know?'

'My husband and I travelled. We spent years travelling. Gives you an eye for that kind of thing.'

'So you went to India?'

'Oh, we went everywhere.' She splashed water over her face and hair, looking out towards the frothing sea. 'Started out in Iran, and just drifted.'

Professor Chandra thought of Steve — 'I'm a fucking stereotype' — but shook his head: he didn't want Steve in there now.

'I've never done that,' he said. 'I've never not known where I was going.'

'It's fun,' said the woman. 'But you've got to feel free to be free, you know. And if you feel free, you can be anywhere.'

'I'm Chandra,' said Chandra, realising this sort of talk no longer alarmed him.

'Dolores,' said the woman, holding out her hand. 'Dolores Blum.'

He accepted her dripping hand.

'So what are you studying here, Dolores?'

'Plain old yoga. Good old yoga, I should say. How about you?'

' "Being Yourself in the Summer Solstice".'

192

'Oh, that sounds beautiful. *Being Yourself in the Summer Solstice.*'

He could see her stretching out the words in her mind, as if admiring the sheen on a strip of satin. 'It's something I struggle with,' she said, 'being myself.'

'Really?'

'I guess we all do. It must be so nice to be yourself, I mean really be yourself.' She stretched out her legs, brushing his thigh with her toe. 'It must be like floating.'

The men who knew nothing about economics left, easing out of the water like hippos from a mud-hole. Chandra tried to relax, leaning back his head, running his hands through his hair. Relaxing wasn't something he was good at, not without a novel or a glass of cognac in his hand. There were massage tables on the deck above them, but Chandra disliked massage. It always left him in pain and more stressed out than before.

'So what was it you were telling those bros?' said Dolores. 'Something about finance?'

'Oh, it was nothing,' said Chandra. 'I'm an economist, that's all.'

'There's a certain type of person that doesn't like being corrected,' she said, eyes twinkling.

'I know,' said Chandra. 'I'm one of them.'

'Course you are, honey. It's called being a man.'

Chandra pursed his lips. This was the sort of thing Radha would have said.

'Hey,' said Dolores, reaching out her hand. 'I didn't mean to upset you.'

'No, no, no,' said Chandra, blinking hard. 'It's all right. It's perfectly true, that's all.'

'Well, hey, it's true of me too. Anyway, I can't stand all this bullshit about being beyond opinions. *There's a garden beyond right and wrong* . . . Sure there is, but I've never seen it.'

'I suppose I should learn when to keep quiet,' said Chandra.

'You know who's the most opinionated person I know?' said Dolores. 'My husband.'

'Oh?'

'And he's a monk.'

'Can one be a monk and a husband?'

'If you're a Zen monk,' said Dolores. 'Sure.'

'So you live in . . . a monastery?'

'Of course!' said Dolores. 'What did you think? Don't these look like the breasts of a nun?'

Professor Chandra tried desperately to think of a response, something like 'They certainly don't,' or 'My thoughts exactly,' but this would sound either sleazy or plain ridiculous from his lips, so he reverted to habit and shifted uncomfortably.

'Actually, I'm not a nun at all. I'm a monk's wife, which isn't the same thing. But you should come visit us,' said Dolores. 'Our place is ten thousand feet high in the mountains. Colorado's best-kept secret. You can just lose yourself up there, forget the rest of the world exists. Not bad for a girl from Honduras.'

'We're doing meditation here,' said Chandra. 'But I don't think it's my kind of thing.'

'We do the simple kind. You just sit. It's good

194

for a lot of things. We had a young man the court ordered into rehab, but they let him come to us instead. Was with us two years and never used again. Ended up going to college. He's a programmer now.'

The mention of college reminded him that his afternoon session was probably starting. He hadn't even thought about his critical voices yet.

'I'm sorry,' said Chandra, 'I think it's time for me to go.'

'Sure, honey,' said Dolores. 'You got duties.'

'Don't you?' he said. 'I mean, won't your yoga be starting?'

'Of course. But who goes to all their sessions?'

'Exactly,' said Chandra, who had attended every scheduled lecture and seminar from the onset of his BA to the end of his PhD. 'Who does that?'

The two sat together for another hour, talking and looking at the seabirds and the waves. Dolores showed him how to count his breaths, how to observe the beads of sensation flowing across his skin. He told her about India and China, about the difference between Tiger and Cub economies. He told her about Jasmine too, though not Radha.

They left the hot tubs when it was time for dinner, and it was only as they crossed the deck that Chandra realised he and Dolores were naked, yet talking away like old friends. They even dressed in front of one another, Dolores slipping into a king-sized bra while he brushed his hair with his hands and put on his blazer. When they were clothed and he could look at her once more, he concluded that Dolores was a handsome woman. No, a *beautiful* woman, soft but strong, wise but wilful, just irritating enough to keep him on his toes. He liked the two tiny moles on her neck, the roundness of her ears (it was rare to have round ears, wasn't it?), the smoothness of her elbows.

As they walked back to the dining hall, Dolores told him she meditated for two hours a day, sometimes more.

Chandra whistled.

'Oh, that's nothing,' she said. 'My husband does a minimum of four.'

'Four hours!' said Chandra.

'And he's still not easy!' said Dolores. 'Who would he be if he didn't meditate? An axe murderer, probably.'

Chandra wanted to say, 'He's a lucky man,' but faltered at the last instant, changing it to, 'I'm sure he's a good man.'

'Well, that's what meditation teaches you. There are no good men or bad men. We're all kind of the same.'

'We are?'

'I think so.'

They reached the dining hall. Dolores stopped and looked towards the river.

'I'm going to pass on dinner,' she said, and patted her stomach. 'Better take care of the mind instead.'

'Oh,' said Chandra. 'Oh, I see.'

'But it was delightful meeting you, honey. And you've got to come to our place. You've just got to. You'll love it.'

Dolores took a pen from her handbag and wrote her number on an old bus ticket. Chandra folded it and put it in his wallet before writing his own number on a business card. They stood looking at each other for a few seconds before hugging. Chandra held on to her a little longer and a little tighter than he had expected to, and when he let go there was a lump in his throat.

'Oh, honey,' said Dolores who, for a moment, looked as sad as he felt. 'That's just the way it is.'

Professor Chandra knew exactly what this meant. She was married and he was lonely, and had they met at another time . . . but this was true of about a thousand other things. There were so many paths his life could have taken. It wasn't worth thinking about.

'Goodbye, Dolores,' he said, surprising himself by executing a neat European demi-bow.

'Goodbye, Chandra,' said Dolores, and puckered up her lips before walking away.

Chandra ate by himself, even though he could see the rest of his group in the dining hall, chatting animatedly. When he finished he returned to his room and lay on his bed, counting his breaths and observing his critical voices.

His father. That was the first. Then his mother, though in a different way (more tears and more guilt). At least four uncles, his grandmother, all his schoolteachers including the dreaded Professor Joseph at Hyderabad who would call him 'duffer' and twist his ear even when he gave the *right* answer and shout, 'Office clerk!' at anyone he deemed stupid enough never to rise above said station.

After school, it was pure carnage. His wife, obviously, and his colleagues, scores of reviewers he had never met, several secretaries, especially Daphne with the permanent cold and transparent nostrils who pronounced his name 'Candour' and hadn't once made eye contact in seven years; then the anti-capitalists and the liberals who'd never read a word he'd written but disagreed with all of it anyway; and finally, his children . . . the most unforgiving critics of all.

He understood it now, that he had internalised those voices, that he was his own worst critic, but there was something Rudi Katz had missed. As Chandra had explained to the group, he was a highly successful man, at the top of his profession, but he had risen to these heights entirely through being hard on himself; those hours of caffeinated self-punishment in the library, digesting near unreadable books, writing until his hand literally bled. It was an ethic he had tried to instil in his children, the necessity of working twice as hard as their peers, but they did not understand. The world was a different place to them. They had gone to the finest schools he could find, and not the *Stalky* & Co. beat-the-lazy-out-of-you type either. It had all been about compassionate rearing and child-centred mollycoddling. And the result? Sunny had pursued success, yes, not out of necessity but due to a sociopathic drive Chandra had never understood. And as for the girls, they simply wanted out, had taken a sledgehammer, in different ways, to the walls of the home he had mortgaged his entire life to build.

But try telling that to Rudi Katz . . .

⋆ ⋆ ⋆

Professor Chandra returned to the yurt the following morning after breakfast. The chairs and cushions had been moved to the perimeter. There was a table near the door with a stack of thin pieces of cardboard on it, and two bowls, one filled with pens and the other with safety pins.

'Take one of each,' said Rudi, who was sitting on the floor near the door with his knees hunched to his chin.

Chandra did, and sat with his back to the wall, eyes closed, counting his breaths.

'Take your card and pen,' continued Katz, 'and write your name at the top. Then write down all the negative things that have been said about you in the past two days. If you can't remember, or you're one of the lucky few about whom no one had anything bad to say, then try to think of other hurtful criticisms you remember receiving in life. Keep it short and snappy. Note form. And when you're done, pin it to the front of your shirt, like this. Okay?'

Chandra could hear Pam's voice complaining, but then he heard the word 'Gucci' and laughter, so perhaps she was parodying herself. The atmosphere felt lighter than before.

He put his head down, trying to remember. The only person who had criticised him was

Pam, but he found it hard to recall anything specific. She had lost her temper, then stormed out of the room. He remembered she'd told him he was acting like her father. Was that right? Or that she *felt* he was like her father, which was a different thing. But in any case, he could hardly write 'Like Pam's father.'

What else? Had Daisy or Bryan said anything? Not Bryan. Daisy said she felt sidelined by his dialogue with Pam, but he couldn't write 'Sideliner'. Someone had told him he believed he was more important than the rest of them. Who was that?

SELF-IMPORTANT, he wrote, unable to remember.

SUPERIOR.

He recalled another now.

THINK EVERYTHING IS ABOUT ME.

It was a short list, would make him look as though he had a big ego if he left it at that. He needed more. The Texan guy to his left seemed to be writing a novel. Chandra thought about things Radha might say, or Jasmine.

POMPOUS.

DOESN'T LISTEN.

DOESN'T GET WOMEN (that was his own, but he was sure one of them would have said it).

THINKS HE KNOWS EVERYTHING.

THINKS HE'S RIGHT ALL THE TIME.

CONTEMPTUOUS.

ARROGANT.

Something from Sunny, perhaps.

WEAK.

Yes, that was what Sunny would say. Maybe

even 'Loser'. Should he write LOSER?

Chandra looked up. Elke, he saw, had already pinned her 'shame sheet', as he thought of it, to her blouse. She seemed to be enjoying it, sticking her flat guilty chest out, practically begging them to judge her. Chandra could not read her sheet from where he sat, but he guessed the word MURDERER was on there somewhere. Was that why she had come here, in search of execration? Or had she genuinely come to be healed?

'Right,' said Rudi, though the Texan was still scribbling. 'I think we're all done. Pin your lists to your chests — don't stab yourselves — and walk around the room in any direction. When you meet someone, stand in front of each other and decide who's going to go first. That person will read the other's list and tell them the *opposite* of what it says. You got that?

'Please understand that the purpose of this exercise isn't to lie or butter the other person up. The purpose is to learn who we truly are in our hearts when our critical voices aren't distorting our perceptions.'

Pam raised her hand.

'Do we have to mean it?'

'Yes,' said Rudi. 'Yes, you do. You can't force it, but I think you'll find it's not so hard after all. Try it. You might like it. Anyone else? Okay, good. Let's begin.'

Professor Chandra watched while the others converged on the centre of the room. How quickly these Californians moved, how eager they were to do as they were told, broadcasting their feelings without the slightest idea that in a totalitarian state mental privacy would be the first thing to be abolished. But he sounded like Radha now. No, he sounded like a cop-out, still standing by the wall. What was it Jean used to call men like that? Wallflowers. 'Stop being a wallflower, Charles,' she'd say.

He stepped forward. Already he could see a red-headed woman brushing away tears. A tall ruddy-faced man called Andy, one of the few who looked approximately Chandra's age, stepped towards him and took off his baseball cap.

'Hey,' said Andy.

'Hey,' said Chandra.

'You want to go first?'

Chandra stared at the cardboard tied to Andy's denim shirt. It read, WITHDRAWN. ALOOF. TALKS IN THIS ANNOYING WAY. KEEPS STARING. PEOPLE THINK HE'S JUDGING THEM ALL THE TIME. LOOKS LIKE HE HAS A GUN.

Andy looked up and shrugged.

'So what are you gonna do?' he said.

'Andy,' said Chandra, and realised he felt relaxed in this man's company. 'Andy, Andy, Andy.'

They were giggling now, the two of them, like schoolboys.

'Andy,' said Chandra. 'You're a great guy. You're friendly and warm. You've got a nice deep voice, a great accent too. I like the way you look at me. Very direct, not hiding anything. I think you're very accepting of people and very peaceful. I can't imagine you ever shooting anyone.'

Andy grinned.

'I think you've got to put things positively,' he said, 'The last part.'

'Oh,' said Chandra. 'Then you look like the sort of man who prefers knives to guns.'

They high-fived. Chandra couldn't remember the last time he'd high-fived anyone. Jasmine, probably, a decade ago.

'A peacemaker,' said Chandra. 'A diplomat. A good, gentle man. How's that?'

'Much better,' said Andy. 'And you, Chandra, am I saying that right? You, Chandra, are . . . wow, nice shirt. Let me say that first. Hey, this is a great way of looking at women's breasts.'

Chandra, who hated such jokes, chuckled in spite of himself.

'Seriously, you're a good man,' said Andy. 'I know that already. I like you.' Andy's clear blue eyes twinkled into his. 'You're easy-going, good-humoured, and humble. You care about people. You've got a good heart. You're a gentleman, kind and respectful to women, kind to darn near everyone, and you're a human being, strong sometimes, vulnerable sometimes, but magnificent, especially when you're at your most fragile. I mean, what could be more magnificent than that?'

Chandra nodded.

'Okay, friend?'

'Great. Thank you, Andy.'

'Thank you, Chandra.'

They shook hands and moved on. He was glad they hadn't hugged. It felt more genuine this way. Why should such a simple exchange of compliments be occasion for high drama?

Bryan was walking his way now, with his broad surfboard smile and a lime-green T-shirt.

'Chandra,' said Bryan.

'Hey,' said Chandra, an old hand at this now.

He looked at Bryan's sheet, which bore the words (in very small letters), SMUG. FAKE. PRETENDING HE'S GOT NO PROBLEMS.

'Bryan,' said Chandra, 'you're a warm, genuine guy whom I'm feeling very fond of. Really, it has been a pleasure to meet you and I know you're as human as the rest of us, even if you don't feel the need to wear your troubles on your sleeve. You're not concealing anything. You're just a big-hearted, generous man.'

'Oh, man,' said Bryan, slapping him on the arm. 'You got me.'

Chandra felt a rush of irritation, and realised why at once. Bryan *was* fake. This was nonsense.

'Chandra,' said Bryan, 'you're a good, humble . . . '

But Professor Chandra wasn't listening.

And now Bryan was hugging him, whispering more mellifluous homily, like a game-show host before he moved on to the next contestant.

And on it went. Some were better than others, but none engendered that early euphoria he had experienced with Andy. Most disappointing of all, people often used the same words to describe him. 'Humble' appeared regularly, and Professor Chandra knew he wasn't humble. He could be whimpering and pathetic, contrite and penitent, but not humble. If he'd been humble he would still be a research assistant at the LSE.

Even Elke, when the two met, said something platitudinous, and Chandra found himself disappointed that her card was free from the words MONSTER and BABY KILLER, containing only COLD, ALOOF, and SCARY: clichés and cop-outs, easy to repudiate.

Only Daisy said something interesting when she told him he was 'An old-fashioned man who believes that women are simply different to men and should be loved instead of understood. In many ways that's more realistic, and I find nothing weak about you at all. You are so strong for coming here and being so honest. The things you said moved me, and I'm not easily moved. Go in peace, Professor Chandra. Go with God.'

The end was a little much for him — and didn't it suggest he was in the last throes of life? — but he appreciated her sentiments. At least she had meant it. He tried to say something equivalent in response, but kept using the word 'warm' (as opposed to 'cold') and couldn't think of the opposite of 'racist', so he said, 'You appreciate lots of different cultures,' which caused her to look at him suspiciously.

But it was almost over now. Chandra could hear Rudi Katz praising everyone and felt relieved . . . until he saw Pam. But he'd known it all along. They'd been avoiding one another, shooting surreptitious hurt-filled glances. Andy was walking towards him, rubbing his hands together and saying, 'Well, that was kind of fun, wasn't it?' to which Chandra replied, 'Sorry, Andy. I think I forgot someone.'

'Sure,' said Andy. 'No problem.'

When Professor Chandra turned around, Pam was directly in front of him, her large brown eyes like the twin barrels of a mascara-lined gun.

'Hi, Pam,' he said.

'Hello.'

'I'm sorry I missed you.'

Pam winced. 'I could see you looking at me.'

'Then I'm sorry for doing that.'

Sighing, Pam looked at Chandra's card and said, 'I guess I'll start then.'

'Sure.'

'Chandra,' she said, somehow looking him in the eye while still reading his card. 'You are self-important, superior and pompous. You think everything is about you. You never listen, and you don't get women. You think you know everything. You think you're right all the time. You're contemptuous and arrogant, but you're not weak. You only pretend to be weak.'

Tears were running down her cheeks.

Chandra put his arms around her, shutting his eyes, holding her to him.

'I'm sorry,' he said. 'I'm sorry for everything.'

He didn't know how long they remained like that. Pam was crying, shaking, but when he let her go she wiped smeared make-up from her cheeks and smiled at him. She didn't seem embarrassed.

The workshop was over. A young man with a pointed black beard arrived with a camera and a tripod. Rudi Katz introduced him as 'My son, Max.' Everybody laughed. Everybody was laughing at everything now. There was a thick

206

euphoria in the room.

'Scooch together, people' said Max. 'Tall ones at the back, short ones at the front.'

Professor Chandra stood beside Pam. They weren't talking or touching, but he wanted to be with her. Rudi Katz was at the front, not far from Chandra. His teeth were gleaming. He looked tired and happy. Chandra still didn't think Katz was the legend everyone said he was, but he appreciated him more now. Chandra had never spoken about himself in public like this before. He wasn't sure if he'd learned anything new, or that he'd march into the summer more himself than before, but he had done something different. And he had met Pam, and Dolores. That seemed important.

'You're all beautiful,' said Max. 'Beautiful!'

Rudi Katz stepped forward from the group and hugged his son, and now everyone was hugging everyone, with Katz moving from participant to participant, thanking them for coming, telling them goodbye.

'*Chandra!*' said Katz, laughing with his mouth wide open. 'Well done, sir. Well done.'

They shook hands; no hug. Chandra doubted Katz had called anyone else 'sir'.

'Thank you for everything,' said Chandra. 'It was a great experience.'

'Keep it going,' said Katz. 'Just be you. What else is there?'

Katz shrugged, and now Chandra laughed for no good reason too. 'Thank you,' he said.

Rudi Katz patted him on the shoulder, and moved on to the next person.

Professor Chandra ate lunch outdoors at a wooden table, facing the sea. Bryan was with him, as were Pam, Andy, and Sally, who turned out to be very funny, with a deep uninhibited tonsil-revealing laugh. They were in a raucous mood, including Chandra who asked the group if all of them knew who Mindy Kaling was.

'Oh, my God,' said Pam, taking out her iPhone. 'Jesus!'

'Daisy was right,' said Chandra, looking at the image Pam had thrust in his face. 'She does look like you. Only ten years older.'

'She's pretty,' said Sally.

'Oh, yes, said Chandra. 'Certainly.'

Daisy was eating by herself at a table closer to the ocean, her fine grey hair blown vertical by the breeze.

'I read her book,' said Sally. 'She says, if you love something put it in a cage and smother it with love till it either dies or loves you back.'

They all laughed.

'That sound like you, Pam?' said Bryan.

'Yeah,' said Pam. 'Anyone else you haven't heard of, Chandra? Taylor Swift? How about Beyonce?'

'How about John Maynard Keynes?' asked Chandra.

'British economist,' said Pam, sounding bored. 'Discovered the multiplier effect.'

'Yes,' said Chandra.

'I go to Stanford,' said Pam.

'One sec,' said Chandra, standing and heading

towards two women carrying yoga mats. 'Excuse me,' he asked them. 'Is Dolores in your workshop by any chance?'

'Dolores,' said one of them. 'Yeah. She left.'

'Oh,' said Chandra, trying to hide his sadness. 'That's a shame.'

'She's a blast,' said the other.

'Thank you,' said Chandra, returning to the table where Sally was showing them all her tattoo.

'I got it done ten years ago,' she said, and held out her ring finger on which was tattooed 'ISIS'. 'I'm just really into ancient Egypt. How was *I* to know?'

'How do you manage at airports?' said Andy.

'I wear my ring and hope nobody looks underneath it,' said Sally.

'So,' said Chandra to Pam, quietly, 'are you heading home now?'

'That's right,' said Pam.

'Do you still think you need more money?'

'I think I need more freedom,' said Pam. 'I need to leave home.'

'Get away from your father.'

'Yep,' said Pam. 'But it's not his fault. That's one thing I learned. Like it's not your fault you never heard of Taylor Swift, it's not his fault he doesn't really know me. I mean, he can only know what he understands, right? I just need to forget about what he sees. I need to see myself.'

'Yes,' said Chandra. 'I suppose that makes sense.'

'I don't mean cut him off,' said Pam. 'I mean forget about his approval. Forget about him making me feel bad about myself.'

'Do you think I made my daughter feel bad about herself?' said Chandra.

'How should I know?'

'If you had to guess.'

'Yeah,' said Pam. 'I think so.'

'But it's not my fault.'

'Actually, it kind of *is* your fault. You keep judging her by your standards. She's not you. She's not a guy. She's not from India.'

'That's why you didn't like me asking if you were Indian,' said Chandra.

'What really pissed me off was when you said I was selfish and ungrateful,' said Pam.

'I'm sorry.'

'Well, don't be,' said Pam. ''Cause it's true. But so are you, Chandra. You ever thought of that? Just 'cause you never yelled at your dad or told him he was full of shit, does that make you better than me? And maybe you should have. Maybe you should have told him to go fuck himself.'

'Maybe,' said Chandra, trying to imagine himself saying that to his father.

'You said it with such confidence,' said Pam. 'Like you knew everything. Like you'd got everything figured out. You wouldn't be here if you'd got everything figured out, would you?'

'I'm not sure why I came here,' said Chandra. 'Someone dared me to. But I think I really came because I'm confused, even though I'm too old for that.'

'Maybe you're never too old to be confused,' said Pam.

'Amen to that,' said Andy, eavesdropping. 'I'll be coming here till the day I die.'

'Anyway,' said Pam. 'I'm gonna take another dip in the hot tub before I leave.' She stood up. 'It was nice to meet you, Professor Chandra.'

They hugged. Chandra watched as Pam went around the table and hugged everyone else.

'I've got to go too,' said Bryan, whose suitcase was beside him. 'Walk me to my car, Chandra?'

'Of course.'

They set off, passing the reception where Ronnie with the ponytail waved at them.

'I'm going to New York,' said Bryan. 'To see my son.'

It was the first time Chandra had seen Bryan look vulnerable. He felt sorry for him now, wished he hadn't judged him so harshly.

'It's a long flight,' said Bryan. 'I don't care. I need to process.'

At the parking lot Bryan rolled a cigarette, leaning against his car which, predictably, was a convertible.

'I wonder if I need to process,' said Chandra.

'We all do,' said Bryan. 'It's no big deal. You just need some time out, think things through. Let it settle. You know?'

Chandra shook his head.

'I suppose I don't do much processing.'

'You're a busy man.'

'You never told us much about your son,' said Chandra.

'I don't see much of him. I had him young, before I knew who I was.'

'Right.'

211

'He's fourteen and doesn't think much of his old man. I'm gonna stay in a hotel, see if he'll talk to me this time.'

'You've done this before?'

'Yeah,' said Bryan, laughing. 'You could say I've done this before.'

'I get it,' said Chandra. 'I've got a similar problem.'

Chandra looked at the sea. He wished he had spent more time looking at the sea while he'd been here. It resembled a rug now, something he could roll up in a child's dream. Looking at it made him wish he had taken a different path in life. What had he wanted when he was a boy? Certainly not to be an economist.

'Being hated is the worst thing,' said Bryan. 'You always think you deserve it. Well, I do. Catholic.'

'God, I'm exhausted,' said Chandra. 'I'm just plain exhausted. I feel like I've been here months.'

'Yeah, it has that effect sometimes,' said Bryan. 'You need to relax now. Go easy on yourself.'

Bryan didn't look relaxed. He looked stressed.

'It'll be okay,' said Chandra.

'How about you? You going to see your kids any time soon?'

'I'm going to Hong Kong,' said Chandra, whose flight left in six days. 'It's where my son lives.'

'Wow. The Far East. What does he do there?'

'He makes money.'

'Nothing wrong with that.'

212

'No, there isn't.'

'So you've just got the one son?'

'And two daughters,' said Chandra. 'One of them's young and having a hard time. The divorce hurt her a lot. The other one I don't really see.'

'Ah, okay,' said Bryan. 'I know how that goes.'

'Bryan,' said Chandra, taking out a business card from his wallet. 'I want to wish you the best of luck in New York. I don't know what happened with your son, but I think that even if you don't manage to see him, he'll know you came and that will be good. Whatever mistakes you've made . . . *if* you've made mistakes . . . '

'I did.'

'I only want to say, what can we do except try?'

But he didn't mean any of this. Chandra had been trying all his life. All those hours in the library, the cigarettes, the illnesses due only to exhaustion, the praise that had no effect on him, the criticism that did, the envy of his peers, the hours he'd spent envying them, and the work, and yet more work, rolling his rock up a hill while others took a cable car. But how many happy people had he met here? Or was it only unhappy people who came to Esalen?

'I'm lonely, Bryan,' said Chandra. 'And I chose it.'

'We choose everything.'

'I don't know if that's true,' said Chandra.

'But sometimes there's only one choice.'

'Right,' said Chandra. 'Right.'

'Okay, buddy,' said Bryan. 'Here's my number.

213

Let's stay in touch.'

'Thanks,' said Chandra, doubting they would; he couldn't imagine visiting Bryan in San Francisco. 'Good luck.'

'You too.'

Professor Chandra extended his hand, wanting them to part on his terms, but at the last moment he leaned forward and hugged Bryan, realising how few men he had hugged in his life, his son included.

He walked back to his room and fell asleep at once, waking at four in the afternoon when he got into his car and drove away, saying goodbye to nobody else. He couldn't bear any more emotion. Bryan had been right. He needed to process.

Professor Chandra felt more exhausted still when he reached UC Bella Vista, which would be his home for only a few more days. He tried to sleep, putting on the airline mask that used to belong to Jean, but couldn't. It felt as if his mind was filled with a new, coltish energy. He thought about getting up and making notes about strings and critical voices, but instead he just lay in bed, imagining the sea was still outside his window.

10

Professor Chandra spent the summer solstice in his garden, listening to the radio. He wondered if he was becoming more himself. He didn't think so. Instead, it seemed, he was becoming more Western like Pam, thinking about things it had never occurred to him to think about before: his father's parenting style, his parents' marriage, whether he had been traumatised, or bullied, or neglected.

But perhaps it wasn't a Western thing. Didn't teenagers in Bangalore wear short skirts and drink white wine and canoodle in bars and vomit into drains? Yes, it was a generational thing; this was what had caused Pam to leave the workshop, when he had called her — and by inference, her generation — a shallow spoiled ingrate. Since Radha had vanished from his life, his biggest, most secret fear had been that he was wrong; that she and Pam and their cohorts understood key principles his generation did not; that all their rebellion and self-analysis had taken them to some other level he could not touch. Yes, they lacked conviction, but maybe this was their strength; maybe there was bravery in this; maybe conviction was the recourse of those too terrified by life to face the confusion head on.

But no, that wasn't it at all. Pam had said it very clearly. It wasn't about whose generation was better. That was all a giant, floppy red

215

herring. Every generation was the same: insecure, powerless, frightened, bewildered, born to die. The only difference between himself and Pam was that Pam had admitted it, had said it loud and clear. She blamed her father. And Chandra had hidden, had pretended he had no feelings towards his parents other than unquestioning filial loyalty and gratitude. And this wasn't true. How could it be true?

So what were his feelings . . . ?

His father was a cruel man. Chandra knew this, though he had never said it before. There had been no one to say it to. Not his mother, who had quietly suppressed not only her own feelings on the matter but her son's too, a practice South Asian wives had maintained for centuries. Not Prakash, who barely spoke about anything until he was old enough to talk about politics (although now, Professor Chandra wondered if Prakash's obsessiveness wasn't an escape from his emotions). Not his friends or colleagues, who saw him as far too accomplished to have been bullied by anyone, a view Chandra had always been loath to correct. Not Jean, whose attitude to everything had always been 'Stop whining and just get on with it.' But maybe this was why he had married her, secure in the knowledge that she would never dip her finger into the well of his pain.

Chandra was pressing his fingernail into the webbing between his thumb and forefinger. He did this when he was nervous, or confused; sometimes he would draw blood. His father used to do it to him — a fact Chandra hadn't registered in fifty years. He would walk up to Chandra and press his thumbnail into the flesh of his hand, always grinning, sometimes ruffling his hair as if it were a boy's game, and if Chandra cried out or struggled his father would spit, 'Sissy,' and cuff him over the head before sending him on his way.

'For God's sake, Chandra,' he muttered, shaking his head. Some parents used switches and canes to beat their children. Others used hammers. His grandfather always used a leather belt, or so his father had said. There had been a boy in Chandra's class with burns on his arm from cigarettes. What was he whining about? He was being a . . .

But it was his father's voice he heard now . . . 'Sissy', 'lazy', 'ungrateful', 'stupid', 'selfish', 'crybaby', 'pathetic', 'dunce', 'slovenly', 'wicked', 'slothful', 'foolish', 'idiotic', 'dumb-head', 'duffer'. These words might as well have been branded onto his brain. His critical voices were so *obvious*, and yet he had spent a lifetime ignoring them. Rudi Katz was a genius.

Professor Chandra's visiting professorship was over now. He would fly to Hong Kong soon, and then on to England. The timing felt auspicious, if unnerving. Chandra's biggest fear was that he was, in fact, hardly different from his father. He had never hit Sunny, it was true, but he had called him names, had spoken with a similar contempt.

It had always enraged him that Sunny hated cricket, and still did, preferring activities with unpronounceable names like Krav Maga,

217

capoeira and Zumba. He used to literally run away from the ball, which was all the more unbearable given that Chandra had named him after India's former captain, Sunil Gavaskar. He used to call Sunny the same names back then: 'sissy', 'wimp', 'pathetic', 'namby-pamby'.

Chandra's father used to sneer at him on account of his grades which, initially, were mediocre. When he was twelve his father had smashed a badminton racquet against the wall and called him a 'knuckle-headed imbecile' before marching into his study and slamming the door five times. Chandra's mother had sat beside her crying son and told him, 'Your father knows you can do it. He's only disappointed. You just need to apply yourself, Chandu.'

Together they made a plan. Chandra would improve his grades and, in time, would take the IAS exam, following in his father's footsteps and becoming a civil servant. When he knocked on his father's door to tell him the news, his father said, 'This idiot? Tell him to take the cleaning toilets exam!'

It was the reason Chandra could never bring himself to clean a toilet, even today, something Jean had never understood, always attributing it to his Brahmin sensibilities.

In his teens, Sunny had begun to take an interest in economics. It didn't occur to Chandra that he was trying to win his father's approval. He regarded it as normal that a boy of Sunny's age should be fascinated by differential levels of human capital investment across Newly Industrialising Countries and responded as he would to any promising undergraduate — with withering contempt.

'There are monkeys in the Amazon who know more economics than you,' he said.

'I'm trying,' said Sunny.

'Yes,' said Chandra. 'You are.'

When Sunny gained a place at the LSE, Chandra had mocked his choice of degree, Business and Management. 'We could come and visit you at Woolworths,' he'd said, before asking, 'Do you *write* your essays, or just highlight them?' and 'Do you call yourself students or interns?'

'I'll be out-earning you within five years,' Sunny had replied, extending his hand to signal a wager.

'And you'll still be working class,' said Chandra, clapping his son's cheeks between his palms.

After his degree, Sunny was offered a position with Salomon Brothers as a strategy consultant. Three years later he sent his father a copy of his pay cheque above which he drew a smiley face. It revealed that he had made good on his promise and was out-earning his father, at least in terms of base salary. Chandra sent an email in response:

Good for you. Don't forget money isn't everything. Look after health. Spend wisely. Consider investing in an education at a later date. Best, Dad

The following year, Sunny moved to Hong Kong where he joined a hedge fund, working sixteen hours a day. He and his father saw each other

219

only twice a year, but even then they tended to argue. Whenever Chandra tried to speak about economics, Sunny would retort with, 'The real world doesn't work according to models. It works on happenings, events, moments. All that matters is what's in play — '

Chandra would put his fingers in his ears when he heard this, knowing the words 'Now!' or 'Stat!' were coming, accompanied by a vicious finger-snap.

Paradoxically, this was also when Sunny's deviation towards the mystical began. That Christmas he presented every one of his family members with a book called *The Secret*, by someone called Rhonda Byrne, handing them out with the air of a man who had not only seen the light but had trapped, bottled and sold it. It was also then that Sunny began to shave his head and to talk with a distinctly South Asian lilt.

In 2008, following the crash, Sunny went silent, refusing to respond to emails or SMS's. When Chandra called him at work he was informed that Sunny was no longer employed by Ponsford & Sons. Professor Chandra made a few notes before calling Sunny's mobile. This was a delicate matter. He did not want to say anything hurtful or ill-considered.

1. It's not your fault. Whole world is hard hit.
2. But I did warn you.
3. Will help find you another job. Don't worry.
4. Come home for a while? Might do you good.
5. As stated, I did warn you (so in a sense, it *is* your fault).

6. It's all right. Part of learning process. You're not a complete idiot (joke).
7. General philosophical statement. Ideas? Quote Mandela? Keynes? Jobs? 'Turn your wounds into wisdom.' Yes, excellent.
8. Another joke. Play by ear. Best jokes = spontaneous.

'I resigned, Dad,' said Sunny, before Chandra could deliver point two. 'I've set up my own management school: The Institute of Mindful Business.'

'The what?'

'It's about positive affirmation.'

'What?'

'You bring your desires into being.'

'What the hell are you talking about, Sunny?'

'Do you know why we're in recession, Dad?'

Chandra did know. He had been speaking about Mortgage Backed Securities on Sky News that morning.

'It's because of negative thinking,' said Sunny.

'Quite the opposite,' said Chandra. 'It was due to a marked *excess* of animal spirits.'

'I don't think so,' said Sunny. 'I think the world *chose* depression. It started in the mind and it manifested.'

'But I'm trying to tell you that isn't what happened,' said Chandra. 'No one was depressed. They all thought the bubble would go on for ever.'

'I'm not talking about economics.'

'Well, I *am*.'

'I'm talking about the mind.'

'Sunny, I'm sorry you lost your job. If you need to come home for a while — '

'I didn't lose my job.'

'It isn't your fault. You didn't do anything wrong.'

'There's no such thing as right or wrong, Dad. Only the consequences of our actions.'

Chandra looked down at his notes.

'Success isn't the result of our successes — '

'Success is the result of our thoughts,' said Sunny.

'What is all this bullshit?' said Chandra, pushing his notebook away.

'People pay good money to hear this bullshit, Dad. I've helped dozens already.'

'Then they're idiots,' said Chandra. 'Why would anyone pay for that?'

'You'd be surprised.'

They spoke again the following week, and it was more cordial. But as time went by, Sunny began to speak almost exclusively in sound bites, saying, 'We are already living the life we were meant to live, the secret is to *know* this.' And, 'Money is psychic blood — a money clot is as dangerous as a blood clot.'

'Are you arguing against a high savings rate?' said Chandra, recalling his recent rather regrettable spat with Krugman.

'I'm talking about the heart,' said Sunny.

'Good Lord,' said Chandra.

In spite of all his outrage, there was one thing Professor Chandra could not deny. The Institute of Mindful Business was a success. Sunny was forever on a first-class flight to Beijing or Paris

222

or, every couple of months, London. But Chandra was still convinced his son was a charlatan, albeit an excellent one, or else he had gone quite mad, irredeemably so.

What Chandra couldn't figure out was his own role amidst all of this. Jasmine had said Sunny wanted to 'beat him'. Was that it?

Chandra wondered if this was true of himself: he had always known he was trying to win his late father's approval, but had he been trying to beat him? Was it victory he craved instead of approval, to smother his old man's grave with prizes and accolades and doctorates and seventeenth-century cottages and hefty consulting fees, to shut his cruel contemptuous mouth for ever and ever, amen?

But it wouldn't work. It couldn't work. Chandra knew that now. And if Sunny was trying to beat him, this also wouldn't work. Professor Chandra needed to tell him that. He needed to sit his son down and share what he had discovered, to break the cycle, to apologise — yes, why not? He, Professor Chandra, who rarely apologised to anyone, would apologise to his son. Perhaps this was why he was going to Hong Kong.

★　★　★

It was a sixteen-hour flight and Professor Chandra was rarely able to sleep on planes. When he landed, all he could think about was having a bath and a small glass of wine. Sunny wasn't there to meet him, but had instructed

223

Chandra to take a taxi, emailing him directions in Chinese which Chandra had printed and now gave to the driver.

They drove across the bridge between Lantau and the mainland — a journey Chandra remembered from his last visit, a shameful four years ago — and traversed east across Hong Kong Island. This didn't feel right to Chandra. Sunny's apartment was in 'the Mid-Levels', one of the city's most desirable spots, a flock of designer skyscrapers and serviced apartments with polished lobbies and doormen. Chandra remembered an uphill climb, but instead they passed between a set of vanilla colonial-style buildings that would not have been out of place in Bombay. They stopped by a pastel-green building which was a mere three storeys high instead of the desired seventy.

'What is this?' asked Chandra.

'Heong Gong Business School,' said the driver.

'I'm sorry,' said Chandra. 'I want to go to the Mid-Levels.'

The driver held up the printout and said once more, 'Hong Kong Business School.'

'Mid-Levels,' said Chandra.

A man was tapping on the window of the car. 'Professor,' he was saying, smiling like gently heated plasticine. 'Professor.'

Chandra rolled down his window. 'Yes?'

'*Hey*,' said the man, who was Chinese and in his early thirties, but had a British, public school-educated accent. 'Great to finally meet you.'

The man opened Chandra's door, leaving him little choice but to step outside into the heat.

'And you are?' said Chandra.

'Professor Martin Cheung. Dean of the Business School.'

Martin Cheung was wearing a blazer with jeans, the uniform of the newer mould of managerial schemers, the ones who had transformed universities into the intellectual equivalent of oil companies.

'I see,' said Chandra. 'Look, I think there's been some mistake. I'm supposed to be at my son's place, in the Mid-Levels.'

'Oh, don't worry,' said the man, paying the driver. 'Your son's inside. I'm sure he filled you in.'

'He did no such thing.'

'Well, what can I say? I'll let him explain. Welcome to Hong Kong, Professor, or *foon ying*, as we say here. Dr Chandrasekhar is waiting for you upstairs. I'm the reception committee.'

Martin Cheung laughed while Chandra glared. In front of them was a stone staircase on which a seemingly endless supply of girls in tiny shorts and T-shirts passed up and down while two white men leaned on the balustrade and drank from Starbucks mugs. Business lecturers: they had that smug look about them that said, *While you were busy learning things, we were getting rich.* 'F.I.L.T.H' he muttered under his breath, an acronym he'd once tried in front of Sunny with disastrous results — Failed In London, Try Hong Kong.

'All right,' said Chandra. 'Let's go then.'

They filed up the stairs into a hallway at the end of which was a conference room as cold as a meat factory. Two female students stood on either side of the doors, one with a tray of champagne flutes, the other with a stack of flyers. Chandra took one of each.

Hong Kong Business School/Event
'The Neglect of the Mind in Contemporary Economics'
A Masterclass with Dr Sunil Chandrasekhar, Director of the Institute of Mindful Business.
Starts: 14 July 2017 — 19:00
Finishes: 14 July 2017 — 20:30

Professor Chandra looked at his watch: the talk was today and started in six and a half hours, except his watch was on London time, which meant it had started half an hour ago.

Inside the room, row upon row of students were sitting in those steel chairs with red upholstery found in business schools everywhere. Sunny was in an armchair on the podium dressed in a cream linen jacket and purple silk shirt. His head was shaven and he wore his usual prescription-free glasses, but there were creases on his forehead now that even the hundred-dollar moisturisers he used couldn't erase. Sunny was becoming middle-aged. Chandra felt at fault, as if it were the task of a father to prevent this.

'Raise your hands,' Sunny was saying. 'Who works hard? Come on? Who?'

Every hand in the room was in the air. At least half the audience were wearing suits, even though the semester had ended, which was typical of MBA students. They were fond of questions like 'Can this be summarised in a single sentence?' or 'On what page of the handout is this?' Any sign of rigour had them running to their parents who'd write letters complaining the course was 'not hands-on enough', meaning their children were too stupid to understand.

Economists younger than Chandra had discarded years of training so these Mediocre But Arrogant rich kids from France, Greece and South Africa could return to their Management Consultancies with pieces of paper confirming they'd spent a year as a foot soldier in the war against intelligence.

'So let's try an exercise,' said Sunny, who didn't seem to have noticed his father's entrance. 'Close your eyes. You are in darkness now. Try to feel the end of your nose. Don't touch it. Just feel its presence; know it exists.'

Chandra sat near the back, ignoring Martin Cheung who was trying to escort him to the VIP seats at the front. He looked at the flyer in his hand once more and then it dawned on him: Dr *Sunil Chandrasekhar*. As far as Chandra knew, Sunny had never gained a doctorate.

'Now imagine the tip of your nose is illuminated like a flash-light. What can you see in the blackness now? It depends on you. What you see is what you desire. All you have to do is let it manifest.'

Professor Chandra could see a bed. A plush

227

multi-cushioned bed floating in the centre of the sea. And on that bed he saw himself.

'Now, open your eyes.'

Sunny slipped deeper into a subcontinental accent as he continued: 'So, welcome to the world of your desires. They don't go away once you open your eyes. They are you and you are them. You can as little escape them as you could the tip of your nose.

'All our lives we've been told to feel ashamed of our desires. All our lives we've been told we are too ambitious, too greedy. As small children we were taught self-abnegation, self-denial. We learned this everywhere, from our teachers, our religions, our parents.'

Nonsense, thought Chandra. This from the boy who had an electric BMW tricycle at the age of seven.

'We were taught to be grateful for what we had, ashamed of wanting more, ashamed of being ourselves. 'Don't enter the race,' they tell us. 'You'll probably lose. Sit aside and watch the runners instead. Just give up, just give up, just give up.''

'You see, as you demonstrated only moments ago, we all work hard. We all strive. But who has everything they want? Who looked into the blackness and saw their lives exactly as they are now? And why? It isn't through lack of striving, I can tell you. It's through a lack of believing. You haven't allowed your dreams to come true.'

This, Chandra remembered with an involuntary snort, was what Sunny had told him after his accident, talking from the lobby of the

Mumbai Oberoi; that he had willed the bicycle into being.

'And this, ladies and gentlemen,' said Sunny, 'is what modern economists fail to understand. Why? Because they don't take into account the human mind. Ask yourself this. How does anything happen out there in the world of objects? How do I move this cup, this glass, this microphone, this chair? That's right. I *decide* to move it. And I make this decision with my mind. Economists say we're all subject to their models, but the truth is we make our own models, and we can unmake them, every day. The secret is to know our own desires. To own them. When we own our desires, we can be the change we want to see.'

Professor Chandra was fairly sure this was a quote from Gandhi. Now the MBA students would go home believing the Mahatma's core message was 'Get what you want.'

Sunny tapped his head and closed his eyes.

'The treasure house is within. Thank you.'

The room applauded. Sunny stood and applauded too, pointing out individuals in the audience and laughing, putting his hand on his heart and saying, 'You! You! You!' before bowing, his hands pressed together in namaste, and sitting down.

A woman in a red trouser suit on the front row was standing with a microphone in her hand, thanking Sunny along with 'our sponsors', which seemed to include every bank in the developed world, before inviting questions.

Martin Cheung raised his hand at once, which

meant the question had been planted.

'Dr Sunil,' he said, which made Chandra wince, 'I think we all know that we, as individuals, *can* think ourselves successful.' A cheap trick, thought Chandra; a way of convincing these weak-minded MBA's that they agreed with everything his son had said. 'All successful businesses, after all, attribute their success to positive thinking, at least in part. But can the same be said of entire nations? Is this why Asia is rising, or why much of the world is in recession? How far can your theory be taken?'

Sunny's eyes had been closed during the question, but now he opened them as if deigning to return to the human plane once more.

'A nation is nothing but a dream of the people,' said Sunny. 'Its leaders guide its dreams. George Bush left America weak and depressed, so look what happened to their economy. Narendra Modi gave Indians hope, and look what has happened to India's economy. These are over-simplifications, but what I am saying is simple. We think together. We dream together. What is a river but millions of drops of water, and what is a nation but millions of people? Our nations' fates are formed by the aggregate of its people's thoughts, and, as always, negative thoughts bring negative fates. This may sound harsh, but it's a natural law, I'm afraid.'

So growth rates, thought Professor Chandra, were subject to the will of the people. He wondered what else this might apply to. Infant mortality? Volcanic explosions? Tidal waves? Cricket scores?

A young woman in a blue blazer was on her feet now. She held her iPhone aloft in her right hand, speaking from notes on it, presumably. It made Chandra think of the Statue of Liberty.

'My name is Claudette Brown,' she said, in a French accent. 'I'd like to thank Dr Sunil on such a thought-provoking lecture. Really, there's so much to think about here, so much to *process*. I wonder whether you're actually talking about *genius*. And maybe this is what we neglect nowadays; maybe we're killing genius in business and we need to let it flourish again. When we think of Steve Jobs or Mark Zuckerberg, it almost feels like a different era now, like they might not have been allowed to exist today . . .'

Professor Chandra listened while Sunny explained that *he* was a genius and everyone who had assembled here to listen to him could be too if they would only pay him huge quantities of money to show them the way. And now he was telling a story about Deepak Chopra who had said about him, 'He puts the whiz into wisdom,' with regard to Sunny's digital detox programmes and spiritual productivity seminars.

When Chandra relaxed his eyes, half-squinting, he didn't see a shaven-headed man in early middle age any more but an attention-seeking little boy. Of course Sunny had wanted his father to see this. He was trying to reverse his own strings, strings Chandra had fashioned with his bare hands, layering one over the other until they were tough as ropes. Professor Chandra hung his head, feeling only embarrassment, and worse, shame, but now everyone was clapping; some were whistling, or making that undergraduate 'whooping' sound that was impossible for anyone with an IQ over eighty. The collective noise sounded like a circular saw, passing first through his right ear and then his left.

The woman in red was closing the event, thanking the sponsors once more, telling the audience how lucky they were that the fabulously busy Dr Chandrasekhar had managed to take time out from his hectic schedule to be there, and now Sunny was surrounded by admirers, shaking hands, posing for selfies, and Martin Cheung was looking for Chandra, beckoning him over. Screwing his flyer into a tight ball before dropping it into his champagne glass, Professor Chandra hauled himself to his feet and fought his way across the room.

'Dad,' said Sunny, taking off his glasses and holding out his hand. 'How are you?'

'Exhausted,' said Chandra. 'Why didn't you tell me about this?'

'What?'

'Your talk. I'd have taken an earlier flight.'

Sunny raised his eyes to heaven. 'I did, Dad. It was in the email.'

Martin Cheung and the woman in the red dress laughed, as did three sycophants who were also listening intently.

'The one in Chinese?'

'No,' said Sunny, his smile tightening. 'The one in English.'

'I didn't get any bloody email.'

'You sure, Dad?'

Chandra wasn't. Sunny's emails were often

pages long, usually including zealous pastings of his articles.

Sunny turned to the others. 'Allow me to introduce my father,' he said. 'Professor P. R. Chandrasekhar.'

'It's a pleasure to finally meet you, sir,' said the woman in the red dress. 'My name's Susan Katto. I'm the Associate Director of IMB.'

'Oh, how do you do?' said Chandra, wondering what IMB was before remembering it was Sunny's company: the Institute of Mindful Business.

'We've all heard so much about you, sir,' said Susan Katto.

'You must be very proud of your son,' said Martin Cheung.

'Oh, very much, very much,' said Chandra, glaring at Sunny.

'Have some champagne,' said Sunny, in the way you'd stuff sweets into a crying child's mouth.

'So what were your thoughts on Dr Sunil's presentation?' said Martin Cheung, handing Chandra a warm glass of Moet.

'Oh, excellent,' said Chandra. 'Very nice.'

'So you agree?' said one of the sycophants, a balding be-suited student, probably French or Italian or Greek (it was hard to tell with MBA students — mediocrity was a great leveller).

'Oh, Sunny is quite right,' said Professor Chandra. 'Of course, the mind *is* a rather neglected area of economics. But economics is a science. We tend to stick to describing what people do rather than what they think. Perhaps that's rather backward of us. I quite agree that one should be positive and so forth, but there are certain things that are rather hard to change, not to say impossible.'

'Like what, sir?' asked Susan Katto.

'Well, if there is only one bottle of champagne in the room, not everyone's going to get a glass, regardless of how much one desires it. That's all I'm trying to say — some things just are and we have to accept them, and this, I'm afraid, includes those foolish sets of laws we call economics.'

They were all looking at Sunny now, who had picked up the champagne bottle as if about to feed the five hundred. 'I believe everything is attainable,' he told them. 'Everything. I've seen businesses double productivity just by repeating simple affirmations. And as I'm sure my father knows, there is never only one bottle, or two bottles, or even ten bottles. Growth is potentially unlimited.'

Chandra nodded. 'Yes, certainly, but there's also something called *effective* demand, and if we start spending money that isn't there, well, we all know where that leads. It wasn't a lack of positivity that caused the crisis. It was too *much* positivity. Sometimes we have to be content with what we have.'

'Which some would call defeatism,' said Sunny.

'And others would call maturity,' said Chandra.

Martin Cheung snorted in an attempt to conceal his laughter. Even Susan Katto was smiling. This was always Chandra's advantage

234

when he went up against Sunny. Sunny wasn't good at humour, which had been Chandra's speciality for decades. He always began his speeches with a joke. It helped establish the audience's allegiance. Liberals forgot he was an evil neoliberal, competitors forgot their envy. It made strangers warm to him, trust him. He could see it already in the faces of the students.

'Anyone who has taken a course with IMB,' said Sunny, 'learns the most important truth of all — that you can be whoever you want to be. There are no mediocre people, only mediocre expectations. Imagine if Steve Jobs or Barack Obama — '

'We can't all be Steve Jobs,' said Chandra. 'And yes, Obama . . . but what about the three hundred and twenty-three million Americans who didn't become President?'

'They didn't believe,' said Sunny.

'You can't have three hundred and twenty-three million Presidents, Sunny,' said Chandra. 'No amount of positive thinking will change that. It isn't all about the mind. Much of success is just luck, or having the right parents, or being in the right place at the right time. Nobody tells you this, but it's true.'

The students were laughing now, probably at the reference to 'having the right parents'. But Sunny had turned away, was looking at his iPhone. Professor Chandra shut his eyes, knowing he was in trouble.

11

He went home by himself that night, claiming he was too exhausted to attend the dinner, which happened to be true, but it felt like a lie when he said it. A driver took him to Sunny's apartment on the forty-sixth floor. Chandra fell asleep without even changing his clothes and awoke on Saturday morning to find Sunny with his mountain bike slung over one shoulder, drinking some juiced green sludge and wearing Lycra shorts.

'Where are you going?' said Chandra.

'Chi Ma Wan.'

'Chi Ma What?'

'Wan,' said Sunny. 'Out with clients.'

When Sunny left, Chandra ran after him to the landing saying, 'You forgot your sports watch,' but the lift doors had already shut. He watched the countdown: Floor 46, 45, 44, 43 . . .

He spent the morning in front of the television until, at lunchtime, two young Filipina women called Wendy and Melissa arrived to clean and cook lunch. He tried his best to talk to them but they replied in polite, embarrassed monosyllables. Chandra wondered if they had families, or if they were as alone as everyone else in this city.

The Mid-Levels, where Sunny's apartment was, consisted of row after row of high-rises, each craning its neck over the next in pursuit of an unimpeded glimpse of the sea. To Chandra it

236

didn't look like the sea. It felt industrial, or digital, something out of a video game. He found himself missing California, longing to be back at Big Sur.

In the afternoon, he visited the sauna on the ground floor before scouring Sunny's cavernous living room for thrillers or mystery novels, but most of the books were on motivational techniques or management. There were magazines in the bathroom, including the *Economist*, but this was the last thing Chandra wanted to read.

Venturing into the bedroom, he discovered two more shelves, mainly history and biography, books on Akbar, Churchill, Abraham Lincoln, the Pilgrim Fathers, Marco Polo, Charlie Chaplin, Andy Warhol, histories of the Civil War, the stock market, the Boxer Rebellion, and the Provincial Insurance Company.

Professor Chandra was impressed. He hadn't realised Sunny read so widely. But he still couldn't find any novels, not even a Stephen King or a Jeffrey Archer. Drawing back the curtains, he found one more shelf of books on the windowsill, sandwiched between statues of the Laughing Buddha and Jesus.

These were his books: *The Economics of Poverty; Who's Afraid of the Big Bad Market?; India and Other Dreams; Why the Third World Matters; Globalise, Mobilise; Fast Unto Bankruptcy;* and *After the Flood*.

Chandra picked up *After the Flood* and thumbed through it. He was so used to the way undergraduates treated books that at first he thought nothing of Sunny highlighting several passages and making notes in pencil in the margins. It was difficult to decipher his shorthand, which used personalised abbreviations like ↑ for 'growth' and 't4' for 'therefore,' letters so tiny they suggested shameful secrets. Chandra feared that closer inspection might reveal sarcastic addendums, but instead it was clear that Sunny had simply wanted to understand. They were the comments of a diligent student, one Chandra had spent half a lifetime deriding.

He ended up asking the doorman to call him a taxi, and spent the rest of the afternoon in an Indian restaurant eating masala eggs on toast and trying to speak Punjabi with the waiters. When Chandra returned to the flat, Sunny was still not there, but Melissa the cook was making pizza and singing a song in Tagalog. Chandra tried to talk to her about Hong Kong, Chinese food, Sunny (which made her even more tight-lipped), and the possibility of the entire island being destroyed by a tsunami, at which the poor girl, who couldn't have been older than nineteen, looked ready to cry.

Eventually he slipped away and returned after Melissa had left, falling asleep in front of the television while watching cricket. When he awoke his son was complaining to nobody in particular about how Melissa had nicked his Japanese knives.

'Wouldn't know Usuba Bōchō from Boko Haram,' he said.

'*Sunny!*' said Professor Chandra, forcing

himself off the sofa. 'Where have you been?'

'I told you,' said Sunny, opening a bottle of orange San Pellegrino.

'Are you hungry? There's pizza left. She cooks well, this girl.'

'I ate with the others.'

'Oh?' said Chandra, suspecting this was a lie. In his experience Sunny never socialised merely for the sake of socialising.

'Yeah, dim sum.'

'I like dim sum.'

They stood staring each other down in the kitchen, two wounded prizefighters pretending to talk about food.

'We can go for dim sum tomorrow, Dad.'

'Great,' said Chandra, as Sunny headed for the bedroom. 'Looking forward to it.'

Chandra went to bed, terrified Sunny would realise he had been snooping in his room and cancel dim sum. He got up early, busying himself in the kitchen preparing dosa, milky coffee and an improvised chutney from green chillies, spinach and lime (it was the maids' day off). Sunny did not surface until eleven, by which time Chandra was wearing an apron and had his head inside the oven looking for even a trace of dirt (those women were unfeasibly efficient).

'Morning, Dad.'

His son was wearing an Oxford University sweatshirt, tennis shorts, and an airline mask pushed back onto his forehead.

Chandra poured coffee into an IMB mug in a thin noisy stream before warming a dosa on a pan and handing it to his son. They ate in air-conditioned silence at the kitchen table.

'Sunny, I hope you weren't upset by our joust the other day.'

'What joust?'

Chandra spooned chutney onto his own plate. 'I just thought I said a few things that might have — '

Sunny took out his iPhone. 'What are you talking about, Dad?'

'Oh, nothing,' said Chandra. 'It was very interesting, your talk. So many things I'd never thought about before, the subconscious mind and all that.'

Sunny put his phone on the table. 'Just because I have a different opinion to you, it doesn't mean I have to grow up, Dad. Growing up doesn't mean becoming you.'

'I agree,' said Chandra. 'Absolutely.'

Sunny switched on the espresso machine, a rebuke to the South Indian coffee Professor Chandra had made.

'Sunny,' said Chandra, 'for a while now, since Esalen, I've been thinking about — '

'Esalen,' said Sunny, brightening. 'Yes, how was it?'

'It was wonderful. Well, it was weird too. It made me remember things I'd forgotten, how maybe my father wasn't the best father. He was unkind to me.' He cleared his throat. 'I mean, he was good to me as well, but I just thought, I simply wondered . . . maybe I'm one of your critical voices?'

'My what?'

'Like when you tell yourself you're not good

enough, or you're silly, or you're an idiot.'

'I don't tell myself those things, Dad. I practise positive thinking. I thought you knew that.'

'Yes, I know, of course. But I mean, I wonder why you need to do it at all?'

'It's my vocation.'

'But maybe it's because of me,' said Chandra. 'Maybe I made fun of you too much. I never meant any harm. My father did it to me and I thought nothing of it, so I did it to you.'

'Maybe everything isn't about you, Dad,' said Sunny. 'You ever think of that?'

Sunny pressed a button on his coffee machine and now neither of them could hear anything. It sounded like a plane taking off. Chandra remembered Sunny telling him how much the machine cost — it was as much as Chandra's first car.

'I did,' said Chandra. 'But I think that's a cop-out.'

'Cop-out?'

'Sunny, all I'm saying is, I know I've hurt you, and I'm sorry.'

Sunny sipped his espresso, his gold bracelet gleaming in the sunlight.

'No, Dad. I don't think you have.'

'Oh?' said Chandra, realising, for the first time, that this couldn't possibly be true.

'Not at all,' said Sunny. 'It's a shame you and Mum couldn't work it out, but I was always fine. Maybe Rad felt it more because she's younger, but I never had any major problems. I have clients who had bad parents. It isn't you.'

241

'Right,' said Chandra. 'Well, that's good.'

Sunny looked at his watch.

'Shall we go?'

They took a taxi to Central, spending half an hour going up and down the giant escalator that climbed halfway up the hill. Chandra had been on it before and found it magnificent, but his son stared into his iPhone for most of the time, his face inscrutable behind his Ray-Bans. Even on a Sunday, Sunny was dressed very well in black woollen trousers and a blue Lacoste polo shirt. It must have been something he had learned from his father, who was carrying his blazer over one arm in spite of the heat.

'Maybe we'll see Melissa here,' said Chandra, gesturing to the Filipino maids who filled every inch of pavement as well as sections of the road.

'There's a quarter of a million of them, Dad.'

It was like this every Sunday, apparently, when the maids took their day off, a giant refugee camp. As always when confronted with the poor, Chandra felt a tinge of envy. They looked so much happier, these women, with their boxed lunches and transistor radios and falling-apart guitars.

'A hard life,' he said, to compensate for this sentimentality. 'Hard work.'

'We all get the lives we choose,' said Sunny.

Bullshit, thought Chandra, and replied, 'Yes, I suppose that's true.'

'It's not a conscious process, if that's what you're thinking,' said Sunny. 'And it can be changed. If these girls spent an hour a week at the IMB they'd be working there in a year.' Sunny pointed at the International Financial Centre, those twin skyscrapers that faced off across the sea.

'Maybe I should take one of your classes,' said Chandra.

'Maybe you should.'

'It's pretty different to what we learned at Esalen.'

Sunny raised his Ray-Bans, though only for a second. 'Really?'

'I don't know,' said Chandra. 'Esalen seemed more psychological, I suppose.' He wanted to say 'rational'.

'Everything is psychology,' said Sunny, to which Chandra could not answer, as his stock phrase used to be, 'Everything is economics.'

Chandra tried to count to ten, and got to four. 'So you really think those women chose to be domestic workers?'

'Yep.'

'Or the Jews chose the Holocaust?'

'I think that's an emotive example.'

'I suppose it is.'

'The thoughts we think habitually leave deep grooves in the subconscious,' said Sunny, putting his phone away. 'If we're always thinking how useless we are, this becomes a subconscious belief that manifests in reality. It's a natural law. I only observe it.'

'So all those women became maids because they had low opinions of themselves?'

'Not necessarily. Maybe they were born into poor families. Maybe they wanted to be maids.

243

How should I know? All I can say is the minute they begin *thinking* they can be something else, it'll start to happen.'

Professor Chandra didn't know what to say to this. He felt like patting his son on the head and saying, 'There, there.'

'Will this work for me?' he said, though he couldn't imagine himself being anything other than an economist.

'It'll work for anyone.'

At the Yacht Club they ate a buffet lunch accompanied by four different wines, though Chandra drank only a single glass. There were fifty tables in the room, all with an array of crystal glasses and lush tablecloths. Sunny spoke Cantonese to the waiters while Chandra made approving comments like, 'Excellent,' or, 'Quite the polyglot,' remembering how he used to give Sunny a hard time for not being bilingual like the two Gujarati girls at his school.

'Sunny!'

A young Chinese couple had approached their table and were doing everything but kiss Sunny's hand. Sunny introduced them.

'I can't believe you're his father,' said the woman.

'Yes,' said Chandra, 'since he was born.'

'He's like a father to *us*,' said the man, before snapping his fingers and miming holding a pistol. 'Who da man?' he asked Sunny.

'You da man,' said Sunny.

'No, *you* da man.'

'These two,' said the woman, shaking her head.

'I hope you're practising,' said Sunny.

'Every day,' said the man, 'or we wouldn't be here, would we?'

'Look after yourselves,' said Sunny, that subcontinental inflection returning to his voice.

'Friends of yours?' asked Chandra, after they had left.

'Clients.'

'Ah.'

It crossed Professor Chandra's mind that Sunny might have asked them to do this, like the planted questions at his talk.

'So Jaz is going to a community college, I hear,' said Sunny.

'Her SATs didn't go according to plan.'

'So she's staying in Boulder.'

'For a while. She can transfer when her grades improve.'

Sunny signalled to the waiter for more green tea.

'I told her to come here. I could have given her an internship for the summer.'

'Yes,' said Chandra, deciding on a second glass of wine after all. 'I think she's depressed. She needs to strike out on her own instead of being stuck at home.'

Sunny shook his head. 'We get the lives we choose.'

'I don't think she chose this,' said Chandra, looking at the enormous pile of rocket leaves and avocado on Sunny's plate, a tremendous waste of a sixty-dollar buffet.

'Like I said,' said Sunny. 'It's not a conscious process.'

'So if I tell myself I'm happy every morning, I'll be happy.'

'That's an over-simplification. But yes.'

'Then why hasn't it worked for you?'

Sunny was looking over Professor Chandra's shoulder, raising his eyebrows as if to acknowledge an acquaintance.

'I've already told you, Dad. I practise what I preach and I preach what I practise, and I'm happy because of it.'

'Yes, of course. But even Rudi Katz admitted he felt unhappy sometimes.'

Sunny put a forkful of leaves in his mouth. 'Who is Rudi Katz?'

'My teacher at Esalen.'

'Perhaps his method isn't as effective as he thinks it is.'

'Isn't it more complex than that?' said Chandra. 'What about all the terrible things that happen to people? How does someone who has been raped or lived through a war just tell themselves they're happy?'

'It doesn't happen overnight.' Sunny placed his fork at a perfect forty-five degree angle to his knife. 'But if a severely traumatised person says their affirmations every day, their life will begin to change. The same is true for Jasmine, and for you. Do it for long enough, and your desires will manifest.'

'So if I desire to be Prime Minister of India . . . ?'

'What do you actually desire, Dad?' said Sunny. 'Your deepest desire.'

'To be with my family. To see my daughters, both of them.'

'Then I will write some affirmations for you to say. It will manifest.'

Professor Chandra stared at his son, searching for signs of doubt and finding none.

'I don't think you believe all this, Sunny,' he said. 'You've done very well for yourself and I'm proud of you, but I don't think you believe everything you say. And I do think you're unhappy.'

'What kind of father tries to convince his son he's unhappy?' said Sunny.

'A father who bloody cares,' said Chandra. 'A father who wants to know his son. Nobody can be this perfect, Sunny. Nobody can be this in control. Nobody is happy all the time.'

'Did I say I'm happy all the time? I'm happy ninety per cent of the time, and when I'm not, I work on it.'

'Okay, fine. Nobody is happy ninety per cent of the time. Who even knows? It's more complex than that.'

'So you think I'm a fraud,' said Sunny, his adult face replaced by a child's for an instant.

'No,' said Chandra. 'No, I don't believe that. I think what you do is very helpful, positive thinking, subconscious thinking. All I am trying to say is — '

Sunny picked up his phone and answered it, even though Professor Chandra hadn't heard it ring. Chandra's head hurt. He closed his eyes and tried to count his breaths. If he had a heart attack now Sunny would only tell him to think positively.

'On the twenty-fourth,' said Sunny. 'Yes, *vado*

direttamente in palesta.'

'I mean,' said Chandra, even though Sunny was still on the phone, 'don't you ever have doubts? Don't you ever think, 'What if I'm wrong about this?''

Sunny put the phone down and called the waiter over, signing for their lunch.

'Are you all right, Dad?' he said.

'I'm not feeling so good.'

'We'll get you some treatments. It'll help.'

They had massages using hot stones and aromatherapy and sounds from the rainforest. Professor Chandra fell asleep in the middle, but when he awoke he did feel better, though he still had a headache, probably a result of the wine.

They went to the steam room afterwards, wrapped in towels and sitting in silence, Sunny's six-pack beside Chandra's one-pack.

'Any news from Radha?' said Chandra, trying to sound as casual as possible.

'She doesn't want to see you, Dad.'

'Where is she?'

'It doesn't matter.'

'Of course it matters. I have a right to know where my daughter is.'

'Then affirm it, Dad. It will manifest.'

'My daughter will manifest?'

'Yes,' said Sunny.

They reverted to silence. As the seconds dripped on, Chandra tried to remember if Sunny had ever had any spiritual inclinations as a child. Theirs had been a secular home, without puja or Diwali or even Christmas carols. When he was nine or ten Sunny had had an imaginary friend called Moonie (the converse of Sunny) who lived in the lampshade. Moonie hated cricket, economics and Indian food. Sometimes Sunny would bring Moonie to the dinner table, tucked into the top pocket of his shirt; he would whisper to him, usually while Chandra was talking. Once Moonie spilt ink all over Chandra's desk, which led Chandra to mime breaking Moonie's back with his fingers before handing his dead body to Sunny who buried him in the garden, crying all the while, before finding him 'reborn in the sink' the following morning.

This was the only religious experience Chandra could remember any of his children ever having. But it was possible that this had been Sunny's true calling all along, that he had never been interested in business or finance or money, that Chandra had ruined it all by making himself the centre of his son's world. Perhaps, then, Sunny's deviation in the direction of mysticism was inevitable; it was the one direction in which his father could not follow, an arena where there could only ever be one winner.

Observing his son, Chandra was struck once again by how middle-aged Sunny looked: the receding hair, the washed-out appearance in the eyes. It was a look Chandra knew only too well. It was to do with loneliness, the absence of the touch of a loving hand.

He remembered an incident from when Sunny was nineteen and at university. He had returned home for Christmas in his second year and the five of them had eaten lunch together wearing Santa hats. Chandra, somewhat drunk on sherry, had begun to mock LSE lecturers (which equated to mocking Sunny), describing one as 'five brain cells short of half-witted', and doing an unfortunate impersonation of him which led Sunny to say:

'So are you suggesting that Professor Martinez is a homosexual?'

'Oh, God, how should I know?' said Chandra, not wanting to speak of such a thing in front of the girls.

'Because if you are,' said Sunny, 'that's a very hurtful comment.'

'I wasn't,' said Chandra.

Jean, Chandra noticed, was looking at him very seriously.

'What the hell are you talking about, Sunny?' he said.

'I'm saying I'm gay,' said Sunny.

Chandra had stared at the turkey, its missing left shank, the pink ribbon Radha had tied around its neck. This was a trial, he concluded, an ordeal by fire and bird. But Professor Chandra was no stranger to challenges. He was accustomed to thinking fast under pressure, had digested more examinations than most people had Christmas dinners.

'That's wonderful, Sunny,' he said. 'I'm proud of you, of whatever you choose to do.'

'So you think,' said Sunny, 'that I chose this?'

Chandra had looked down at his plate for ten leaden seconds before his son, eldest daughter and wife collapsed into peals of laughter while Jasmine looked up in confusion.

As far as Chandra was concerned, the episode

had been a way of outing *him*, the family fool, the patriarch with less dignity than the partially disembowelled turkey on the table. Since then, however, Sunny's sexuality had remained a mystery. Though he was convinced the rest of the family knew everything, all Chandra knew was that Sunny had never brought a girlfriend home, or a boyfriend. There was the possibility that he was asexual, or 'self-sexual', terms Professor Chandra had discovered via Google, but how was *he* supposed to know?

As the silence in the steam room lengthened, Chandra noticed that Sunny shaved his chest as well as his legs. He made a note to Google this too, when he got the opportunity.

'All right, Dad,' said Sunny, sighing. 'Yes, I have doubts, and yes, I get lonely, and yes, I get sad, and no, I'm not perfect, but who are you to tell me I'm not happy?'

'I'm sorry for doing that,' said Chandra. 'I was tired. I wasn't thinking straight.'

'I'm trying,' said Sunny. 'I've built a good business.'

'You're doing splendidly,' said Chandra. 'You out-earn me by miles, it's true.'

'It isn't just about money,' said Sunny. 'I believe in what I do.'

'I believe in it too. I just hope you have enough friends and you don't keep it all inside. I get lonely sometimes, you see. That's why I'm saying it.'

They left the club an hour later, going back to the apartment where Chandra took a nap. When he awoke, Sunny was pedalling on the exercise bike in the living room. Chandra poured himself a small brandy from the bottle he'd bought at the duty free and had been planning to give to Maurice, the head porter, on his return.

'I've never seen your workplace,' he told Sunny.

'Maybe you will.'

'Or we could go to Macau. I've never been there.'

'Yes,' said Sunny. 'We could.'

'Maybe it will manifest,' said Chandra.

Sunny continued to pedal, his face unreadable.

'So what affirmations should I say, Sunny?'

'I've told you before, Dad. Affirm your deepest desires. Just make sure you say them every day.'

The phone rang. Sunny hopped off the bike in a single movement and answered in Cantonese, saying, '*Wai*,' and then, 'Oh, hi, Mum. Yeah, he is. He's just having a little drink. Okay, sure.'

Sunny passed the phone to Chandra.

'Hello, Jean,' said Chandra. '*Lei ho ma?*'

'Charles.'

The moment he heard her voice, he knew it was serious.

After putting the phone down, Chandra collapsed onto the sofa, his face in his hands. 'Dad,' Sunny kept saying, but it was minutes before Chandra was able to look up and explain. He kept thinking about those books that Sunny used to read in primary school called *Choose Your Own Adventure*. They contained passages like 'The dragon paces towards you with outstretched wings. *If you try to poke his eyes* out with your fingers, turn to page 86. If you turn around and run screaming, turn to page 92.' And then you turned the page and found out you were dead, or you poked the dragon's eyes and he dissolved and you realised he was a hologram. And on it would go.

This was life, it seemed. It didn't matter what decision you made because the consequences were determined by someone else whose imagination far outstripped yours. Who could have foreseen Aids or Ebola? Or that someone would fly a plane into the World Trade Center one fine Tuesday? And who could ever have predicted that Professor Chandra's youngest, sweetest, most loving daughter, who at the age of five used to fall asleep wearing 1930s-style aviator goggles in imitation of her heroine Amy Johnson, would ever do something like this?

Jasmine had been arrested while under the influence of something called crystal meth. She had been stealing money from her mother, and when this wasn't enough had broken into a burger joint at night with two companions and raided the cash register. Now she was facing charges of breaking and entering and petty larceny.

Crystal meth, Jean had said, was not the sort of drug girls like Jasmine usually took. It was a poor person's drug, but Jasmine had been keeping some unlikely company recently. 'I don't even know where she met them,' said Jean.

'So she's become a . . . ' Chandra replied, unable to say the words 'drug addict'.

'We think she has a problem,' said Jean. 'Yes.'

Sunny helped him to find a flight. It left after midnight, which meant he would just make it. He'd have to change in San Francisco. They took a taxi together to the aiport. To Chandra's relief, Sunny didn't tell him to say his affirmations; his comments were the usual platitudes: 'Don't worry,' and 'She'll be all right,' which, coming from Sunny's lips, were almost enough to bring Chandra to tears.

They hugged at the airport. 'Call me when you get there,' said Sunny. 'And take care of yourself, Dad.'

'Thanks, Sunny,' said Chandra, as Sunny gave him that finger-pistol gesture whose meaning Chandra still hadn't deciphered. 'I'm sorry I couldn't stay longer.'

'So am I.'

'You take care of yourself too. I worry about you, Sunny. I can't help it. I worry about you all.'

When he reached security, Chandra turned, expecting to see that Sunny had gone, or was talking on his iPhone, but instead his son was smiling and waving at him. Chandra tried to hold this image in his mind for as long as possible, but once on the plane his thoughts turned to Jasmine. As always, he couldn't help blaming himself, except this time he suspected he was right: this time it really was his fault.

12

Professor Chandra awoke on the ground in San Francisco. He was dehydrated, had eaten nothing for sixteen hours but airline coffee, peanuts, and a limp disinfected sandwich, and had not changed his clothes.

He fell asleep in the taxi to Boulder, arriving in the middle of the night with no one to greet him. He had to knock several times before Steve emerged, pulling a black polo neck over his head. Jean followed, wearing the Garfield slippers Chandra had bought her for Christmas in the mid-nineties. Her hair was longer now, though still blonde. They did not hug. She simply said, 'Jasmine's in bed. Her trial's on Tuesday.'

He tried to ask her about meths.

'Meth,' she corrected.

'You ever see *Breaking Bad*?' said Steve.

'Course he hasn't,' said Jean, putting the kettle on.

Her hands were still rough as old gardening gloves. He'd always liked this about Jean, her practicality.

'It's dangerous as hell,' said Jean. 'Can be addictive the first time you take it.'

'Good God.'

'Meth is addictive,' said Steve. 'But Jaz is no junkie. She just went off the rails.'

'What do you mean she went off the rails?' said Chandra. 'Why didn't you stop her?'

'We didn't know,' said Jean. 'She just got steadily worse, Charles. It was so . . . gradual.'

'Have you ever taken this drug, Steve?' asked Chandra, moving to the breakfast bar and sitting on a stool.

'Oh, no. It was mainly bikers who did it in my day. Today's kids are different. Drugs aren't exciting to them. They just want to get high, get out of it.'

'But Jasmine isn't an addict, is she?' said Chandra.

'We don't know,' said Jean. 'We think it's more a psychological thing. A protest maybe.'

'I want to see her,' said Chandra.

'You look like you could use a bath, Charles, and a drink.'

'No drink.'

He had thrown up somewhere over the Great Lakes, the result of instant coffee, anxiety and an empty stomach.

'*Charles?*'

He had fallen asleep again, his face on the kitchen counter. Steve took his arm, leading him into the hall. Chandra had never been this far inside the house. Steve was running him a bath, laying towels on the edge of the tub for Chandra's head.

'Don't lock it, okay?' said Steve.

The bathroom looked cavernous and filled with heavenly light. There were jasmine petals floating on the surface of the water, spirals of golden oil beneath. He got in, turning off the tap before lowering his head onto the towel.

It was the divorce. Surely it was the divorce. In

256

Chandra's experience, Westerners didn't like to admit that divorce was bad for children. But now he sounded like Prakash, who always claimed that Indians were not as individualistic as Westerners. But Chandra had read in the *Hindu* about something called a 'desi divorce' which was popular among the younger generation: the married couple would remain together only in name, sleeping in separate beds, often taking lovers, an arrangement known to everyone save their parents and children.

There was music coming from behind him, deeper inside the house. Janis Joplin. Jasmine had played this album every day when she'd visited him in Bella Vista. She'd told him Steve claimed to have seen the singer in concert in 1972, which was impossible seeing as she died in 1970. 'Try-hard prick,' she'd muttered, after which Janis Joplin became Professor Chandra's favourite singer. He listened to her in his rooms sometimes, when he missed his daughter,

He lifted himself out of the water and put on his pyjamas before padding barefoot and wet-haired down the corridor, following the music.

'Jasmine?' he said, standing in front of the door, his voice a croak. 'Jasmine? It's Daddy.'

He opened the door. Jasmine was lying on the bed wearing white flannel pyjamas. Her hair was longer than he remembered, almost to her waist. Chandra sat beside her on the bed, his hand flat against the hand-embroidered bedspread he had bought for her in Dhaka.

She was staring at the skylight. He tried to

think of something to say. 'So, drugs, eh?' didn't feel like a good opener.

'You're going to tell me you don't understand, aren't you?' she said.

Her room was so bare. There was a fern plant in one corner, a hard chair, and a torn poster on the wall showing the phases of the moon. She had been here for three years but there was so little trace of her in the room.

'What does it feel like,' he said, 'this meths?'

Jasmine sighed, then blew a strand of hair ceilingwards. It landed on her mouth and she chewed it before pulling it out.

'You really want to know?'

He nodded.

'It's like you're in it. You're just in it.'

He looked at her, wondering if she was saying unintelligible things on purpose.

'You're right in there, Dad. In life. You're not on the outside any more.'

He closed his eyes, wanting to understand.

'Can I try it?'

'No, Dad. You can't.'

'Why did you do it? The break-in?'

'It seemed like a good idea at the time. I never thought anyone would care. I just wanted to do something crazy.'

He put his hand on hers, resisting the urge to tell her how stupid she'd been.

'I'm scared, Dad, in case you're wondering. I could go to jail. I know I messed up.'

'It won't happen.'

'How do you know?'

'I won't let it.'

'What are you going to do? Smuggle me into Mexico?'

'We'll get good lawyers,' said Chandra. 'You're young. You're from a good family. You're sorry. It'll be okay.'

'I don't think sorry is a defence, Dad.'

'It is,' he said, raising his voice. 'Remorse. They take that into account.'

She turned away from him, facing the wall. He put his hand on her shoulder. She was trembling.

'Never mind what I said,' he said. 'Forget it. I will take care of everything. Just sleep.'

He lay on top the covers facing his daughter's back, her hair touching his face. After a few minutes her breathing deepened and Chandra stared at the square of black night he could see through the skylight. He had neglected Jasmine, the small one, the quiet one, the tiniest baby he had ever seen. He thought of that blue vase in the hospital, those little white petals. She looked tiny even now.

★   ★   ★

Chandra checked into a hotel the following morning, and from that moment on he was busy. He and Steve spent hours vetting lawyers, sifting through testimonials on Google. In the end they chose a woman recommended by one of Steve's customers who spoke in short, clipped sentences and smoked incessantly.

When the trial came, however, it was a cursory affair. Any lawyer would have done. The judge said everything Chandra hoped she would

— that Jasmine was young and foolish, that this was her first offence and that she had clearly been under strain, corrupted by poor influences. Jasmine stared back at her as if the whole procedure were too predictable for words. Chandra worried that the judge might take this as an affront, but she didn't seem to care. She sentenced Jasmine to two weeks of community service and a court-mandated rehabilitation programme, looking her in the eye and saying she was confident there would be no repeat offence.

They went out for hamburgers and milkshakes afterwards at a faux-1950s diner, as if treating a child after a visit to the dentist. Jean, for once, seemed flustered, spilling her Diet Coke all over the table and making comments like, 'Well, I must say I'm relieved it's over,' or, 'Community service sounds all right, doesn't it, Jaz?' to which nobody replied. Halfway through the meal Jean's mobile rang and she walked to the back of the restaurant to answer it before summoning Jasmine over. Radha. Chandra pushed his jalapeño burger away in protest.

When the bill arrived, Professor Chandra announced his decision to remain in Boulder for the following weeks. Jean told him it wasn't necessary, but this time Jasmine spoke up, saying, 'Why don't you stay at the house, Dad? There's room.'

'I'll be all right where I am,' said Chandra, feeling hungry again, though they had already taken his burger away.

Every morning from then on, Chandra drove

Jasmine to community service. She was capable of driving herself, but it was the only opportunity he had to be alone with her. She would give him a report of her day on the way back. Usually she'd been out in national parkland, picking up litter, painting signs, putting up fences.

'It's not so bad,' she always said. 'Everyone's pretty cool. Seriously, Dad, it's not what you think. I've met some really nice people.'

'Yes, yes, of course,' he said, imagining a flock of amiable psychopaths.

'They are. You should hear some of their stories.'

He did, all about women who couldn't afford healthcare for their children, or had abusive husbands they couldn't leave for financial reasons, or who had lost their jobs or homes or savings in the recession. He tried not to feel guilty about the last part — that was his critical voices talking.

In any case, Chandra was far more concerned about the rehabilitation centre where Jasmine would spend three months in the company of 'other addicts'. Steve said the good centres were more like spas, with arts and craft and music alongside various types of therapy, but Chandra worried nonetheless. The more skiers, the slippier the slope, was his belief. The idea that Jasmine could be 'cured' by talking about drugs for hours every day was highly suspect. There was every chance she would leave able to synthesise her own cocaine in the greenhouse while Steve watered his LSD plants in the nude, his liberalism dangling for all to see.

Chandra was in the hotel's sauna, wrapped in a towel, when the solution came to him. He returned to his room at once and found his wallet where he had kept her number.

'Dolores,' he said. 'This is Chandra. We met at — '

'Well, well, well, the Professor of Esalen! How are you? Breathing the joy?'

'Not really.'

'Well, that's all right too, isn't it?'

'Yes, I suppose it is,' he said, slipping back into cuckoo talk against his will.

'So how are you?' said Dolores. '*Where* are you?'

'I'm in Boulder.'

'Boulder! That's wonderful! Come see us. You must.'

'Well, that's the thing,' he said. 'We've had an emergency.'

To his relief, Dolores did not say a word until he had finished.

'Wow,' she said at last. 'Sounds like you've been through the wringer.'

'It's not her fault,' said Chandra. 'But — '

'Oh, of course not. But I mean, it sounds like y'all are struggling. How's the mommy doing?'

'She's okay. She's worried about a relapse. We all are. She thinks rehab might even make things worse.'

'And is this what you think?' said Dolores.

'I suppose it is,' said Chandra. 'And then I remembered what you told me about your place and I thought I'd ask.'

'I see,' said Dolores. 'So, if I understand you correctly, you're wondering if Jasmine could come serve her court mandate with us.'

'Would that be possible?'

'Well, does she want this too? Have you raised it with her?'

'Not yet,' he said. 'I wanted to check with you first.'

'Theoretically it could work. I mean, we don't have anyone else in those circumstances at present, so there's what you might call a vacancy. But it's not so simple. First, the mommy has to agree, and then you've got to get the court to give the all-clear. And then we've got to agree, which means we've got to meet the girl. Now, I know she's the apple of your eye, but if Saul or I get the sense the kid's likely to use again when she comes to us, then it's got to be a big old no.'

'I understand.'

'So she lives in Colorado?'

'Yes.'

'And the misdemeanour was in Colorado?'

'Yes, Boulder.'

'Well, that helps,' said Dolores. 'But don't forget it isn't easy living in a monastery. It's practically a prison. Up at four, rain, shine or snow, and we get plenty of all three. Every day will be a struggle. And it won't work unless she wants to meditate. If she thinks it's all baloney . . . '

'Jasmine doesn't believe in anything,' he said, feeling depression heading his way.

'Well, that sounds about perfect.'

'It does?'

'You heard of 'beginner's mind'?'

He shook his head, forgetting she couldn't see him.

'It means a lack of preconceptions. It's a good thing.'

'Oh, I see.'

'I'm just giving you the bad news first, honey. This could all work out. Let's *try* to make it work, okay?'

'Okay,' said Chandra.

⋆ ⋆ ⋆

Professor Chandra called the house, telling Steve he was coming over. While driving, Chandra tried to rehearse what he might say, but however he phrased it, it sounded ridiculous on his lips. He had printed out some information about the monastery in the hope that this might make him look more like a respected academic and less like a crackpot He could imagine Jean saying something like 'Honestly, Charles, do you even have the slightest idea what you're talking about?'

He couldn't think of a response apart from 'I've got a feeling this will work out,' which was only two steps away from 'The universe has already said yes.'

Jean was out when Chandra arrived, so he waited for her in the kitchen with Steve. He and Steve did not hug or shake hands. It was different without an audience; the faux-warmth between them had disappeared.

He opened his briefcase, prepared to martial his argument.

When Jean arrived she was carrying her yoga mat and was dressed in sweatpants instead of those awful leggings that students seemed to think appropriate for tutorials nowadays.

Chandra executed a nervous namaste, a throwback to the nineties when he used to laugh at her pronunciation of Marjaryasana and Patanjali (he regretted all of this now).

'So you're still studying yoga?' he said.

'I'm a yoga *teacher*, Charles. Didn't you know that?'

'Oh,' said Chandra. 'That's wonderful.'

'Actually,' said Steve, 'Jean has her own studio now. We decided it was a good investment.'

'Everyone does yoga in Boulder,' said Jean.

'Of course, it's not one hundred per cent authentic,' said Steve, switching to that faux-familiar tone now that Jean was present. 'But it's quite a revolution, when one thinks about it. Extraordinary that such an ancient practice could become as American as apple pie.'

'Well, I'm not American,' said Jean. 'All I'm about is posture and core strength. We keep our third eyes closed in my class.'

'But it's still an awareness practice, isn't it, honey?' said Steve.

'You become more aware of your body,' said Jean, 'yes, but there's nothing cosmic about that.'

'Jean's wiser than we give her credit for,' said Steve.

'Thank you,' said Jean, who looked tired. 'Anyway, what have you got there, Charles?'

Chandra had already opened his briefcase, rehearsing his arguments in his head. He handed her the printouts. 'I had an idea about Jasmine,' he said. 'I met a woman at Esalen, you see, in the hot tubs.' He was probably blushing now. 'I mean, she's a nun. She lives in the mountains, and she said Jasmine could serve her rehabilitation at their monastery, feasibly. They've done it before. The courts allow it. It's very good for young people who've had problems with drugs. Very calming.'

Chandra had no idea what Jean's opinion on monks was. She was staring at the printouts and frowning.

'It doesn't say anything about rehab on here,' she said.

'It's not an official thing,' said Chandra. 'It's just something they do occasionally. I thought it'd be better than leaving her in the company of addicts.'

'I think so too,' said Steve.

'This place is in the middle of nowhere,' said Jean.

'Exactly,' said Steve.

'Have you ever even been there, Charles?'

He shook his head. Jean sighed.

'Honestly, honey, I think it's a wonderful idea,' said Steve, but then his mobile began ringing and he took himself outside, talking rapidly about order numbers and bouquets.

Jean sat opposite Chandra at the bar. She was still looking at the printout, but he sensed she wasn't taking anything in.

'I don't know, Charles. Do you really want her so far away from us?'

'It isn't so far. A few hours' drive.'

Jean shook her head. 'Jasmine won't like the idea.'

'What *does* Jasmine like?'

Jean nodded.

'Sunny wasn't like this,' said Chandra, 'or Radha.'

'They take after you, Charles,' said Jean.

'Perhaps.'

'Charles, when did you ever hear me say I liked anything?'

Chandra stared at her in confusion.

'I didn't like chemistry. I just did it. I thought it was boring. I didn't like ballroom dancing. I just did that too; I can't even remember why. I didn't like ice cream; I just said I did because everyone likes ice cream. I didn't know what kind of music I liked, not really. Politics . . . I don't know. Maybe I had opinions, but I never *liked* it.

'I was exactly like Jaz, Charles, just drifting my way through life. Jennifer was the confident one. Me, I just faked it, way more than you realise. I always felt like everyone else had an identity and I was only . . . tagging along. I was nearly fifty when I realised yoga was what I wanted to do. *Fifty*. God, you didn't even know, did you?'

Chandra shook his head.

'Christ,' said Jean, 'if there'd been meth in my day I might have taken it myself. Well, there was, I suppose, but drugs just weren't a part of my world. *Nothing* was.'

He'd been a part of her world. He wondered if she'd liked him, or if she'd been faking that too. Perhaps he had been nothing more than a raft

267

for her to hold on to.

'I wish I'd spent more time with Jasmine,' he said. 'I could have helped her find out what she liked.'

'She doesn't like economics, Charles.'

He looked up, met Jean's eye.

'I'm sorry,' she said. 'I'm on edge. I know you are too.'

'I just mean if I'd spent more time with her she might have felt more appreciated,' he said. 'Less invisible.'

Jean had said she felt invisible once, he remembered. It was during a counselling session. He hadn't understood what it meant at the time.

'Maybe she wanted to be invisible, Charles. Maybe she wanted to hide.'

Chandra shook his head.

'She's hardly seen me all these years. I was so obsessed with myself, my work.'

'It's not your fault, Charles. Or if it is, it's *our* fault. Nobody's blaming you.'

'I'm blaming me.'

'Well, that won't help Jaz much, will it?'

Jean looked at the papers in her lap once more.

'Look, Charles,' she said. 'Go and see this place. Just the two of you. And *talk* to her. Try. If she likes it, if she actually says she wants to go, then we can give it a shot. I mean, if the place looks all right to you.'

'You don't want to come?' said Chandra.

Jean shook her head. 'Maybe you're right, Charles. Maybe she does need to spend more time with you. She doesn't listen to me any

268

more. I don't think she even likes me much.'

'I don't know if she likes me much either.'

'Well, let's just see, said Jean, putting the printouts on the counter.

⋆   ⋆   ⋆

They drove up that Saturday, heading for the town of Cove, eight thousand feet high in the Sangre de Cristo Mountains. Chandra read out the entry on Wikipedia to Jasmine while they ate their sandwiches at a rest stop.

The land, thousands of acres of it, was owned by a billionaire called Maurice Powers. He'd bought it 'because of the energy there', which he claimed was more powerful than anywhere else in the Americas, and had extended an invitation to any spiritual organisation to come and build on it. Cove now boasted nine Tibetan Buddhist monasteries; two Theravada centres (one Thai, one Burmese); a Hindu ashram; a Catholic monastery; a Temple of Consciousness institute; a Sivananda ashram; an Episcopal mission; a Shumei institute; an Academy of On; and the Cove Zen Centre, run by Dolores and Saul Blum.

'Sounds like Epcot for loonies,' said Jasmine.

Chandra grunted, unwilling to say anything negative, though he quite agreed.

'You don't have to go there, Jasmine,' he said, giving her what he hoped was a reassuring smile. 'Just see what you think of it. Don't worry.'

'I'm not.'

When he'd tried to sell the idea to Jasmine,

he'd argued that people would be gentler there, that it would be a less punitive environment than a rehab centre. She would be a free member of a community instead of an inmate. This had been working until she saw the schedule.

'They hit you with sticks in Zen,' said Jasmine.

'Not here,' said Chandra. 'I don't think so.'

He showed her a picture of Dolores, which seemed to help, that broad smile, her lips upturned as if to say, 'Me, a Zen nun? Well, if you say so.'

'You don't have to do anything you don't want to do, Jasmine.'

'Yes, I do. It's this or rehab.'

'Yes, I'm afraid that's true.'

'Well,' said Jasmine, 'I guess I shouldn't have fucked up then.'

They drove for two more hours until the elevation increased and they felt the air become colder and thinner. The mountains were visible, blocking the horizon, and there were no other cars in sight, only wilderness ahead, a road to nowhere.

They passed a marijuana dispensary, legal in Colorado, and Professor Chandra pretended not to notice when Jasmine's head swivelled. He tried to focus on those operatic, full-bosomed peaks; if Jasmine lived here she would see them every day. He wondered what this would do to her. It could drive a person mad, being so far from civilisation. You might start talking to the snow and the sky.

By the time they reached the foothills the road was in shadow, the mountains blotting out the horizon. His headlights on high, Chandra turned onto the narrow road that led to the centre. It soon became a dirt track, clogged with river water and stones.

To their right they could see the entire valley, the corn stalks and aspen leaves and grasslands drained of colour in that artificial twilight brought on by the mountains. To their left it was all forest land, inclining upward. They passed a Catholic hermitage, the sign instructing visitors to keep silent until they reached reception. Further ahead they saw a statue of Ganesha, so incongruous in this place that Chandra laughed until he saw Jasmine's face. She looked scared now, staring at the directions in her lap, though they didn't need directions any more.

'It's beautiful here,' he said, in that same voice he'd used to tell her that having her ears pierced wouldn't hurt a bit.

'We're miles from anywhere,' said Jasmine.

'Yes,' he said. 'How does it feel?'

'All right, I suppose. It's quiet.'

The monastery was on their left, a swing board with the words COVE MOUNTAIN ZEN RETREAT (CLOSED) painted on it in white. Professor Chandra turned onto the gravelled track that led up the slope.

He remembered how Jasmine had told him she would have loved to go to summer camp, how she had missed all that by being born in England. But the truth was that Jasmine had never been an extrovert. She liked to spend a lot of time in her room. Other people exhausted her. She rarely said a word in group settings. But

271

now, if all went according to plan, she would be moving into a commune where she would be forced to live with others all day long.

They left the car in the parking lot and walked the rest of the way up the slope, heading for the building in front of them, a black wooden bungalow with a single oblong window, like a giant iPhone. There was a sign welcoming visitors to the monastery, advising them that intoxicants were prohibited on the premises.

Chandra slipped off his shoes and opened the door. The first thing he saw was a huge painting from floor to ceiling of a Japanese god with murderous red eyes and a scimitar in his hand, like an anarchist at a WTO summit. To their left was a trestle table that could have seated twenty. A shaven-headed man was sitting in front of a laptop. He wore a checked shirt and, apparent when he stood up, shorts, which surprised Chandra.

'Chandra, right?' said the man. 'And you must be the lovely Jasmine.'

'Pleased to meet you,' said Chandra.

The man laughed which, in Professor Chandra's experience, was what spiritual types did when they didn't know what to say.

'I'm Saul, Dolores's husband.'

'Ah, yes,' said Chandra, with only the faintest tinge of jealousy.

'And our oldest resident, which is why I'm not at zazen with the others.'

'Well,' said Chandra, 'it looks like I'm the oldest now.'

'Oh, really? So you're eighty-one?' said Saul,

272

grinning. 'It's okay. I know I don't look my age. It's the mountain air, I guess, and lots of miso soup. Look at the Japanese. They always look ten years younger. So how was the drive down?'

'Oh, very nice. Beautiful countryside here.'

'And how about you, Jasmine?' said Saul. 'Did you like what you saw?'

'It was all right,' said Jasmine.

This was her stock answer to all questions nowadays, which he supposed was a Generation X thing, or was it Y? (It worried him that they were reaching the end of the alphabet.) You have to care, he wanted to tell her. If you don't care about anything, you aren't — what was her expression? — 'in it'.

'Want to see the zendō?' said Saul. 'Maybe sit for a few minutes, see how you like it?'

'Sure,' said Chandra before Jasmine could answer. 'We'd love that.'

'Wonderful.'

Saul led them out, following a brick pathway lit by solar lamps. The sky looked much bigger here, vaguely threatening as if a giant spacecraft was waiting in the wings, preparing its attack, the darkness absolute save for two or three budding stars.

'You'll be able to see the peaks in the morning,' said Saul. 'They're magnificent. Just wait.'

Jasmine was trailing behind, staring at the monastery and its buildings,

'So,' said Saul, 'this is our zendō.'

In front of them was a raised wooden building with a covered veranda running around its outside. It was set apart from the rest of the site, surrounded by bare earth. Like the main building, everything was black and right-angled.

'There's a lot of ritual to follow,' said Saul, 'but I don't want to overwhelm you. They're sitting zazen now. You know zazen?'

'I don't think Jasmine does.'

'It's very simple. You just sit. Got that?'

'Try to count your breaths,' said Chandra, remembering what Dolores had told him.

Jasmine scowled while Saul walked up the zendō's steps, handing them slippers from a wooden cupboard. He pulled the screen door aside. The only light came from the candles on the altar where there was a golden statue of the Buddha. The room was colder than Chandra had expected, full of silent, brown-robed monks.

Saul bowed, took two steps left, turned and bowed again. Chandra did the same, feeling ridiculous. He didn't look at Jasmine, but suspected she had her hands in her pockets. He hoped she wasn't looking at her phone.

Around the zendō's perimeter was a raised wooden bench with black cushions placed at intervals. Saul pointed to the two nearest the entrance and said, 'These are yours.'

Chandra slipped off his shoes and sat facing the wall like the others. He waited until Jasmine was sitting beside him before closing his eyes.

They meditated for twenty minutes or so, but Chandra kept falling asleep. He'd think he was awake until he realised he was doing something unlikely, like talking to a tiger, and would open his eyes, trying to blink sleep away. After a while he decided it didn't matter any more. He'd had a long drive. Why shouldn't he sleep?

When the gong sounded, Jasmine touched his shoulder. She had turned around and was putting her slippers on. Chandra followed her outside, stopping to bow in various directions, copying Jasmine who was copying the monk ahead of them. There was something intimate about engaging in all this rigmarole with his daughter. He supposed she wasn't used to seeing him so helpless. But that wasn't true. He was helpless in most places save for universities. No, it was the sudden, categorical equivalence between the two of them. Sitting on that cushion they were just two confused people trying to still the madness for a while.

Dolores was waiting for them outside. She was wearing the same brown robe as everyone else, though her head wasn't shaved. In fact, she looked exactly as he remembered her, warm and fulsome, though somewhat incongruous in this place.

'Professor,' she said, hugging him. 'So glad you made it. And here she is! Here's the famous Jasmine!'

Dolores put out her arms and, to Chandra's surprise, Jasmine tumbled into them.

'So how'd you find zazen, honey?'

Jasmine shrugged. 'It was all right.'

Chandra noticed that a couple of the younger monks were listening with interest.

'How was the space in your mind?'

'It was all right,' said Jasmine. 'Yeah.'

'I think you can do better than 'all right',' said

275

Dolores. 'How did it feel?'

Chandra wanted to say something, like 'Try,' or 'Answer the question,' but he counted his breaths instead, getting to two.

'It was big,' said Jasmine.

'Ah,' said Saul, and Chandra wanted to say, 'Bisto,' but refrained.

'Expansive?' said Dolores.

Jasmine nodded. 'Yeah.'

'Vast,' said Chandra.

'That's wonderful, honey,' said Dolores, and hugged her again.

They had missed dinner, but Dolores gave them some soup in the kitchen after which she sat at the table and explained the schedule for the following day.

'Zazen is at five, but you'll likely be exhausted from your drive and the altitude takes its toll, so sleep if you like. Just try to come for breakfast at seven thirty. After that someone will show you around the monastery and then Jasmine and Saul can have a little chat in the tea room.'

Professor Chandra wanted to talk to Dolores on his own, but after dinner she left to go to her home outside the monastery's grounds. 'Means we can have wine,' she told him, with a wink. In any case, he doubted he could stay awake much longer. Dolores had been right about the air.

Saul took him to his room, and led Jasmine away to the 'women's dormitory', perhaps to ready her for the experience of life without privacy. Chandra wished they were together. He wanted to interrogate her about this business of 'expansiveness'. It sounded like drug talk to his ears.

Professor Chandra hadn't thought to bring a book, so he went straight to sleep and for the first time in months, perhaps years, slept all the way through the night without interruption. It was eight o'clock when he awoke, which meant he was late.

Chandra rushed to the main building where he found Jasmine already at the breakfast table, sitting with Saul and Dolores while the monks cleared the plates away.

'Jasmine was up for zazen,' announced Dolores.

'Seems she likes it,' said Saul.

Chandra poured himself some coffee and tried to make eye contact with his daughter.

'You okay, honey?' asked Dolores.

'Never better,' said Chandra.

'You should know we've come to a decision,' said Saul. 'As of this morning, we have invited Jasmine to join us.'

Jasmine returned his gaze in that neutral way he had come to expect, revealing nothing. He looked back at her, wondering if he had lost her for ever.

'That's wonderful,' he said.

13

Professor Chandra returned to Cambridge late in August to prepare for the Michaelmas term. He called Dolores every week to check up on Jasmine. The report was always the same; that she'd been up every morning for zazen, that she was 'a natural'. Saul was convinced that she'd done it before, that this was the case with most who took to meditation so easily, but Chandra was allergic to talk of past lives. He was simply happy his daughter had found something she liked and, most of all, that she was out of harm's way.

When Dolores asked him if he was glad to be home, Professor Chandra told her the truth: after being around his children for so long, he was finding it hard to live in that empty house by himself. 'Then don't be alone,' said Dolores. 'It's not rocket science.'

It was something Jean had suggested several times, which was probably why he'd never done it, but the following week Chandra called Ram Singh and told him that if he was still looking for new accommodation, he and his fiancée Betina Moreira could rent the top floor of the house for a hundred pounds a month.

Since Betina's move to England, they had been living in Ram's bachelor pad with three other Indians, whisky-guzzlers who filled their living room with games consoles and made a

278

single communal meal each day in the pressure cooker. Betina was grateful for the escape, and Ram proved himself an excellent lodger: discreet, respectful, and not in the habit of talking economics, largely because he knew so little about it. Betina was more affectionate; she would massage Chandra's shoulders, make him smoothies from spirulina and goji berries and, worst of all, attempt to talk to him about his feelings, clasping his hands in hers and looking into his eyes before asking, 'How is your heart?'

Most of the time, however, Chandra enjoyed their company. Even when he was grumpy and told them he wished he was on his own they would only laugh and Betina would make him a cup of hot chocolate, with some gummy bears in a silver thali bowl on the side.

In October, Chandra failed to win the Nobel Prize once more, losing out to a man known for his attacks on the Chicago School, to which Chandra de facto belonged. The winner described his contribution to the discipline as based on 'the recognition that economic agents are human'. 'I intend to spend my prize money as irrationally as possible,' he said. To Chandra's surprise, he felt no rancour at all when he read this in *The Times*. He even felt happy for the man.

In November, Betina presented him with a framed quotation by the biologist George Wald, who had won the Nobel fifty years ago. It read:

What one really needs is not Nobel laureates but love. How do you think one gets to be a

Nobel laureate? Wanting love, that's how. Wanting it so bad that one works all the time and ends up a Nobel laureate. It's a consolation prize. What matters is love.

'What the hell do you want me to do with this?' said Chandra, who had come to a similar conclusion himself but would sooner be damned than tell Ms Moreira this.

'You keep it on your wall, Chandu,' said Betina. 'Just keep looking at it, so it seeps in.'

'I don't want it to 'seep in',' said Chandra, 'or anything else.'

'I used to be sceptical too, sir,' said Ram. 'But I've found such things can be very effective.'

'Will you shut up, both of you?' said Chandra, who was sitting at the kitchen table trying to read an email from the Master, informing him that Caius was having a 'college silver' weekend:

We will be making use of some of the rarely used but eminently valuable silverware owned by the College. Amongst them will be our collection of 'silver marrow spoons'. We are aware that bone marrow will not be to everyone's taste or dietary inclination. Should you not wish to partake, please indicate 'No bone marrow' on the form below. Simultaneously, do bear in mind the College has only 14 silver bone marrow spoons, and that these will be allocated on a first-come-first-served basis.

Professor Chandra did not know what his position on bone marrow was and deleted the email without filling in the form. He had a dozen more messages to read, but Ram and Betina were still hovering in the kitchen, which was never a good sign.

'So . . . we've been thinking about your birthday,' said Betina. 'We thought we could host a small gathering here. Just a few close friends. Intimate. Romantic.' She did a little waltz around the kitchen. 'A fun, lovely evening.'

'I don't want a party,' said Chandra. 'I don't want to do anything.'

'But it's your seventieth, Chandu.'

'It's true, sir,' said Ram. 'How many seventieth birthdays does a person have?'

'Well, in any case,' said Chandra, who had prepared a lie for exactly this eventuality, 'I've just been on the phone to my daughter and she wants to take me out in London, something about a West End show and dinner.'

'Why don't you bring her here?' said Betina. 'That would be so much nicer, wouldn't it?'

'Yes,' said Chandra, who hadn't thought of that. 'Yes, it would. But she's only in the UK for one night. Transit to the US. There wouldn't be time.'

He could see Betina working out the logistics. This was the problem with finance graduates. They were sharp in all the wrong places.

'Your daughter . . . ' said Ram, also thinking, only more slowly. 'You don't mean the one you haven't seen in all this time?'

He'd told Ram about it once, after a bottle of wine.

'Oh,' said Betina. 'But that's wonderful!'

'I don't want to talk about it,' said Chandra, and went upstairs to his study, the one place he could be certain Ram and Betina would not enter.

★ ★ ★

Jasmine had sent an email, which meant she was awake, though it was three thirty in the morning in Colorado.

To:prchandra101@cam.ac.uk
From:jazzzz@gmail.com

Subject: Xmas

Hey Dad,

Just saw your mail. Everything's fine. Don't worry if you can't get me on the phone. There's not much reception up here and I can hardly keep it on during zazen, can I? As for you, I take your point, but the whole reason behind having a mobile is . . . it's mobile. If you leave it in a drawer or only turn it on when you want to make a call, it sort of defeats the purpose, doesn't it?

Thanks for the pictures. I do miss home, yeah, but it's hard to miss anywhere when you're here. You spend so much time inside your head that it's like you're in every place at once. You live in your memories a lot.

It's getting cold now. The snow hasn't hit yet, but it will. Not looking forward to kinhin when it does, and at five in the morning! I'm pretty sure I saw a mountain lion last week. Don't freak out. It was miles away, and they only attack if they mix you up with a deer or something, and that only happens when you're jogging.

I saw a couple of hunters yesterday too with bows and guns, God knows why they need both. They were going after bears, they said. Saul says he respects them seeing as they kill all their own meat and don't bother with the industrial agricultural system blah blah blah. I guess he has a point, but he says a lot of stuff just to be controversial, like you wouldn't expect a roshi to say he respects hunters so he's got to go ahead and say it. He is a genuinely weird guy, even Dolly says so. He just does his own thing, has a PhD in maths, and he told me the other day he used to be a professional juggler.

Saul also says George Soros thinks there's going to be another crash, or depression, or recession, or whatever it is. Is this true?

Christmas could work, yeah. Dolly says it's okay. You could have your own rooms at reduced cost. The thing is that Mum wanted me to come to Boulder but I don't think I'm even allowed, so I was thinking, if it wouldn't be too weird for you, maybe you could all come up to Cove. We could ask Sunny too. I know he said he wanted to visit. It's just an idea, but it could be fun, all of us

283

having Christmas together. Don't you think it could be fun? Or maybe it's silly. I don't know.

Miss you loads, Dad.

A big hug. Be good! Be healthy! Be happy!

Jaz xoxoxo

This 'Be happy!' Hari Rama spiel was new, the result of his daughter's recent conversion, but at least she was communicating. She seemed to have forgotten that this was all his doing, that she had barely known what Zen was prior to his intervention.

Chandra had been unable to convince his lodgers (or dislodgers, as he thought of them) that he didn't give a damn about turning seventy, but it was true. What he did care about was Christmas.

His born-again daughter was right. It would not do for her to go back to Boulder, even if she were allowed. There were too many temptations there, too many drug fiends and hoodlums. But Jasmine's idea of a family congregation in Cove was interesting. He doubted Jean would be enthusiastic, though Steve would probably love the idea of spending Christmas in a Zen monastery.

Chandra considered emailing the two of them together, but couldn't bring himself to do it. He wrote to Jean instead, telling her about Jasmine's idea. 'Of course Steve must come,' he said, somewhat high-handedly, as this was hardly up to him. 'Give me an all-clear and I'll write to Sunny. It could be good for Jasmine, to host us in her 'own place'.'

He turned to his upcoming lecture, making some final notes on 'the Economics of India's Southern States', trying to think of a good economist joke to open with, preferably one he hadn't told before. He used to use the one about the woman whose doctor tells her she has six months to live and advises her to marry an economist and move to Kansas. 'Why?' says the woman. 'Will this cure my illness?' 'No,' says the doctor, 'but those six months will feel like a lifetime.' But after his divorce and his heart attack, Chandra had been on the lookout for something less depression-inducing.

Chandra Googled on until lunchtime, reading joke after joke but finding little to his taste. Too many were replete with genuine hatred, which was hardly appropriate, while the rest were simply unfunny, probably written by economists. At one thirty, he saw he had a new email from Jean, who must have just woken up.

To:prchandra101@cam.ac.uk
From:jeanjeanie@aol.com

Subject: Xmas

Hullo Charles,

I'll have to check with Steve but I don't think it's a bad idea. You're right. It would definitely be good for her. I'll email Sunny if you like, but you're the one he listens to. Try to put your foot down. He'll do it if you don't plead with him, and I know you know what I mean.

I've finally given up coffee, which has, you'll be glad to know, made me a lot calmer. Steve and I drink matcha in the mornings instead. You make it from powder and whip it with a shaving brush, well, something that looks like a shaving brush. It tastes weird but it's good for you.

Look after yourself,

Jean

Delighted, Professor Chandra wrote back to Jasmine at once.

To:jazzzz@gmail.com
From:prchandra101@cam.ac.uk

Subject: Xmas

Dear Jasmine,

Well, it's all settled. I'm coming, so is your mother, and we'll stay until Christmas is over. We're so looking forward to it, all of us. I'm still working on Sunny, but if you could drop him a line that would probably help. Try to butter him up a little. I guess you know what I mean.

Seventy on Thurs. Getting old. Been riding the damn exercise bike in the bedroom. Read

Twilight. Boring, I thought. Vegetarian vampires is a stupid idea. Going to try Hunger Games on your recommendation. This is the good thing about getting old. Read what the hell I like. No guilt any more. Done my bit.

Look after yourself. Keep meditating. Stay away from bears, lions, and anything else that looks like it might eat you. Can't wait for my holiday. Becoming a sentimental fool in my old age but you fellows are the only things that make me happy nowadays.

Love, Dad

P.S. You ever drink something called matcha? All the rage, I am told.

Professor Chandra began composing his email to Sunny. He could hear Betina making lunch in the kitchen, singing to herself in Portuguese. She and Ram were talking about getting married the following summer. He was happy for them. Ram Singh, he knew, had no delusions of grandeur. He just wanted to get by, finish his PhD, find a high-paying job within an unscrupulous institution, raise a family and get old and die with a minimum of terror or fuss. It was, Chandra was beginning to believe, a laudable non-ambition.

To:sunnysideofthestreet@imb.co.hk
From:prchandra101@cam.ac.uk

Subject: Jasmine

Dear Sunny,

Good of you to call the other week. Seems like you're doing a roaring trade out there. The world needs positivity these days and you're much in demand. Proud of your successes and ideas as always. I've been saying my affirmations. Not sure if I'm getting it right. Trying to remind myself of my good qualities and so on. Also trying to do it for the economy, FTSE and so forth. All our stock needs to rise, n'est-ce pas?

Was talking with Jaz. She's doing okay out there. Talked to the head honcho too. Guy by the name of Saul. Nice chap. Bit pompous. Says Jasmine's coming along well, settling in, calming down. No drugs of course, which is the most important thing, but she's also found something she likes. Bit of meditation does everyone some good, doesn't it?

I do think she could use her family from time to time, that's the only thing that's missing. Been out there on her own for too long. Thing is, Jaz wants us all to come for Christmas and she particularly wants to see you, big brother and all that, in the non-Orwellian sense of course. Looks to you for guidance as you know and, well, she's hoping you might come, be proud of what she's doing and whatnot. It's her new life and she wants to show it to you.

Plan is that all of us, your mother, me, you and S, land up in Colorado on 23 Dec and stay a few days together. The monks have heard so much about you, expert on the mind etc., and I think they'd even like you to give a small talk, if this is of interest to you.

With all love and best wishes,

Dad

P.S. Saw your Chopra fellow on the YouTube the other day. Very strange chap. Not sure I understand what he means by 'quantum' in this context, but each to their own. More anon.

He hoped this would do the trick.

★   ★   ★

On the morning of his birthday, Professor Chandra allowed Betina and Ram Singh to serve him a breakfast of scrambled eggs, salmon and champagne in bed, where he stayed until lunchtime. He didn't answer his phone except for when Jasmine called, and took out his iPad only once. There were messages all over Facebook and several emails 'congratulating' him, which he found irritating. It was hardly an achievement to reach seventy: all one did was try not to die. A great many emails were from younger colleagues and old PhD students he hadn't heard from in years, all angling for something, a fellowship or a reference.

In the afternoon he went into college.

Maurice, the head porter, presented him with a card which read:

Esteemed, Sir,
We look forward to seeing your face for many more years to come, smiling out at us from the Gate of Humility. With kindest regards, the Lodge Staff

He opened the rest of his mail in his rooms. The handwritten notes touched him more than any of the digital messages. Some were obviously insincere, like those from his old colleagues in Chicago, his rivals in India (the Bengali included), and his brother, though Prakash's note contained no mention of imperialism or Monsanto and was written in his wife's handwriting. Saul and Dolores had sent him a blue silk scarf and Jasmine had gifted him the remaining books from the *Twilight* series. As was her habit, she had written him a poem too:
Nobel Sir, it began, which made him wince:

So you're seventy today, whoever would
　have thought it?
Don't worry about a thing, everything's as
　it ought
To be, it's a question of karma
Ask Dolores who sends a kiss, you old
　charmer
I can't wait to see you and give you one
　too
We're so far away these days and I miss
　you

290

It's getting cold now, the zendō has icicles
So look after yourself, Dad, and stay away
    from bicycles.

Professor Chandra printed the poem, with the words 'Nobel Sir' cut out, and pinned it to his wall. He switched on his computer and skimmed through more birthday wishes, including ones from his insurance company, bank, travel agent and, to his relief, Sunny.

To:prchandra101@cam.ac.uk
From:sunnysideofthestreet@imb.co.hk

Subject: Happy birthday!!!

Hi Dad,

Sorry not to call. The time difference, and I've been in this bloody thing all day, conference on neuro-programming or something, which is boring the hell out of me. But what can I do? I said I'd be the keynote and I can hardly walk out before everyone else has had their turn, can I?

So, seventy years old. Many congratulations and happy returns. I hope you're enjoying yourself, wherever you are.

Apologies too for not replying earlier about Cove. I had to sort out my schedule, but I'd love to come to Colorado for Xmas and, with a little bit of juggling, I'm pretty sure I can make it. Like you say, it would be good for Jaz and, to be honest, I

291

think it'd be good for me too. Been feeling the strain lately. Not sure why. Feels like I woke up and twenty years had gone by and I'm thinking, how did I get here? And, what do I do now? Mid-life crisis maybe, I don't know. Or maybe I just don't want to be in Hong Kong any more, miles away from anyone. Got to think about these things, I suppose.

Anyway, cheerio, old man, and see you soon(ish). Try to say those affirmations before you go to bed. 'I am young.' 'I am healthy.' 'I am happy.' 'I am a masterpiece.' It'll do you good and much more in the long run. Sometimes I forget to say mine. Ridiculous, I know, but, well . . .

Okay, dear Professor, got to go. Happy birthday again!!!

Love,

Sunil

This was unprecedented from Sunny, an admission that he was confused and unhappy and had no idea what he was doing in life. But at least he was coming. That was the most important thing, in the short term.

Professor Chandra sent a quick reply, telling Sunny he was delighted and couldn't wait to see him at Christmas, and then ran a brush through his hair before setting off down the staircase. He had drinks with the Master at four in honour of his birthday.

It was getting dark as he crossed Tree Court, entering the Master's Lodge into which he hadn't set foot since the day of his accident. The Master was waiting for him in front of the fireplace, an open bottle of champagne and two glasses beside him.

'Welcome, Chandra,' said the Master, standing. 'And a very happy birthday.'

'Thank you so much, Master,' said Chandra.

'So, seventy!'

'That's right.'

'Well, you know what George Eliot said — that the years between fifty and seventy are when you're always being asked to do things but aren't decrepit enough to turn them down.'

Chandra laughed, clenching his fist inside his blazer pocket.

'Haven't seen much of you since you left for the States though,' said the Master. 'You're working on a new book, aren't you?'

'I put it on hold,' said Chandra.

'For health reasons?'

'Actually, no,' said Chandra. 'I've been having something of a change of outlook.'

'Well,' said the Master, rubbing his hands together in the manner of an evil genius, 'what could be more fitting for a septuagenarian?'

Chandra laughed. 'It has been troubling me that much of my work is intelligible only to a relatively small number of individuals,' he said. 'And my fear is many of us economists no longer strive to be understood, and in this respect we are becoming rather like the occultists of old, thriving on obscurity, trusting the common man will simply accept our judgement rather than entering into a dialogue.'

'Well, I suppose I *am* one of those common men,' said the Master while Chandra, who agreed heartily, mumbled, 'Oh, certainly not.'

'But surely putting our trust in experts is simply a fact of modern life, Chandra. Lord knows, I have no idea how my computer works.'

'The fact of the matter is, Master,' said Chandra, 'that in the nineteenth century the economist was a polymath. He was typically a natural scientist, a linguist, a man of God, a philosopher, *and* a mathematician. I am simply wondering whether economics doesn't need to restore some humanity to its dismal science.'

'Well, here's to that,' said the Master, raising his glass. 'It would be an understatement to say I'd be fascinated to read what you had to say on this matter.'

They clinked their glasses together and drank while Chandra settled back in his armchair, realising that, for once, he had little else to say. It felt surprisingly comfortable.

Since Esalen, he had continually been asking himself how many of his opinions were actually his own, and how many were his critical voices manifesting in his mind; those of former tutors and mentors who had rammed their views into his skull. It made him wonder what he actually did believe. And then there was Sunny with his affirmations which Chandra had begun to say in the mornings, and Jasmine with her 'Be Happy, Be Snappy' patter. And of course there was always Radha, that permanent resident in his brain, constantly reminding him that every thought he had was proof he belonged in a maximum security ward for the ideologically deranged. The end result was that he had barely written a word in months.

The Master refilled their glasses and asked Chandra about Brexit, to which Chandra replied, 'To be honest, Master, I have no idea,' and when the Master came at him with a follow-up about America, Chandra answered, 'It's both fascinating and terrifying to watch history unfold, isn't it?'

The truth was that he was tired of his own opinions now, tired of having to have opinions at all. But he could see that his reticence was causing the Master, who like most academics was incapable of mere banter, considerable consternation.

'Well,' said the Master, at last. 'I do enjoy these chats.'

'As do I, Master,' said Chandra, already a little drunk.

'And happy birthday, my friend.'

'You too,' said Chandra, realising this made no sense but not caring.

After taking his leave, Professor Chandra walked back through the college which always took on a dark, foreboding character in winter. He lay on the sofa in his rooms, looking at the bottle of claret he had laid out but now lost all desire to drink. He put the kettle on instead and began scanning through his emails again, simply for something to do. There were more birthday wishes, one from Bryan, which made him laugh:

Once in a century, a man is born who burns brighter than all the rest, who shines with wisdom and brilliance, and today that man would like to wish you a very happy birthday.

Perhaps this was why Chandra had never liked his birthday. It always felt like an invitation to evaluate his life rather than celebrate it, to assess his worth, and all he could ever think about were the things he *hadn't* achieved, as well as the things he should achieve, and could, if only he worked harder. When he was a child his father never gave him toys as presents, just pens or exercise books, or biographies of men who had reached the very pinnacles of their professions, like Einstein or Napoleon or Ramanujan. It was only his mother who seemed to believe it was acceptable for him to be a child, but she always supported his father in the end.

'He's doing it because he wants you to be a success,' she would tell him. 'It's to remind you.'

'Remind me of what?'

'That you have to work for it, that nothing good comes without struggle. It's good for the soul.'

It was a phrase his mother was fond of. Chandra used to say it to his students sometimes when they complained of exhaustion or stress or hinted at impending nervous breakdowns. When he himself was studying for his PhD, he would lock himself in his office on his birthday, working until early morning, driving himself on with cup after cup of coffee, cigarette after cigarette.

Remembering this, Professor Chandra spooned

instant coffee into his 'Keep Calm and Study Economics' mug before adding milk and hot water and returning to his desk. He was thinking he might watch a movie on his computer instead of reading, but it was then that he saw the email.

To:prchandra101@cam.ac.uk
From:roastedmango11@gmail.com

Subject: Happy seventieth

Hi Dad,

I'm sorry I've been out of touch for so long. I needed time to work some things out. I hope you're not angry. Sunny told me about the plan for Christmas. I'd like to come, if you want me to. I'll understand if you don't.

I hope you've had a lovely birthday.

Radha

14

Professor Chandra spent most of that night drafting a reply to Radha's email, an ill-advised three-page gush about how happy he was to hear from her, telling her all about Esalen and Hong Kong and Jasmine. He ended it by giving the Englishman's apology, that tawdry syntax implying it was all in the victim's head:

For anything I might have done to upset you, I am truly . . .

After sending it, he suffered an hour of excruciating regret until Radha replied with the single line,

Looking forward to seeing you, Dad.

Over the following weeks, Chandra found himself in higher spirits than he had been in years. It was only when the time came to fly to Denver that his anxiety returned. Ram drove him to the airport and, on arrival, pressed a pill into his hand and urged him to take it with a glass of wine on the plane but not to tell Betina. And so, for the first time in life, Professor Chandra found himself under the influence of a powerful tranquilliser called Xanax, which caused him to miss all his meals and to wake up on the ground in Denver ravenous, thirsty, and feeling as if all his emotions had been pressed and folded away.

After a bottle of sparkling water and a plate of pad thai from a place called City Wok, Professor Chandra rented his usual SUV and commenced the five-hour drive to Cove. It was midnight by the time he got there, crawling along at five miles per hour, terrified by the black road in front of him, the liquid stares of animals in his headlights. Chandra had forgotten that America could look like this. He remembered the icy sidewalks of Chicago, the frozen lakes of New England, but this was more like the Himalayas. Not only was there the darkness to contend with, but also the preternatural brightness, that ever-present snow that resembled a living organism.

The first thing he noticed was Steve's Lincoln Navigator, hulking hearse-like in the parking lot. He parked as far away from it as he could. Reaching the monastery, he found a map pinned to the door to help him find his cabin. Nobody had waited up for him. Professor Chandra walked by the light of the storage lamps before reaching something that looked like a tree carved into the shape of a house, a hundred metres behind the snow-covered zendō. Everything inside was wooden, rough and knotted, though furnished in an elegant, if austere, Japanese way, with a low desk and a black meditation cushion in front of it.

There was a hole in the floor with a stepladder that led to a subterranean bunker, a bed fixed halfway up the wall. To get into it, Chandra had to swing his legs sideways off the ladder. He found a bathroom at the bottom too, big enough for a medium-sized dog with a short tail, and somehow succeeded in brushing his teeth before getting into bed.

★ ★ ★

He was awoken a few hours later by a woodpecker, quite an eccentric fellow by the sound of him. He would peck once, wait until Chandra was returning to sleep, then do it again, a loud, decisive strike. When Chandra sat up, the woodpecker pecked harder, making a sound like an electric drill, and then paused before beginning again with those slow, solo attacks.

Professor Chandra lowered himself to the ground and showered before putting on his blazer and slacks and climbing the ladder. When he opened the door he found it was still dark. The moon had disappeared and the only light came from the zendō where a group of monks were walking along the veranda in single file, their shaven heads bowed. Dolores was at the front, stately in her robes. Chandra saw Jasmine behind her and almost called out. Her hair had been cut short, though it wasn't shaved like the others. She looked so focused, her steps serious and precise.

And now he saw Radha, second from the back, her hair long and thick as he remembered, those saucer eyes that he had known since she had to stand on tiptoes to see him. For several seconds, all he could feel was love, overwhelming in its intensity, until he remembered the last two years and began to feel angry and frightened in equal measure. When the monks began to file into the zendō, Professor Chandra followed, climbing the steps and taking off his shoes.

Inside, the monks were taking their seats, their backs turned, facing the wall, the room lit only by candles. Chandra stood beside the statue of the Buddha, looking from brown-robed back to brown-robed back. It was easy to find Radha with her long tail of hair, all brushed and shiny and neat. He stood staring at her before going outside again, kicking at the snow on the path, and returning to his room.

Professor Chandra slept for a further two hours before leaving his hut once more. This time, the sun was up, warming his forehead, and Jasmine was only a hundred metres away, sweeping snow from the path in her monk's robe. When she saw him she skipped towards him, eyes shining.

'Dad!' she said, throwing herself into his arms in a way she hadn't in years. 'I'm so glad you're here!'

He ran his hand over her hair. 'Aren't you cold? It's so short.'

'I shaved it off. It was liberating. It's grown back a bit now. It's all right. I usually wear a hat.'

He shook his head. 'I hardly recognise you.'

Jasmine put an arm around him. 'Radha's here, Dad.'

'I know.'

'And Sunny. He's rented a place a mile away. Mum and Steve went there for breakfast. It's a little McMansion.'

He should have seen this coming. Sunny would never consent to join a company at the bottom rung, so he'd set up a rival one and appointed himself CEO.

'He just wanted everyone to have somewhere to go,' said Jasmine, as if reading his mind. 'There's a TV there, and you can't drink alcohol inside the monastery. He's being considerate.'

'And they're there now, Steve and Jean?'

'Yes.'

'And Radha?'

'Radha's waiting for you to take her.'

'Right,' said Chandra.

Jasmine shifted so she could look into his eyes. 'You seem tired, Dad. I hope you slept all right. It can be hard at first, the altitude.'

'It was the bloody woodpecker.'

'The what?'

'He was right outside my door, the lunatic. Pock pock pock.'

Jasmine smiled. 'I think that was the han, Dad.'

'Han?'

She led him up the zendō's steps to the veranda.

'Here.' A block of wood was hanging by a string from one of the rafters, a mallet beside it. 'Someone hits it in the morning,' said Jasmine, 'and it goes clack . . . clack . . . clack. Then it gets faster till it's like clack-clack-clack-clack. You're supposed to get to the zendō by the third round. Actually it was me hitting it this morning.'

Chandra stared at the writing on the wood which had almost worn out in the middle:

302

Let me respectfully remind you, Life and death are of supreme importance. Time swiftly passes by and opportunity is lost. Each of us should strive to awaken. Awaken! Take heed! Do not squander your life.

He nodded. These were terrifying sentiments, impossible to argue with. He wished he had read these words fifty years ago, though, in all probability, they would have meant nothing to him then.

'Shall we go and see Rad now?' said Jasmine. She pointed to the bungalow to the left of the zendō. 'We're sharing.'

Chandra nodded and stared at the mountains on the horizon as they walked. He wished he could be like them, cold and impassive. Taking off his shoes outside the building, he tried to count his breaths. He wondered if he had squandered his life. He wondered if his daughter still loved him or if hate had cooled into mere indifference.

Radha was in the bathroom when they entered. He could hear the taps running. The twin beds had been sloppily made. The furthest had a battered grey Samsonite suitcase on it which might have belonged to him once, a pair of jeans and a black bra on top.

'I'll see you later, Dad,' said Jasmine.

'You're going?' said Chandra, but Jasmine had already shut the door.

When he was seven he had stood outside the deputy headmaster's office waiting to be beaten. The cane had a brass ball at the end of it and it was rumoured that the deputy, a Mr S. T. 'Stinky' Srinavasan, used to heat it in a fire first. Chandra had hyperventilated in front of him, and Stinky Srinavasan had slapped him and let him go. Chandra told everyone he had been caned 'unto death'. This was how he felt now, waiting.

He crossed to the armchair in the corner. There was a leather-bound notebook on top of it which he opened and saw Radha's big round handwriting, unchanged since fifth grade. *I'm getting sick of his shit*, he read, and put it down quickly as the bathroom door opened.

'Oh,' said Radha.

Chandra was happy to see she didn't look older, but there was a fragility about her eyes now, as if she had lost a layer of hardness. She was dressed in a vest and black jogging pants; he could see the muscles in her arms, a scar on her bicep. Her hair fell halfway down her back but was shaved underneath on one side. He wondered if she had become a terrorist.

'It's good to see you, Radha.'

'You too, Dad.'

They looked at one another, uncertain whether to hug. Eventually Radha sat on the bed, facing him. Chandra stared at his hands. It was like those first moments before a lecture to a capacity crowd.

'So when did you get here?'

'A few days ago,' said Radha. 'I wanted to meditate for a while.'

'Oh, that's good.'

'It's been peaceful.'

304

'Where are you living now?'

'New York.'

'Oh, New York.'

'Brooklyn. We live in Brooklyn.'

It was too early to ask about the 'we'.

'I heard you were in an accident,' said Radha.

'A bicycle hit me. My fault.'

'But you're okay now.'

'Yes,' said Chandra. 'No problems.'

'That's good.'

He thought of his week in hospital, how it had destroyed him that she hadn't called. How could she not have called? And why would anyone do that to their hair?

'I suppose you think I deserved it.'

'Dad . . . ' said Radha, looking past his shoulder. 'Shall we go to Sunny's?'

'Yeah, sure. Why not?'

Her winter coat was on the floor, one of those black puffy things that looked like it might be bulletproof. She had a bobble-hat and mittens too.

'I thought we could walk, Dad. If you're up to it.'

He put on his trench coat and they trudged out of the monastery in silence until they reached the road. The valley looked so far away, all those houses, the couples arguing in bedrooms. He wondered if that was why people became monks — to escape the noise. The snow was undisturbed and the light sharper now, making everything around them feel two-dimensional.

'I can't really meditate,' said Chandra. 'I think

305

about too many things.'

'Me too,'

'Jasmine is good at it, I think.'

'She's taken to it. It's been good for her.'

'I hope she doesn't stay here too long, though. There's nothing here.'

Radha began to walk faster. He had said it to annoy her, he realised.

'So you've been in New York,' he said. 'Brooklyn.'

'A year, something like that. I met someone in Paris.'

'You were in Paris?'

'I thought you knew.'

'I didn't know anything.'

He couldn't keep the anger from his voice. Clods of snow were dropping from the trees, so big they sounded like bodies. He hoped they wouldn't see a bear.

'I didn't really live anywhere for a while,' said Radha. 'Squats, then in a van. We went all over the place, demonstrations, protests, that kind of thing. Then I got tired of it.'

'Yes,' said Chandra. 'That kind of thing can get repetitive.'

'I met this guy in Paris. Marco. I came to New York with him.'

'So you live together?'

'Yes, but not for much longer.'

'You're moving?'

'I'm moving. He's staying.'

'Oh.'

'Like I said in my mail, Dad, I should have got in touch earlier. I just couldn't bear any more arguments, you know what I mean?'

'I also don't like arguing,' said Chandra, folding his arms.

'I couldn't stand you telling me I was living my life wrong, or that I'd grow out of it, or that I was an idiot.'

He wanted to say, 'I never said anything of the sort,' but instead he watched while Radha lit a cigarette and blew a cloud of smoke out in front of her, a cow's breath on a Cambridgeshire paddock.

'Give me one,' he said.

'No.'

Chandra stopped, picked up a small flat stone, and threw it into the trees. He hadn't thrown in a long time. It hurt his shoulder. Radha picked up one too and threw it. When she was little they would go down to the lake and have competitions. Sometimes they'd pretend there was a monster in the water, 'the Loch Ness Tyrannosaurus', and the game would be to hit its head. Jasmine had never liked games like that, and Sunny was always too competitive. He'd had more fun with Radha.

The road began to rise up the mountainside.

'Take it easy, Dad,' said Radha. 'You're really not supposed to walk on the first day here. The altitude.'

'Now you tell me.'

He put his hand on her shoulder, breathing hard. The sky looked transparent.

'So,' he said, coughing. 'What does he do, this Marco?'

'We're breaking up. I thought you got that.'

She tossed her cigarette and stepped on it. 'He's a lawyer.'

'What kind of lawyer?'

'The rich kind.'

'How about you? You working?'

'Not much these days. Activism still.'

'Oh,' he said, wondering if she was a part of the 'Antifa' that he had read so much about. 'That sounds interesting.'

'It was, kind of, but I got fed up with it all. That's why I came here early, to have a think about it.'

'Oh,' he said. 'You decide anything?'

'Only that there's no point preaching to the converted. But also no point trying to change people who don't want to change.'

'Yes,' said Chandra, wondering if she was talking about him.

'I decided self-care's the most important thing. Everything else flows from that. But I still want to make a contribution. If we all do nothing . . . '

Chandra was desperate to suggest going back to university, a decent Master's degree at a good institution, which he would happily finance. He tried to focus on walking.

When they were halfway up the hill they got a glimpse of what could only have been Sunny's rental home. It was built from stone, no bigger than any suburban house, but with spiral towers on both sides and mock battlements at the top. A small creek ran through the front yard, a miniature drawbridge over it.

'For fuck's sake,' said Radha.

Radha and Sunny had stopped fighting after Sunny moved to Hong Kong, but they often spoke to each other with cold contempt. They still shared a mutual concern for one another's well-being, but the sort one had for a terminally ill prisoner released on compassionate grounds.

Jean met them at the door, holding a cup of tea. She kissed Radha on the cheek and made as if to shake Chandra's hand before hugging him. They entered a cavernous living room with a bare Christmas tree in one corner and two leather sofas in the middle facing a TV that covered most of one wall. A Jack Lemmon film was playing.

'Hey,' said Sunny, coming down the stairs wearing jogging pants and a crisply ironed white shirt (a look Chandra had all but patented over the last forty years).

'Hi,' said Chandra, hugging him and asking, *sotto voce*, 'Where's Steve?'

'Out walking,' said Sunny, his voice reassuringly cold.

Jean sat on the sofa holding a cup of tea on her lap. 'So how have you been, Charles?' she asked.

Chandra was about to answer when he noticed the look of wariness on Sunny's face. This was the first time he had seen his parents in the same room for a very long time.

'Sunny,' said Chandra, 'this place is incredible.'

'My assistant found it,' said Sunny. 'I thought we'd need a space just for us.'

This was their original family, he realised, the

309

four of them from before Jasmine was born, sitting together in a room. For all the sadness and discomfort, this was something. But now Chandra could hear Steve singing in the hallway, his voice deep and loud. 'Lo, lo, lo, la, la.' The alpha back from the hunt.

'Hello, all,' said Steve, lolling a final bar. 'Hello, Chandrasekhar.'

Chandra stood and shook Steve's hand, aware that Radha and Sunny were watching him.

'Nice to see you, Steve,' said Chandra.

Steve wasn't wearing his Californian attire today, just a grey sweater and jeans, an average white guy on an average day.

'This place is almost like Rishikesh,' said Steve. 'Well, I suppose it's nothing like Rishikesh at all, but you know what I mean. To think I never knew Cove existed.'

'I'm thinking of reserving a plot for the IMB,' said Sunny. 'We'd fit in here.'

'No, you wouldn't,' said Radha. 'These are spiritual centres.'

'As are we — '

'You run a business school.'

'The whole world's about business,' said Sunny. 'We can't change that. But we can change the way we *do* business.'

Radha raised her eyes to the heavens. Chandra wondered if she knew how fragile Sunny was these days. It didn't look like it.

'Does it remind you of Esalen, Chandrasekhar?' said Steve, sitting on the arm of the sofa beside Jean. 'The vibe?'

'My God!' said Jean, in a tone that suggested

310

he'd been caught trafficking cocaine. 'How was it?'

'Actually, I know all about it already,' said Steve, tapping his nose. 'Got my sources. Heard you kicked up quite a storm.'

'Well, hardly.'

'It's wonderful, Chandrasekhar,' said Steve. 'You've taken your first steps into a wider world.'

Chandra dug his nails into his palm.

'It's a beautiful place, isn't it?' said Steve. 'I miss it. When I lived there the therapies were even more confrontational, brutal, you could say, like having a mirror pressed right up into your face. Can't say I always liked what I saw.'

'Yes,' said Radha. 'I can imagine.'

He felt the edge of Radha's hand against his, remembered shouting her name into the sea.

'It was very beneficial,' said Chandra.

They ate lunch in the open-plan kitchen with its view of the valley through patio doors. Chandra could not talk. All his words seemed to have descended into his heart. He found himself alternating between annoyance and relief that Steve was there.

'She seems to be settling in splendidly,' said Chandra, a from-the-rough non-sequitur that everyone understood.

'She's doing very well,' said Jean.

'And she can re-sit,' said Sunny. 'If she wants to.'

'In a way it's a good thing this happened,' said Steve. 'It means she won't go off the rails later in life.'

'There's a Christmas party tomorrow, Charles,'

311

said Jean. 'Outside the monastery. At Saul's house.'

'Then dinner here,' said Sunny. 'Just the family.'

Radha wandered onto the patio and lit a cigarette while Jean dished up shortbread with ice cream. Chandra put on his coat and scarf and joined his daughter.

'I went through hell when I gave up smoking,' he said.

'I've told myself I'll stop when I'm thirty-five, or when I have a baby.'

Radha looked the same to Chandra, except for the hair. He couldn't imagine her being thirty-five, or pregnant, let alone his age.

'So things are really over with this — '

'Marco. Yes.'

He wanted to hug her as he had hugged Pam, to tell her that he couldn't assure her that everything was going to be all right, but that he loved her and always would.

'Did you think about a PhD?' he said. 'It might be a good time to . . . '

Radha tossed her cigarette into the snow, and stared at the valley. He knew he shouldn't have said anything, that she was angry now, but he couldn't help it. This was the way it would go, the way it always went. When she turned to leave he had no choice but to follow her back into the house.

Sunny was doing the dishes and Steve and Jean were upstairs, Skyping with Steve's relatives. Chandra sat in the living room by himself, changing channels on the television while Radha helped her brother in the kitchen.

Sometimes it seemed that the two of them could only get on well when there were no adults around, as if their bickering was only a performance for the older generation. They were flicking water at one another now, doing impressions of characters from *The Muppet Show*. If only he could have kept them like this.

Chandra found an old Cary Grant movie, and lay down on the sofa. To his surprise, he awoke an hour later with a duvet over his body, remembering nothing of the film. It was charcoal grey outside, that early winter evening treachery.

Sunny was sitting on the other sofa, looking at his iPad.

'Where is everyone?' said Chandra.

'They're all back at the mon,' said Sunny, not looking up. 'Want me to drop you?'

'Sure.'

Chandra did not move. He was too exhausted. Sunny put his iPad down, seeming more relaxed now that they were alone.

'Are you all right, Dad?'

'Overwhelmed,' said Chandra.

'At seeing Rad?'

'At everything.'

They sat in silence for several minutes, the only sound coming from an owl somewhere outside. It pleased Chandra that Sunny could be himself when the two of them were together, but he worried for his son. It must be exhausting to have to wear such heavy armour in public.

'He's pompous, isn't he?' said Sunny. 'Steve, I mean.'

'Yes, he is,' said Chandra. 'But he means well.'

'It's weird, seeing him with Mum.'

'I'm sorry, Sunny,' said Chandra. 'This must be hard.'

'I'm more worried for you.'

'And I'm worried about Radha,' said Chandra. 'I don't know how to talk to her.'

'Well, now is your chance.'

They put on their coats and scarves and drove back to the monastery, past the Hindu ashram and Saul and Dolores's house. Chandra still had no idea what to say to Radha. They had spent so many years arguing about politics that it felt as if they had no other way of communicating.

When he knocked on Radha's door he found her meditating on the floor, an Indian shawl over her shoulders.

'Oh,' he said. 'Sorry.'

'Come in, Dad,' said Radha.

They sat opposite one another again, Chandra fidgeting, playing with the spot where his wedding ring used to be. Radha was doing exactly the same although, so far as he knew, she had never worn a ring. It was probably a gesture she'd learned from him. She'd even held her cigarette the way he used to. They had the same scowl too, the same laugh.

'Why are you so angry with me?' said Chandra.

She looked away. 'I'm not. I was. I'm not now.'

'Why?'

'You know why.'

'Because you believe in Marxism and I believe in trade. So what? I am not a fascist. Could you imagine me sending people to their deaths?'

'No,' said Radha softly. 'I could imagine Prakash Uncle doing that.'

'Oh,' he said. 'Oh, well, that's different.'

'I thought I was rebelling against you, but I just went from one big man to another.'

'I'm not like that now. I know what you're talking about, but I am not like that now.'

'It was never about politics, Dad.'

'What then? Tell me.'

'Dad, I can't deal with this at the moment. Later, all right?'

'You can't deal with anyone, Radha. Instead of dealing, you just disappear.'

'Dad, stop it, please. We'll talk about this later.'

'Look what happened to Jasmine, Radha. Think what I've been through. And all you want to do is torment me.'

'No, Dad, that's not it at all. But can we just talk about this later?'

'And you smoke, and you swear at me, and you think it's fine. 'The old bastard, just say anything. He has no feelings.''

This was the way he always used to talk to her, and he was slipping back into it. They were too close, Radha and he, too similar; it made him less guarded, as if it didn't matter what he said.

'I know you have feelings, Dad, and I won't smoke or swear in front of you if it bothers you so much. I just have a headache now and I'm tired and I think I'm getting a cold and this is too much. I do want to talk to you, but not like this, not now.'

'You said in your email that you were sorry.'

'I am. But only for not being in touch. That was wrong of me.'

'You've been so pampered. It's my fault. I brought you up to be like this. If I talked to this Marco of yours he would say the same thing, I'm sure.'

'I have to get out of here.'

Radha moved towards the door, slowly, but with all the finality of an ocean liner heading out to sea.

'No, Radha,' he said. 'Come on. Let's talk this over.'

'Dad,' said Radha. 'It's fine. I'm just going to dinner. We can talk later.'

'No, Radha. Come on.'

'Dad,' she said, her hand on the door knob. 'I'm just going to have fucking *dinner*. Jesus Christ, I can't believe you brought Marco into it!'

'Yes, yes, I am not allowed to say anything.'

'It's because of *you*, Dad. If I hadn't had this giant patriarch for a father I wouldn't have gone from one fucking abusive man to another. You get it now?'

'What do you mean, 'abusive'? You are calling me an abuser?'

'Yes.'

He stood up. 'How dare you.'

Radha left. The burst of night air was sharp and cold. Chandra pressed his hands to his face, wanting to pull out his hair. Instead he sat on the bed and punched the pillow several times before standing, smoothing out the creases in his blazer and trousers, and heading for the main building.

316

It was much colder now, and just as dark as last night. Without the storage lamps he would have been quite lost. Reaching the main building he kicked off his shoes and squinted through the glass door until he caught sight of Radha. She was pointing at the painting of the Japanese demon and laughing. Her eyes were still so huge. He'd had a song about them when she was little. 'Big eyes, big eyes, they're better than the TV/Big eyes, big eyes, you're getting very sleepy.'

Professor Chandra wanted to leave but he couldn't find his shoes any more. It was too dark, and though there were several pairs there, none seemed to belong to him. He started kicking them in frustration before giving up and shoving a pair of boots onto his feet, not bothering with the laces, not caring who they belonged to. He stumbled through the darkness to his cabin and, once outside, took the boots off and threw them as far as he could into the trees.

Inside, he bolted the door and climbed down the stepladder before throwing himself onto the bed and closing his eyes.

15

Professor Chandra awoke on Christmas morning. The snow-capped mountains were clearer today, leaning over the monastery like inquisitive old men. Chandra walked to the zendō in his tennis shoes, finding his calfskin brogues in the lobby of the main building and remembering how he had hurled some poor unfortunate's boots into the snow. He would look for them later, assuming they weren't already submerged. It had snowed afresh in the night.

Jasmine was in the kitchen unloading the dishwasher. She was wearing jeans and a cotton shirt, but with her inch-long hair she still looked monkish to Chandra's eyes.

'Merry Christmas, Dad,' she said.

'Merry Christmas, Jasmine.'

'Dad,' said Jasmine. 'There's something you should know. Radha's gone. She left before zazen. I mean, her suitcase is still in the room, but her phone's off, and she's not at Sunny's.'

'Oh, my God,' he said.

'Dad, it's all right. Look, here's Mum.'

Jean was striding into the room, taking off her woolly hat and stuffing it into her pocket, blowing on her fingers. Steve followed behind her in a yellow jumpsuit, which made Chandra think of Goldfinger.

'Morning, Charles. Morning, Jaz. Merry Christmas.'

'Radha's gone,' said Chandra. 'We had a fight.'

'Oh, Charles,' said Jean. 'Not again.'

'It isn't like that, Mum,' said Jasmine. 'She'll be back.'

Chandra thought of Pam, of how when she walked out of the workshop the others had assured him she would return, and how when she did he had been glad he hadn't suppressed his feelings. But this was Radha. When Radha stormed out of a room it could take years for her to return.

'It *is* like that,' said Chandra. 'I'm sorry, Jean.'

'Oh, Charles,' said Jean, and pressed his arm although, he noticed, she wouldn't look him in the eye. 'You mustn't push it.'

'I know,' he said. 'I know that now.'

'She's too strong-willed, that one,' said Jean. 'She's just as dramatic as you are, Charles.'

'So let's go look for her,' said Steve. 'Come on, Chandrasekhar, what do you say? Here comes the cavalry?'

'If she's hitch-hiked she could be anywhere,' said Jean, who used to hitch-hike herself, a habit that, in Professor Chandra's opinion, was about as sensible as taking meth.

'Nonsense,' said Steve. 'She'll be out walking somewhere and we'll bring her back, won't we, Chandrasekhar?'

'Yes,' said Chandra, looking at the ground. 'Yes, we will.'

In the lobby he noticed that Steve was putting on a pair of bedroom slippers. Chandra was about to tell him how wet it was, before he realised why. He had thrown *Steve's* boots into the trees. He would look for them when they got back.

In the parking lot Professor Chandra's SUV was covered in snow, a wall of it around his tyres, while Steve, with that calculated prescience common to all men of dubious character, had parked his Lincoln under the cover of two fir trees. Chandra got inside while Steve threw a can of 'Starbucks Doubleshot Espresso' into the back and started the engine.

'So what do you think of TTIP, Chandrasekhar?' said Steve, putting the car into reverse.

'What?' said Chandra, staring out the window at the huge drifts of snow.

'The Transatlantic Trade and Investment Protocol,' said Steve.

'Partnership,' said Chandra automatically, still staring, imagining he might see his daughter crouching behind a tree like a sniper in a war movie.

'Yes, exactly,' said Steve. 'You a fan?'

'I don't know,' said Chandra. 'It will be good for trade flows. But please, do not discuss this in front of Radha.'

'Sure,' said Steve. 'Sure. Of course, I mean, I don't think all leftists are against it. It's more complicated than that, isn't it?'

Chandra shook his head. Such questions were not worthy of answers.

They reached the main road. The sky was almost white, the valley beneath them too. They passed the Hindu ashram and the turn-off to Sunny's, his house a hulking monolith at the top of the hill.

'Interesting guy, your son,' said Steve finally. 'He's rented that whole place for himself.'

'For all of us,' said Chandra.

'Well, that's generous. I suspect he likes being on his own, though. So do I. Grew up sharing a room with four others and couldn't stand it.'

Steve turned on the radio and began to hum, a gesture that, in Chandra's opinion, was far too quotidian under the circumstances.

'Yes,' said Chandra. 'Sunny has done very well for himself.'

'You must be proud of him.'

'Of course.'

'Bit of a narcissist though,' said Steve, turning right.

'What? What's that?'

'Sunny. I mean, he's a good guy but he's . . . you know, like a caricature, wants everyone to know how important he is. My guess is he's vying for your attention. Quite common amongst the children of successful men. He'd be in real trouble if he wasn't successful.'

'Sunny is fine,' said Chandra, counting his breaths and getting to four. 'Thank you, Steve.'

'Yes, of course. I didn't mean anything by it.'

'Let's just find my daughter, please.'

They continued in silence, past the Tibetan monastery. Chandra rotated his gaze between the anorexic trees on one side, and the valley on the other.

'Steve,' he said, 'you have every right to speak your mind. You have been more of a parent to Jasmine than I, and, frankly, I could do with some advice. And I have not thanked you yet for sending me to Esalen. I needed it. If I hadn't have gone I wouldn't have realised how poor a father I've been.'

'Nonsense, you're doing great!' said Steve. 'The important thing is that you're here for them. What more could anyone ask of you? God knows you're a better man than I am.'

Chandra used to have a Professor at the LSE who would say to him, 'You're a better man than I am, Gunga Din Din Din.' Was Steve resorting to racial slurs now?

'There,' said Steve, slowing down.

'There what?'

Steve pointed to the right. Professor Chandra saw only a canvas of snow, a low hill behind it.

'The footprints.'

'Oh,' said Chandra. 'Oh, yes.'

There they were, deep and black in the fresh powder. It irritated Chandra that Steve had proved himself the superior tracker.

'I'll wait here for you,' said Steve, 'if you don't mind.'

Chandra looked at Steve's feet. 'Sure,' he said. 'Sure, Steve.'

He stepped out of the car and over the gutter. Hardly dressed for a Captain Scott adventure himself, he tried to place his shoes in his daughter's footprints, avoiding the ankle-deep drifts around him. There was a solitary cloud ahead, slightly pink, the only colour in this place.

Chandra was panting and sweating when he reached the top of the hill. Looking back, he saw Steve's Lincoln like a huge abandoned black boot in the snow. There was a parking lot ahead, a sign advising visitors to take care of their valuables, and another behind it which read, SMALL BUDDHA SHRINE (500M). He could see Radha's footprints continuing towards the shrine and, his shoes saturated now, he headed towards it.

Chandra remembered a cartoon he'd seen in the *New Yorker* in which a man climbs a sheer cliff face to meet a guru who tells him, 'Buy low, sell high, stay diversified.' This was his sort of joke, though he doubted any of his family would have found it funny, Steve included.

He could see a building in front of him now, almost square and made entirely of glass except for the roof. He could make out a large vase of flowers and a statue of the Buddha inside.

'Dad, get in. It's freezing.'

Radha was standing in the doorway dressed in a baggy grey sweater and army pants, her hair tied back, snowflakes buzzing around her face. She was holding the door open for him. He felt afraid, a doomed disciple in the presence of a famously short-tempered ascetic.

It was warm inside. There were rugs on the floor, a mandala on the north wall, all elaborate in a washed-out, threadbare way. The statue was not of the Buddha but of a woman in the lotus position with one arm outstretched, a crown on her forehead. Radha had made a nest for herself on the floor with cushions and shawls. There was a thermos beside her, a bag of sandwiches and some fruit.

'I thought you'd gone,' he said.

Radha was leaning against the wall, the

radiator behind her. 'I just wanted a change of scene. It's clearer here, more peaceful.'

'Cold to walk all the way.'

'I've got a good jacket.'

'I thought you'd gone,' he said once more.

'Oh, Dad,' said Radha. 'It's okay.'

He was about to cry and she could see it. When she put her arms around him he had the sensation that it was the bronze goddess herself, climbed down from the altar. All his life seemed to be inside the grey inch of sweater he could see on her shoulder.

'I'm sorry,' he said.

'I know,' said Radha.

'I'm sorry. I love you.'

He shouldn't have said sorry a second time. It brought him back to his senses, his sharpness returning. She was the one who had turned her back on him. She was the one who had banned everyone else from breathing a word about her doings and wrongdoings. Two years. She had defeated him and she knew it.

Radha seemed to sense the change and let him go. He sat down cross-legged, his hands on his knees.

'I just didn't like what you said about Marco, Dad.'

'Who?'

'The guy I was living with, remember? The hard-working, decent corporate lawyer.'

He had no memory of saying anything about Marco.

'I remember you saying he wasn't so decent,' said Chandra.

'No, he wasn't, Dad. That's all there is to it. Actually, there's a lot more to it, but God knows why you should have any opinion about it. You don't even know him.'

'Did he hit you?' said Chandra.

'No, I hit him a couple of times.'

'Oh.'

'He was an asshole, Dad. Just take my word for it.'

'All right.'

Radha sighed. 'He was about fifteen years older and he'd made a lot of money and it gave him this crushing sense of certainty. Whatever I did, he told me I would 'learn' or I had a 'way to go', or he'd pat me on the head and tell me it was cute that I got so agitated about things. I was living off him, and he thought that meant he could take out all his shit on me. He was this big swinging man and I was just a silly little brown girl throwing eggs at the cops, which meant he could treat me with contempt. Sound familiar?'

It did, but Chandra didn't think this made Marco an 'asshole', not yet. He moved his head in that South Indian double helix designed to convey everything at once.

'I'm not blaming you, Dad. I'm just saying there's a pattern. Like you get used to men putting you down so you go looking for it. You choose the thing you're trying to get away from, because it's all you know, because you've grown up associating contempt with love. Yeah. It took about a year of therapy for me to figure this out.'

'Maybe I should also have therapy,' said Chandra.

'Well, you did, didn't you? You and Mum?'

Chandra looked at the cushions on the floor, the thermos beside them.

'How did you know that?'

'Oh, Dad, it's nothing to be ashamed of.'

When he was a child Chandra had believed his parents had everything under control. Now he knew they'd been as lost as he was. Humans were like those snowflakes against the window, buffeted by winds no one understood.

'Merry Christmas, Dad.'

'Merry Christmas, Radha.'

They looked into each other's eyes until Radha looked away and said, 'You can't know this, but I was even angrier with Mum than I was with you, Dad. I couldn't believe she left you for that . . .'

'Yet you decided to cut *me* out of your life.'

'That's why,' said Radha. 'I'm closer to you. Don't you see?'

'No,' he said. 'No, I don't see at all.'

'All my life I believed you were all-powerful, Dad. It was like I couldn't see myself because your shadow was always in the way. I kept trying to break you. It felt like that was the only way I could be me. But I couldn't. It was impossible, and that pissed me off. But then Mum did it. She did it so easily. She just dismantled you. And it hurt to see you like that. I wanted you to fight back but you just got more . . . I don't know . . . defeated. I just needed to get away. I needed to focus on me. It sounds selfish, I know.'

There were tears in her eyes, huge pools.

'I suppose it wasn't easy to see your father so

326

pathetic,' said Chandra.

'You weren't pathetic, Dad. You were just human. That's what I learned.'

Once, when she was little, Professor Chandra had dressed up in a Santa Claus outfit. Radha and Sunny had taken him for the real thing, quite star-struck. For one wonderful half-hour he had spoken in that pseudo-drunken baritone common to all Father Christmas impersonators and they had stared up at him as if he were no less than a perfect being.

'Yes,' he said. 'I had to learn it too.'

'I was mad at you for being human. And I was also mad at you for pretending you weren't. I don't get it, Dad. Why do you all do this? Why do you pretend you've got everything down?'

'Down?'

'Like you know everything. Like everything's under control. Like you've got no frailties and no doubts and no . . . anything. What *is* that? I mean, I actually believed it. How dumb was I? I really thought you were some kind of god. And don't say everyone sees their parents like that — it isn't true. There are certain types, like you, and Prakash Uncle — and Marco. It's just so . . . convincing but, I mean, how can everything be under control? How? For anyone?'

'I had a heart attack last year,' said Chandra. 'I couldn't control that. It was terrifying. I think people like me, and Prakash, maybe Marco, we don't want to be frightened.'

Chandra hadn't known he could talk like this. He had been brought up on emotional blackmail: his grandmother, his father, two if not

327

three of his aunts and uncles. He was a master of it himself, of scrolling between pathetic, pitiable, intimidating, unreasonable, and mortally wounded. But now he and his daughter were simply talking.

'I guess I was doing it too,' said Radha, 'for a while. It was bullshit, the whole thing. I mean, it was never about politics. I was just trying to break you.'

'Well, it worked,' said Chandra.

'It *didn't*. You just got bigger. Bigger than I could ever be. And I don't want to be big, Dad. It's exhausting.'

'Yes, it is,' he said. 'I actually thought I could do it, you know. I thought if I tried hard enough, worked hard enough, I could control everything. I thought it would work on your mother too, I didn't realise she didn't care whether I won the prize.'

'You thought if you won the Nobel then everything would be all right with Mum?'

'I thought she'd come back if I won.'

For years Chandra had had a vision of himself in white tie and tails with Jean in a silver sequinned gown bowing before Carl XVI Gustaf while his children applauded and couples the world over hugged in front of TV screens knowing that in Stockholm two beings were glowing with a light so perfect that the universe would always be benevolent and secure in its moorings.

'That's mental,' said Radha.

'I know.'

'I'd be proud of you if you won the Nobel, Dad,' said Radha.

'It isn't important.'

'I *know*,' said Radha, looking into his eyes.

'What could I do?' he said, spreading out his hands. 'I thought it was everything.'

'You did it to us too, Dad,' said Radha. 'You made us feel that because we hadn't achieved as much as you we weren't as important.'

Professor Chandra wanted to crawl under the cushions and emerge in his bed in Cambridge, or better, in the office with a pile of work and a cup of triple-strength coffee.

'Yes,' he said. 'I can see that.'

He closed his eyes, imagining his daughter dancing on his body, drunk with blood. She had taken it all now, his years of training and striving, the thousands of pages he had filled with a soft pencil in an over-heated office, the confusion he had never admitted to, the heart he had driven to failure, to breaking.

'It's okay, Dad,' said Radha. 'I just needed to say it.'

'I'm proud of you,' he said. 'I'm proud of you for knowing all this, all these things you are telling me. You know so much more than I do. I am trying to learn this kind of thing too. It's difficult but . . . it's nice to know you're doing it while you're still young.'

'Dad,' said Radha. 'I'm just trying to be normal, you know? A normal person.'

'But you're not,' he said. 'I don't think you are normal at all.'

'Neither are you,' said Radha.

'At Esalen they called me a character.'

Radha laughed. 'You *are* a character.'

'Maybe we all are,' said Chandra.

'Steve isn't,' said Radha. 'He's so fucking ordinary. He's normal.'

'I don't blame Steve,' said Chandra. 'He's been good to Jasmine. And to me in some ways. He drove me here. He's waiting for us on the road. I threw his boots into the trees so he's in his slippers.'

Radha snorted. 'You threw his boots into the trees?'

'It was an accident.'

'Go on, Dad,' she said. 'You can say it. It's okay.'

'Say what?'

'Come on. Steve's a prick. Say it.'

'What is this, Radha? Of course not.'

'Go on, Dad. Just for you, me, and the goddess over there. Say it.'

'Steve's a prick,' said Chandra.

'Again.'

'Steve is a bloody fucking prick.'

Radha grinned. Chandra grinned back.

'Shall we go to the monastery?' he said. 'I'm hungry.'

'I want to stay and meditate for a while, Dad.'

'What about Christmas?'

'It's not even ten o'clock.'

He looked at his watch. It was true.

'So I'll come back for you, when you're ready?'

'It's a half-hour walk,' said Radha. 'I'm fine.'

'It's cold.'

'Thank you for coming, Dad.'

It was like the end of a job interview. 'Thank

you for coming, your CV's in the shredder.'

'So I'll see you later.'

'Yes, of course.'

He lifted himself to his feet and crossed to the door. Radha was already on her cushion, wrapping her shawl around her shoulders.

There was no sun or even pink in the sky now, but there were several more clouds, which made the valley look smaller. He felt like the yeti as he lumbered his way down the slope, his feet so wet he didn't care where he stepped any more.

Professor Chandra was shivering when he reached the car. Steve had tilted his seat back and was listening to the radio, but sat up when he heard the door slam.

'You find her?'

'Yes,' said Chandra. 'She was meditating.'

'Shall we wait for her?'

'She'll be all right.'

Steve turned off the music and restored his seat to the vertical. 'Great,' he said, and put the Lincoln into gear.

'Steve,' said Chandra, as they pulled away. 'I am sorry for punching you. It was wrong of me, and everything you said about me was correct, my need for power and so on. You were quite right.'

'I appreciate you saying that,' said Steve.

Chandra laughed.

'Is something funny, Chandrasekhar?'

He was remembering how Radha had made him call Steve a prick.

'But I had my reasons, Steve.'

'And I apologised, Chandrasekhar.'

331

'I mean Jean,' said Chandra. 'You took her. It was a cruel and cowardly thing to do.'

'This really depends on your definition of cowardly, my friend.'

'I've no idea what you're talking about, Steve.'

Steve stopped the car. The Hindu ashram was on the other side of the road, a stone's throw from the monastery.

'You're right, Chandrasekhar. We lied to you and it was wrong. And yes, I was angry that you hit me. It felt childish. Grown-ups don't hit each other.'

'I'm not saying you deserved it, Steve, all I am saying is that I had my reasons. In any case, as I told Radha, Jean is much happier with you. You look after her in ways I never could.'

'I don't think Jean *needs* looking after any more,' said Steve. 'She did, but then a time came when she didn't, and maybe it was you who got her there.'

'So I brought her to you,' said Chandra.

'In a manner of speaking.'

There was a snowman with a piece of tinsel around his neck in front of the ashram, except now Chandra realised it wasn't a snowman at all but a statue of Ganesha, his trunk poking up through the snow like a periscope.

'I just mean that maybe your marriage ran its course, Chandrasekhar. It happened to my first marriage too. My ex is with someone else now and she's happy. I have no hard feelings. I'm happy for her. I've explained this to Jasmine — that divorce isn't as abnormal as we make it out to be. That humans weren't meant to be life partners. I've told Radha too.'

'Have you spoken much with Radha, Steve?'

'A little, yes. She's come to the house.'

Steve switched on the engine and began to drive once more.

'Listen, Chandrasekhar, they're not my children. I know that. But I love them. Not like you, perhaps, but in my own way, and I have a role in their lives. But I couldn't replace you if I tried. I hope that's enough for you.'

Chandra nodded. 'You will never know any of them the way I do, Steve.'

'I know.'

He thought of Steve coaching Jasmine to take drugs, of how terrified she'd been in court, of how he'd found her crouched by a dumpster, staring at the moon.

'But you spoke to Radha about me?'

'Hardly.'

'Yes or no?'

'I listened to her, Chandrasekhar. Perhaps that's the difference.'

'The difference between what?'

'You seem angry, my friend. Ask yourself what need isn't being met?'

'My need for an answer, Steve.'

'Then, yes,' said Steve, 'I have spoken to Radha about you. I've spoken to all of them. They love you, of course, but they resented you, and I understand that. My children resented me for a time.'

They were entering the parking lot now. Steve parked the car beneath the same fir tree as before.

'But why do my children resent me?' asked Chandra.

'I think you know why.'

'Tell me.'

'Like I said,' said Steve, 'you're a wonderful father; but you've got to stop trying to control them. I'm always telling Jean this. If you just give them a little space, they'll come back to you. No one likes a judger. No one likes a tyrant.'

'You think I'm a tyrant?'

'It's not a noun situation. This is adjectival.'

'And what is that supposed to mean?'

'It means,' said Steve, 'from all I've heard, that there were moments when you were tyrannical, and I think that probably pushed them away from you.'

'Well, this shows how little you know my family, Steve.'

'Chandrasekhar — '

'Your pronunciation of my name is horrendous.' He opened the door. Snowflakes blitzed against his cheek. 'And if you're looking for your boots, they're in the trees.'

Chandra marched back to the main building where Dolores waved at him from the office window. He waved back, hoping she wouldn't see what a rage he was in.

When he reached his cabin Chandra took a shower before getting into bed and pulling the covers over his head. He fell asleep at once, exhausted after his hike up the hill.

When he awoke, somebody was climbing down the stepladder.

'Charles?'

He did not move. If he did not move, she might go away.

'Charles, I know you can hear me.'

He hoped she wouldn't pull the covers away, leaving him in his vest and shorts like a small boy after gym class. He focused on his breathing . . . one, two, three.

'How could you throw Steve's boots away? I know you resent him, but of all the petty, stupid things you could do . . . I mean, what are you, some kind of kid? He didn't bring any other shoes. What if I took *your* shoes, Charles? Charles? I know you can hear me.'

He counted twelve more breaths. She was still there, staring at his lumpen form beneath the duvet, those mounds and craters like the surface of the moon. But now he could hear her leather pumps on the steps, her footsteps on the floor above his head, the door opening and slamming, his whole hut shaking.

He waited. Was she really gone? Or was it a trick?

No. He was alone. Jean had left. Again.

Chandra went back to sleep, sinking into the mattress, convinced he was at sea with choppy grey waves outside his porthole. Somebody knocked twice, a half-hour apart, waking him both times, but no one came in. He heard voices, someone speaking in German, or what he thought was German, someone else shouting about there not being enough vegetables. A car pulled up and a voice yelled, 'Merry Christmas,' and laughed as if they had said something hilarious.

When he got out of bed it was 1.37 p.m. on Christmas Day and he was late. The party at Saul and Dolores's house had begun.

Professor Chandra shaved and showered before putting on his blue blazer, grey slacks, and black knitted socks once more. He wore a tie too, the one the Master had presented him with at Cambridge. He would be the only person at the party wearing a tie, but it was Christmas, after all. Standards had to be maintained.

Professor Chandra left his hut and saw Steve hunched over in the trees, poking at the snow with a stick.

'Steve,' he said.

Steve raised a hand in greeting. Chandra noticed he was wearing gumboots, presumably borrowed.

'I think they're over there, Steve,' he said, pointing right.

Steve shuffled over and began stabbing once more. Chandra stomped through the snow and began to help, kicking at the earth before squatting and using his hands. It took five minutes before Steve found them; they looked waterproof, at least, and had been lying on their sides. Steve took them in his gloved hand and began to walk away.

'Steve,' said Chandra, and shuffled over to him. 'I didn't realize the boots were yours. I'm sorry. Really. I don't want to fight any more.'

Chandra was panting, his breath white like fine cigarette smoke.

'There's nothing to say,' said Steve. 'It's normal. All of this. Of course you don't like me.'

'That isn't true,' said Chandra, but he knew it was a lie — of course he didn't like Steve.

'We just have to try to be grown-ups about it,' said Steve.

'I suppose I haven't done a good job of that so far.'

'I'll try to leave the five of you alone tonight. It'll be weird for Jean if I don't come at all, but I'll give you a few hours.'

'Thanks.'

'I really have a lot of respect for you, Chandrasekhar. But I guess I don't like you so much either. Not now.'

'I understand that,' said Chandra.

'I also have feelings. I know you're the hurt one, but this hasn't been easy for me either.'

'Yes,' said Chandra, not caring at all.

'I guess you'd happily punch my nose again, wouldn't you?'

Chandra visualised knocking Steve onto his back, a trickle of blood running from his nose onto the snow.

'We don't have to be friends,' he said.

'But we can be diplomats,' said Steve.

'Politicians.'

Steve put out his hand which Chandra grasped and shook, looking him in the eye.

'Well,' said Steve. 'I'm going to try and dry out my boots before the party.'

'See you later, Steve,' said Chandra.

He set off down the path, knowing Steve had to go that way too but not caring. It felt good not to have to apologise any more. His shoes and socks were soaked, but it didn't matter. Anger was circulating through his body and he liked it.

It was even colder on the main road without the shelter from the buildings. The mountains were covered by a thick layer of charcoal cloud. Saul and Dolores's house, a large bungalow made of black wood, was set partway down the slope that led to the valley. Chinese lanterns lined the driveway, burning through the greyness and drizzle. Chandra knocked. When the door opened he smelled sherry and cake.

A big black smelly dog leapt out at him.

'Lama!' said Saul, from the doorway. 'Lama, stop that. Sorry, Chandra.'

'No problem,' said Chandra, smiling at the beast and wishing he could call the pound.

'Come in, come in!'

'I forgot to bring the presents,' said Chandra, taking off his shoes and realising he had left them all in the hut, including the two bottles of wine he'd bought in Napa.

'Oh, no, you're all we need. We keep it simple here. Come in, please. It's dismal out there.'

He stepped into the hallway and followed Saul, who was holding the beast by the collar, to the drawing room where there was a fake silver Christmas tree as high as the ceiling and three sofas in a semicircle on which several monks were gathered. Bing Crosby was playing, a huge log burning in the fireplace, and Dolores was walking towards him in a sleeveless silvery-green dress that made her look like a mermaid. She kissed his cheeks and led him by the hand into Saul's study where she shut the door and looked him up and down.

'Now, you're not to take this too hard, but we've got a few problems.'

'Radha.'

'No, not Radha. Jasmine.'

'Jasmine?'

'It's bad, but not that bad. It seems one of our people caught her smoking a joint this morning.'

Chandra looked for somewhere to sit, but the desk and chair were too far away.

'Oh, God,' he said, stepping backwards into the bookcase and knocking two hardbacks onto the ground. 'How could this happen?'

'It's only marijuana,' said Dolores. 'Not meth. Marijuana's legal in Colorado, in fact, but it does violate the terms of her being here, so we've got to take this seriously, for her sake and for ours. The upshot is that she'll have to go home for a while, like a suspension. She can still come back to us, but she's got to know it's serious first.'

'This is terrible,' he said, unable to look at Dolores. 'Terrible.'

'Oh, no. Sit here.' Dolores wheeled out the swivel chair from behind the desk. 'And drink this.' She pushed a brandy into his hand. 'It'll be okay. It's just a little glitch in the matrix, that's all.'

'And Radha?'

'She's consoling her sister back in the dorm. It's all good. They'll be here in a while, by which time our goose will be on its third life and my chances of being reborn in the human realm as good as gone. I mean, it's one thing to kill a bird, but to torture the poor creature in its afterlife . . . '

'So none of them are here?'

'They'll come.'

'Why did she do this?'

'It's Christmas,' said Dolores. 'This is what happens at Christmas.'

Chandra watched as his glass fell from his hand, the golden liquid falling in a narrow column like a sword. He found himself following it, tumbling onto the floor, his hands first, and then his whole body.

'Chandra!' said Dolores.

He was on the carpet now, looking at the legs of the chair while Dolores slipped a cushion beneath his head. He wasn't in any pain, he noted, with relief: this wasn't a heart attack.

'You just take it easy,' she said.

Chandra closed his eyes. He could hear Dolores calling to her husband.

He hadn't felt this helpless since the bicycle incident in Cambridge a year ago, but he'd had a heart attack then, even if he hadn't known it at the time. But now there was nothing wrong with his body. It was his family, and this was far, far worse.

Saul was in the room now, the dog too, hovering over him, threatening to lick his face until Saul grabbed its collar and dragged it out of the door. 'Here,' said Saul, returning and pushing another glass of brandy into Chandra's hand.

'Thanks,' said Chandra, and took a long, grateful swig.

Closing his eyes, he felt almost peaceful, conscious only of the aftertaste of brandy in his mouth, the past seventy years like an unpleasant dream he could barely remember. This was what he'd longed to do at so many departmental dinners, so many tutorials and lectures. To lie on the floor and close his eyes. But now he could hear Jasmine's voice in his head, picture her face, that tiny, delicate flower, and he had to get up. The show had to go on. Taking another swig of brandy, Chandra allowed Saul to help him to his feet.

'How are you feeling now?' asked Saul, massaging his neck with one hand.

'Good enough,' said Chandra.

16

Steve and Jean arrived an hour later. Steve was wearing his boots. He'd taken a blow-dryer to them, in all probability. Jean refused to even look at Chandra and went straight for the dog who was lying on the rug by the fire. Jean loved dogs. It was on his list of reasons why she had left him.

Jasmine and Radha arrived not long afterwards and, for once, Jasmine did not go to the kitchen. She sat by herself looking at a photo album, her demeanour saying 'stay away', though not aggressively. Chandra wanted to go to her, but knew he should wait — she'd come when she was ready.

Radha sat beside Saul who was sitting beside Chandra. She managed to maintain her part of the conversation while simultaneously saying nothing of any importance. Chandra felt proud of her. It was a trick it had taken him years to master. Saul was telling her about his time in the Marine Corps.

'I just loved blowing things up. The truth is, I was desperate to go to Vietnam, so I was first in line, but they sent the first ten to Okinawa. And Okinawa just happened to be the home of karate. So there I was, not speaking a word of Japanese, learning karate from a teacher who didn't speak a word of English. At the end of every class we'd sit facing a statue of the Buddha for anything up to an hour. It was only a decade later, when I was an anti-war activist, that I realised this was Zen.'

Sunny wasn't there. Chandra had been afraid of this.

Dolores ushered them all into the conservatory. Her goose was cooked, she said, with a grin.

Chandra joined the others, taking his seat at one end of a long mahogany table, with Saul at the other.

It was a beautiful setting, the glass windows, the acres of snow outside, the bowls of flowers and incense. Saul was making a speech, but Chandra couldn't listen, unable to think of anything save for Sunny's absence, Jasmine's predilection for narcotics, and Radha, who seemed to be meditating at the table. Professor Chandra considered meditation an excellent opportunity to compensate for his forty-year sleep deficit or to work on unfinished papers, but he couldn't help believing meditation was best suited to those with less mind to be mindful of: sociologists, for example, or geographers. But now that *two* of his daughters were devotees, he would probably have to reconsider.

'And so,' Saul was saying, 'I wish you all a bon appetit, and a peaceful and happy holiday.'

Saul looked at Chandra as if inviting him to add something, but Chandra turned to Jasmine, sitting to his left, and said, 'Are you all right, Jaz?'

'I'm fine,' said Jasmine. 'I mean, I'm in trouble again.' She leaned backwards, her profile a line drawing against the Colorado winter behind her. 'But that's what life is, isn't it, Dad? Just one

343

stupid mess after another. Maybe a few breaks in between, but they're really just more storms gathering.'

Chandra sighed. It was so dark outside now, and his daughter was so bright. He hated to hear these words from her lips, but he knew she was right, quite right.

'I'm proud of you,' he said, taking hold of her hand. 'I'm so proud of you, Jasmine.'

'Thanks, Dad.'

'I mean it,' he said. 'I am sorry, Jasmine. I haven't given you enough attention. My marriage. Radha. It all got in the way.' He looked at Radha who was talking to Dolores with animation.

'But you're making it up with her, Dad. She told me you had a good talk this morning.'

'Yes,' he said. 'Yes, we did.'

'That's great, Dad.'

'No,' he said, tightening his grip on her hand. 'No, that isn't what I want to say. Forget about that. What I mean is, things got in the way and I wasn't a good enough parent. I was a better father to them than I was to you, but look how you turned out. You're wonderful.'

'But I haven't *done* anything, Dad,' said Jasmine. 'I'm the only one. The rest of you, you all stand for something. You all do things in the world. Me, I'm just . . . whatever.'

'What are you talking about?' he said. 'You believe in this place. You're in your home now.'

'They're kicking me out.'

'No, they're not,' said Chandra. 'You'll be back by January. We'd do the same if we caught

344

you taking drugs in our university.'

'Drugs is why I'm in here.'

'It was only marijuana,' said Chandra. 'It's okay. Everything's okay.'

'Dad, last night Sunny asked me where I saw myself in five years' time.'

'He asks everyone that.'

'And I didn't know. I said maybe I'd be here and he looked horrified.'

'It wouldn't be so bad,' said Chandra, also horrified. 'Anyway, it's your choice. You can still go to university, or you can be a monk. It's up to you.'

'Nun, Dad. I'd be a nun.'

'Oh,' he said, thinking how much worse this sounded. 'Just as long as it makes you happy.'

'Dad, does your job make you happy?'

'I don't know,' he said. 'I suppose it doesn't make me happy or unhappy.'

'So maybe it doesn't matter what we do, or whether we're successful. Maybe it just doesn't matter.'

'What is this?' he said, shaking his head and laughing. 'Why do you all talk like this?'

After dinner Dolores brought out a sticky toffee pudding and Chandra ate a spoonful before looking at his watch and saying, to no one in particular, 'I'm going to get Sunny.'

'Charles, let him be,' said Jean. 'We're having dessert.'

'How about we join you?' said Steve. 'We finish our dessert and then we all go.'

'No,' said Chandra, standing. 'I'm going to get Sunny.'

He could hear them all protesting — that mob of ex-wives, cuckolders, daughters and monks — but he strode into the hall regardless and laced up his shoes before realising he didn't have a car. To his relief, Saul appeared, giving him his keys before he could ask. Chandra opened his mouth to thank him, then saw the dog approaching, a purple rind of tinsel wrapped around his tail, and fled.

It was black outside, and Professor Chandra drove on the left side of the road the entire way there, only realising his mistake when he was turning into Sunny's driveway.

When Sunny answered the door he had his phone fixed beneath his chin.

'François,' he was saying, gesturing to Chandra to come in. 'Talk to me, baby; what's the drill? That's bullshit and they know it. No, that's not good enough. Don't drop the ball on this number just 'cause it's Christmas, okay? All right. Call me back. *A bientôt.*'

'Merry Christmas, Sunny,' said Chandra.

'You too, Dad. I got so caught up I almost forgot.'

Chandra could smell something cooking in the kitchen.

'Turkey,' said Sunny. 'For tonight.'

'Right. But what about now? What about lunch?'

'Lunch is for wimps,' said Sunny, a line from *Wall Street* that Chandra knew only too well (twenty years ago Sunny used to speak almost exclusively in *Wall Street* dialogue).

'People are asking for you,' said Chandra.

Sunny tapped his phone. 'Got a deal brewing.'

'You can bring your phone.'

'I don't think it's my scene, Dad.'

'Sunny, come on,' said Chandra, suddenly exhausted. 'Of course it's your scene. Radha is there, and Jasmine, and your mother. It's Christmas.'

'But everyone's coming here, aren't they?'

'Yes, yes, they will. But if you come now we can all take our time.'

'I've got to keep an eye on the turkey, Dad.'

'It smells done to me.'

Chandra was fairly sure caterers had delivered it pre-cooked and Sunny was just keeping it warm. Probably he'd been expecting them earlier, hoping to lure them away from Saul's house. He wondered if Sunny was afraid Chandra might upstage him at the party, or if he simply wasn't interested.

He remembered a party he and Jean had hosted not long after moving to Cambridge. Jean had been nervous, practising lines in front of the mirror like 'Pleased to meet you,' and 'What would you like to drink?' He had kept an eye on her throughout the party, making sure she was never alone or stuck with a Boho (Bore Of the Highest Order). She'd even been enjoying herself, he believed, until he had decided to pick a fight with a visiting professor from Calcutta (short, fat and convinced free trade was equivalent to armed robbery). The two had argued until one in the morning, long after Jean had gone upstairs where she'd suffered a mild panic attack, worsened by the fight from downstairs that she couldn't help but hear. Sometimes Chandra traced the initial breakdown of his marriage to that evening, thirty years ago.

'Dad, why don't you sit down? I'll get you a drink.'

'Sure,' said Chandra. 'Why not?'

For a man who didn't drink, Sunny had a lot of bottles. There they stood on the rosewood sideboard, twinkling like a line of chorus girls. Chandra sat on the sofa, leaning back into the cushions while his son mixed him a brandy and soda.

'Sunny,' said Chandra. 'How are you? Seriously.'

'I'm great,' said Sunny, and grinned wide like a character from *The Muppet Show*.

'But in your email you said — '

'I'm thinking of leaving Hong Kong, that's all.'

'Oh,' said Chandra, wondering if his business was in trouble. 'What for?'

Sunny sighed. 'You were right, Dad. I'm lonely. I've been there too long. I want to be in the UK or the US, somewhere I know people.'

'Sunny,' said Chandra, 'I know this is none of my business, but — '

'No, Dad. I'm not seeing anybody. It's just me.' Sunny had been looking past him all the while, but now made eye contact. 'I'm not so good with relationships, Dad,' he said. 'I don't think they're for me.'

'Don't say that, Sunny.'

'Everyone has strengths and weaknesses. Relationships aren't one of my strengths.'

348

'Heavens,' said Chandra. 'I'm sure you're better than I am.'

'I doubt that.'

'Nonsense, Sunny. You just haven't met the right person yet. It's all about . . . '

Chandra was about to say 'compatibility', interlocking his fingers to illustrate his point, when he realised Sunny was telling him his strings. Strings weren't something one could contradict. They had to be undone patiently, with love. He took a swallow of brandy.

'It doesn't matter,' said Sunny. 'We all have a purpose. Winners fulfil their purpose. Losers don't.'

'I don't want you to win, Sunny. I want you to be happy.'

Sunny smiled. His face looked watery and weak, as if a swipe of a hand could wipe him away.

'I'd be so happy if you moved to London,' said Chandra. 'I wish we weren't all on opposite ends of the earth.'

'Maybe Rad will come back too,' said Sunny. 'She said she's thinking about it.'

'Sunny,' said Chandra. 'I know everything has been about the other two recently, but you're my son; you're so important to me. Don't forget that, please.'

Sunny smiled. 'So how about you, Dad? You seeing anybody?'

'Oh, God,' said Chandra, wanting to add 'of course not' before realising it was a legitimate question. 'No, no, I'm not.'

'Gotta get back on that horse, Dad.'

'Horse?'

'Back in the saddle. You know, the game.'

'I don't know,' said Chandra. 'I suppose you're right. Anyway, have you heard about Jasmine?'

'Mum told me.'

'I think it was my fault.'

'How could it be your fault?'

'It happened after I fought with Radha. I think it stressed her out.'

'Stress is something she's got to learn to deal with,' said Sunny. 'Anyway, it was only a joint.'

'But Dolores says they're suspending her.'

'She'll be back. It's okay.'

Chandra closed his eyes. 'I just think sending her to Boulder's the worst punishment anyone could think of. Boulder's where it all happened, where her drugs friends are, her old haunts, her pimps.'

'Pimps?' said Sunny.

'Isn't that the right word?'

'I don't think so.'

Chandra put down his drink. 'I should be getting back,' he said. 'They'll all be here soon. I've just got to pick up my presents from the monastery first. You sure you don't want to come with me?'

Sunny nodded.

'All right,' said Chandra. 'See you soon.'

They walked to the door where they hugged in a way they hadn't in years. Chandra wondered if it could always be like this, whether if Sunny moved to London they could have a different relationship, one where they were loving and open and didn't need to speak in code. He decided it didn't matter. The important thing was this moment.

In the car he ran his hands through his hair and took several deep breaths. The dark ice on the road was treacherous and invisible, but at least he remembered to drive on the right. It took only a few minutes to reach the house, but when he looked at his reflection he saw the face of a man who'd been driving for hours.

The party had livened in his absence. New guests had arrived, residents from other centres. Music was playing, a song by Fleetwood Mac that Chandra remembered from when the children were little. Dolores and Radha were dancing with a group of teenagers, and two middle-aged white women were sitting on the sofa with Saul. They introduced themselves as 'Parvati' and 'Meenakshi' from the Hindu temple. To his annoyance, neither of them seemed impressed by the appearance of a bona-fide Indian.

Jasmine was sitting with two of the other monks, drinking hot apple cider and laughing. She looked better now, a carefree young woman. Chandra poured himself some mulled wine and Dolores caught his eye, beckoning him to follow her to Saul's study, as before.

'Are you okay?' she asked.

'I think so,' said Chandra. 'How about you?'

'Oh, I'm doing fine. I had a good talk with your ex, you know.'

'Oh, God,' said Chandra.

'I think she does the angry thing to cover up how much she blames herself.'

351

'I doubt that,' said Chandra. 'She blames me.'

'Maybe she blames herself too.'

'Hey,' said Chandra. 'Where are they?'

'Oh, they just went to lie down for a while back at the monastery. They're all right.'

Chandra stared at the floor, trying to dispel the image of Jean and Steve lying down. Dolores had beautiful feet, he noticed, perfectly proportioned, a silver ring on her little toe. He liked the way she was wearing her hair tonight. He could see her neck this way. Her hair was silver like her dress, a curvaceous Joan of Arc in figure-hugging armour.

'Sunny wouldn't come,' said Chandra, and told her about their talk. 'I can't help him. I wish I could.'

'Hey,' said Dolores, putting her hands on his shoulders. 'You're doing great. You made all this happen. So what if there's been a few hiccoughs. You seized your moment. If you miss those moments they're gone for ever.'

Professor Chandra leaned forward and kissed her on the lips. To his horror and delight, Dolores kissed him back. It lasted about ten seconds before she pulled away and said, 'Well, not bad, Professor C.'

'I am sorry,' he said. 'Truly, Dolores, I should not have done that. You are a married woman.'

'Yes, you should and you know it. Now get back to your family and forget about it, honey.'

'Yes,' said Chandra. 'Yes, of course.'

'Come on, you naughty fella.'

They returned to the living room where Chandra found Radha who had stopped dancing and was talking to Saul. To his surprise, he did not feel guilty at all, standing there between his prodigal daughter and the man *he* had cuckolded, not even when Saul smiled warmly at him and asked how his evening was going.

Chandra hoped no lipstick had rubbed off on his lips.

'We should be getting to Sunny's soon,' he told Radha.

'You're the boss, apple sauce,' she said, a little drunk.

Chandra thought of his wife, those parties they used to have that would go on until midnight, that wonderful smell of perfume and cigarette smoke and university-grade wine. Those were the days, he thought, before recalling the night of the Bengali Boho which returned him to reality.

'I've got to go back to the monastery,' said Chandra. 'I have presents.'

'Jaz and I can walk to Sunny's,' said Radha. 'Maybe smoke a doobie on the way.'

Saul laughed and they all looked at Jasmine who was swaying to the music in the corner, her eyes mostly closed.

Saul held out his car keys with what Chandra believed was a knowing glance, and Chandra returned to the hallway and outside, relieved not to encounter Dolores on the way. Night had truly arrived now, and as he drove up the hill to the monastery he kept imagining that the shadows to his right and left were giant, skulking bears. He parked beside Steve's Lincoln and realised he had no flashlight, and no idea how to turn his phone into one.

Getting out of the car, Chandra began to thread his way through the darkness like Theseus in the labyrinth. He wondered if Steve was the Minotaur, or Jean, but came to the conclusion that it was probably all of them, himself included.

When he reached his hut he felt as if he had not been there in weeks. He shimmied down the stepladder to fetch his bag of gifts and staggered back through the monastery, an ageing Santa in reverse. As he passed the zendō he heard a voice call out to him.

'Charles.'

She was standing between two fir trees near the main building. All he could see was the glowing stamp of a cigarette.

'Jean,' he said, heading towards her. He couldn't remember the last time he had seen her smoke. 'Can I drive you to Sunny's place?'

He could see her so clearly now, this woman with whom he had shared his life. She looked small out here in the woods, with the impenetrable black valley behind her. She turned towards the parking lot. He could smell her perfume.

'Okay, Charles,' said Jean, and it sounded like her old voice, the one before Cambridge. 'Steve's going to join us later anyway.'

They walked towards the parking lot in silence. He took the keys from his pocket.

'I miss you,' he said.

'Let's get going,' said Jean. 'It's freezing.'

'Yes,' said Chandra. 'Yes, of course.'

He unlocked the door to Saul's Ford and started the engine. Jean did not get inside. He

354

couldn't see her face, only her back. He wondered if she was lighting another cigarette. When he got out of the car Jean was looking down towards the valley. She seemed fragile and confused, her face yellow in the car's headlights.

'I'm sorry,' she said, still not looking at him.

'It's okay.'

'I mean, I'm sorry for it all, Charles. This has been hardest on you.'

'But I'm glad you're here,' he said.

'I don't mean that. I mean everything. Steve. Everything. I'm sorry, Charles.'

'I'm such an ass,' said Chandra. 'I've ruined our lives. I ruined your life.'

'No, you didn't. I've hurt you horribly. You didn't deserve this. Everybody knows it. I'll be sorry for ever. You don't believe me, but it's true.'

He was shivering and so was Jean. He could actually hear her teeth clanging together.

'Are you happy with Steve?'

'Sometimes. Often. I don't know him as well as I know you, that's all. But he has more time for me. His life isn't so outward.'

'I'm trying,' he said. 'I'm trying to be different.'

'I've noticed.'

Jean reached into her jacket and took out a packet of Salem's before changing her mind.

'You don't have to be different for me, you know, Charles.'

'I know. I think I'm doing it for me.'

'Good,' said Jean. 'Good for you.'

'I wouldn't have, if you hadn't left.'

'So maybe I did you a favour.'

Jean got into the car and Chandra joined her, putting it into gear. They did not speak until he'd turned onto the main road.

'So you'll stay with Steve?'

'Yes, I think so.'

'And you'd never come back to me?'

'Is that what you want?'

He slowed to a crawl, the huge December moon filling the windscreen. The question felt hollow. He'd been asking out of habit, he realised.

'Have a think,' said Jean. 'You might be surprised.'

'I will,' he said, and he meant it. It was a question he had never asked himself before.

⋆　⋆　⋆

When they arrived at Sunny's place, Radha and Jasmine were already there. Sunny was standing in the doorway, wearing a Santa hat.

Chandra set down his bag of gifts. 'We're here,' he said, somewhat superfluously.

'I'm glad,' said Sunny. 'Merry Christmas.'

'Merry Christmas,' said Jean.

In the living room, Radha and Jasmine were lying on the sofa with their arms linked. E.T. was on the television and the fire was burning with perfect yellow flames that suggested Sunny had bought some special designer wood. Jean sat on the sofa beside her daughters eating a minced pie with a thimbleful of brandy brought by Sunny.

Professor Chandra sat opposite while Sunny gave him a glass of the champagne he seemed to have in abundance, and some smoked salmon on toast. The Christmas tree, he noticed, had been trimmed with tinsel and baubles and lights. There were presents beneath it too, and now Sunny was adding Chandra's gifts to the pile, humming Nat King Cole's 'The Christmas Song' under his breath.

'We should have opened the presents this morning,' said Jean, who was sitting next to Jasmine.

'We would have,' said Sunny, refilling Radha's glass, 'if somebody hadn't gone AWOL.'

'Sunny,' said Radha, 'you didn't even turn up for your own birthday party.'

'There were too many people!' said Sunny, who had booked a room at the LSE when he was nineteen but run in the opposite direction when he saw it filled with drunken, dancing strangers.

'I didn't even consider having a party this year,' said Chandra.

'Oh, Charles,' said Jean.

'Oh, Charles, nothing,' said Chandra. 'It was my birthday.'

'Quite right,' said Radha.

'Why, Dad?' said Jasmine. 'It was your seventieth.'

'I just didn't feel like it,' said Chandra. 'The thing about your birthday is you get to do whatever you want. I didn't want to be around just anybody. I wanted to be around all of you.'

'And now you are,' said Radha.

'Well, we should thank Jaz for this,' said Jean.

357

'It was Jaz who made this happen.'

'Hear, hear,' said Sunny, and raised his glass. 'To my little sister and her new weird life. To Jasmine.'

'To Jasmine,' everyone repeated, with the exception of Radha who merely put her arm around her sister's shoulder.

'I'm happy everybody's here,' said Jean. 'It's been a funny year, but this isn't a bad ending.'

'*Hello?*' said Jasmine. 'I kind of, you know, fucked up. What are you talking about?'

Radha laughed. Chandra hadn't heard Jasmine talk like this in a while. He wondered if her suspension had turned her into a teenager again. He didn't mind, so long as she stayed away from drugs.

'What I want to know is where you got the joint *from*,' said Jean. 'You live in a monastery.'

'Mum, there's a weed dispensary down the road,' said Radha.

'I brought it with me,' said Jasmine. 'Sorry, but I did. It was a kind of insurance policy.'

'There's an insurance policy down the *road*,' said Radha.

'Can we stop talking about this now?' said Jasmine.

'Leave it, Mum,' said Radha, before Jean could speak. 'Jaz is right. There's no point going on about it.'

'We just worry,' said Jean. 'Parents worry, you know.'

'Jesus!' said Jasmine, who really did look like her old self now. 'I'm not going to do it again and I feel like shit about it, okay?'

358

'Okay,' said Jean, though she looked as if she still had plenty to say.

'I have some news,' said Sunny. 'I'm moving back to London.'

Chandra raised both hands in the air in triumph. Sunny had said 'the US or the UK' earlier. This was definitive.

Chandra looked at Radha, trying to will her to say the same. She met his gaze.

'Well,' said Chandra, standing so he could survey the entire room and step out of Radha's eye-lock. 'I am very happy about so many things. But most of all I'm happy to be here now with all of you, especially Jean. I know it hasn't been easy for all of you to watch us separate. Well, maybe I didn't know. But I know it now and I want to say I'm sorry, from the heart, and I'm very, very glad we can be together anyway. And I am glad Steve is here too, or will be here, to share this holiday with us.'

'Assuming nobody punches him,' said Jean.

'Yes,' said Chandra, noticing no one else appeared to know what Jean was talking about and feeling mildly disappointed. 'This is my seventy-first year,' he continued. 'So much has happened, and so much has changed.'

'You became a hippie like me,' said Radha.

'Except he's got a job,' said Sunny.

Radha gave Sunny the finger while Chandra continued.

'I realise now,' he said, 'that my mistake was in thinking that I had nothing else to learn in life. I think if there's nothing new to learn, there's probably no point being alive at all. An hour ago

Jean was asking me why I've been doing all these new things, and I said it was for me, but maybe it was for all of you too. I'm not even sure what I mean by that, but I think it's true.'

Chandra could hear a car pulling into the driveway. Steve.

'I suppose I expected my life to be different at seventy, but what I want to say is that it's perfect the way it is. With all of you here. So . . . Merry Christmas. Merry Christmas to you all.'

Professor Chandra lifted his champagne glass, now empty, and held it aloft, looking at Jean and each of his children in turn, their faces lit by the muted television. He tried to imprint the moment on his mind so he would never forget it. There had been so many like this . . . in Chicago, in Cambridge. They'd been a family so long, and most of it, some of it, much of it, had been wonderful. Even if this was the last moment they ever shared together, he would have this memory. He would always have this memory.

17

The following morning they all began to leave, one by one. Professor Chandra hadn't expected this.

But last night had been a success. Sunny had served them all a mammoth, quite over-the-top dinner, including turkey, champagne and baked Alaska. Afterwards they sat in the kitchen and Chandra and Jean told stories about their children, things only they could know. For a short while he and his former wife had held hands beneath the table where no one, Steve included, could see. Chandra loved her, but not in the way that he used to, and when she let go of his hand he didn't miss it.

Later, they played charades in front of the fire. Steve acted out the entirety of *Titanic* in two minutes, which moved Chandra to clap Steve on the back in a way that was almost entirely non-violent. For a while he felt something fraternal towards his cuckolder, like a half-brother, or a stepbrother, which moved him to go upstairs to call Prakash, though he hung up after only two rings. Phoning a Third World nationalist on an imperialist holiday was never a good idea.

They shifted to the basement after midnight. There was a ping-pong table there, which was Chandra's number one game now that he was too old to play cricket. To his surprise, Steve wasn't bad at all, and Chandra found himself having to strip down to his undershirt to gain more leverage. It was important to strike the ball at shoulder height if you wanted real power in your smash. He'd been telling people this for years.

He was disappointed when, at two in the morning, everyone announced they were calling it a night, as he could happily have gone on until dawn. But Jasmine put her arm around him and said, 'You need to go to bed, Dad,' which was code for 'You're drunk.'

But he felt fine this morning, fresh as a woodpecker. And yet everyone was leaving. He hadn't realised Steve and Jean had planned to return to Boulder so soon, and of course Jasmine was going with them on account of her suspension, which didn't seem so bad now, not to anyone.

And so here he was, hugging his youngest daughter and trying not to cry as she got into the back of Steve's Lincoln with her inch of black hair.

'Bye, Jean. Bye, Steve,' he said. 'Take care of yourselves.'

'All the best, Chandrasekhar,' said Steve.

'Look after yourself, Charles.'

By the time Dolores came over and put her arm around him, the Lincoln had disappeared from view. He wanted to tell her how sad he was, but last night's misadventures were still fresh in his mind.

'Well, Professor,' said Dolores. 'It's been quite something.'

'Thank you for everything, Dolores,' he said. 'This couldn't have happened if it wasn't for you.'

'My pleasure,' said Dolores. 'You look after yourself, Professor Chandra. You're a very special guy, you know that?'

Dolores's arms were around him, hugging him tight without any apparent self-consciousness. When they separated he found he couldn't make eye contact with her and, after mumbling a few non-sequiturs, he excused himself and went to his cabin, trying to get the thought out of his mind that perhaps life with someone other than Jean wasn't as impossible as he had imagined.

Shortly before lunchtime, Sunny left too. He had booked a holiday in Hawaii, some remote island outside the tourist trail that boasted eco-tourism and swimming with dolphins. Chandra hoped he wasn't going alone, but knew not to ask.

'I'll miss you,' he said. 'I always miss you, Sunny.'

'Thanks, Dad.'

'I know I shouldn't worry. I know you'll be all right.'

Sunny took off his sunglasses.

'Is anyone really all right, Dad?'

Chandra did not know what to say to this. He was trying to think of a reply when Sunny stepped to one side to answer his phone and began speaking in Cantonese.

Chandra looked up at the sky, which was mostly blue today, and saw a couple of geese flying overhead. Sunny finished his call and put the last of his bags into his rental car.

'I'm sorry I go on about things,' said Chandra. 'It happens at my age. I just want you to be happy, Sunny, but that doesn't mean you have to be anything different. Just be yourself. That's enough.'

'I'll see you in London,' said Sunny.

'I can't wait.'

'Ciao, Dad.'

'Ciao,' said Chandra.

Chandra stood in the parking lot until Sunny's car was a tiny dot on the horizon. He realised that Radha had not been there to see them all off, but even as a child she had hated goodbyes. Sometimes she would stay in her room and refuse to come out when he left for a conference.

He found her outside the zendō. She was walking the perimeter, her head down, looking at her feet.

'Hi, Dad,' she said. 'On your own?'

'We're the only ones left.'

'So we are,' said Radha.

'Are you going back to New York?'

'In a few days. I'm going to stay here and meditate some more.'

Radha was wearing a hooded sweatshirt and jogging pants, her hair tied back.

'I'm going to New York,' said Chandra. 'For New Year's.'

'Yes,' said Radha, 'you said.'

He had announced it last night, a pure fabrication. He'd told her he had been planning it for weeks.

'We could go together,' said Chandra. 'I have a car.'

Radha reached the zendō's steps and sat on the lowest one, cupping her face in her hands. Chandra sat beside her. They looked up at the mountains.

'Are you nuts?' said Radha.

'Maybe still a little drunk.'

'You want to spend the trip fighting? The free market, remember? You're for it. Me, not so much.'

'We can't fight all the time.'

'You sure?'

'Even if we do, it's better than being apart,' he said, smiling.

'Dad, you just made that up, didn't you, about your New York trip?'

'Yes,' he said, hanging his head.

'Look,' said Radha, 'we can give it a try. Let's see if we can get to New York without tearing each other apart.'

'How long will it take us by car?'

'A couple of days.' Radha shuffled closer to him, so their arms touched. 'At least. Why don't we fly instead?'

'I don't like flying.'

Radha looked up at him with those saucer eyes that so resembled his own.

'Road trip, Dad?' she said.

'Yes,' said Chandra. 'Yes, I'd love that.'

Acknowledgements

This novel began with the Hemera Foundation whose marvellous fellowship made everything possible. My warmest, deepest thanks to everyone there, in particular Andrew Merz and Dan Halpern, who helped me plan my two pilgrimages to the US, and my two mentors Charles Johnson and Anushka Fernandopulle. To all the companions who helped me on my way with beds, rides, hugs, laughter, dinner, advice and that most essential of all things, spiritual companionship: Mauricio and Maria, Thomas, Jamie, Fannie-Lee, Jay, Carmen, Swamiji, Ramesh, Yuval, Diego, Sita, Rudy and Denise, Linda, Praveen, Stan, Ryan and Carmen, Athmeya, Arun, Ngugi, Kevin, Simon and Pia, Tom and Bird. I could write pages about your kindness and humour and love and generosity.

My thanks and *metta* to all the meditation teachers I have learned from — before, during and after my travels: S. N. Goenka, who gave me a new life so many years ago; Thich Nhat Hanh, who became the guiding spirit for my American pilgrimages; all the nuns and monks at Deer Park Monastery, as well as the other teachers I met there who moved me so deeply; Sister Jewel, Larry Ward, Rev. Angel Kyodo Williams, and Rev. Earthlyn Manuel; all the assistant teachers on the Vipassana courses I sat and served on while writing this novel; the nuns and monks at the Vajrapani Institute, the Crestone Mountain Zen Center and the Zen Center of New York (Reynold, Christian, Nick and Ven. Drolma in particular); Mark Matousek, my wonderful teacher at Esalen; and lastly, to two spiritual companions and teachers who died while I was writing this novel, Leonard Cohen and Prince Rogers Nelson — may you both rest in bliss.

A big thank you to my earliest readers: Stephan, my companion in the adjoining room while I wrote the first draft; Prashant, my much-loved friend and confidante for a glorious twenty-five years now; my wonderful agent Margaret for her patience, insight and persistence; everyone at Vermont Studio Center for such enthusiastic feedback after my first ever reading from the novel (Sam Lipstye and Larissa Svirsky in particular); Steve Potter who read more than one draft and who has been a loving, therapeutic presence in my life for almost a decade now; and to our friend and now neighbour Carrie for her constant support and companionship. My thanks to everyone at my Berlin café and home away from home, Factory Girl, where I wrote much of this book and am sitting now; to Evelyn Somers at the *Missouri Review* for giving Professor Chandra his first home; and to Jacob and Anna at the Pigeonhole, and to Ingo and Martin for support and savvy advice.

With deep gratitude to everyone at Chatto & Windus and Random House USA: Monique, Whitney, Sam, Jane, Fran and my brilliant editors Clio, Susan and Becky. The three of you plus Margaret were and continue to be my dream team. My thanks to the porters at Gonville & Caius College, Cambridge and to the organ scholar, Luke, who overheard us talking and explained where in Cambridge a person would be most likely get hit by a bicycle. A final thank you to my old, deeply loved friends who kept me sane while I was at my most frazzled: Mark, Max, Marie, Sofia and Mutlu, and my long-term guardian angel, Nick. Finally, all the love, hugs, thank yous and kisses I have to Divya, the only one with me on all of my journeys, the keeper of my bliss.

We do hope that you have enjoyed reading this large print book.

Did you know that all of our titles are available for purchase?

We publish a wide range of high quality large print books including:
Romances, Mysteries, Classics
General Fiction
Non Fiction and Westerns

Special interest titles available in large print are:
The Little Oxford Dictionary
Music Book
Song Book
Hymn Book
Service Book

Also available from us courtesy of Oxford University Press:
Young Readers' Dictionary
(large print edition)
Young Readers' Thesaurus
(large print edition)

For further information or a free brochure, please contact us at:
Ulverscroft Large Print Books Ltd.,
The Green, Bradgate Road, Anstey,
Leicester, LE7 7FU, England.
Tel: (00 44) 0116 236 4325
Fax: (00 44) 0116 234 0205

NOONDAY

Pat Barker

London, the Blitz, autumn 1940: As the bombs fall on the blacked-out city, ambulance driver Elinor Brooke races from bomb sites to hospitals trying to save the lives of injured survivors. But Elinor sees little of her husband Paul as she works alongside long-time friend Kit Neville — and in this time of death and chaos, the normal boundaries seem like they're crumbling. Meanwhile, Paul believes that a child is dead due to a decision he made; and when a psychic says she sees the ghost of a boy hovering around him, he's inclined to give her words weight. As the bombing intensifies, the constant risk of death impels all three reach out for quick consolation. Old loves and obsessions resurface, until Elinor is brought face to face with an almost impossible choice.